BITTEN

by

Alan Moore

D1464229

Independently published on Amazon KDP in 2018.
ISBN: 9781980200895

DEDICATION

To Amber, Georgina, Chloe and Thomas

ABOUT THE AUTHOR

Born in Surbiton in 1944, Alan Moore lives in Barnes with his wife, Amber. They have two daughters and a son, who between them currently have two boys and two girls. Alan was educated at Oundle School in Northamptonshire and at London University, where, as an external student, he obtained a BA (Hons) degree. Thereafter, for 25 years, he single-handedly ran his own book publishing company, which at one point was producing up to 20 books a year.

CONTENTS

Chapter 1 .... *1*

Chapter 2 .... *9*

Chapter 3 .... *25*

Chapter 4 .... *33*

Chapter 5 .... *43*

Chapter 6 .... *59*

Chapter 7 .... *72*

Chapter 8 .... *85*

Chapter 9 .... *100*

Chapter 10 .... *142*

Chapter 11 .... *166*

Chapter 12 .... *191*

Chapter 13 .... *223*

Chapter 14 .... *238*

Chapter 15 .... *250*

Chapter 16 .... *261*

Chapter 17 .... *275*

Chapter 18 .... *294*

Chapter 19 .... *319*

Chapter 20 .... *342*

Chapter 21 .... *366*

Chapter 22 .... *388*

Chapter 23 .... *399*

Chapter 24 .... *413*

Appendix 1 .... *424*

Appendix 2 .... *428*

CHAPTER 1

Pinned to the door of a warehouse in the northern suburbs of Kazan, capital of the Republic of Tatarstan, was a large piece of cardboard on which had been scrawled, in red paint, the words, '**OPÁSNOST': DERZHAT'SYA PODAL'SHE!** [DANGER: STAY AWAY!]' Inside the warehouse, it was gloomy and the atmosphere was heavy with dust and the smell of cordite. Untidy piles of small wooden boxes with rope handles jostled for space with stacks of long rectangular crates. It was difficult to find a way through them. Once he had reached the other end of the building, the visitor stopped momentarily and stared. A beam of sunlight, radiating from a chink in the roof, illuminated a package standing against the back wall. A strip of the wrapping paper had been torn away. The man was transfixed by what he saw. In the shaft of light, through the tear in the paper, peering out from under arched brows and following his every move, were two soft deep brown eyes.

* * *

At the end of July in a popular bar on Via Maggio in Florence, two men sat at a table drinking their cocktails. They were Roberto Mattioli and Giorgio Belori, who worked part-time as art dealers. 'Italy's done for!' exclaimed Roberto. 'The country has voted to leave the EU hoping to revitalise its economy and reduce the national debt – but nothing's going to change. We'll still have a failing economy and our national debt is just going to get bigger and bigger. The fact is we've had no economic growth since we joined the euro twenty years ago – a complete balls-up if you ask me, for a country as large as Italy.'

'And all the while immigrants from Libya and Tunisia,' said Giorgio, 'are pouring into Sicily and Lampedusa in their thousands, and no one lifts a finger!'

'Well, what do you expect? Bureaucrats in this country are lazy and inept. They take so long to deal with anything that the decisions they eventually make are pointless.'

'Yes, it's crazy, isn't it? Last year there were over 100,000 applications for asylum – and only about 25 per cent have been approved so far, due to the Ministry of Interior's incompetence and time-wasting. Of course, it's the taxpayer who foots the bill for housing these wretched people.'

'What about the politicians?' asked a young man, who was sitting with two other young men and a girl. Roberto and Giorgio looked surprised. 'Excuse me for butting in,' he continued, 'but I couldn't help overhearing what you were talking about. The thing is it seems to me that most of our problems are caused by the bloody politicians.'

'Too right,' said Roberto. 'By and large, they're an ineffectual and ignorant bunch. One thing's certain: they're no longer trusted by the electorate. They're—'

'—dishonest,' said another of the young men.

'And what's worse, they're corrupt. They use public money to pay for the holidays they spend in five-star hotels and the expensive gifts they buy for their partners and children—'

'It pays for their visits to prostitutes, as well!' the girl chimed in.

'If you ask me, darling,' someone nearby shouted, in Italian with a strange accent, 'they're all the same. Two-timing creeps! Useless bastards! They all talk the same old bollocks!' Drinking pints of lager, the people at his table, which was covered with empty glasses, roared with laughter. 'Bollocks!' they shouted in unison.

Disregarding the rowdy interruption, the third young man exclaimed, 'The economy's down the tubes. Most of the banks are on the verge of collapse because they've made so many bad loans, the politicians are disreputable and two-faced, the bureaucrats do as little work as they can get away with, the judicial system is inefficient and far from impartial, the—'

There was a further interruption, this time in French. 'They're *all* fucking bastards, especially the bureaucrats! We should know, we're from Brussels.'

'What about unemployment?' asked Roberto.

'Of young people, you mean?' Roberto nodded. 'Well, when students like us leave university, we're highly unlikely to find employment. There are too many of us chasing too few jobs. In other words, there's rising youth unemployment, which is inflated further by members of our generation leaving the countryside and heading for the towns and cities in the hope of finding work. If they fail to get jobs with regular salaries, there's no way they can afford to rent even a single-room flat, and many of them end up as down-and-outs on the streets.'

The Belgian stood up. 'Let's drink a toast to the bureau-*craps* of Brussels.' He raised his half-full pint glass. His companions guffawed with delight.

'There seem to me,' said the tall studious-looking girl, 'to be only two areas in the economy that do well – the black market and organised crime. Tourism, of course, is a major contributor to our imports – but not for much longer, I think. According to *La Nazione*, visitors are complaining about a drop in hotel and catering standards, the rising cost of meals, unfair car hire costs, more and more immigrants, the theft of money and mobiles, too many viral infections, and so on.'

'Well sorry, darling,' said one of the other Belgians, 'we're tourists and we think Florence is fantastic. We don't recognise these complaints. They're just …'

'A load of BOLLOCKS!' he and his friends screamed. This time, other people in the bar joined in and laughed.

Raising his voice, Giorgio said, 'What about the Earth and the way it's been treated – is being treated – by mankind? Are you—'

'You mean global warming?' interjected the first Belgian. 'According to the Americans, that's a load of—'

Giorgio stood up with an angry expression on his face. 'Look, you lot, can't you keep the noise down and stop making silly comments? We're trying to have a *serious* conversation.'

'Oh dear, we've upset him. *Tout va bien chérie.* Just for you, sir, we'll lower our voices.'

Giorgio sat down. 'What I was going to ask is are you students concerned about the damage being done to the Earth?'

'Yes,' said the third student. 'It's something we feel really strongly about – so much so that on 24th of August we're going to have simultaneous protest marches in Rome, Milan, Turin and Florence. Although many of those taking part will be students, we're hoping to organise a coming together of people of *all* classes and backgrounds. And the main purpose is to urge the Government and big business to take action on global warming.'

'Not just sit there,' the first student exclaimed, 'like other European countries and do nothing to protect the environment.'

'That's right,' said Roberto. 'None of us are doing anything constructive to try and reduce melting glaciers, the rise in coastal waters, floods—'

'—the ever more frequent earthquakes, landslides and violent storms,' interrupted the second student.

'And let's not forget,' the girl exclaimed, 'Vesuvius hasn't erupted for three quarters of a century!'

'When it blows, it'll be as catastrophic as the 79 AD eruption,' someone added, cheerily.

'It may well be,' Roberto said. 'Anyway, it's time Italy realised that these dangers will result in many of our seaside resorts and tourist attractions being overrun by rising tides – places like Herculaneum, Porto Ercoli, Portofino, Otranto and, of course,

Venice and Venice Lido.'

'Don't worry,' said the third student, 'we'll be doing everything we can to persuade the Government to confront these problems. In our own way, we're going to save the environment.'

'That's good to hear,' said Roberto, 'don't you think, Giorgio?'

'Yes, really good.'

'I know someone who'll be delighted by the stand you and your friends are taking on behalf of the environment.'

'Who's that?' asked the first student.

'Claudia, my daughter. She's an ecologist.'

* * *

A few days later, in the Library of the Castello di Montezano near Poggibonsi in the Province of Siena, Boris Ouspensky shook hands with a small, wiry, silk-suited man with gelled black hair.

'I've checked the warehouse,' Ouspensky said. 'I can assure you everything's there that should be.'

'Including the picture?'

'Yes, including the picture.'

'Good. So now we work out a deal. What are the items you have for sale? How much do you want for them – always remembering that I expect a decent discount?' asked the local Mafia boss, Luca Baldini, with a smile as lethal as his occupation.

'Well, I'm offering you – er – let me see.' Ouspensky looked at his mobile. 'I'm offering you

100 Kalashnikov AK-471s; 50 rocket launchers; 200 rockets; 50 hand grenades; 100 Dragunov sniper rifles; 50 Makarov pistols; and 100 Saiga carbines. As to price: I'd be happy to accept $500,000 for the lot – which represents a considerable discount off the black-market price.'

'Yes,' said Baldini, referring to a small notebook he had taken from the inside pocket of his jacket, 'it does. And that makes me very happy. One question: where did you get all the stuff from?'

'The army.'

'The army? I take it the weapons aren't second-hand and haven't been used on military exercises.'

'Oh no, they're brand new. As I understand it, they've come straight from an armoury near Moscow.'

'Good. Glad to hear it. Now what about the picture?'

'Well,' said Ouspensky, 'I'm selling it on behalf of the Bratva. It's not their sort of thing, of course, and how they got hold of the picture in the first place I don't know. After all, the Russian Mafia are not noted for their love of art. What they like is money! Which is why they've instructed me to sell the picture for as much as I can get. Apparently, it's a famous lost masterpiece that's extremely valuable and will be of great interest to wealthy art collectors. The problem is I've never sold a work of art before, so don't know where to start. Have you any advice?'

'Let me help you. I have quite a few contacts in the art world and I'm sure I can get you the best price. Of course, we'll need an expert to examine the painting. If he or she confirms that it *is* genuine and then someone goes ahead and buys it, obviously I'll expect you to pay me a sizeable commission – but we'll discuss that later. You tell me when you're ready and I'll send a couple of my guys to collect the picture from your warehouse.'

CHAPTER 2

Thursday 15 August

Two weeks later, on the day of the Ferragusto public holiday, the weather in Florence was hot and sultry, with an ambient temperature of 33°C and a relative humidity reading of 76 per cent. Many shops and restaurants were shut, but most of the museums were open without charge. The majority of businesses were closed for two to three weeks. Laughing, dancing, eating, picnicking in the parks were the order of the day. Complimentary drinks with *ciccheti* were available at cocktail bars. Free watermelon was to be had in Piazza del Carmine in the Oltrarno area, and on the Arno Beach beside Piazza Poggi a sandcastle-building competition was taking place. Florentines had escaped to the relative cool of their 'seaside', to avoid the searing heat of the city.

On San Miniato Hill, where there was a slight breeze, the tall, slim, middle-aged man felt the sudden feathery touch on his forehead. Brushing the insect aside, he hissed under his breath, 'For Chrissake! Not you again! You drove me nuts the last time I was here.'

On the way from Pisa International Airport, Scott Lee had made his customary stop-off at Piazzale

Michelangelo, the large elevated terrace that overlooks Florence from the east. He walked to the perimeter balustrade and gazed. He always had the same reaction: the view was breathtaking, more so even than the Manhattan skyline of his native New York. The overhanging haze of pollution did not impair the elegance and splendour of the historic Renaissance city, whose landmarks were as familiar as old friends: the green and listless river glistening in the sun; the ancient three-arched bridge surmounted by its line of irregular buildings; the central dominating red-brick, white-ribbed dome; the scattering of towers; the brown-red terracotta roofs; the many-windowed, ochre-washed façades; the thickets of dark green trees – cypress, laurel, pine – against a backdrop of undulating hills. The panorama ranged before him never failed to evince gasps of wonder and admiration, from visitors and Italians alike.

What an awesome place, thought Scott. There was a 'beep' from his mobile. He had received a text from Laurence: 'Just wondering where you are.'

'Jeez, I'm late! I gotta go,' he said out loud. He sent a return text: 'On my way. Be there in ten mins.' He ran across the square and jumped into a waiting taxi, which drove off down the Viale Michelangelo, past the Camp Sportivo to the Ponte San Niccolò and the north side of the Arno.

* * *

In Rome, Roberto's 29-year-old daughter, Dr Claudia Mattioli, gazed out of the window at the Egyptian obelisk and the twin Baroque churches in the Piazza del Popolo, and thought how fortunate she was to work in such beautiful surroundings. Turning her attention again to her laptop, she looked over the notes she had made for her forthcoming article to be syndicated to various national newspapers.

Some observations on the effects of climate change

1. Since the 1990s a tenth of the Earth's wilderness area has been destroyed by humans.

2. If humans continue to burn fossil fuels at the current rate, the Earth will return to the climate conditions of the Eocene Epoch which lasted from 56 to 33.9 million years ago. The Earth's temperature is rising: the rate of increase in the Northern hemisphere is more than 0.2°C per month. The Earth hasn't heated up this quickly since the end of the Dinosaurs. Carbon is pouring into the atmosphere faster now than during the hottest period in the past 66 million years.

3. All along the mid-Atlantic coast, trees are being killed in those areas where there is a rapid rise in sea level.

4. The risk to America from rising seas could triple by the end of the century and up to 15 million people would be …

'Claudia!' A short man in a rumpled suit entered the room. 'I'm afraid I have some worrying news.' He was the Director-General of the Institute of Ecology, Dr Ettore Ravegnani. 'Can you kindly come with me to the lab and see what Giuseppe has discovered?' Claudia stood up. She was at least 15cm taller than Ettore. The black satin blazer and trousers she had on emphasised her height. She wore a pair of black-framed clear-lens glasses, which she presumed made her look less attractive and more studious. But any such attempt to deglamourise herself was doomed to failure. Nothing could alter the fact that she had large brown eyes, shoulder-length brunette hair, full lips, a dazzling smile, high cheekbones, long legs and a shapely figure. But aside from being unarguably beautiful, she was academically gifted – and bilingual. Instead of being a model or an actress, she had chosen to be an ecologist. She had majored in science at Harvard and been awarded a DSc by Bologna University for her research into the mound-building skills of the South American ant. Now she was Associate Director of the Institute – the youngest person ever to hold the post.

She followed Ettore through to the lab where a tall fair-haired young man in a white coat was looking into a stereo microscope.

'Giuseppe, can you tell Dr Claudia what you've found?'

'Good afternoon, Doctor.' Claudia acknowledged him with a nod of her head. 'I've been measuring the specimens we've collected in the last fortnight. And I've found that all the species, both vectors and non-vectors, under examination have grown quite noticeably over the past year. Their lengths have increased by an average of 1.5mm. Here's a list I made for you.' He handed her a sheet of paper, which she took and studied.

'A 12.5mm Alaskan? My god, that's something you don't want hiding in your bedroom at night! Such a vicious biter. And as for the African Malaria mosquito, I didn't think it had arrived here yet.'

'Apparently it's been working its way up through

Sicily, Calabria and Campania to here. I haven't established whether the particular specimen I'm in the process of analysing is carrying the *falciparum* virus.'

'It's possible,' said Claudia, 'that these specimens are exceptions to the rule. People can be unusually long and large, so why can't mosquitoes? We need to study further specimens, before we can establish whether or not mosquitoes are definitely growing longer and bigger.'

* * *

In Piazza Santissima Annunziata, as in practically every other part of the centre of Florence, sightseers abounded, despite the heat. They walked under the portico of Brunelleschi's Ospedale degli Innocenti. They looked up at Giambologna's imposing equestrian statue of Grand Duke Ferdinand. They pointed at the bizarre marine monsters and grotesques on the two bronze fountains. They went into the lavishly decorated Basilica to see Michelozzo's ornate tabernacle and the tiny miraculous painting of the *Annunciation* inside.

At the southern end of the square, in his first-floor apartment overlooking the Palazzo Grifoni, Laurence Spencer was oblivious to the activity outside. He was concentrating on reading the previous day's edition of the *Daily Telegraph*. The lofty and impressive drawing room, in which he sat, featured gold-leaf cornicing on the ceiling, heavy red damask curtains in the high sash windows, and a large oval Savonnerie rug in the centre of the polished oak floor. The front door bell sounded and moments later Laurence's factotum, Paolo, ushered in the visitor. 'Hey, I'm sorry I'm late. I hope I haven't gone and messed things up,' said Scott, crossing the room. 'Anyway, how're you doing?'

'Oh, can't grumble, I suppose,' said Laurence, getting up and shaking Scott's hand. 'It's good to see you again. Pity we missed each other last month. Got some serious catching up to do, haven't we?' He waved his hand in the direction of a faded dark-red chesterfield. 'Sit yourself down and have a drink. What d'you fancy?'

'Oh, a bourbon on the rocks, *per favore*.'

Laurence sat down beside Scott. 'And a G and T for me please, Paolo.'

'Well, tell me, how're things in the art world?' Scott asked.

'Fine. In fact, there's been an interesting development, which I'll tell you about in a moment. But how about you? What's happening on the publishing scene? You had any successful titles recently?'

'Yeah. We've sold just over 10,000 of a controversial study of the life and works of Caravaggio. And that's since we published the book in April! The digital version is doing well, too: over 3,500 downloads so far. Then a warts-and-all biography of Pollock we published last fall got this amazing review in the *New York Times* and just sorta took off.'

Paolo, who had the swarthy looks of a southern Italian, offered the two men their drinks on a silver salver. 'Okay, Paolo, that'll be all for now, thank you.' As soon as the door closed, Laurence stood up, put down his drink and strode across the room. 'Scott, guess what? I've had the most amazing luck. I've … but listen! Keep this under your hat. Don't tell a soul, otherwise bits of me will be found floating in the Arno. Understood?'

Scott nodded. 'Sure. But ... whaddya mean about the bits? You're not getting into deep water, are you?' He swallowed most of his drink in one mouthful.

'Quite possibly. You see, I'm on the trail of an extremely important old master painting. For the moment I can't tell you what it is and who it's by. This painting disappeared from Poland at the end of World War Two. It was probably commandeered by Stalin's so-called "Trophy Brigade", who were—'

'Hey, man, that's ... that's awesome! If you do get your hands on it, it's gonna be worth a few bucks, surely?'

'Oh yes, it's ... potentially worth a *lot* of money.' Laurence picked up his gin and tonic and sat down opposite Scott.

'How come you managed to track it down?'

'Through an organisation called Trace-Art, believe it or not.' Laurence took a sip of his drink. 'But there's a snag. We're not talking about your normal "I like this picture and I'll pay you x amount for it" type of transaction. Those involved are hardly the sort of people you find in Christie's or Sotheby's. It's more complicated than that, and the risks are much higher.' He put his glass down on the table beside him. 'The point is, I don't know how, but this wonderful masterpiece has fetched up in the hands of the Bratva, the Russian Mafia, whose normal activities are money laundering and drug trafficking. And they've asked the 'Ndrangheta over here to sell the painting for them ...'

'"Oondrangetter"? That's a strange word!'

'It comes from the Greek for heroism and manly virtue – not qualities you'd immediately associate with the Mafia! Anyway, I find myself involved – and don't forget, keep this to yourself – because in South America I have a Polish-American client, a fabulously wealthy man, who's very keen to buy the painting and give it back to its original owners, the Czartoryski family in Krakow.'

'So how do you plan to proceed?' asked Scott, thinking his old pal was crazy to have gotten himself mixed up with the Mob.

'Well, I'm expecting Trace-Art's agent to call here a bit later. He's an associate of mine and has arranged to take me to some preliminary meeting, I don't know where or who with. Anyway, I feel rotten about going out and leaving you when you've only just arrived. Perhaps you'd like to come along as well. You never know, you might find it interesting.'

'Hey Laurence, don't fret yourself on my account. I'll be fine. Heck, I'm happy to stay here. I've got some papers I need to run through before tomorrow. So no, go to your meeting. But remember, watch your back. You can't trust those Mafiosi guys.'

'Oh, I'll be careful.' Laurence rose to his feet. 'Seriously, though, Scott, I'd like you to come with me. Your impressions of what goes on at the meeting and the people who are there will, I know, be perceptive and … and thought-provoking. I guess what I'm trying to say is that I'd value your company.'

'Well, in that case …'

'Good man!' cried Laurence, patting Scott on the

back. 'Now let's freshen up before Signor Casti arrives on the doorstep!'

* * *

The Trace-Art agent, Filippo Casti, an art authenticator and restorer, called at the apartment in Piazza Santissima Annunziata at 18:30 and, having quickly shaken hands with Laurence and Scott and alerted them to the possibility that the planned meeting might be a waste of time, led the two men at a brisk pace across the square, down the bustling Via dei Servi, round the east end of the Duomo, along the Via del Proconsolo past the fifteenth-century Palazzo Pazzi-Quaratesi, to the Badia Fiorentina, where heavy scaffolding and green plastic sheeting around the 70-metre high campanile signified that *Lavori di Consolidamento e Restauri* were in progress. Standing at the top of the steps in front of the entrance to the Cloister of the Oranges were two big men in well-cut dark grey suits, one larger than the other, who Frederico approached and conferred with. The shorter of the two turned and knocked on the large oak doors to the church, softly at first but, getting no response, with increasing vehemence, until eventually one of the doors was flung open to reveal a member of the Carabinieri – a high-ranking officer, if the amount of gold braid and buttons on his shoulders was anything to go by. This doggish man, with dark brown eyes, protruding ears and matted black hair, conducted Laurence, Scott, Filippo and the two doorkeepers past a painted panel, one of Filippino Lippi's finest works, and a series of masterpieces of Renaissance sculpture, up the steps to the chancel and into a small room on the right-hand side, formerly the sacristy.

Standing to attention with a click of his heels, the policeman introduced himself. '*Buonesera.* I am General Bruno Malatesta, and I am in charge of the Carabinieri Stolen Arts and Antiques Unit. It is my concern to secure this picture while it's here in Italy.' Turning to a lanky bespectacled man in a scruffy raincoat, he continued, 'This is Signor Boris Ouspensky. He's our contact in Russia. His job is to act as messenger for the businessmen in Moscow who have the painting.' Ouspensky bowed his head stiffly. 'Organising the transfer of the picture undercover from Russia is Signor Baldini.'

'It is my pleasure,' Baldini said, with a sequined smile.

General Malatesta waved his hand in the direction of the two men in grey suits: 'Signor Baldini's assistants, Mario and Giovanni. And here,' he indicated a man in a vivid checked jacket and dark glasses, who was seated at the table, 'is Signor Pennington.' No explanation as to his part in the proceedings was forthcoming.

An attractive, raven-haired woman of about 30, hovering in the shadows at the back of the room, remained unacknowledged by everyone. 'And the lady over there?' asked Scott.

Malatesta replied, 'Oh, yes. That's Ms Maruichi.'

Pennington rose from the table and approached Laurence. 'Mister Spencer, no necessity for you to innerduce yourself. Your reputation precedes you,' he drawled. 'If anyone can verify whether this picture is genu-ine, I believe you can.'

'Thank you, Mr Pennington. It's always a pleasure

to meet a fellow art dealer.' They shook hands.

Baldini looked Scott up and down. '*Scusi,* your name is?'

'Scott Lee.'

'And where are you from?'

'New York.'

'Ah, New York. You are here on holiday or working?'

'Working.'

'And what is it you do?'

'I'm a publisher, *un editore.*'

'Ah, *un editore.* Good.' Again, Baldini presented that flashing smile.

Pennington turned to Scott. 'I see you dress smart like a city slicker, so I suspect you ain't poor. I bet you get paid a heap of greenbacks. Isn't I right?'

'I'm not sure that's any of ...' Scott thought better of completing the sentence. Instead he said, 'Well, I have to admit I do make a fairly decent living.'

'And what is your business in Italy, if you don't mind me inquiring?' asked Baldini.

'Well, I'm going to try and arrange with the Uffizi Gallery for my firm to publish a series of books on some of its most important paintings.'

'Who do you deal with? Gennaro Lombardo?'

'Yeah, that's right.'

'I know this Lombardo. He's a nice guy.'

'Yeah, he's okay, I guess, although he can be ... difficult.'

'Difficult? Yes, I think you say right.'

'Mister Spencer.' Ouspensky spoke for the first time. 'On a different subject: you know Raphael's self-portrait in Hall 66 of the Uffizi?' Laurence nodded. 'We agree, I'm sure, that it is a pupil's copy of the painter's image in the *School of Athens* mural in Rome. It is not copied very well. There is too much thickness in the neck and shoulder. Is it not so?'

'Yes, it is. Also, if I recall correctly,' said Laurence, 'there's something odd about the appearance of the chest: it has a wavy line running down it, doesn't it?'

'Yes. That's because the pupil tried to alter the shape of the young man's robe.' Ouspensky glanced around the room at the faded and patchy frescoes. 'Anyway,' he said, turning to face Laurence again, 'we are concerned not with the ordinary Uffizi picture, but with a different cup of tea, as you English say. This is an extraordinary painting of a young man. His look is, how do you say, enigmatic. He is well dressed, he has style. The warm tones of his flesh, the fall of his hair, the fold of his sleeve, the fur collar of his robe: these are the undoubted touches of a master craftsman – which is hardly surprising as the master craftsman in question is Raphael, one of the greatest artists of all time. And the painting we are dealing with here, Raphael's *Portrait of a Young Man*, is one of the most valuable missing paintings in the world. It is worth millions!' Ouspensky reached into his inside coat pocket and pulled out an envelope. 'Here are some photos to prove we have the picture. But be warned!' he said. 'The photos I show you now are not good. Much better photos, and a video clip if you want, can be supplied – but *only* when my contacts in

Russia have received a nonreturnable goodwill payment of 750,000 dollars, which is a tiny percentage of how much the picture is worth.'

Laurence looked briefly at the photographs, then handed them to Scott. 'These prove absolutely nothing,' Laurence said. 'They aren't direct photographs. They are reproductions, very poor ones, of a not very clear illustration taken from some book or other – an art encyclopaedia maybe. Don't you agree, Scott?'

'Yeah, they're scans. You can see by the colour depth.'

'Frankly Mr Ouspensky,' Laurence said brusquely, 'I'm surprised your contacts in Russia haven't made a better show of proving they have *Portrait of a Young Man* – even if, as seems pretty likely at this moment, they don't! Quite why we,' he indicated the others, 'should be subjected to this pathetic charade is beyond me. But I'm sure these busy people here, like myself, have more important things to do with their time.'

At this Baldini (pretending to be outraged), Pennington and Malatesta rounded on Ouspensky.

'You think we're stupid?'

'You ain't got no evidence! God damn it! What dumb-arse kinda game are you playing at?'

'We have come here for nothing. It's ridiculous!'

Obviously shaken, Ouspensky began speaking earnestly. 'I assure you, my contacts have this painting in Russia, and ... and will supply proof of its existence when they are receiving the payment required of 750 ...'

Laurence interrupted, 'Look, Mr Ouspensky, let me make it *picture* clear: my client is *not* going to pay *anything* until I advise him that the Raphael exists and is genuine. And the only way I am going to be convinced enough to do that is if I see the painting for myself. Amongst other things, I have to make sure it's not a fake, a pastiche or a product of Raphael's workshop pupils and that it bears all the hallmarks of the style he developed when he was in Rome. So, when your contacts have been informed of my position and it dawns on them that they have no alternative but to show me the picture, no doubt you'll let me know. Now, I must go. Scott, are you coming? Goodbye everyone.' As Laurence turned, Giovanni and Mario stood between him and the door, but Baldini waved them aside. Laurence opened the door and stepped through to the chancel. When, moments later, Scott left with Frederico, he noticed that Ms Maruichi was talking animatedly to Pennington.

* * *

Back at the apartment, Laurence handed Scott a bourbon on the rocks and a small bowl of olives. 'Sorry about the waste of time,' he said.

'Oh don't worry about that,' Scott replied, sitting down with drink in hand. 'I found it all quite entertaining. If you ask me, I reckon this Ouspensky guy is on a fat commission. I'd say the Russkies have the Raphael all right, and they sure as hell want to convert it into big bucks.' He picked an olive out of the bowl, put it in his mouth and chewed, before dropping the stone onto a small silver salver on the coffee table in front of him. 'The sooner you verify the painting's authenticity, the quicker they'll get their spondoolies.' He raised the glass to his mouth and swallowed the contents. 'It doesn't make sense for them to protract matters. I figure it's Ouspensky's own initiative to ask for 750 grand, and I bet you if he gets it, he ain't intending to give any of it to charity!' Scott scooped up a handful of pistachio nuts from another bowl that Laurence offered him.

'I don't know,' said Laurence. 'I think it's more likely they don't actually have the Raphael, and they're trying to pull a fast one. I mean, once a thief, always a thief. Dear Mr O and his Russian arms-smuggling, cyber-attacking, drugs-trafficking associates are doubtless banking on one of the would-be buyers of the painting being mad enough and gullible enough to pay up three quarters of a million for nothing!' Laurence sat down and sipped his gin and tonic. 'After all, considering who Mr O's Italian contacts are, I hardly think it likely anyone is going to ask for their money back, if there is no portrait – do you?'

'Not unless they have an absolute hankering to be riddled with holes! But heck, it's not inconceivable ...' Scott got to his feet and waved his empty glass in the air. 'Mind if I grab another?'

'No, please help yourself.'

'Can I get you one?'

'No, thanks. I'm fine.'

Scott went over to the bar and poured himself another bourbon. 'As I was about to say, it's not inconceivable that the Russkies do have the painting and it *is* by Raphael.'

'Well, of course, that's ... that's what we all hope is the case.' Laurence sounded more animated. 'Once

I'm convinced we're dealing with the genuine article, I'll be doing my damnedest to buy the portrait for my client. As it's a sealed-bid auction, I'll just have to make sure my offer is higher than anyone else's!'

'I take it if you *are* successful, you're in for a big fat pay-out.'

'Yes, quite a tidy sum. The thing is I want to do something worthwhile with the money. The trust fund I started up a little while ago, together with the generous commission I'll be due to receive from my client, once the authenticated portrait has been delivered to the Czartoryski Museum in Krakow, will help me establish an Art Foundation – the *Spencer* Art Foundation – something I've dreamt of doing for quite a while now. It'll be a fitting bequest from someone who's spent his life buying and selling paintings for other people.'

'Fitting bequest? I would have thought it was far too early for you to be considering such things. You're only 56, for Chrissake!'

'Well, it will take several years to set up the Foundation – and who's to say I'll still be around when it's up and running? The decision is out of my hands.'

CHAPTER 3

Friday 16 August

Next morning, after a restful night, Scott spoke briefly to Laurence. He said he was due to see the Managing Editor of the Uffizi's Publications Department at 11:30. Before and after that, he had meetings with booksellers and publishers. He didn't expect to be back until about 18:00. They embraced one another, then Scott hurried down the stairs and out into the piazza.

After calling, as arranged, on the manager of the Libri d' Arte bookshop in Piazza Duomo, Scott made his way down the Via dei Calzaiuoli to the Piazza della Signori. He was early for his appointment with Lombardo, so he took the opportunity to call Claudia. 'Hi, honey! Sorry I didn't get to call you yesterday. The plane was late and unexpectedly Laurence took me to a meeting he had been asked to attend. How're things with you?'

'Fine, thanks. We've got a bit of a panic on here at the moment. There's been a marked increase in …' She stopped in mid-sentence. She knew how information of that sort disturbed Scott, so she thought it best not to mention what they had discovered at the Institute. '… in global warming, and as a result more and more creatures are migrating to Europe from the sub-tropics. At the Institute, we have to keep a record and make an analysis of each inflow. As you know, I'm also busy preparing for the talk I'm due to give in Rome on climate change.'

'Well, honey, don't get so involved with the Earth's problems that you forget all about me! I miss you. I want to see you. Can't we get together? How about if I come to Rome for the weekend?'

'No, no, not this weekend!' Claudia said, forcefully. 'I have too much to do.' Then, more softly, 'Next week is a different matter. I have to go to Florence, because I need to collect insect samples from the river area and elsewhere. I'll let you know exactly which day – also the arrival time of my train, so you can be a darling and collect me from the station.'

'Of course I will, honey. And although you'll be working, I trust we'll be able to … you know … make out. Will you be staying in your family's flat?'

'Yes. Which means—'

'Jeez!' Scott exclaimed, looking at his watch. 'I've gotta go, honey. I'm late for a meeting. Love you. See you next week.' He ended the call and went into the Piazzale degli Uffizi, where, outside in the blazing sun, there were seemingly endless lines of jostling tourists. Despite being accused of queue jumping, Scott managed to force his way through to the Uffizi Entrance Hall. Inside he found more tourists awaiting their turn to enter the Gallery. In the absence of air conditioning, the place was sweltering. Scott had to push past people – many of whom were sweaty and fractious – in order to reach the bookshop on the right-hand side. This was crowded, not just with potential customers, but also with people making their way to the Gallery exit. Beckoning Scott to join her, one of the shop assistants opened a door at the back of the shop and led him along a passageway to another door. 'This is Signor Lombardi's office,' she said.

Scott's meeting with the Uffizi's Managing Editor did not go well. Lombardo was an awkward person to deal with. A little man in big boots, he was by degrees pompous and arrogant. When he felt the impact of his own words required special emphasis, he would puff out his chest, place his hands on his hips and adopt a disdainful, head-back stance, as if he was imitating Benito Mussolini.

'Signor Lee, I *must* insist you pay reproduction fees. We have no arrangement *unless* you pay for copyright usage of photographs.'

'Okay, Signor Lombardo, I understand where you're coming from. Even so, if I may, I'd just like to go over again what's on offer here. We're proposing that the Uffizi and my company work *together* on a joint undertaking basis. Normally this means expenses and profits are split fifty-fifty between the parties. However, what I'm suggesting is a lot more generous for your side than ours ...'

'That surely is for us to decide, Signor Lee.'

'Yes, of course it is. The fact is, though, my company's offering to pay *all* the production costs of the venture – yet give you *half* the profits! This has gotta be a fantastic deal. It's like having Christmas all over again! There's only one condition: we'd like the

Uffizi to arrange copyright clearance of the photos of the paintings we choose to include in the book. Surely you don't have a problem with this? It's not an unreasonable request, given that the photos are to be taken by the Uffizi's own recommended photographers?'

'I regret I can't agree with this!' exclaimed Lombardo, striking his *Il Duce* pose once more. 'The Uffizi will allow use of these photos *only* if *you* pay repro fees to our photographers.'

'If we have to pay production costs *and* repro fees,' Scott said with a hint of irritation, 'we might as well publish the books ourselves – and forget altogether about co-publishing them with the Uffizi!'

'If you are publishing books like this, the Uffizi will require an appropriate sum of money for the reproduction of *its* paintings – and if that is not forthcoming, we will have no alternative but to sue your company for substantial damages!'

Jeez, thought Scott, *what the fuck am I doing wasting my time with this puffed-up jerk?* He looked at his watch and said pleasantly, 'Signor Lombardo, why don't we go and have an early lunch somewhere and hash this over? It sure would suit us both if we could come to an amicable agreement.'

But Lombardo was determined. 'Taking lunch is a nice idea, *grazie* – but please be advised, I will not change my mind. You *must* pay repro fees!'

* * *

That same morning, at Castello di Montezano, Baldini addressed Malatesta, Ouspensky, Mario, Giovanni, together with his crew of *soldati* and their *capo*: 'I just wanted to make you aware of a recent development. Our friends in the Bratva – through their agent Boris Ouspensky – have offered me a batch of surplus weapons that they want to sell off. I've agreed to buy the weapons at a very favourable price. Unusually, Boris also offered me a painting, which he says is a missing masterpiece and extremely valuable. Now, as many of you will be aware, I know absolutely nothing about art. Rather than look at paintings or sculpture, I prefer to watch football or boxing. However, to sell Boris's painting for what I hope will be a lot of money, we need to prove it is genuine and not fake. Fortunately, we think we may have found an expert to do this for us. If that proves to be the case, I shall want to deal personally with the expert. But first, we have to collect the painting from Russia. That will be the responsibility of Gennady Alexandrov and Ms Mariuchi, who are away today in Calabria. Bruno, you and your men will protect and secure the painting when and while it's in Italy.'

* * *

In her office with its beautiful view, Claudia was compiling her notes on the environment. It was late in the day. It was quiet. No one else was in the Institute offices. She wrote:

5. There is now definite evidence that renewable energy can make global warming worse. Large-scale GM tree plantations, soil modification, bioenergy crops: they all add to the on-going damage of global warming.

6. Together with global warming, climate change and greenhouse gas emissions are major problems that mankind has created and is still not addressing effectively.

7. Climate change is gradually moving the North Pole. As ice melts and aquifers [layers of rock that hold water] are drained, the Earth's distribution of mass is changing.

8. Greenland's ice sheet is melting. Half of its surface is now liquid. Huge hunks of ice break off and their movement causes earthquakes.

9. Pollution of the sea has an adverse effect on marine wildlife – as seen in the corals of the Great Barrier Reef.

10. Air pollution harms human health (those particularly affected are walkers, cyclists, asthma sufferers, children and older people with breathing difficulties). It is caused by carbon dioxide emissions and other greenhouse gases being released into the Earth's atmosphere when fossil fuels – coal, gas, natural gas, petrol, diesel – are burned. Among other consequences, it creates acid rain, which generates environmental harm, principally to forests and lakes.

11. As the climate has warmed, so some types of extreme weather – e.g. severe thunderstorms, hurricanes, tornadoes, tropical cyclones, windstorms, winter storms, tsunamis – have become more frequent and extreme, with increases in overall temperature, intense precipitation and drought.

12. Global warming, …

Claudia looked at the time on her laptop. *Mio Dio*! she thought. *It's almost 20:30. I must get this finished and go home.* Tapping rapidly at the keyboard, she completed the final sentence:

… climate change, greenhouse gas emissions – these are

problems that man has caused and is still not confronting effectively or with any urgency.

Claudia's parents lived in the Tuscan city of Pistoia. Sara, her mother, was bedridden and, because Roberto was nearly always away working, she hardly saw anyone during the day except the cleaner. Claudia had a guilty conscience about not visiting her mother on a regular basis. She knew she was putting her own interests first. Apart from that, she dreaded hearing for the umpteenth time that she should stop having aimless affairs and get married! On the few visits that Claudia made to Pistoia, her mother, without fail, expressed her wish and hope that Claudia would settle down with someone of her own age and give birth to a succession of bright and beautiful *bambini*. To her disappointment, Claudia had become involved with Scott Lee, an American, who was almost twice her age.

Claudia had been drawn to Scott when they first met, in March, at a publisher's party in Rome for the launch of a book on environmental art. It was not difficult to see why. Being an American, he was different. He had an unusual sense of humour. He was good company. Unlike some of his compatriots, he did not try to dominate the conversation and shout down other people when they were talking. He was kind and generous. He was dependable and practical. And, notwithstanding the air of cool shrewdness and aplomb with which he conducted his business dealings, he was a romantic at heart. He was also, unlike most of the Italian men of her acquaintance, who had usually been 'fast' in several senses of the word, a considerate and caring lover.

Claudia worked on her notes until after 21:00. She also read her emails, including one from the Institute's office in southern Italy:

Situation here not great. Little whiners no longer just a nuisance. Now a major threat - with regular increase in no. & size. Many different species coming over from sub-tropics on weekly basis. More & more humans being bitten. Virus infection rife. In circumstances shldn't we make public aware of seriousness of situation & recommend measures to be taken to reduce risk of being attacked?

She replied:

Am preparing list of recommended precautions 4 general distribution. When ready, will email U copy. Meanwhile suggest U call on hotels, pharmacies, supermarkets, restaurants with outdoor dining areas, etc. & advise them 2 stock up with repellent creams, wipes & sprays.

She locked the offices, went downstairs and hailed a taxi. Seven minutes later, she arrived at her destination. Overlooking the peaceful wooded Piazza d' Azeglio, the Mattioli family apartment was on the third floor of a splendid nineteenth-century building, which was distinguished by its old parquet flooring, beautiful fresco ceilings and original carved doors. Claudia went inside and the first thing she did was to call her mother.

CHAPTER 4

Saturday 17 August

At 07:40 the next morning, Claudia received the following text:

Am aware this is bit sooner than discussed, but I think U should go 2 Florence 2day 2 investigate situation there, & catch & forward 2 us as many specimens as poss. Yrs Ettore

Claudia's first reaction was: '*Accidenti*! There goes my weekend!' She had planned to complete her notes on global warming and begin her article for the *Journal of Ecology* on 'The Life Cycle of the Mosquito'. But going to Florence did have its compensations. First, she loved the city, and secondly Scott, who loved her, would be waiting for her there. *So lovemaking, rather than note-taking, will be my main preoccupation for the next few days,* was her thought – and she smiled as she anticipated the carnal pleasure there would be in exhausting her older lover with her sexual demands.

She sent Scott a text:

Ettore wants me visit Florence 2day. So if convenient will catch 16:00 train arriving SM Novello at 17:30. Cxxx

Almost immediately she received an answer:

Fantastic honey! Have no fear, I'll be there at the station to meet U. Can't tell U how much I long 2 see you again. Tanto amore - S

* * *

'Mario, can you fetch the chef, *per favore*,' Baldini asked. 'Meanwhile, Giovanni, you and a couple of guys bring the tables out here. Each table sits four people, so ... let me see, I'm expecting 22 and possibly another two ... so we want six tables. By the way, who's putting up the marquee?"

Mario, who had returned with the chef, answered, 'Conti Awnings and Canopies, boss.'

'Well, call them and tell them if they're not here in five minutes, something nasty is going to happen to them! Now, chef, I want you to note down ... have you got a pen and some paper?'

'Yes, sir.'

'Good. I want you to make a note of the food I'd like you to prepare for tomorrow's lunch. For the antipasto,' Baldini continued, 'we'll have a selection of sliced cold meats, tomato crostini, white bean and – you're not keeping up with me, can't you write faster? – white bean and tuna salad, and fava beans and pecorino. For the pasta course: *gnocchetti* with spinach, noodles with chickpeas, *strapponi* with wild boar, and *pappardelle* with *cavolo nero*. We'll have some fish. Let me see, what about crayfish in a pan, seafood stew, and fillets of sole *Fiorentina*? For the main course: I think we'll have pork steak with black olives, roast duck with—'

Mario returned. 'Boss, the marquee people are here. Do you want me to deal with them?'

'No, Mario. Send them to me right away. Now, Chef, where were we?'

'We'd got to roast duck, sir. But sir, I think we have too many dishes, no? After all, there are only 20 guests—'

'Allow for 24 – and I want them to be *inundated* with food and wine.' Giovanni and another man started bringing in the tables. 'There's nothing worse than going to a special lunch party and finding there isn't enough to eat! Giovanni, arrange the tables in a circle, will you? Don't forget we need something to put the food on – longer tables, four of them, which can be placed lengthways around the tables in the middle, so that you have a circle within a square.' Mario came back with three men. 'These the marquee people? Right. Mario, instruct the steward to lay the tables with Venetian lace tablecloths and red and gold place settings, together with cut-crystal and gold goblets. Now, as for you lot. You were supposed to be here over an hour ago. Let me tell you, if you had been another five minutes late, I would have told you to go ahead and erect the marquee, and then I would have hung each one of you by your balls from the crossbar! In future, remember who you're dealing with. I take it you've fulfilled my request for a cream-coloured sailcloth marquee with terracotta-coloured flooring.'

'*Sì*, signor,' said one of the men, nervously. 'We're sorry we're so late, but we got held up by—'

'I don't want to hear your excuses,' Baldini interrupted. 'Just get on with it, do your job and go! But in the process, make sure you don't damage anything.' He went over to where Mario and two *soldati* were laying the tables. 'Mario, leave that for the moment. These guys are going to put up the marquee – hopefully without smashing the crockery! Watch 'em, will you?'

* * *

That afternoon Laurence went to see Frances Morley in her Grand Deluxe Suite at the Westin Excelsior Hotel. Frances's husband, J. Reynolds ('JR') Morley, an avid collector of *Quattrocento* paintings, was well known to Laurence. Frances, on the other hand, he didn't know, except by reputation. As an MP and long-standing member of the UK Defence Select Committee, she had been well known for her forthright views, particularly on the growing influence in the UK of organised crime.

First, there were the usual social preliminaries to go through: Frances and Laurence greeted each other in the continental manner as if they were long-standing friends. Frances explained that 'JR' was away in Urbino, where he was hoping to buy a rediscovered 'Bagu-etta' ('I think you'll find it's probably a Berruguete,' Laurence commented). Laurence was shown an uncomfortable-looking Louis Quinze-style fauteuil to sit on, and then, with an extravagant flourish, Frances's manservant opened a bottle of Giulio Ferrari Reserva, handed them each a fluteful and then discreetly left the room.

'How can I help?' Frances asked, holding her mobile in front of her and looking briefly at a text message she had received.

'Well, I am wondering whether you can possibly give me some information about smuggling by organised crime groups – particularly of weapons and drugs.'

'That's not your normal field of interest, is it? I mean, I thought you'd want to know who's *stealing paintings*, not running arms or drug trafficking!'

'Well, in a manner of speaking, odd though it may seem, I need to be brought up to date on their criminal activities. Let me explain.' Without revealing too many details, Laurence told her about his interest in a painting (he described it as 'a valuable missing masterpiece') which was being offered for sale by the Mafia.

'My, what an adventurous life you lead! I had no idea that members of the art world have such fun. "JR", in comparison, never seems to do *anything* exciting.'

'It's not always fun, Frances, believe you me. At times it can be awfully boring and unrewarding. Anyway, in the position I currently find myself, don't you think I need to know something about the sort of people I'm dealing with and what the potential risks are?'

Frances nodded her head. 'Where the Mafia is concerned,' she said, 'it's advisable to have one's wits about one. Be inadvertent and before you can say "Al Capone", you'll be history just like him. Although it's a much more sophisticated organisation than of old, the Mafia – and I'm talking here about the current dominant family, the 'Ndrangheta – still doesn't hesitate to remove, by one means or another, anyone who stands in their way.' Laurence sat back, sipped his champagne and listened attentively as Frances summarised the Mafia's various smuggling activities. 'Its bread-and-butter business is arms smuggling. It buys weapons from America, Britain, Germany, Russia – particularly Russia, where there's an explosive mix of economic crisis, unpaid or late-paid workers and seriously lax security controls. Guns that have been appropriated from the manufacturers find their way into the hands of four or five Russian arms agents, who then sell the assorted Saigas, Kalashnikovs, Dragunovs on to the Mafia. It, in turn, sells the guns to ISIS, Al-Qaeda, the Taliban, Boko-Haram, Hezbollah, etc. – whoever's looking to buy weapons secretly and at discounted prices.'

'Is Ouspensky one of those agents?'

'Yes, he is.'

'What about drugs?'

'Drug trafficking is 'Ndrangeta's main activity. Unbelievably, they control 80 per cent of Europe's cocaine traffic. They obtain the drugs mostly from dealers in South America – but they also have contacts with producers in Russia.'

'Are they Mafia as well?'

'Yes, they're members of the Bratva, the Russian wing of the Mafia. They smuggle cocaine from Russia into Italy and then supply it to other European countries such as France, Germany and Spain. 'Ndrangeta also has syndicates in the US and Canada. Basically, it runs a global criminal network, which is involved in not only guns and drugs, but also fraud, counterfeiting, cyber crime, extortion, human trafficking, gambling, credit card and identity theft, etc., etc. You name it, they're into it.'

'You don't mention it,' said Laurence, 'but art theft is presumably one of their criminal activities, and I was wondering why.'

'What happens is that, in order to finalise the sale of weapons or drugs to an interested purchaser, the Mafia sometimes throws in a valuable stolen masterpiece at a heavily discounted sale price as an added incentive. There was a well-documented case of this happening quite recently. It involved a couple of undercover Carabinieri agents posing as drug traffickers. They were in Moscow negotiating with intermediaries about a large consignment of cocaine, when they were approached by two so-called art experts, who said they were acting on behalf of the vendors of the consignment. They wanted to know whether, as part of the overall deal, the agents would like to buy *Madonna of the Hay* – a painting believed to be by Raphael – at an advantageous price.'

'Which if I recall correctly,' Laurence said, 'was a painting once owned by a Victorian ancestor of the late Princess Diana. Then subsequently it popped up in a gallery in Germany, from where it disappeared in the 1920s.'

'Yes, that's right – and it reappeared in the early noughties as part of the negotiation between the art specialists and carabinieri agents in question. The specialists offered the painting to the agents for $15,000,000. In response, the agents said they were prepared to pay half that figure, so long as the sale took place in Italy and was subject to verification, by impartial experts, of the painting's authenticity. The two art specialists and their courier, whose position as a diplomat at the Italian Embassy in Rome gave him safe passage to convey the painting to Italy from its hiding place in Switzerland, were caught and prosecuted for VAT fraud. Needless to say, they didn't reveal the identity of the big fish behind the operation. The painting, incidentally, was found to be a fake.'

Later, in the car on the way back to Piazza Santissima della Annunziata, Laurence reflected upon the precariousness of his position. He was participating in an illegal and inordinately hazardous venture. He was dealing with members of a worldwide criminal organisation, who based on his advice proposed to hold the clandestine sale of one of the world's most sought-after works of art. Much was at stake: his honour, his principles, his self-respect, his dependability – not to mention his professional reputation. Also, he would more than likely forfeit the good opinion and support of his clients and his friends.

Back at his apartment, Laurence sank into an easy chair and asked Paolo to mix him a gin and tonic. The thought uppermost in his mind was: *What* have *I got myself into?*

* * *

Scott had several shortcomings, the principal one being his obsession with Claudia. He found he couldn't be without her. When he was away from her, he felt unfulfilled, aimless, empty. When he was with her, his sense of purpose revived, he was much happier in himself, and he was prepared to accept there was some point to the repetitiveness of everyday existence. Even so, he feared he was not living up to her expectations. Aside from being high-powered intellectually, Claudia was keen on a variety of outdoor activities. She ran, she cycled, she swam, she played tennis, she went horse riding. She also enjoyed sex – to a degree that was highly energetic and demanding. Scott knew he couldn't match her either physically or mentally, and for that reason believed he would lose her to someone nearer her own age, who was better suited and had youth and stamina on his side when it came to raising a family. He was 27 years older than Claudia. Why settle down with an older partner, when she could take her pick from a wide diversity of younger men, who would fall all over themselves just to be introduced to her?

Scott had been waiting for nearly half an hour when Claudia's overdue Trenitalia pulled into the Stazione di Santa Maria Novella just after 18:00. The tedium of this delay, and the aggravation he still felt because of his inconclusive meeting with Lombardo, evaporated as soon as Claudia walked down the platform towards him. Wearing her hair long, she was dressed simply in a coral skater dress with matching sandals. He reached out for her and she fell into his arms. After they had kissed, she stepped back and said, 'Darling, don't get too excited, will you? I afraid I didn't get much sleep last night and I've had a tiring day, so I'd like to have an early supper and then go to bed.'

Scott's face lit up. 'Oh yeah honey, that's a great idea. I've been longing to—'

'No, Scott. You misunderstand me,' she said. 'I plan to go to bed to sleep – not to mess about.'

Scott's face fell. 'But honey, I love you. I want to kiss you, caress you, give you pleasure …'

'*Not* tonight. I need to catch up on my sleep, and while I'm doing that I *don't* want to be disturbed. So, I suggest you sleep in the other room. Now let's go and get something to eat.'

Scott almost cried. This woman he loved was not only beautiful, intelligent, warm-hearted and sensual. At times she could also be heartless, wilful and insensitive. As they were sitting down to dinner in a local trattoria, Claudia leant towards Scott with a big smile. 'Don't look so glum, darling. I was only kidding. We'll have sex tonight, believe you me.' She thought how easy it was for her to excite men and then deflate them.

CHAPTER 5

At 08:15 Scott came out of the bedroom to find Claudia in the kitchen making coffee.

'Did you manage to get any sleep?'

'Yes – in between bouts of strenuous activity!' he said, with a chuckle.

'Same with me. Strangely, I don't feel tired. I feel quite rested. In fact,' she said, going right up to him, 'I'm ready for some more.' She put her hand between his legs and squeezed. 'It *is* Sunday, after all.'

Scott embraced her. They kissed passionately, and were on the point of returning to the bedroom when Scott's mobile buzzed. 'Oh crap! Now who can that be?' He put the mobile to his ear. 'Oh, hi Laurence.' He looked at Claudia resignedly.

'Can we possibly get together sometime today?' Laurence asked. 'There's been a development of sorts in the Raphael business, which I'd like to discuss with you. How about lunch?'

'Great.' Scott looked at Claudia. 'Erm, will it be a hassle if Claudia comes along, too? Thing is, we haven't met up for a while, and before she goes back to Rome, I'd like to spend as much time with her as I can.'

'Yes, of course, by all means bring Claudia – love to see her again. You'll have to fill her in on what's happening – but please, old chap, do ask her to keep it quiet. Shall we say 12:30 here at my flat?'

'Sure, see you then.' Scott caught hold of Claudia's hand. 'Laurence has asked us to lunch at 12:30. That means we have four hours to kill. What the hell are we going to do, I wonder?'

'Oh don't worry. I have a few ideas,' Claudia said. 'But first I'm going to take a shower.'

'I'll join you.'

* * *

Scott and Claudia left her apartment at 12:20, and as they hurried along the Via della Colonna, Scott noticed the sign outside a newsagent's: **'ZANZARI: ALLARMANTE AUMENTO DEL VOLUME E DIMENZIONI'** ['MOSQUITOES: ALARMING INCREASE IN VOLUME AND SIZE!'] He went in and came out with a copy of *Il Tempo,* which he offered to Claudia. 'Honey, tell me what they're going on about, will you? Am I to understand I'm going to be bitten more often in future?'

Setting off at a quick pace, she said over her shoulder, 'Hang onto it. I'll read it later, although if the reporter in question says anything I don't already know about, I'll be surprised.'

'The article isn't aimed at know-alls like you. It's aimed at numbskulls like me!'

About five minutes later they were standing in

Piazza della Santissima Annunziata outside the impressive building in which Laurence rented an apartment. Scott pushed the buzzer. One of the main oak entrance doors flew open and Laurence emerged carrying a battered leather attaché case. 'Sorry, chaps. Just been trying to get hold of you. We're going right past your place and could have picked you up on the way. Hello, Claudia, my lovely.' He kissed her on both cheeks.

'On the way where?' asked Scott.

'A castle midway between Castellina and Poggibonsi.'

'A castle?' asked Scott.

'Yes. Castello di Montezano. It'll take about 45 minutes, if the traffic out of the city isn't too bad – although, of course, there's a big football match on this afternoon, so there might be a few delays. Hope you don't mind. We'll take the A1, then the Via Chiantigiana – which has the most amazing views. Paolo's waiting beside the car around the corner. You probably walked straight past him!'

'But why are we going to a castle? Are we going on a sightseeing tour?' Scott sounded bemused.

'No. We've been invited to the castle for lunch – by Signor Baldini, no less. I'll tell you all about it on the way.' Laurence closed the front door and led Scott and Claudia to a large dark blue Mercedes, which was parked at the beginning of the Via della Colonna with its engine running and emergency lights flashing. Paolo opened the nearside back door for Claudia and then went round the other side to let Scott in. Laurence sat in the front.

As they made their way out of Florence, Laurence revealed that, since the meeting in the Badia, he had not been allowed a moment's peace by either Ouspensky or Baldini, one or other of whom had been calling him almost continuously: Ouspensky to insist that his Russian contacts could not, under any circumstances, let the Raphael out of their possession unless they received the down payment of $750,000; and Baldini to express the hope that Laurence would decide, in the best interests of all concerned, to persuade his client to pay the money.

Laurence had not budged an inch, holding steadfastly to his resolve that no one was going to be paid anything until he had personally seen and vetted the alleged Raphael painting. Thus, deadlocked and at cross purposes, the parties might have remained, had not Baldini rung him late the previous evening to declare that he and his business associates, who he did not identify, would themselves pay the $750,000 – so long as it was understood that if the Raphael was found to be genuine, and only in that event, the money would be refunded. Although he doubted the two men's motives and suspected that the painting, if it existed, was a fake, Laurence felt he had to agree to meet Baldini to discuss the proposal further.

On the autostrada, the occupants enjoyed the soundlessness inside the big car, as it moved smoothly on its way, hardly varying its speed from 150km/h, except when an errant Fiat Panda or Lancia Ypsilon dawdling in the fast lane necessitated a quick application of the disc brakes. After about 25 minutes of sweeping along the A1, they turned off onto the Via Chiantigiano. Passing through Greve, Panzano and Castellina, they turned right for Poggibonsi. Ten minutes later they arrived at Castello di Montezano, the medieval fortress village on a hill that had been transformed into a magnificent five-star hotel, and found Signor Baldini's lunch party was already under way. There were some 20 people circulating in what had been the village piazza, and where, under an extensive crimson-and-gold awning, an ample buffet lunch was presented on flawlessly laid tables. It was an ostentatious display, which was made more striking for being set against a backdrop of dark green trees and olive groves, rolling umber-coloured hills and brilliant cerulean sky. The encircling houses were constructed of irregularly shaped stones with terracotta brick door and window surrounds, together with large rectangular quoins in the corners.

Baldini broke away from a group of guests and came bustling towards Laurence, Scott and Claudia, flashing his now familiar smile. 'Ah, signori, *buongiorno*! This is a great honour. I'm very happy you have joined us!' He shook their hands vigorously and with a forceful grip.

'Signor Baldini,' said Scott, retracting his hand, 'may I introduce my partner, Doctor Claudia Mattioli.'

'Signorina, what a pleasure! I was talking to your father a moment ago and he—'

'Papa is here?'

'Yes, he is. He went into the garden to call someone on his mobile.'

'He's a colleague of yours, then?'

'A business associate, yes, didn't you know?'

Laurence looked at Scott. 'I hope you don't mind me asking, Signor Baldini, but exactly how many people know about the – er …' he lowered his voice, 'painting?'

'I think only ten of these people here.'

'But was it necessary, I wonder, to let anyone else know other than those who were at the Badia on Thursday?'

'The people here are mostly those who *were* in the Badia! Signori Ouspensky, Pennington and Malatesta are here, also *il mio dipendenti* Giovanni and Mario. Those who were not at the Badia,' he said, pointing at the persons concerned, 'are Signor Alexandrov, my friend Caterina, and the signorina's father and his friend—'

Scott interrupted. 'The woman over there with long dark hair who's talking to the elderly man in a brown suit. *She* was at the Badia. Am I right? You told me her name, but I've forgotten it.'

'*Già, è vero.* Her name is Francesca Maruichi. She's talking to Signor Gennady Alexandrov. He's a Russian entrepreneur, who has dealings with the Bratva. I'll introduce you to him later. But first, my friends, you are eating, no? Then afterwards, Signor Spencer and I are having a chat.' Baldini took Claudia by the arm and led her over to the tables under the awning. Scott and Laurence followed behind. 'We have many good things here for you, *tipico di la Toscana.*' Baldini indicated the opulent array of gold tureens on ornate heaters and large china serving dishes laden with food. 'Here are the antipasti and pasta*,* here the *pesce e carni.* And there is plenty of salads and vegetables. It's all very good, no? But I think it is too much for not that many people? *Non fa niente*! You have what you like. Just make your choice and the waiter is putting it on your plate. Then you and your fellow guests will please sit at this table here. *Buon appetito*!' Having said this seemingly without drawing breath, Baldini rushed off in the direction of the house.

'Scott, old chap,' said Laurence, 'you and Claudia organise the starters, while I go over to the bar and get some drinks.'

In the course of a lavishly overabundant meal, which was accompanied by some fine Tuscan wines, Laurence was not particularly surprised to discover from talking to the other guests that, once he had seen and authenticated the Raphael portrait, he would not be the only person interested in buying the painting on behalf of a client. Apparently Hyram G. Pennington had been commissioned to hand Ouspensky a sealed bid on behalf of an American collector, one of the wealthiest men in the world. Something else Laurence found out, and wished he hadn't, was that Ouspensky's Russian contacts dealt in a variety of stolen goods other than works of art, including arms, drugs and radioactive materials. This information he obtained from the two couriers who had been assigned to escort the painting on its journey from Russia to Italy: Francesca Maruichi and Gennady Alexandrov. The latter, after he had drunk a considerable amount of Antinori Solaia, disclosed that the Raphael painting was being thrown in as part of a deal involving weapons, such as submachine guns and pistols. He didn't know exactly what was being sold.

He also didn't know, or wouldn't reveal, the identity of the likely buyer or buyers of these weapons.

Meanwhile, Claudia found, somewhat to her surprise, that her father had left. And so had a man described as his associate, one Giorgio Belori, who Claudia did not know. She thought it strange that Roberto should go without speaking to her – and a pity that he had missed an opportunity, in convivial surroundings, to get to know Scott better. As it was, she and Scott spent most of their time talking to Baldini and Caterina Ricci, a petite dark-haired, brown-eyed, chain-smoking beauty who was clearly more than just a friend to Baldini. While she and Claudia discussed the latest Italian designer fashions, Baldini pumped Scott for details about Laurence's business connections and, in particular, his dealings with the British Royal Family. Scott attempted to feed his curiosity with some harmless information, but Baldini was not so easily satisfied. His questions became more persistent and less easy to fend off, when, fortunately for Scott, Bruno Malatesta came over and joined their table. It turned out that the General, a football fanatic, had been watching the Italian series match between Fiorentina and AS Roma on television, and he could talk of little else.

At about 16:00 Laurence, having circulated amongst the guests, came over to advise Baldini that he would be leaving shortly. 'I wonder if we could possibly have our little chat now,' he said.

'*Ma sì!* We go inside. Just follow me, please.'

The tête-à-tête between Baldini and Laurence took place in the Castello Reception Office. Sipping Picolit and eating slices of *Panforte Margherita*, they sat in ergonomic office chairs beneath LED panel lights and spoke quietly and reasonably to one another. Laurence wanted to know more about what he described as 'the shadows in the background', i.e. Baldini's business associates and Ouspensky's Russian contacts: who they were and, in the first case, how and why they were going to put up the $750,000 advance payment and, in the second case, what other sale items were on offer as part of the transaction involving the portrait presumed to be by Raphael. Baldini talked a great deal, but revealed little of substance. Whereas it was perfectly understandable, he said, that anybody in Laurence's position would want to know who and what they were dealing with, unfortunately he was not at liberty, at that time, to name names or disclose sensitive information. His associates had sworn him to secrecy, and Ouspensky had not revealed who his contacts were, for the same reason. The fact was that his four associates and he had each raised $150,000 and, if Laurence was in agreement, Ouspensky would go ahead and pay the advance, in dollars, to the Russians, following which Laurence would be provided with evidence of the existence of the painting in the form of digital camera photographs on CD. If he found these interesting enough to induce him to see and assess the painting, arrangements would be put in hand to transport it from Russia to Italy by diplomatic courier. Once the painting had arrived in Italy and hopefully been authenticated by Laurence, Baldini and his friends would expect to be repaid their money, interest free, promptly.

Laurence sensed that it would difficult to get Baldini to divulge anything further. The information that both Baldini and Alexandrov had given him would have to suffice, for the time being. Meanwhile, it was evident that if they were to make any progress so far as the painting was concerned, he had to agree to the proposal that the down payment be made by Baldini's syndicate. Laurence's commission in the matter did not include making payments in advance of examining and establishing the genuineness of the painting, and, as no one else was prepared to pay the $750,000, he clearly had no alternative.

'Signor Baldini,' he said. 'On consideration, I think I may be able to go along with your proposal. However, there's one point that needs to be clarified. What happens if the painting turns out to be a fake? There's no way I can persuade my client to cough up $750,000 – unless the painting we're dealing with *is* a genuine Raphael. Until such time as I am satisfied that that's the case, he has given me strict instructions not to make *any* payments at all.'

Baldini opened his arms. 'My dear Signor Spencer, you have no worry. My associates and I, we will put up the money on the basis that the painting is real. If the painting is fake, too bad – we will lose our money!'

Laurence wondered whether Baldini, who appeared to be so laid-back about the matter, would in fact remain so if he and his companions *did* lose their money.

* * *

On their way back, about half a kilometre from Castellina, the quartet in the Mercedes encountered a succession of diversion signs. 'We did come this way this morning, didn't we Paolo?' asked Scott.

'*Si*, signor.'

'Well, I don't recall any detour due to roadworks. It's kinda weird, too, that there's no one *doing* any work!'

'There's nothing odd about that,' said Claudia. 'In Italy it's unusual – if not unheard of – for anyone to carry out road repairs at the weekend.'

'So that means,' Scott remarked, 'some jerk must have come out here this afternoon to stick up these signs specially, even though there's no intention of carrying out any work here until Monday! That wouldn't happen in the States.'

'Yes, but don't you realise there's not an Italian in the surrounding area,' said Laurence, 'who would want, indeed could be bribed, to work on a Saturday afternoon when Fiorentina are playing at home!'

'This way we go now,' said Paolo, rotating the steering wheel, 'is in the wrong direction. It takes us to Poggibonsi. I know this road. It is stony and has *molti curve*!'

Leading to Fioraie and the Natural Forest Reserve of St Agnes, the *strada provinciale* they found themselves on was up-and-down and twisty. However, this was not to be their only cause for concern.

As they approached a 180° hairpin bend, a red Fiat saloon with black tinted windows emerged at speed from a side turning on the left and swung in front of the Mercedes. '*Coglione!*' Paolo muttered under his breath. Pressing the left-hand paddle shifter to change down into second gear, he chased the Fiat into the corner ahead. Halfway round, Paolo accelerated: the engine snarled and the big car lurched, with its tyres flicking up stones, as it surged forwards.

'Careful, Paolo!' Laurence cried. 'Don't forget we have a lady on board.'

'Oh, don't mind me,' exclaimed Claudia, 'I enjoy going fast!'

Scott, on the other hand, was thinking, *Why in this lovely country do they all have to drive like third-rate Sennas, so that a pleasant afternoon outing turns into a goddamned race?*

As the two cars drew alongside on the way up to the next bend, the back window of the Fiat opened slightly and something glinted in the gap. Paolo flipped the right-hand paddle to change up into third. As they hurtled towards the next bend, Laurence noticed that the speed readout reached 150km/h. *Oh my God!* he thought. *Please don't let them push my new car off the road!*

Having expertly drifted the Mercedes round the bend, Paolo accelerated hard up the next incline.

'My man here used to drive karts,' Laurence advised Scott and Claudia, with a grim half-smile.

In a series of thrusts and turns they carved their way up the hill – braking, sliding, accelerating, with the red Fiat in hot pursuit. Just over the brow, the speeding Mercedes was confronted by a large black Toyota SUV, which had triple-loop bullbars across its front and was being driven in the middle of the road. *Jeez, this could end up being rather messy!* was Scott's instinctive reaction as he reached for Claudia's hand and held onto it. Both vehicles braked fiercely, scrabbling for grip on the rough surface. The driver of the Toyota slewed his vehicle across the road with the apparent aim of boxing in the other vehicle. At precisely the same instant Paolo put the Mercedes into a leftward slide, so that its back wheels were spinning on the very edge of the road, from which there was a precipitous drop into the valley below. Scott, who was sitting in the offside passenger backseat, stared into the abyss and the thought occurred to him that he might never have another bourbon. Having somehow swerved around the Toyota, Paolo applied a half-turn of opposite lock, which had the desired effect of straightening the car, and, tapping the paddle shifter through the gears up to fourth with the car going from 60 to 130km/h, he drove towards the first of the 20 or so curves that zigzagged down the hill.

Meanwhile, having failed to restart the Toyota, which had stalled because of the attempted blocking of the Mercedes, the driver beckoned to the occupants of the Fiat. 'Come and give me a hand!' he shouted. Three men got out of the Fiat and went over to help him push the Toyota to one side. A fourth occupant of the car, Primo, a large man in dark glasses who was named after Primo Carnera, the huge Italian boxer of the 1930s, extricated himself from the passenger seat and sauntered over to the road edge. He looked down into the valley. 'They're almost at the bottom of the hill,' he observed, in a deep voice. 'You'll never catch them now.'

'It doesn't matter,' said the driver of the Fiat. 'Our mission is accomplished. We've done our job. We've given them a good scare!'

The man was mistaken. The sequence of events had taken place so rapidly and been handled so dexterously by Paolo that there hadn't been time for his passengers to be alarmed by what was happening. However, once the threat of danger had passed and the adrenaline had stopped pumping, each was affected in a different way. Laurence was relieved that Claudia, Scott and Paolo were unharmed, for their safety had been his main concern. They were innocent parties, he was sure of that. *He* was the intended target of the would-be killers, and if it had come down to it and an opportunity had presented itself, he would have sacrificed himself to save the others.

Of the three, Scott had been the only one to realise the possible danger they faced. He knew how close they had come to slipping off the road and barrelling down the hillside. He smiled at Claudia. 'You okay, honey?'

She nodded. 'Yes, I'm fine.' Initially exhilarated by the speed of the car, Claudia had come back to earth with a jolt. What had the men in the Fiat been trying to do – kill them all? If so, why? And would they be safe from further attack? She had every reason to reflect upon what had happened, as did Scott and Laurence, and on the way back to Florence the three of them tried to figure out who had been behind the apparent attempt on their lives.

'I doubt it was the Mafia,' Laurence said, 'not now I've sorted things out with Baldini.'

'It's gotta be a gang of screwballs,' Scott said to Laurence, 'who have a grudge against you or me – but hopefully not Claudia. Or maybe it's someone who knows about, and doesn't care for, your dealings with the criminal fraternity.'

'Oh, I don't know. I mean, apart from Baldini's lunch guests, who else is aware of my connections with the Mafia?'

'*And* knew we were going to be at the Castello?' added Claudia.

'Well, I think only Messrs Baldini and Ouspensky knew that,' said Laurence, 'although, of course, they could have told any or all of the others.'

'It's gotta be somebody who can count on the heavy mob to run around sticking up unauthorised road signs and trying to force good folk like us off the goddamned road!' exclaimed Scott.

'In that case,' said Claudia, 'whoever it is probably stayed on at the Castello after we left, so he or she would have an alibi. Do you remember who was still there when we left?'

'I guess Pennington and the General were. Also Signorina Mariuchi and what's his name – er—'

'Gennady Alexandrov,' said Laurence.

'Yeah, that's it. I think Ouspensky quit early – not long after your dad and Signor Belori.'

'What about Malatesta?' asked Laurence. 'Don't you find it surprising that the man in charge of the Police Stolen Arts and Antiques Unit should be helping members of the Mafia to arrange the sale of a valuable stolen painting?'

'Oh, there's nothing odd about that!' exclaimed Claudia. 'Corruption is widespread in this country, and it's quite common for members of the Mafia to have friends in the Caribinieri and the *Polizia Municipale*! Malatesta knows what's going on all right, and presumably he's being well paid to look the other way.'

'Pennington is a possible suspect,' said Laurence.

'He wants to buy the Raphael on behalf of his client and earn himself a big fat commission. Maybe he's decided to try and wipe out the competition, i.e. me!'

'But did Pennington know you were going to be at the lunch?' asked Claudia. 'And does he have the resources to pay thugs to do his dirty work for him?'

'Personally, I doubt it,' said Scott. 'No, if you ask my opinion – and I know this sounds crazy – the guy I suspect is … Baldini.'

'But that just doesn't make sense,' said Laurence. 'He needs me to authenticate the Raphael, and after that he'll expect me to make an offer of purchase on behalf of my client. Why, in heavens' name, would he want to have me and my friends driven off the road into the valley below in my brand new car?'

It was a question to which no one had an answer.

CHAPTER 6

At about 04:45 the next morning, Scott was aroused from the depths of sleep by a high-pitched sound near his ear. He sat bolt upright. Claudia stirred. 'What is it, darling?'

'It's a skeeter,' he said, *sotto voce*. 'Mind if I switch on the light and zap the little bugger?'

'If it's been busy biting you,' she said sleepily, 'it's a bitch, not a bugger!'

'Hey, honey, watch your language!' Scott turned on the light and got out of bed.

'It's the female that does the biting—'

'—yeah, I know, while the male goes off swarming with his pals.'

'Oh, so you *do* occasionally take notice of what I say.'

'I'm not just a pretty face, you know!' Scott stood naked at the end of the bed and surveyed the ceiling.

'I can see that!' said Claudia, trying hard not to giggle.

'Now the light's on, hadn't I better close the

window – otherwise every skeeter in Florence will be in here fixing to have me for breakfast?'

'They're drawn to light, that's true – but even when the light isn't on, they'll come in through an open window, particularly at sunset or sunrise. That's when they're on the lookout for a good feed. And what better inducement is there to satisfy their hunger than the scent of human body odour and CO_2 emission?'

'Well, they ain't getting a scent of me!' exclaimed Scott, hurriedly closing the window. Picking up a copy of *La Nazione* that lay on the table, he continued, 'Problem is there must be one in here already, because I sure as hell didn't imagine the whining in my ear!' He proceeded to roll up the newspaper.

'Well, if it was whining, it can't be an *Aedes albopictus*.'

'An *Aedes* what?'

'*Albopictus,* the Asian Tiger mosquito: a nasty customer.'

'Why nasty?'

'Oh, I don't think we need go into that, darling. It'll only increase your aversion to our little friends.'

'No, go on, tell me.'

'Well, a Tiger's difficult to detect until it strikes, because it flies low and makes no sound. Disconcertingly, the bites it inflicts usually turn to boils, which cause discomfort for days and may become infected. It also transmits—'

'Not a gal of much charm, then,' said Scott, scratching his arm. 'Why's it called a Tiger?'

'Because it has stripes on its legs and thorax.'

Scott lunged upwards and swatted at the ceiling. 'Hell's bells, missed! Whatever type it is, it's a helluva big 'un.'

'It's definitely not a Tiger, then. A Tiger is smaller than the average mosquito. It's probably a Banded, which is large and—'

'Honey, *don't* tell me.' Scott scratched his arm. 'All this talk about our pesky whining friends has made me decidedly itchy.' He examined his forearm. 'In fact, I've gotta bite here.'

'You've become sensitised, darling.'

'Sensitive, maybe. But sensitised? What's that?'

'It means the species of mosquito that just bit you has had a go at you previously, and so you've developed a reaction to its bites – a sort of allergy, if you like. Eventually, when you've been bitten by the same species over a sufficiently long period, you'll lose the reaction altogether and become *de*sensitised – or immune.'

'Er, well, that's kind of a comfort, I suppose – even if, meanwhile, I have to endure a helluva lot more bites!' Scott took another swipe at the ceiling. 'That'll teach you!' He tore off a corner of the newspaper and used it to wipe away the squashed insect from the ceiling.

'I take it you come up in bumps,' Claudia asked.

'Yeah, too right – big ugly bumps.' He sat down on the end of the bed. 'When I was last here, I got a bite on my forehead, which came up like a freakin' golf ball. I'm sure glad you didn't see me then, honey.

You would've been put right off.' Scott scratched his arm again. 'Say, have you got any antihistamine?'

'I'm not sure, darling. I'll have a look.'

Claudia swung her long legs out of the bed and walked towards the bathroom. Scott was overwhelmed by her naked body. He reached out for her arm as she passed and pulled her towards him. 'Never mind the goddamned bite!' he said and began to kiss her.

Claudia uncoupled herself and playfully pushed him away. 'Darling, what *has* got into you?' she asked, glancing downwards. 'Didn't we give sir complete satisfaction earlier on?'

'Twice is not enough,' he said, lifting her in his arms and swinging her onto the bed.

'Greedy!'

* * *

After their enthusiastic lovemaking during the night, Scott and Claudia were dead to the world when his mobile pinged at 08:30.

Claudia yawned. 'Oh, darling, don't tell me we've got to go out. I was looking forward to staying here this morning – in bed. I thought we might chat and, you know, have some fun and see how many times we can …'

Wondering if he'd have the energy left to make love once, let alone several times, he said, 'Great idea, honey. Maybe we can get down to some serious record-breaking another day. Right now, I'm going to grab a shower. Then I must do some work, go and see some booksellers, that sort of thing. The text, incidentally, was from Laurence. He's asked us to dinner.' Scott scratched at his arm. 'I just wish I'd put some antihistamine on this earlier this morning. Look at it!' He indicated a large angry swelling, at least five centimetres across, on his right forearm.

'Darling, you weren't joking when you said you come up in bumps, were you? Quickly, let's see whether there's any cream in the bathroom. If not, I'll fling on some clothes and pop round to the pharmacy in Borgo Pinti.'

* * *

Claudia found she had no cream, so she went to the chemist. When she came back with some antihistamine gel, Scott was in the bathroom. 'I'm having a shave, honey,' he called out behind the closed door. 'If you need anything, just come in and get it.'

'Okay.' Claudia thought she'd take the opportunity to look through her emails. First in the Inbox was this message:

Institute of Ecology, Rome

Re: Mosquitoes - URGENT

C - We've caught more specimens in net traps. Some even larger than those discussed on Thurs. There R 11 different species. Increase in av length over past 12 months is 2.5 mm. Gallinippers in partic R worryingly big. Specimen we hv is 17.5 mm long - an increase of 3.5 mm on last year's av length. What R Gallis doing here anyway? Isn't continental America their normal habitat?

Lab also spotted 2 alarming developments: increase in no. of gynandromorphs[1]; & males of several different species R developing female proboscises.[2]

Ettore suggests U observe breeding grounds alongside Arno 2 see whether there R unusual behavioural patterns, then visit Venice 2 investigate canals. Wd be helpful if U could catch live specimens & send them 2 us for analysis.

Here, as U know, there's been steady increase in mosq population as well as in no. of people bitten. U know, 2, members of press R saying more & more vehemently on daily basis that problem is not being dealt with effectively enough by CC. Well, today Mayor has asked Institute to advise on what remedial actions shld be taken. (5 new cases of dengue admitted 2 Polyclinico this morning, which means currently there's total of 16 cases in Rome.) Ettore rang Mayor straightaway & suggested he shd issue guidelines 2 members of public on how 2 protect themselves from being bitten. So next week Mosquito Awareness Campaign is 2 be launched on TV, radio, social media, etc. & notices R going 2 be posted in hotels, banks, restaurants, bars, supermkts & other public places. Unfortunately, because Council is so chronically short of funds, mass distribution of leaflets to all residents, shops, businesses, etc. is not poss.

If U think Ne other action shld be taken, let Ettore know asap. Pls don't bother 2 ackowledge this, even tho I'm crazy about U & hang on yr every word! NRN - G

Claudia smiled at the concluding sentiments. Giuseppe Corti was a 26-year-old Piedmontese, who, in common with several other male employees at the Institute, including Dr Ravegnani, was charmed – one

---

[1] Gynandromorph: an organism, especially an insect, which has both male and female characteristics.
[2] Proboscis: the mosquito's piercing and sucking mouthpart.

might even say bewitched – by her.

'Something funny, honey?' asked Scott, who was standing in the bathroom doorway with an electric razor in his hand.

'Only Giuseppe,' said Claudia. 'He's the Laboratory Analyst at the Institute. I think he – erm – fancies me.'

'He's not the only one. Join the queue, Giuseppe. But tell me, does he have anything *positive* to say?'

'Yes. Ettore wants me to check out the mosquito situation both here and in Venice. So, instead of going back to Rome on Monday morning, I'll be using this as my base for the next week at least.'

'Gee, that's wonderful,' said Scott. 'Maybe we'll get to spend more time together – assuming you're not too preoccupied with your blessed skeeters, Laurence isn't knocked off the hillside in his new Mercedes, and the guy at the Uffizi doesn't drive me nuts!'

'Why don't you come with me to Venice for a couple of days? We could stay at the Danieli – such a lovely hotel!'

'Yeah, that's a great idea! I reckon it'll take me a couple of days to do a deal with Lombardo or to fall out with him completely – so, if it's okay with you, honey, I say we go on Wednesday and come back Friday.'

'Agreed.'

'Fine. You go freshen up, while I call the *Stazione* to reserve seats. I'll try the Danieli, too – but, don't forget, it *is* high season and we may be plumb out of luck.'

'I realise that, darling, but please give them a buzz.'

She stroked his cheek and gave him a quick kiss on the mouth. 'Then, when I've had a shower, maybe we can give each other a buzz. Laurence won't be picking us up for at least an hour.'

Scott smiled. 'You know, honey, if you keep this up, you'll wear me out and I won't be able to satisfy you any longer ... I'll have shot my bolt!'

'More than likely,' she said, smiling. 'Now go and ring the Danieli like a good boy.'

* * *

Before she and Scott went to join Laurence for dinner, Claudia quickly looked through the article in *Il Tempo*:

Entomologists meeting in Milan this week say that the indigenous mosquito population is now greater than it has been at any time during the past 65 years. Another worrying development is mosquitoes generally seem to be larger than they were last year.

There are reports of similar increases, both in volume and size, in other EU countries and in the USA and South America. Apparently global warming is to blame. The rise in temperature worldwide is having a twofold effect: species of mosquito that previously have survived only in the tropics and subtropics are being carried on warm fronts to temperate zones; and in those zones, because there is more rain and less prolonged cold weather during winter months than there used to be, mosquitoes generally are becoming larger, longer living and more numerous ...

The article continued in much the same vein, reporting what Claudia already knew. 'Old hat!' she said to herself, as she tossed the newspaper into the recycling bin. The possibility that the article was aimed at or could be of interest to people who knew nothing or very little about the mosquito problem hadn't occurred to her.

'Aren't you ready yet, darling?' she enquired, with a touch of irritation in her voice.

* * *

As they enjoyed dinner on the terrace of the L'Altro Ristorante in Via Ghibellina, Laurence, Claudia and Scott discussed a number of topics: whether national museums and galleries should charge higher entrance fees, the Italian sense of style, the art of the Etruscans, the skeletons at Herculaneum. Inevitably the conversation turned to the subject of mosquitoes.

'Claudia,' Laurence said, 'I've been meaning to ask your opinion about something – something you're bound to know about.'

'Well, I'll try my best!'

'I haven't mentioned it before, but about three weeks ago I visited Ghana to see a—'

'You took your anti-malarials, I hope – before, during and after?' she asked anxiously.

'Oh yes, yes. I may have missed one or two, that's true, but overall I took my pills when I was supposed to. Actually, it's mosquitoes and Malaria I want to ask you about. Is there—'

'What were you doing in Ghana, for Chrissake?' interrupted Scott.

'I went to see a man about a painting! It turned out to be quite an adventure, I can tell you. I was invited by a chap who owns a cocoa bean estate outside Sunyani in the Brong-Ahafo Region. This chap wanted me to authenticate and value a painting of his that he said was by – believe it or not – Piero di Cosimo. Now I ask you, a fifteenth-century Italian oil painting hanging on a wall near Sunyani in Ghana! Who would have thought it? Anyway, I went there to check it out – on behalf of an important client who's mad about Italian Renaissance art. It's just a shame the painting turned out to be a forgery! Fortunately, my client was happy to pay my expenses.'

'Wow, buddy!' exclaimed Scott. 'You certainly lead an interesting life. Publishing by comparison is goddamned dull stuff!'

Claudia leant towards Laurence and put her hand on his. 'What was it you wanted to ask me?'

'Well, I wondered whether you knew if there's any truth in the news reports that mosquitoes are so much on the increase in Italy that they could soon become a major menace.'

'Yes, and not just in—'

'What?' cried Scott. 'Do you mean to say these wretched creatures, not content with attacking me once or twice a night, are now likely to do so in large numbers over and over again?'

Ignoring Scott, Claudia continued: 'They're definitely on the increase, not just in Italy but throughout Europe. In Rome, at the Institute where I work, we've recorded an extraordinary growth in the numbers of the bitten as well as of the biters! Attempts at containing the situation have so far met with little success. So Laurence, to answer your query:

I have no doubt that mosquitoes have the potential to become a major threat.'

'But why have we got this problem?' asked Laurence.

'It's a question of temperature. Mosquitoes thrive in warm environments. They look for and choose to inhabit places where it's warm and they are able to flourish. So, with European countries becoming hotter due to global warming, many unfamiliar species of mosquito – including some from the subtropics – are making their way northwards.'

'And what's anybody doing about it?' asked Scott, imagining himself covered in nasty suppurating bites.

'Well, next week will see the launch in the mass media of a nationwide campaign to arouse awareness of the increased mosquito activity. The idea is to give people advice on how best to protect themselves and their properties against mosquitoes. There's also a plan to spray as much of the countryside as possible – that's if the Government can find enough insecticide which is harmless to humans and doesn't have adverse effects on the environment.'

'How do you mean, honey – there *isn't* enough insecticide that can be used safely, is that what you're saying?'

'Yes. The only chemical spray there's sufficient stock of, is Malathion, which is by no means 100 per cent safe. In the three to four weeks it remains in the environment, not only does it have adverse effects on us, it also kills beneficial, harmless insects such as bees and butterflies and is highly toxic to aquatic organisms. To make matters worse, it appears that mosquitoes, and the viruses and parasites they carry, are becoming resistant to Malathion. Skeeters, as you call them, seem to be able to adjust to everything we throw at them. They …'

'And do we have the mosquito that spreads Denger?' asked Laurence.

'It's actually pronounced Deng-ee. Yes, that's the Asian Tiger, which you've no doubt read about in the newspapers. There's also another type of mosquito that carries the Zika virus – and, worse still, we've found an example of an anopheline, the mosquito that transmits Malaria to humans, which was eradicated from Italy more than fifty years ago.'

'What?' said Scott. 'I never knew they ever had Malaria in Italy!'

'Oh yes,' said Claudia. 'After all, "Mal'aria" is an Italian word which was first used in the mid-1700s. It means "bad air". The disease was rife in Italy for centuries until 1962, when the last case was resolved. In the 1940s Malaria killed hundreds of thousands, even millions, of Italians. Most of the deaths occurred in the south, where the deadly *falciparum* parasite predominated. Ironically, the famous nationalist from the south, Camillo Cavour, who founded the modern Italian state, was a victim.'

'How many more victims will there be, I wonder. Quite a few, by the sound of it. I suppose what will happen is – erm …' Laurence sought to find the appropriate word, 'unpredictable.' He looked at his watch. 'Heavens, it's 22:55! Time to turn in. If you two wouldn't mind …'

'No, of course not,' said Claudia. 'It's been a long

day and I think we're all ready for bed, aren't we darling?' She gave Scott an artful smile. 'It's been lovely seeing you again, Laurence. We've had the most delicious meal. The food was outstanding. Thank you. Thank you so much.' She kissed Laurence on both cheeks.

'Yeah,' said Scott, 'time to call it a day. Great food, beautiful place! *Grazie mille*, pal.'

Laurence paid the bill and they left the restaurant.

CHAPTER 7

At 06:10 the next morning, Claudia, without waking Scott, who was still asleep, put on a cream-coloured jumpsuit and left the apartment with a sports bag slung over her shoulder. She walked down to the Arno, and at Ponte San Niccolò she headed east alongside the river, past the Biblioteca Nazionale Centrale, to the small public gardens on Lungarno Cristoforo Colombo. As she walked under the dark canopy of plane trees, she could sense, rather than see, the mosquito activity. Going over to the river at the edge of the gardens, Claudia noticed that dank puddles of water had been left on the bankside pathway by overnight storms. What also drew her attention was a cloud of mosquitoes swaying menacingly just off the bank above an area of riverbed that was all but dried up, except for a few scattered stagnant pools. Removing an ultra-zoom camera from her bag, she proceeded to take close-up photographs of the swarm. She then slid sideways down the steep incline to the riverbank. Having reached the bottom without mishap, she pulled out of the bag three metre-length aluminium tubes, which she screwed together. Onto one end of the assembled pole she fixed a cylindrical muslin net with a hinged lid. To the pole she attached, by means of plastic clips, a pullback. This had at one end an oval ring and at the other a small hook which slotted into a flange on the net lid. She walked along the path and stood parallel to the mosquito cloud. Pulling down on the ring and thereby opening the lid, she reached out with the net as far as she could and passed it through the mass of insects slowly and cautiously, in order not to attract their attention. She did not want suddenly to find herself at the centre of the swarming insects. Having retrieved the trap, she went to her bag, unscrewed the net from the pole and shut it hastily in a portable vivarium which was inside the bag. She watched as the net lid opened slightly and about 150 mosquitoes, of varying shapes and sizes, poured into the clear plastic container. Then, using an electronic pipette, she transferred pupae from some of the stagnant pools to a specimen jar containing slightly salty water. She was about to make a note in her diary of the time, place and weather conditions, when she heard yelps followed by an anguished voice shouting in English, 'Stay! This isn't a game. Stay there when I tell you!' In the middle distance she discerned a man chasing along the bank after something fluffy. As they came closer, Claudia could see that the object of pursuit was a lolloping grey-and-white Bearded Collie, which kept looking behind it and yelping. The man, who was middle-aged and paunchy, was running with short, irregular strides – stumbling almost – as if he was on the point of exhaustion, but reluctant to stop to catch his breath. As the dog came nearer, Claudia noticed that a strange oscillating haze encircled its body. Red in the face and panting heavily, the man cried out, 'Sit, boy! …SIT!' – an order that the dog obeyed to the extent of slowing down to a walking pace, despite being in an obvious state of panic. On reaching the dog, the man caught hold of its collar with one hand and with the other stroked the dog's head and back. 'You're a naughty boy, aren't you, running away li …' The man stepped back in horror. His hand was covered in blood. The dog was being attacked and bitten by a horde of mosquitoes, some of which were turning their attention to the man. The realisation of the perilous position of both animal and man had hardly registered in Claudia's mind, when the black squirming cloud that hovered over the riverbed lurched towards the bank. Claudia ran towards the man, pointing at the dark spiral and shouting, 'Quick! Throw the dog in the water – then get away as fast as you can!' Unhesitatingly, but with some difficulty, the man picked up the frightened dog, staggered to the edge of the bank and threw the animal into the low-lying river. Fortunately, the dog landed in water up to its shoulders and was able to dip beneath the surface and drown the insects that clung to its body. Meanwhile, the man and Claudia, who had grabbed her sports bag, ran along the pathway towards Ponte San Niccolò – with the helical swarm in hot pursuit. Just before the Bagno Communale, at the point where the tree-lined public gardens end, they turned right, climbed up a rough track and reached the relative safety of the busy Lungarno Cristoforo Colombo. Claudia turned to the man and, raising her voice above the din of the traffic, asked, 'Are you okay?' The man, clearly shaken, nodded. 'We'll be safe here. Mosquitoes don't usually like loud noise. I'm Claudia Mattioli, by the way.'

'Michael Hardwick, from London. I'm staying in Florence for a couple of weeks.' They shook hands. 'I … I've never seen anything like it, signorina,' he shouted. 'For mosquitoes to attack like that – you know, all together – is most unusual.'

'It is indeed. It's the sort of thing you expect to happen in Alaska, not here.' *Thank goodness,* thought Claudia. 'Swarms there contain hundreds of thousands, if not millions, of big vicious biters – who altogether can feed on a caribou calf until it has no blood left in its body.'

'I reckon global warming is to blame. It's causing creatures to alter their normal behavioural patterns.' Mr Hardwick looked towards the river. 'How about my dog? Will he be all right, signorina?'

'I'm sure he will. A bit dazed, perhaps, but otherwise fine. It would've been a different story, if you hadn't thrown him in the water.'

'That was thanks to you, signorina. I would never have thought of taking such action. *You* saved his life. I really am most grateful. I …'

'Lovely dog, isn't he? What's his name?'

'Caesar.'

'That's quite appropriate, given what just happened. If my memory serves me correctly, Julius Caesar rather enjoyed swimming. Anyway, I don't recommend that you let this Caesar go for a doggy paddle – not while there's a chance of further attacks. I suggest you wait a few moments for the mosquitoes to disperse or move on, before you fetch him out of the water. Now I must dash. It's been nice meeting you, Signor Hardwick, even if the circumstances have been somewhat fraught!'

'Signorina, once again I thank you very much for rescuing us. I wish you all the best.' He turned to get his dog and go back the way he had come.

'Signor Hardwick,' Claudia called after him. 'In view of the bites you've sustained, I recommend you go to the Santa Maria Nuova Hospital and have a blood test as soon as possible.'

'Yes, signorina. I'll do that this afternoon.'

Claudia turned round and set off on the 30-minute walk back to her apartment. On the way, she reflected upon the increase in the numbers and size of mosquitoes. She thought of what was going on in Rome and what had just happened on the south bank of the Arno, and wondered how the authorities intended to deal with the problem of mounting mosquito hostility. Were they going to introduce a countrywide spraying campaign? If so, would they use botanical or chemical pesticides? That was the critical question. In her heart, she knew she could never support the use of chemicals. Man had been down that path before, with life-threatening consequences for humans, particularly young children. It all depended on the Institute. If it failed to make a stand on the issue, she would find herself in an awkward position. Meanwhile, she had to go to Venice and ascertain what the situation was there.

On arriving back at her apartment and, bearing in mind Scott's susceptibility to mosquitoes, Claudia decided it would be best not to tell him about her experience on the riverbank.

After breakfast, they kissed and then each went

their way: Scott to see some booksellers and a printer, before going on to the Uffizi for a further meeting with Lombardo; Claudia to her office to email her report on the mosquito situation to the Institute and to pack up the specimens she had caught for dispatch to Rome by same-day delivery.

* * *

In his suite at the Castello di Montezano, with the help of one of his *soldati*, Baldini made arrangements for the transportation of arms from the Bratva warehouse in Kazan to Reggio Calabria.

In payment for the arms they were supplying, he authorised a bank transfer to the Bratva of the agreed amount of $500,000 – an amount which represented a considerable discount on the black-market price.

He hired a tractor truck, hitched to a large trailer with a false bottom under which the arms could be concealed. The legitimate load, as supplied free of cost by one of the Bratva's 'protected' customers, consisted of eight racks of raw aluminium ingots.

After that, he obtained the relevant international authorisations and permits for road haulage, without which there would be difficulties at the border controls of those countries the lorry had to pass through – Belarus, Poland, Czech Republic, Austria and Italy.

His final task was to organise for his couriers, Gennady Alexandrov and Francesca Maruichi, to fly from Florence to Kazan, collect the painting from the Bratva warehouse, and fly back with a heavily wrapped package accredited with diplomatic bag status and thus secure from the prying eyes of customs officers.

Mario came in with a mobile. 'Boss, its Signor Serge Kuznetsov.'

'Who's he?'

'I think he's one of the Bratva's bosses.' Mario handed him the mobile.

'Hi, Signor Kuznetsov. Just a minute, if you will …' He put his hand over the mouthpiece. 'Mario, has this line been scrambled?'

'Yes, boss.'

Baldini put the mobile back to his ear. 'Signor Kuznetsov – may I call you Serge? … Good. Silly question I know, but has *your* line been scrambled? … Excellent. I don't think we've spoken before, have we? … And you are? … Right. In this business it's essential to know who you're talking to. Anyway, what can I do for you?' He listened and, as he did so, a smile spread across his face. 'Well, that's a *very* interesting proposition, Serge. You say you have 10kg, which you're prepared to sell us at 20 per cent of the going price? So it works out at – er, let me see – $10,000,000. Well, to my mind, we'd be mad to pass up such a generous offer. Transportation might be a problem, though, and … No? You'll organise that? Anywhere in Europe or the Middle East? Well, Serge, if it was *my* decision … But let's wait and see what Calabria's attitude is. After all, it's a lot of hard cash to raise. I'll need to contact our area *capobastone* to see what he thinks. If he's keen on the idea, it'll be up to him to persuade the family in San Luca to cough up the cash. But I'm sure they can get hold of it just like that! After all, they do have some very helpful bank contacts!'

* * *

'Signor Lombardo, I've drawn up a cash flow forecast for the first four titles in the proposed Uffizi series.' Scott handed Lombardo a piece of paper. 'In the left-hand column are the production costs. You'll note that these include repro fees of 475 euros per painting, which is the absolute minimum you said you were prepared to accept when we lunched together the other day. In the right-hand column are the estimated receipts from sales. These are calculated on the basis that we manage to sell out of all four titles, which I estimate may take about twelve to eighteen months to achieve. After deduction of editor's royalties, booksellers' discounts, distribution costs, publicity, advertising and operating expenses, you'll see that the projected net profit figure is only 3,000 euros. Split that equally between us as proposed, and my company, having put up and/or borrowed 73,750 euros to cover the costs of the venture, will some eighteen months later receive the princely return of 1,500 euros – and then *only* if all four titles sell out! That, as you must surely realise, doesn't make sense economically from my company's point of view. Meanwhile, the Uffizi has its name imprinted on the series of books as copublisher, contributes absolutely nothing towards the cost of the venture, and yet receives 27,350 euros for permitting us to use photographs taken by its selected photographers of its own paintings. It also receives its 50% share of the net profits amounting to 1,500 euros, so altogether the Gallery pockets 28,850 euros. It's hardly a deal for me to get excited about, is it? But there's something else that's equally off-putting. If we decide to turn the series of titles into ebooks, there will be substantial online sales, from which you will receive further benefit in the form of royalties.

Also, the ebooks will be a useful tool for publicising the Uffizi and its artworks on the Internet. But I don't know why I'm explaining all this to you in such detail! The fact is my company isn't a philanthropic organisation. It's a commercial enterprise and exists principally to make profits. In this case, if it didn't have to pay unreasonable repro fees to its copublisher, there would be approximately 29,500 euros net profits to be divided two ways – giving my company a respectable return on its money of 20 per cent. I realise the Uffizi would then get 14,750 instead of 28,850 euros. However, 14,750 euros is better than zilch, which I'm afraid is what you'll end up with if you continue to insist on payment of these fees. To put it more succinctly, Signor Lombardo: either you agree, by way of your contribution to this venture, to supply us with photographs of the relevant paintings free of charge, or I'm afraid we'll have to forget about copublishing a series on the great painters of the Uffizi.'

Lombardo handed back the cash forecast. 'It is not right when you say our request for repro fees is "unreasonable". The Uffizi is having to pay photographers to take these photos. Also the Uffizi *always* charges for the reproduction of its pieces of art. It is unbelievable you are asking the Uffizi to provide its professional services free. No, Signor Lee, I'm sorry but I'm not doing business with anybody without receiving payment of our usual repro fees. For us to share in possible profits that are made at some time in the future is unimportant. Nor is our disagreement on this issue a problem. The Uffizi will find another publisher who *is* happy to pay our repro fees, I can assure you.'

There being nothing further for them to discuss, Lombardo showed Scott out. At the side door to the gallery, they shook hands and Lombardo, smiling for the first and only time in their brief association, said, 'I'm sorry I did not come to Signor Baldini's lunch on Saturday. I hear it was a very pleasant occasion. You were there, no? Unfortunately, Signora Lombardo was not feeling well. Anyway Signor Lee, *ciao*. I wish you the best of fortune with your project.'

* * *

Meanwhile, in Rome, Mosquito Awareness Week was launched. The Mayor announced that the City Council had decided to respond to public concern about the number of people being bitten by mosquitoes. A leaflet 'Mosquito Awareness Recommendations'[3] was being distributed. It was going to be displayed in public places and posted on social media. As regards questions about the mosquito problem: they should be addressed to the Institute of Ecology, where, in the absence of Claudia, Ettore had selected Giuseppe as the Institute's representative.

In the library of the Institute, members of the press faced Giuseppe, who sat alone at a long table. 'Can we have the first question please?' he asked.

'Yes,' said a young lady from *Corriere della Sera*. 'Why are we getting this problem?'

'Well, basically it's due to the weather conditions we've been having recently – you know, the extended heat wave coupled with intermittent overnight rainstorms. These have encouraged mosquitoes from

---

[3] See Appendix 1, pp. 425-8.

other countries to breed here.'

'And when,' the Home Affairs correspondent of *Il Messaggero* asked, 'do mosquitoes bite – any particular time of day?'

'Yes, they're at their most active and hungriest during the evening, overnight and in the early morning – but there are mosquitoes that bite during the daytime.'

'What precautions can one take at these times to avoid being bitten?'

'The best advice is don't go outside, if possible. But if you must, then wear light-coloured long-sleeved shirts or blouses, together with long trousers that are thick enough to prevent mosquitoes biting through to your skin. Spray 20% DEET repellent on your clothes and on any exposed areas of flesh. Be careful not to spray any in your eyes.'

'And the home?' asked the reporter from *Leggo*. 'How does one protect one's home?'

'You must keep mosquitoes outside by …'

Giuseppe went on for about 20 minutes answering questions from, among others, representatives of *La Stampa*, *Metro*, *Il Tempo* and *La Repubblica*.

Afterwards, Ettore congratulated him and told him he thought he'd handled a potentially difficult situation very well.

* * *

That evening, Scott called Laurence. 'Hi pal, how you doing?'

'I'm fine. How are things with you?'

'Okay, I guess – although I rather wasted my time this morning. That's because I had a further and, as it turned out, final session with Lombardo. Man, he's a real pain in the butt! I reckon the guy gets a kick out of being awkward. What can I say? We agreed to disagree. The idea of copublishing a series about the contents of the Uffizi is not of interest to him – *unless* I pay all the expenses, including the Uffizi's fees for photographing their own paintings, and he gets practically all the income! I can't tell you how exasperating it is to try and do business with someone who refuses to give an inch. Look, there I am getting all worked up and the guy just isn't worth it! By the bye, as I was leaving, he did say something odd. He said he was sorry he missed Baldini's lunch on Saturday, because his wife was not feeling very well. Now I recall we both heard Baldini say in the Badia that he knew Lombardo and agreed he was difficult – so why on earth would he invite the guy to his lunch party?'

'Perhaps he's another potential bidder for the Raphael,' Laurence suggested. 'After all, the portrait in the Uffizi, which is attributed to Raphael, is just a studio work, a pupil's rather poorly executed copy of another portrait by the Italian master. *Portrait of a Young Man*, on the other hand, is considered by experts such as Fischel and Dussler to be mostly by Raphael and an outstanding example of the studied casualness of his later portraiture. It is hardly surprising, therefore, if Lombardo *is* interested in bidding for the picture on behalf of the Gallery. However, having said that, I wouldn't have thought the Uffizi could *afford* to buy it. I mean, say the bidding reaches $75,000,000 or more ...'

'Wow! That's a lot of dough!' cried Scott.

'Yes, it is. And the Uffizi's annual acquisitions fund is probably less than a quarter of that amount.'

'There's also the question of prior ownership, surely? A renowned public gallery such as the Uffizi would be ill advised to buy, let alone exhibit, a painting that it knew belonged to another gallery. Isn't that the case?'

'It is,' said Laurence. 'Maybe Lombardo is acting on behalf of some private individual – or maybe it's just a coincidence that he was invited to Baldini's lunch.'

They went on chatting for a short while, until Laurence said it was time to go to bed. Scott agreed, and they wished each other goodnight.

CHAPTER 8

Early on the next morning, Laurence received a phone call from Baldini. 'Signor Spencer, *buongiorno*! I have good news! The photos and video are here. So we have only to agree when is a good time for us to meet, and I am making the necessary arrangements.'

'Good news indeed, Signor Baldini. The sooner we view and authenticate this picture the better. So may I suggest we meet today, preferably this afternoon, if that's convenient for you.'

'This afternoon? *Si*, it is very convenient. I will make the arrangements for 14:30 – okay?

'Yes, that's fine. Where shall we meet?'

'I'll ask Mario to find somewhere suitable. And then I'll let you know, hopefully within the hour.'

'Signor Baldini, just one thing: may I bring along Signor Lee and my co-authenticator Signor Casti?'

'Signor Spencer, I'm so sorry but it is not possible for other persons to be with us – for the reason that we have to have very tight security. *Capisci*?'

'Yes, I quite understand.'

* * *

In the newspapers, there were startling front-page headlines: **FOLLIA DELLA ZANZARA** [Mosquito Madness]; **PROBLEMA DELLE ZANZARA CONTINUA: Il Sindaco Lancia la Campagna di Evasione** [Mosquito Problem Continues: Mayor Launches Avoidance Campaign]; **ZANZARE ASSASSINE!** [KILLER MOSQUITOES!]; **AUMENTO DEGLI ATTACCHI DI ZANZARA** [Increase in Mosquito Attacks]; and **BAMBINI MORSI DALLE ZANZARE** [Children Bitten by Mosquitoes]. These, combined with a leading article in *Il Messaggero*, which suggested there was the potential for a full-scale Dengue epidemic, and a breakfast-time TV programme, in which heart-rending interviews were conducted with Dengue and Malaria sufferers, sparked off a countrywide panic and ensured that by midday shops were sold out of netting, window mesh, plug-in mosquito killers, repellents, Piriton syrup, cooling sprays, antihistamine ointment, and benzocaine and hydrocortisone creams.

Having read the front page of *La Stampa* and the *Il Messaggero* article, Claudia opened her laptop and found she had quite a few emails, including a request to contact the Institute.

Claudia made a video call to Ettore, whose familiar craggy features appeared moments later on her mobile screen. 'Ah, Claudia! Thank you for coming back to me so promptly. I trust you're enjoying your latest visit to Florence?'

'Yes, very much so. It's just a pity there's this growing problem in the background. Have you managed to check the specimens I sent you yesterday?'

'Yes, and what is interesting – or shall I say worrying – is that the measurements of your specimens are much the same as those on the list Giuseppe gave us on Thursday. So we're not dealing here with any kind of aberration. There are even one or two species which have experienced an exceptional increase in length – such as the African Malaria Mosquito (up by 1.0mm to 8.5mm), the Banded Mosquito (up by 2.0mm to 11.5mm) and the Yellow Fever Mosquito (up by 1.0mm to 7.5mm). Anyway, I'll email you a list of the various species.'

'Any of them vectors?'

'Yes. There were carriers of Dengue, Malaria and West Nile Fever. Again, I'll send you details by email.'

'And in Rome? Have you caught any vectors yet?'

'No – and I find that extraordinary, considering last week there were 25 cases of Dengue and five cases of Zika virus, and the Polyclinico Umberto's quarantine wing have had to deal with a sudden influx of Malaria cases (nine yesterday). There are definitely vectors in the city. It's just that we haven't found any specimens yet.'

'So what is the plan? What are you aiming to do?'

'At the moment, our priority is to collect as many specimens and as much data as possible from around the country. The information we have so far is not encouraging. In Sicily and Calabria, there are cases not just of Dengue and Malaria but also of Zika virus, Filariasis and Yellow Fever, and it's reported that swarms of half-inch long *Coquillettidia richiardii* have set upon farmers on tractors, grape pickers, fishermen, roadworkers, and so on.'

'And in Naples?'

'There mosquitoes are no longer looked upon as a nuisance. They are viewed as a dangerous menace – and for good reason. There are more cases of Dengue in Naples than anywhere else in the country. There is also a rising number of Malaria cases. A combination of daily temperatures in the mid-30s and constant biting by Alaskan, Banded, Gallinipper and other non-vectors is causing tempers to flare, with a corresponding increase in violence and crime.'

'I take it the police are on hand, in case things get out of hand.'

'Yes, both the police and the army are on standby. And as a precautionary step, a bylaw has been introduced by the Naples City Council, whereby anyone who leaves stagnant water in flowerpot trays or other garden containers will be fined up to 1,500 euros!'

'In the west we know there's a problem in Florence. But what is the position in the east? And in the north?'

'We've not heard much about what's happening in the eastern central province, so I've sent Giuseppe to Ancona, Perugia, Pesaro, Urbino, etc. on a fact-finding tour. I'm hoping he'll send us back some specimens. Our northern representative, Professor Zobi, has already sent us specimens from Milan, including one Malaria-carrying anopheline and two Dengue-carrying Yellow Fever mosquitoes. He is currently en route to Turin and Genoa, from where he will send us more specimens.'

'And what shall I do? Continue to look for

specimens here in Florence?'

'All things considered, I think you should go to Venice. With the pools of fetid water that lie stagnating around the place at this time of year, I'll be surprised if the inhabitants and their many foreign visitors aren't being pestered by our little friends. Of course, when you've finished in Venice, we'll need you back here urgently. You are our expert on mosquitoes, after all.'

Claudia smiled. 'From Florence to Venice – who could ask for more? There may be this ongoing problem in Florence, but, fingers crossed, one hopes there won't be anything worse lurking among the canals!'

'Claudia, sorry, I have to go. I have someone waiting to see me. I'll email you the data about measurements later this morning. Speak to you soon.' The screen went blank.

Claudia looked through her other emails, most of which were junk and she deleted. Scott emerged from the bedroom. 'Honey, I've must go. I'm late. I'll be back at about 15:00. See you then. *Ciao*.' He blew her a kiss and dashed out of the room.

Claudia opened her 'Climate Change' file and continued to make notes for her article:

13. Most people say they are concerned about the environment, but are reluctant to act accordingly. So not enough is done to stop waste being used as landfill. People who reuse carrier bags do so mainly to avoid being charged for a new bag, not because they care about the environment. They are reluctant to

reduce their motor travel either by sharing a vehicle or by using public transport instead. They are deterred from insulating their homes because of the cost. Would it not be better to appeal to people's innate wish to be green and waste-conscious by stressing the overall community benefits of being environmentally friendly?

14. There have been extended heat waves in the Far East. Temperatures have soared as high as 50°C in New Delhi. There have been more heat waves in Europe, where temperatures have reached record highs, such as 39°C in Kitzingen, Germany and 39.7°C in Paris, France. Larger and more numerous wildfires in the US and Canada are starting earlier, lasting longer and destroying more and more …

There was a ping and notification that mail had been received appeared in the top right-hand corner of the screen. It was the promised email from Ettore.

C - here R measurements of specimens U caught:

African Malaria	9.5 mm
Asian Tiger	8.0
Banded	13.0
Inland Floodwater	11.5
Northern House	11.0
Snow	10.0
Southern House	7.5
Spear	11.5
Yellow Fever	8.0

Many of pupae R abnormally large, 2.

Then there R other species we've not had specimens of be4:

Common Malaria	10.0
Eastern Treehole	7.5
Small Woodland	6 .0
<u>Woodland Pool</u>	8.0

What gives rise for concern is fact that specimens I've underlined were found to B carrying diseases of which they R established vectors, i.e. African/Malaria; Asian Tiger/Dengue & Zika; Inland Flood & Woodland Pool/WNF; & Yellow Fever/Dengue & Zika. More worringly, among specimens we found an *anopheles algeriensis* - the killer without a common name. As U know, *algeriensis* used to B found in Med region but seemed 2 disappear in 1950s. The news it has been found again in N Europe is extremely disturbing. I need hardly spell out 2 U what implications R of all this 2 people of Florence & surrounding area.

After staring vacantly at the screen for a few minutes, Claudia closed her email Inbox, opened a new document with a three-column layout and under the title 'Reducing and Managing the Mosquito Problem by Biocontrol'[4] listed the Aims, Pros and Cons of existing biological controls.

She saved and closed the document and, staring

---

[4] See Appendix 2, pp. 429-31

out of the window, reflected upon what she had written. She went into the bedroom, pulled a suitcase from the cupboard and began to pack some things for her trip to Venice.

Her mobile buzzed.

'Claudia, it's Laurence. Any chance of having a quick word with Scott?'

'No, sorry, he's out this morning. You could try ringing him on his mobile or sending him a—'

'I've already rung his mobile,' Laurence interrupted, 'but it seems to be turned off.'

'That doesn't surprise me. He has two important meetings to attend, so he probably doesn't want to be disturbed. I don't know who he's meeting with or what their respective contact numbers are. He should be back around lunchtime. Would you like me to give him a message?'

'Yes, could you? I thought he might like to know that I have a meeting with Baldini this afternoon. He says he has evidence, in the form of photos and film, which proves the existence of the supposed Raphael portrait. Whether he has or not remains to be seen. Anyway, I'll ring you this evening and – if you'll forgive the pun – put you in the picture.'

'No, no. We'll call you from Venice.'

'Venice?

'Yes. I need to collect specimens from the canal areas, together with some facts and figures from the main hospital. We'll be staying at the Danieli for a couple of nights. We'll give you a call this evening.'

'I look forward to it. All the best, Claudia.'

'Good luck with the painting. *Ciao!*'

* * *

At 14:30 that afternoon, Laurence walked through the peaceful, Brunelleschi-designed cloisters of San Lorenzo, which surround a compact garden comprised of small triangles of grass, box hedges and a central, sweet-smelling orange tree. He climbed the stone steps to the first floor and then went up the imposing staircase of Michelangelo's Vestibule to the Laurentian Library, where Baldini had arranged for their meeting to be held. Standing before the heavy carved oak doors at the top of the stairs was Giovanni, the larger of Baldini's two sidekicks, who nodded his head in recognition, opened the doors and escorted Laurence through the Reading Room – a long room lined on either side with oak reading desks and featuring a superb carved-wood ceiling and a terracotta-and-cream marble floor. The thought occurred to Laurence that Lorenzo the Magnificent's great library, containing thousands of codices of Latin and Greek authors and hundreds of manuscripts from the time of Dante and Petrarch as well as others from Florence's remote past, seemed an inappropriate place to be viewing digital camera photos and film-look video. Anyway, there, on a stand, in the study room of this treasure house of pre-Renaissance literature, was a laptop connected to a digital projector that was pointing at a portable pull-up screen. 'Ah, Signor Spencer, it is good to meet you again. I hope our little show in this beautiful place is having a good result. If you are seeing something you like, if it is impressing you, then I am arranging for the picture to come to *Firenze, pronto!*' Apart from Baldini, the only other person in the room was the smaller of his two henchmen, Mario.

Mario pushed a button on the hand controller and a full-colour picture of an androgynous, long-haired young man appeared on the screen. He was dressed in a style that would have been considered elegant and fashionable at the time the picture was reputedly painted, in the first quarter of the sixteenth century. He wore a soft black velvet cap on the back of his head, a white chemise and a gold and brown ocelot-fur gown. His right arm lay on a table with the hand, or part of it – the thumb and forefinger – hanging nonchalantly over the edge. The other three fingers were missing, as if at some stage someone had trimmed the picture on the left-hand side in order to fit it into a new frame. Of the left hand, too, probably for the same reason, only the thumb and forefinger were visible and these appeared to be squeezing a small tuft of fur on the cloak. The gleaming flesh tones of both the face and hands were particularly striking, and the overall impression was one of warm, luminous colouring.

Five more full-colour photographs appeared successively on the screen, each highlighting a particular area of the portrait: the head and hair, the billowing sleeves, the cloak-covered left shoulder, and the view through the window in the background.

The photographs were followed by a video. This opened with a close-up of the painting, from which the camera tracked back to reveal a normal-sized, unframed portrait displayed on an artist's easel and, somewhat incongruously, a grinning Gennady Alexandrov, who was standing beside the easel and holding up a newspaper. After a pause, the camera zoomed in to a point where both the newspaper and most of the painting were viewed together. The newspaper was a copy of that day's early edition of *Corriere della Sera*, with its headline about the launch of the Mosquito Avoidance Campaign in Rome. The camera tracked back again so that Gennady Alexandrov was in full view. Gennady then spoke, looking directly into the camera: 'Mister Spencer, we trust this demonstration is confirming that we have the picture. Balls are in your court, as you say in the UK. If you think the picture is worth a look, we are bringing it to you very soon – if possible by next weekend. Mister Spencer, may I say it was a great pleasure meeting you on Saturday. I am wishing you all the best.' The screen went blank. Baldini looked at Laurence expectantly.

Laurence checked the excitement he felt welling up inside him. What appeared to be Raphael's *Portrait of a Young Man* could be a forgery, he reminded himself, and the only way he would be able to establish whether that was the case or not was to subject the painting to a thorough examination. 'Signor Baldini,' he said, 'you will recall that when we had our meeting at your house last Saturday, I asked you to let me know what other items, apart from the painting, are included in this deal and who the interested parties are. As that information has not yet been forthcoming, I regret I must emphasise that, until it is, I am *not* prepared to examine the painting. Speaking for my client as much as for myself, I can see no reason why we should take any further part in these proceedings, until we know precisely the sort of people and the nature of the transaction we are involving ourselves in.'

Fearing a negative reaction, Laurence was surprised by Baldini's reply. 'Signor Spencer, when I have the picture here and, before you are looking at it, then I am telling you these things you need to know. Telling you now, before the picture is here, is not possible. I'm sorry, but this is the best I can say.'

'That's fine,' said Laurence. 'Although I hope you realise that if I don't like what you tell me, then, subject to my client's instructions, I will obviously not want to become involved in validating the painting.'

'I understand what you say, Signor Spencer. I have respect for your position. I am expecting Gennady and Francesca to bring the picture here next week, otherwise they are not making me happy! Then I will meet with you and speak to you very frankly.'

* * *

The *Italo Treno* on which Scott and Claudia were travelling to Venice left the Stazione di Santa Maria Novella promptly at 14:55. They sat opposite one another at their reserved table for two.

Scott flicked through *La Nazione* and then concentrated on the *Washington Post*, while Claudia tapped away on her laptop. She was composing an introduction to her proposals on how to tackle the mosquito problem in Italy. 'Mosquitoes are prolific pollinators. Therefore environmentally their survival is important to the Earth. They can no longer be viewed myopically as enemies which should be wiped out at all costs. Rather they should be seen as adversaries that need to be subdued, moderated and endured.'

Claudia looked out of the window and watched the

dark green and umber countryside flash by. She thought about her video call to Ettore. She realised she needed to discuss the situation in Rome and Florence with someone who had an unbiased view. 'Darling.' Scott looked up from his newspaper. 'I had a rather disturbing conversation with Ettore this morning.' She then outlined what they had talked about. 'And later,' she said, as she opened her email received file, 'he sent me this.' She passed him the laptop, which he looked at briefly.

'You want my opinion?' Scott asked. Claudia nodded. 'Well, honey, I don't know about you, but I hear alarm bells ringing. These goddamned insects are not only getting bigger. They're also bringing life-threatening diseases with them. Yet the Mayor of Rome issues bland guidelines on how to take evasive action, while the Institute calmly collects specimens, takes measurements and writes reports. And you, honey, go about insisting that we should work *with* skeeters, not against them. It strikes me that no one is dealing with this potential threat to humans with any sort of urgency.' Claudia nodded. She could see that what he was saying was mostly true. 'Given,' Scott continued, 'that folk, particularly in the south of the country, are under mounting attack by an enemy, which, tiny insect though it may be, is the deadliest creature on earth, the Italian Government should surely consider appointing a Committee, or at the very least a think tank, whose business should be to plan a practical strategy for the whole country. I reckon that if nothing immediate and radical *is* done to contain the mosquitoes, they will just become more and more numerous, until there's literally no stopping them! But ... what if it's already too late to act? What if there isn't a darned thing anyone can do about the situation? The consequences are likely to be catastrophic.'

An hour later, the *Italo Treno* rattled across the railroad bridge beside the Ponte della Libertà, which connects Venice with Mestre on the mainland, and pulled into Stazione di Santa Lucia on time, at 17:00.

Finding it more humid in Venice than Florence, Scott and Claudia made their way from the platform to the landing stage outside the station, where they boarded the Line No. 2 Express Waterbus.

As the crowded vaporetto cruised along the Grand Canal, with stops at Rialto, San Tomà, San Samuele, San Marco and San Zaccaria, Scott and Claudia noticed that the water level was lower than on their visit in April. 'The new water defence system seems to be doing its job,' observed Scott. 'In fact, if anything, the water seems to have dropped too much!' Surveying the fabulous vista that unfolded before them, they experienced the elevation of mind which is inspired by the uniqueness of *La Serenissima*, with its weathered palazzi, white domes, green-topped campanile, terracotta towers, narrow streets, cluttered houses – all disparately arranged in the brilliant and translucent Italian light.

Scott and Claudia disembarked and walked across the Riva degli Schiavoni and up the steps to the Hotel Danieli. After they had checked in at the reception desk in the magnificent entrance hall, with its marble pillared arches, crystal chandeliers and oval-patterned glass skylight, a porter led them up the red-carpeted stairs to their first-floor bedroom, which overlooked Rio del Vin. 'I know the rooms on this side,' Scott remarked. 'You get woken up at six in the morning by the refuse collection barge. Shall I ask them to move us?'

'No, darling,' said Claudia. 'I have to get up early tomorrow, anyway.' She looked round the room, with its damask curtains, softly-patterned silk wallpaper, pieces of brown furniture and king-size bed. 'I think it's a lovely room, even if it is slightly dated in style – but look how big the bed is! Plenty of room for some action in that,' she said, taking his hand. 'What say we give it a trial run right now? That's if you're *up* to it. Then afterwards, we can go out for an early dinner at Harry's Bar.'

'You're … you're … insatiable, did you know that, honey?' said Scott.

CHAPTER 9

Thursday 22 August

The following morning Claudia left the hotel at 06:15 and walked along Riva degli Schiavoni. She turned left into Calle Pietà. She noticed the familiar unpleasant smell – the result of many years of the Venetians' use of the canals as a rudimentary sewage disposal system. Looking upstream as she was about to cross the bridge over Rio della Pietà, she was startled to see a dark mass of mosquitoes swirling from one side of the canal to the other. Having watched their frenzied activity for several minutes, she took some photographs with her digital camera. She then continued along Calle della Pietà, branched left into Calle della Madonna and crossed over the Rio dei Greci into the old Greek quarter of the city. Turning right into the *calle* alongside Rio di San Lorenzo, she came face to face with another cloud of mosquitoes, which, though not as large as the one over Rio della Pietà, oscillated wildly. Claudia assembled her custom-made net and, reaching out over the edge of the canal to where the swarm was gyrating, tried to capture some specimens. She had managed to make a successful pass with the net, when two drunks in T-shirts and shorts came reeling along the *calle*, drinking from lager bottles, belly laughing and belching noisily. One of them threw his bottle onto the ground and, cursing loudly, stamped on the bits of broken glass.

Suddenly the swarm, which they were too inebriated to notice, veered towards them and pounced. Within seconds, the pair were covered from head to foot with seething mosquitoes. They staggered about, flailing their arms and yelling obscenities. 'Jump! JUMP into the water!' Claudia shouted, but they were too preoccupied to comply. Claudia quickly put the net down, checking to see that the lid had closed securely on the specimens trapped inside. She took a large canister from her bag, ran over to the men and proceeded to spray the extra strong repellent all over them. Gradually, the mosquitoes dispersed. Having heard the men's cries, an inhabitant of one of the houses came out to ask whether she could be of any help. Claudia asked her to phone for an ambulance urgently. The two unfortunates were not a pretty sight. Blood-sated mosquitoes, which they had swatted in their panic, were squashed onto their clothes, their bare arms and legs, and their swollen faces. One of the men was unable to see because his eyelids, bitten on the outside and jammed on the inside with dead or partly alive mosquitoes, had been transformed into two angry red bulges that completely covered his eyes. The other man, who was shaking uncontrollably, dropped to his knees, spitting out dead insects and retching violently.

A strident two-tone siren, increasing in volume, echoed through the canal. The ambulance, a motor launch painted in orange and yellow, came round the corner from Rio del Pestrin and pulled up at the landing stage. Three men – an emergency care nurse and two technicians – got off and surveyed the scene. '*Zanzare*?' the nurse asked.

'*Sì*,' Claudia replied, 'but it's a bad attack. They have both been bitten many, many times. The man on his knees, as you can see, is in shock. Please, they need to be taken to Intensive Care immediately. Their histamine levels must be dangerously high, and it's likely that some of the mosquitoes which bit them were carrying dangerous viruses.'

'Don't worry! We'll get them there as fast as possible,' said one of the technicians, as he guided the shaking man onto the launch and his companions carried the other man aboard on a stretcher. As the ambulance moved off, the nurse cried out, 'Signorina, you were lucky they didn't attack you.'

'I know,' Claudia shouted back, with a quick perfunctory half-smile. Although outwardly calm, inwardly Claudia was disturbed by what had occurred. Twice she had witnessed the concerted, seemingly arbitrary aggression of a mass of mosquitoes. *Is it possible,* she asked herself, *that females, and maybe also gynandromorphs, are now swarming* as a prelude *to carrying out large-scale attacks on human beings?* She watched as, sounding its siren, the ambulance passed out of view.

Having placed the net in the portable vivarium, she walked to the end of the *calle*, along Borgoloco San Lorenzo and into Fondamenta San Severo. There she found minor mosquito activity, a few small swarms. On the pathway, however, there was a large puddle of water, in which comma-shaped larvae were darting about. Using an electronic pipette, she removed specimens from the puddle and transferred them to a small amber bottle.

Crossing over Rio di San Severo, Claudia headed back to the Hotel. To ease her sense of foreboding, she stopped outside the Church of San Zaccaria and gazed at its elegant façade, one of the masterpieces of the Renaissance. As she was standing there, a man dressed in the distinctive costume of a gondolier stopped on his way across the Campo and asked her for the time. Claudia looked at her watch. 'It's 06:15.'

'I don't know why I get up so early!' he exclaimed. 'If I manage to pick up a fare before lunch, I shall count myself lucky. I tell you, it's just not worth sculling a gondola these days. Business is so bad.'

'Why is it?' she asked. 'Surely some of the millions of tourists you get here every year are keen to go on a gondola?'

'They *were* – but that was before the mosquitoes came. Now tourists go for a ride as a dare or for a bet – and either way they're not going to pay very much, if they run the risk of a possible mosquito strike.'

'How much are they prepared to pay?'

'Well, whereas just a short while ago we were charging 80 euros for a 40-minute ride, plus 40 euros for every additional 20 minutes, now we're lucky if we get 25 euros an hour. Locals still use us from time to time, in an emergency, and then only after haggling over the fare!'

'The drop-off in business must be worrying,' Claudia said. 'When I first came to Venice about ten years ago, there seemed to be gondolas with happy people on board in practically every canal.'

'They were the good times. Nowadays the tourists complain, especially about our charges – but they have no conception of how hard it is to make a living as a gondolier. The boats aren't cheap. They cost anywhere between 35,000 to 50,000 euros to buy and—'

'But that's crazy,' exclaimed Claudia. 'At the rates you charge, it must take years to recoup your outlay—'

'—or to pay back the bank the money you borrowed to buy the boat! There's the fact, too, that prime gondola sites sell for 20,000 euros or more – or at least they did before we were faced with the menace of the mosquitoes. Another problem is that for the first time since the war, the Regata Storica, which is a great source of income for us gondoliers, has been cancelled – because of the wretched mosquitoes!'

'But surely,' Claudia declared, 'they're more of a nuisance at night-time than during the day.'

'Yes, that used to be the case. Mosquitoes would appear at dusk and stay active until dawn. Traders setting up their stalls in the Rialto Market and their early customers were a favoured target, as was anyone who went for a ride in the dark on a gondola lit by lanterns. A friend of mine, Matteo, a gondolier like me, was taking a Danish couple down Rio di San Barnaba in the evening, when a swarm struck – and the man died. In the space of two and a half minutes he received more than 500 bites, and he had a major allergic reaction. Matteo said that the man's skin reddened and quickly developed rashes and large angry blisters. His lower legs swelled. He gasped for breath, and clutched one hand to his chest and the other to his throat. Then he sort of choked – and collapsed.'

'Clearly he had an overwhelming anaphylactic attack. How about Matteo and the woman? Were they bitten?'

'Yes, but nowhere near so badly. Matteo told me afterwards that the man worked as an attaché at the Danish Consulate here. He was reputed to be an incorrigible casanova and, believe it or not, the woman he was with in the gondola was ... the consul's wife!'

'A relationship which presumably would not have come to light had the poor man not died.'

'Yes, it's ironic. I hadn't thought of it like that. Anyway, what was I about to say? Oh yes, the pattern of these attacks has changed. Now people are being pestered throughout the day, by smaller groups of mosquitoes. Even the pigeons in Piazza San Marco have been targeted! And the attacks aren't just restricted to the city area. On Burano, where my parents live, people have been harassed indiscriminately both on the canals and in the *calli*. On Murano, the story is the same. My aunt works in the glass factory there, and she's been set upon several times. During one such assault, her dog, which she loved more than anything else in the world, was bitten, became infested by horrible worms and died of massive heart failure. It's a crap world we live in, isn't it, signorina? Personally, I blame those greedy capitalists who chopped all the rainforests down. Anyhow, signorina, it's been nice talking to you. I'd better be going. Mario and some of the other gondoliers are expecting me at a meeting they're holding at Bacino Orseolo. I hope you manage to enjoy your stay, signorina, without being too bothered by … you know what. *Ciao*!'

On the way from Campo San Zaccaria to the Hotel, Claudia introduced herself to various people who were going to work – café bar staff, hotel employees, shopkeepers and ferry pilots, among others. She asked them how they were coping with the heatwave and the mosquitoes. She was surprised by some of their answers – especially the suggestion that the weight of 20,000,000 tourists a year is causing Venice to sink into the Lagoon, and this, combined with the global rise in sea levels, brings the city ever closer to ruination.

When Claudia got back to the Danieli, the night porter, Luigi, who she knew from her previous visit in the spring, welcomed her. '*Buongiorno,* signorina! You're up bright and early!'

'Yes. I couldn't sleep, so I went for a walk by the canals. How are you, Luigi?' They shook hands.

'*Così così.* I was not too well about a fortnight ago. I had some sort of viral infection. But,' he said, adopting a confidential tone, 'I'm not the only one. In the past month, there've been a number of unexplained illnesses among both staff and guests. Some have been so poorly that they've had to be taken to hospital. It's not been a happy time, and with so many people staying at the Hotel, we've found it difficult to maintain our usual high standards.' The internal phone rang and Luigi became involved in a conversation about obtaining opera tickets for one of the Hotel guests, so Claudia waved and went upstairs. She entered the bedroom and looked at the clock on the bedside table. It was 07:05. She knelt beside the bed and kissed Scott's forehead. He stirred. 'Morning, lazybones,' she said. 'I'm glad the rubbish people didn't wake you, after all. Shall I order breakfast?'

'Yeah, please, honey.'

Claudia rang room service.

Scott got up and went into the bathroom, while Claudia sat at her laptop and began to make notes about her experiences that morning. What had happened and been said weighed heavily on her mind. Staring blankly out of the window at the buildings on the other side of Rio del Vin, she felt a growing sense of her own powerlessness. She knew that urgent action had to be taken to suppress the mosquito swarms, but there was no way she could endorse a renewed all-out war. In that event, she would have to declare herself a conscientious objector.

There was a knock at the door and a waiter brought in breakfast on a large wooden tray, which he set down on the glass-topped round table in the centre of the room. Claudia called Scott. When he came in from the bathroom, he could see that something was troubling her. 'Honey, you okay?' he asked.

'*Sì, mio caro!*' she said. 'I am just a little surprised by the extent of what a gondolier I was speaking to earlier calls the menace of the mosquitoes. I mean, people here are having a rough time. At night, despite the heat and humidity, windows are kept shut and rooms are sprayed in order to keep the mosquitoes at bay. But during the day attacks take place indiscriminately in the open, on the canals and in the *calli* and piazzas, at almost any time. That is disturbing, because, as you've heard me say often enough, most species of mosquitoes are normally active from dawn to sunrise and sunset to dusk. Luigi – you know, the night porter downstairs – says there have been outbreaks of various unknown illnesses in the hotel, among staff as well as guests. He says some cases have had to be referred to hospital. And that's somewhere I must go – to check out which, and how many, mosquito-borne viruses have been recorded, what the mortality rate is, and so on. I think I should go and get the details today. And it would help me to collect data and samples more quickly, if, rather than try and find my way through the *calli* and over the bridges, I had someone experienced to take me round the canals. Do you think we could possibly hire a boat? It would make life a lot easier.'

'There are a couple of folk,' said Scott, 'that I have appointments with this morning – a printer and one of our authors. Afterwards, I'll see what I can do about getting hold of some form of water transport. In view of the state of affairs here, I can't imagine tourists are queuing up for trips on the canals, so it should be relatively easy to hire a boat – and, hopefully, at half the usual rate! Anyway, I expect to be back by about 13:30. What say we have a quick lunch and afterwards go to the Hospital by boat, assuming I've managed to hire one with a driver.'

'That'll be great.'

'Now, how about some tea – or would you prefer coffee?'

After breakfast, Scott gave Claudia a quick kiss and hurried off to his meeting with the printer. Claudia rang through to the day porter, Ottavio, and asked him to arrange for a special courier to make a delivery for her to an address in Rome. After she had packed the specimens, she rang the Ospedale Civile and made an appointment to see the Registrar at 15:00. She then sat at her laptop again and continued to make notes about her early morning encounters.

* * *

'Hello … Hello? It's Luca Baldini here … from Tuscany in Italy. Can I speak to Serge Kuznetsov, please. Kuz-net-sov. My Russian pronunciation is not too good …'

Baldini drummed his fingers on the table as he waited a long time for a response. 'Serge? Oh good! I thought I'd never get through to you … Yes, I'm fine, thank you. I just wanted to confirm that the family in San Luca have okayed the deal, whereby we buy 10kg of weapons-grade plutonium-239 with reduced critical mass at a cost of $10,000,000, which the Bratva will transport and deliver anywhere in Europe or the Middle East free of charge … Destination for the material will be advised within the next few days … I believe it may be Iran … Yes, I understand … we're to pay the money to Bruno Ouspensky as and when you confirm the material is ready for shipment … My friend, it's good to do business with you … Have you any questions? No? Good. I'll wait to hear from you. Let's hope everything goes according to plan … Best wishes to you, too. *Ciao.*'

* * *

Scott came back at 13:10. 'Hey, come and see what I've got you, honey!' He took Claudia outside to the hotel's landing stage, where a stylish wooden motor launch was moored. 'I'm borrowing it from the hotel

– also the driver. I didn't think you'd fancy paddling about in a kayak! Apparently the boat was made in the 1950s. Isn't she beautiful? The driver will be back in an hour. He's just getting something to eat.' They walked beside the waters of the Bacino San Marco, past Piazzetta San Marco and Giardinetti Reali, to the Calle Vallaresso.

In the elegant and airy Gran Veduta dell' Acqua Ristorante the *capo cameriere* showed them to a table on the terrace, from which they had a glorious view across the sunlit lagoon to the fabled Cipriani Hotel on La Guidecca. Over a simple meal of *prosciutto crudo di San Daniele e fici* and *spaghetti con vongole*, they discussed Laurence's involvement with the 'Ndrangheta, Baldini's lunch party, the car chase that followed, and whether the painting, supposedly by Raphael, could be genuine or not.

As they talked, they watched vaporettos coming and going from the Vallaresso landing stage, with mainly tourists getting on and off.

'Why's it called a vaporetto?' Scott asked.

'The word means "little steamer",' Claudia answered. 'Vaporettos used to run on *vapore* – steam.'

After lunch, Scott and Claudia returned to the Danieli and went aboard the motor launch. Having welcomed them, the driver cast off and headed for the Ospedale Civile. From the Riva degli Schiavoni they turned right into Rio di Palazzo Laterano, passed under the Bridge of Sighs and progressed along various canals until they reached Rio di San Giovanni, where the driver moored the boat. Claudia and Scott walked the short distance to the Hospital – an enormous building with an elaborate façade. When they arrived at Reception at shortly after 15:00, Claudia told the girl behind the desk about her appointment, and they were shown along a myriad of passages to a large, comfortable office at the rear of the building.

The Registrar, a serious-looking, grey-haired man of about 50, was helpful and businesslike. Over the past month, he said, 472 people had consulted the Accident and Emergency Department with what he called idiopathies, illnesses of unknown cause, for which antibiotics are not recommended as a means of treatment. The symptoms of these illnesses had included, with varying degrees of acuteness and occasionally with several symptoms combined, earache, chesty cough, fever, gastroenteritis, aching muscles, headache and sore throat. Seventeen patients had been kept in overnight for observation. None had died or developed any life-threatening disease. More seriously, the Hospital had treated 937 victims of mosquito attacks, ranging from those who, in 52.5% of cases, had received from one to ten bites each to those who, in 42.5% of cases, had received more than 50 bites, i.e. multiple bites. A minority of those attacked had developed virulent tropical diseases: currently in the Hospital's Quarantine Wing there were eighteen cases of Dengue, sixteen cases of Malaria and three cases of Yellow Fever. The Registrar handed Claudia a list of the number of people bitten and, where applicable, the virus they had been infected by. The number of deaths was also given. Claudia looked at the list and then passed it to Scott.

Claudia asked whether the person who was

recorded as having died from anaphylaxis had been the Commercial Attaché at the Danish Consulate. The Registrar nodded his head. She then asked him what the up-to-date condition was of the two men who had been attacked that morning beside Rio di San Lorenzo. The Registrar said that one was in deep shock, the other had lost his sight, and both were giving rise for concern.

Scott, who was studying the sheet of statistics, looked up suddenly and asked, 'Are the media aware of these figures?'

The Registrar looked appalled. 'Good heavens, no!' he exclaimed. 'We don't want the public to panic – and that's precisely what will happen if sensitive information like this gets into the hands of the gutter press!'

'Yes, but a hospital like this has a duty to safeguard public health,' exclaimed Claudia. 'I agree you don't want to cause a panic, but surely you ought to alert people to the dangers of mosquito bites. It's not my business, I know, but I should have thought, at the very least, you ought to be conducting some sort of poster campaign and issuing toned-down press releases about the incidence of Malaria, Dengue and Yellow Fever.'

'Yeah,' said Scott. 'It's just *not* in the public interest to hide the facts. I mean, folk have a right to know—'

'*If* you'll excuse me,' interrupted the Registrar, 'I have other more important matters to deal with. I believe I've given you the information you requested, so, if you don't mind finding your own way out, I'll bid you good afternoon.' With that he turned his attention to the pile of papers on his desk and the interview was terminated. Finding their own way out of the Hospital proved difficult and they had to ask five times for directions.

When they were outside the building, Claudia said, angrily, 'He seemed to be more interested in reeling off statistics than in saving lives. Maybe that's unkind – but petty bureaucrats in this country never do seem to view humans as anything other than units.'

'Not just in this country, honey! Now let's get on board and do some serious sightseeing. Hey! What is it with this nasty smell?' Scott asked, pinching his nostrils and pulling a face.

'Rather off-putting, isn't it?' replied Claudia. 'I'm afraid it's particularly bad when the weather's hot.'

'It smells like seaweed – or something worse. Cap'n, can you take us on a quick tour of the place please?' The launch set off and headed west via Rio di Santa Marina and Rio di San Giovanni Laterano out into the Grand Canal, under the Rialto Bridge and past the palazzi that lined the banks on either side. After they had passed Ca' Rezzonico, they noticed that on the opposite bank some workmen with pneumatic drills and a small JCB were digging a trench from Calle degli Orbi towards the Grand Canal. The noise they were making bounced back and forth from the surrounding buildings. Scott turned to the driver. 'Cap'n, can you slow down for a moment? Those guys who're digging a trench – any idea why? Are they planning to divert water from the Grand Canal into the smaller canals that have almost dried up?'

The driver nodded his head. '*Si,* signor, I think is possible,' he said, manoeuvring the launch as close as he could to the Ca' Rezzonico dock, without blocking other boats.

'I think it's more likely they're digging the channel for a sewage pipe,' said Claudia. 'They—'

'Jeez! Do you mean to say they intend to flush shit into the canal?'

'I'm afraid so. It's a fact that 90% of Venice's raw sewage still goes straight into the canals, including the Grand Canal. So that's why, when the weather's hot and you're walking among the backstreet *calli*, there's a smell that's not very pleasant.'

'Yeah, I noticed it was pretty bad,' said Scott, 'when we were going along the smaller canals to the Hospital.'

'The smell arises from a mixture of *merda*, dried seaweed and uncollected decomposing garbage. The pollution of the water is compounded by the addition of chemicals and detergents, which are responsible for killing off the fish and upsetting the marine plant life.'

'Isn't there any way of getting rid of all this filth?'

'Well, most of it. Fortunately, that's because twice a day the tide sweeps about 65% of the waste out into the Lagoon. Even so, in high summer, when the canals are low, there's a definite threat to public health – especially from our little whining friends, who just love the odours, not just of humans, but also of dirty water!'

There was a sudden burst of shouting from the

opposite bank. The three workmen were waving their arms back and forth. Then one of them collapsed, and his two colleagues knelt beside him, still waving their arms about and shouting. Passers-by went to help them, but hurriedly stepped back. Others raced off down the *calle*.

'Heck, he musta put the drill through his foot or something,' Scott suggested.

'No, I don't think so, Claudia said. 'It looks to me as if they're trying to ward off a swarm of …' she remembered Scott's aversion, 'bees or wasps. And maybe the man passed out or had a heart attack.'

'Bees or wasps. As long as it isn't our little whiny friends!' Scott signalled to the driver to move on. A siren sounded and a water ambulance sped by with its blue light flashing. 'You know, honey, I getta distinct feeling of unease about this place. It's as if we're due a storm – but it's more than that. It's hard to explain.'

Claudia looked at him, with a puzzled expression. 'Well, it's certainly humid enough for a storm – but otherwise I don't sense any difference. The place seems to me to be just the same as usual,' she said. A few minutes later the motor launch branched off from the Grand Canal onto some of the smaller canals, stopping from time to time so that Claudia could make notes of where the breeding areas were in the stagnant backwaters and beside the *calli*, or get out to examine the standing water on the pathways.

They arrived back at the Danieli at about 17:25, and the driver was on the point of mooring the boat, when Claudia said, 'Darling, do you mind if we visit the canals I walked beside this morning? There was quite a bit of mosquito activity there and, although I captured some adult specimens, I didn't get enough larvae.'

'Sure, honey. Which canals were they?'

'Della Pietà and … San Lorenzo.'

'So, if we take a left along here into della Pietà, I guess we can double back into San Lorenzo. Isn't that correct, Cap'n?'

The driver answered, '*Si,* signor,' and pushed the throttle forwards. Prow lifting, the boat surged through the water.

* * *

Meanwhile, as the *passeggiata*[5] was taking shape on the quayside of Piazza San Marco, a southeasterly sirocco blew in from the Adriatic and had the happy effect of dispersing the gathering mosquitoes. The downside was that the humidity increased considerably, and it felt as if a huge, stifling PVC tarpaulin had enveloped the Laguna Veneta. In the various wards or sixths of the city, people were affected by the heat in different ways. In the grounds of a large care home in Cannaregio, patients who were taking their evening constitutionals were overcome by the sultry conditions and many passed out or suffered heat

---

[5] *Il passeggiata*, or the stroll, takes place on weekdays in the early evening in Piazza San Marco, under the colonnades when it is cold and towards the quayside when it is warm. Two lines of people form and each approaches the other from opposite directions. As the lines overlap, the people intermingle. Thus an opportunity is provided at the end of the working day for friends and acquaintances to walk and talk together in one of the most magnificent squares in the world.

exhaustion. In Santa Croce, in the Giardini Papadopoli, two couples argued about whose prior right it was to sit on the only remaining communal bench. The taller of the two men was so incensed by not getting his own way that he punched the other man to the ground and, despite the women screaming for him to stop, repeatedly stamped on the man's face with heavy duty boots until it was just bloody mush and barely recognisable. In Campo San Polo, at the top of the campanile, a young man, exasperated by his girlfriend's non-stop whiny voice, shoved her away violently and, losing her footing, she collided backwards with the parapet balustrade, toppled over it and plummeted 25 metres onto the grey flagstones below. In Dorsoduro, in the sweltering kitchen of a restaurant just off Rio di San Barnaba, a commis, who was momentarily blinded by perspiration, chopped off his forefinger and thumb. In another kitchen in the nearby Campo Santa Margherita, the chef, who was described as 'sweating like a fat man in a sauna', went berserk and charged through the restaurant hacking at customers indiscriminately with a 28cm slicing knife. In Piazza San Marco outside the historic cafés, tourists sipped exorbitantly priced lagers and other cold drinks and watched people taking part in the *passeggiata*. At a table for four, a man mopped his face and exclaimed to his fellow drinkers: 'Good Lord, it's so *bloody* hot! A case of oh to be in England now that August's there – and where it's a damned sight cooler than here! I put it down to El Nina, or whatever it's called, making the ocean hotter, also the weather and the air, and shifting the whole damned lot this way.'

At another table a fat, middle-aged woman was

telling her companion in a loud voice that she wasn't going to join the communal walkabout, because her clothes would become even more soaked than they already were.

The sirocco whirled round the square. Awnings were ripped, parasol sunshades uprooted. In the Doge's Palace Arcade there was a kerfuffle as two overheated gays pushed and shoved each other. Rude names, swear words and accusations of betrayal were bandied about. Other people became involved and one or two punches were thrown. A couple of urban policemen arrived on the scene and tried to calm everyone down, without much success.

But these various incidents were of little significance, compared to what was about to happen.

In the southeast of the city, something occurred which would change Venice forever. On Fondamenta Rio della Tana, a crimson-faced, inebriated resident swayed back and forth in front of his house and stared disbelievingly at an area of standing water on the *calle,* which had been liberally sprinkled with oil but was nonetheless wriggling with hundreds of comma-shaped pupae. For someone whose family had been tormented for weeks by mosquitoes this was the final straw. A road builder by profession and choleric by nature, he decided there and then that he had had enough. He stormed into his house and reappeared with a large commercial flamethrower. He pumped up the pressure, turned on the jet and lit the paraffin vapour. He took aim and, from close range, blasted three arcs of bright orange flame at the large puddle. The first missed the water completely and set fire to the small wooden lean-to shed, in which he and his closest neighbours kept their refuse bins. The second arc lit the oil on the water. The third ignited a pile of empty fish crates that someone had left standing on the *calle*. The man blinked stupidly at his handiwork. The hot wind fanned the three separate blazes. Burning shards were driven through the open windows and doors, not just of his own house, but of adjoining buildings as well. Curtains, carpets and other combustibles burst into flames. Before long, sparks from burning floors and roofs were raining down like confetti. Wooden boats that were moored on the nearside of Rio della Tana caught light and, in turn, set fire first to the fuel left by motorboats on the surface of the water and then to the boats on the opposite side.

The sirocco blew more strongly and the flames spread by leaps and bounds. Burning ash and debris swept across the canals and along the *calli*. In the main dockyard area, people in fear for their lives jumped into the water, as the wooden piers ignited and boats and petrol pumps exploded. Remorselessly, the flames swept through Campo San Biagio and its Church, into the Naval History Museum, where the remains of ancient wooden galleys burned fiercely and, confronted with the fire's sudden manifestation, rats and mice ran from their hiding places. Birds – blackbirds, pigeons, plovers – flew from their nests. Seagulls squawked overhead, above the blaze. Dogs and cats ran down the narrow pathways. People on the higher floors of buildings found themselves trapped; and to escape choking to death or being burnt alive, some chose to fling themselves into the knee-deep canals below, often landing head first in the foul sludge that lay directly under the surface of the green water. The oppressive air soon filled with the screams of those who opted to stay indoors. A thick swirling pall of smoke enclosed their houses. Inhaling toxic gases, some were asphyxiated – but not before superheated air scalded the soft tissues of their mouths, throats and lungs, burnt their hair off and scorched and cracked their skin, until it shed in flakes and fragments. Others died fighting for breath and drowning in flames. As their bodies were cooked, the fat under their skin melted, the thin tissue of their eyelids was destroyed, and their liquid eyeballs boiled and burst. With their charred bodies rupturing, the victims were granted momentary relief from the excruciating pain when their nerve endings were cauterised. Then, almost immediately, they went into neurogenic shock, multiple organ failure set in and death came not a moment too soon. One after another, humans, like candle flames, were snuffed out.

On Calle de la Pegola, in a third-floor bedsit with bars in the windows, a young mother clasped her two babies to her chest and cried helplessly, as flames licked at the entrance door and flickered between the floorboards and the room filled with the acrid smoke of smouldering foam rubber. Close by, on the fourth floor of another deathtrap, an old man begged his wife, who had locked herself in the bathroom, to come out and jump with him into the canal below; but he was unable to persuade her and, rather than leave the woman he had lived with for 45 years, he stayed and they held each other close, as they slowly suffocated.

Fanned by the wind, the fire had built up a terrifying momentum. It next consumed Palazzo Querini, San Martino Church and the old Arsenal dockyard, where in the thirteenth century, at the height of Venice's power, one galley a day was built and work was provided for 16,000 men. Then the Arsenal itself was scorched and blackened and partly destroyed, as were its tower and its magnificent Portal, the first notable Renaissance structure in the city. The sirocco blew even more strongly, and the flames raced through the network of intercommunicating *calli*, *corti* and *salizzade* that lie beyond the Arsenal, thus establishing a fiery front from the Church of San Giovanni in Bragora in the south to the Church of San Francesco della Vigna in the north. Narrow confines, where buildings lean against one another and there are only short spaces between the open windows of adjoining houses, are a happy hunting ground for a wind-driven conflagration.

Those who had seen or sensed the approaching danger fled while they could. Among their number was the man who started it all with his flamethrower. He was crying as he ran and muttering repeatedly, '*Che cosa ho fatto*? [What have I done?]' Sirens, alarms, church bells, the haunting bong of the Marangona from the Campanile sounded throughout the city. More and more residents of the eastern islet ran from their homes: some to moored boats or to the nearest waterbus, motorboat or *barca* landing-stages, others to the Grand Canal and the Rialto and dell' Accademia bridges – all trying desperately to escape to the western islet or to Guidecca, the Lido, the islands or Mestre. People fled from their homes, carrying treasured possessions. Those who were empty-handed slid into the deeper canals and swam through the filthy water to the Canale di San Marco, where in many cases they were hit by passing speedboats and drowned. Museum staff tried to choose which of Venice's many famous and influential works of art they should or could rescue. Meanwhile, soldiers and policemen, who had been called in to act as a deterrent to those bent on thieving, decided discretion was the better part of valour and joined in the frenzied exodus. Thus looters, with wet scarves over their mouths and noses, were free to take anything of value that they could lay their hands on. But, delaying too long to gather as many treasures as possible, they found themselves enclosed by the onrushing flames and were burnt to death. While the sun set and electric power began to fail, panic and pandemonium reigned.

At about the same time as the fire reached the Arsenal complex and Claudia had completed the business of collecting larvae from the pools of water on Salizzada dei Greci and Fondamenta dei Furlani, she and Scott decided to take temporary shelter from the hot dry wind in the Church of Sant' Antonin. 'Phew! Someone's got a bonfire going,' observed Scott, sniffing the air. Inside the empty building, there was a welcome coolness amid the gloom and the stale smell of incense and candle wax. Claudia sat down on the end of a row of chairs, opened her sports bag, took out her notebook and began to write.

Scott, who was standing beside her, said, 'It's funny you're not religious. Most Italians would be kneeling and crossing themselves.'

'I dare say,' said Claudia, in a fierce whisper, 'but, as you know, I'm a pantheist. I believe Nature and God are one and the same thing. I have no time for the Church and its ceremonies. All that kneeling and eating wafers! *Nature* orders our lives, not God.'

'Hey!' He tapped her on the shoulder. She looked up with a frown on her face, and he leant down and kissed her on the mouth. 'You're beautiful, you know that,' he said, 'especially when you're so … so intense!' Leaving her to make her notes, he went on a tour of the church. He was in the chancel, looking at the altarpiece, when he suddenly called out, 'There's a heck of a ruckus going on outside. Can you hear it? Also I think I … yes, I can smell burning. Look!' He pointed at the ceiling. 'There's smoke seeping in through those vents up there. That's not coming from any goddamned bonfire!' He ran down the aisle and went out through the west door. Claudia got to her feet, picked up her bag and followed him.

On turning the corner to go round to the back of the Church, they were confronted by a wall of leaping flames and thick black smoke, which stretched as far as the eye could see. Running towards them were people escaping from the raging fire. Ear-piercing screams and the sound of collapsing masonry and timber joists filled the air. 'Jeez!' Scott cried. 'How the hell did this start? Most of the city at this end seems to be ablaze, and the wind is driving the flames towards the centre. My God, what a catastrophe! Honey, we need to get outta here fast!' He grabbed Claudia's hand, and they turned round and ran to Fondamenta dei Furlani, where the boat was moored. There was no sign of the driver. They jumped aboard, and Claudia cast off, while Scott went to the front, inserted the ignition key and pressed the starter button. The engines didn't fire. He tried six or seven times, without success. 'Goddamned piece of crap!'

he yelled. 'The freaking carburettors must be flooded!' People were running past them towards Riva degli Schiavoni. Behind them, the School of Art, the houses in Calle dei Furlani and the Church of San Giovanni di Malta were all burning. 'We gonna have to make a run for it.'

Claudia came up to the front of the boat. 'Let me try.' She pressed the starter button and the engines fired instantly.

'Hey, the magic touch! Well done, honey.' He kissed her on the cheek. She sat in the passenger seat. Scott simultaneously slammed the throttle forward and turned the steering wheel, with the result that the boat swerved out into the canal almost on its side in a great wave of spuming water. They swept down Rio della Pietà, under the bridge and out into the Canale di San Marco.

'I've just thought. I need my files from the hotel,' Claudia cried. Scott nodded. He pulled back on the throttle, turned the boat and, easing the throttle forward again, returned to the Danieli landing stage.

Dense, choking smoke was swirling in the wind. A stone's throw away, the fire had reached the Church of San Zaccaria. People charged backwards and forwards along Riva degli Schiavoni, clutching suitcases and household objects. There were shouts and screams for help. Scott and Claudia leapt from the boat, ran into the deserted, blacked out hotel and collected some belongings from their smoked-filled bedroom. On their way out through the foyer, Claudia noticed something. 'Look!' she said, pointing at two black shoes that were sticking out from behind the Reception counter. They went to investigate. 'O

Madre dell' Inferno, no!' Luigi was lying on his back, with blood from his battered skull seeping onto the floor. By his side was an open cash box, which contained some loose change. Drawers in the counter had been pulled out. Papers had been thrown everywhere.

'Looters,' Scott said, kneeling down and feeling Luigi's pulse. A few moments later, he looked up at Claudia and shook his head. Thick black smoke poured in through the windows. 'Honey, we *must* go, otherwise we gonna get fried!' He took her by the arm and, with Claudia peering over her shoulder at the counter, dragged her outside. On the landing stage, he pushed her into the boat and jumped in after her. A crowd of people, who were waiting for the next waterbus, followed his lead and jumped on board as well – so many, in fact, that the launch was in danger of sinking. 'Hey, can you get off, please? This is a private boat, not a waterbus,' Scott shouted, but his uninvited passengers stayed put. A burly man, who he recognised as a waiter from the hotel, stood at the stern of the boat and dissuaded any further would-be fellow travellers from boarding. 'For Chrissake, hightail it outta here, honey,' Scott shouted, 'before we go under!'

'Where are we aiming for?' Claudia asked, pushing the throttle as far forward as it would go, whereupon the overladen boat moved sluggishly out into the Canale di San Marco.

'I was going to suggest,' Scott replied, 'we went to Marco Polo Airport – but just look at the chaos out here. It'll take us hours! I propose we head for somewhere that's out of harm's way, such as Giudecca, always assuming we don't bump into one of those goddamned liners. It's the longer of the two islands ahead. It normally takes about ten minutes to get over there, but today, with all this traffic in the canal, I reckon it'll take considerably longer. What we'll do is drop this lot off at the San Giorgio landing station, and then go round the corner into the Canale della Grazia and park in the Cipriani's private harbour. I know the assistant manager there. He's American. We can get a drink in the bar – I'm sure we'll both need one by then – and work out what we're going to do next.'

'I think you should find out what the situation is,' Claudia said. 'I mean, find out whether there are any flights from Marco Polo or Treviso still available. If there are hundreds of people waiting for flights, then we'll know it's not worth going to either airport. Anyhow, some way or other I want to go back home as soon as … *Mio Dio*, this is unbelievable!' One of the many small craft in the water darted across the bow of the launch and Claudia managed to avoid a collision by a hair's breadth. Scott pushed his way through to the front of the boat.

'Okay, honey! Let me take over,' he said, sensing that the confusion was making her nervous. They swapped positions and, while Scott was manoeuvring through what amounted to a mobile obstacle course on water, three fire tenders set off from the City Fire Station, but had no chance of getting through canals that had been transformed into swirling tunnels of flame. Fighting the fire was further complicated by the fact that water levels in the smaller canals were unusually low, as Scott and Claudia had noticed, and therefore the fire hydrants on some of the *calli* did not have sufficient pressure to work effectively. At its northern end, *il incendio* burnt its way round the extensive Campo Santi Giovanni e Paolo, through the adjoining San Zanipolo church and onto the Scuola Grande di San Marco, where the Ospedale Civile is located. There patients, who were in the process of being moved out, were badly burnt and, in many cases, asphyxiated, along with hospital porters and other staff engaged in their evacuation. Inside, administration staff, including the Registrar, who had been attempting to save the Hospital's records on disk and paper, were trapped and roasted alive by the searing flames.

Meanwhile, Claudia and Scott continued on their perilous journey through the mayhem on Canale di San Marco. 'Where are the police?' Scott asked. 'They should be out here on the water directing these jerks!' A few moments later, they were faced with a difficult decision. They came across two boats that had collided. The members of each crew, six people in all, were floating in the sea. 'Please help us!' one of their number, a woman, cried out. She was holding onto a man, whose head was slumped forward and dipping in and out of the water.

Claudia put her hand on Scott's forearm.

'No way, honey! It's crazy even to think of it. The goddamned boat'll sink!'

'Please,' shouted the woman. 'My husband has been injured. He's losing a lot of blood.' Scott pulled the throttle back. As the launch drifted to a standstill, there was no let-up in the seafaring activity around it. Boats of all types passed continuously on either side. A jet ski sped by, narrowly missing two of the people in the water.

'Maniac!' Scott screamed. 'Jeez, what a dope!'

Beckoning with her hand, Claudia called out, 'Come on. Come and join us. We'll help you get on board.'

'This is a major mistake, honey,' Scott muttered. 'The boat's already very low in the water.' The four people other than the woman and her injured husband – they were all men – needed no further encouragement. Managing somehow to weave their way in and out of the boats that constantly streamed by, they swam over to the launch and tried to clamber on all at the same time. The side of the boat plunged under the surface and water poured in. 'Hey, one at a time, you idiots – or you'll sink us!' yelled Scott, angrily. The men drew back slightly and waited until each in turn was pulled aboard.

'Can someone give me a hand, please?' the woman asked. 'I don't think I can hold onto my husband much longer. My arms …' She and the injured man were inundated by the wash of a large cabin cruiser that went by at speed. When they reappeared, the woman was coughing and spluttering.

'Okay,' said Scott, taking off his shirt and shoes, 'I guess I'm gonna have to get them.' He stood on the bow of the boat, looked both ways to see that nothing was coming and dived in. He swam over to the couple easily enough, but the return journey was another story. Swimming on one's back in wildly undulating water while holding on to a large, semi-conscious man is in itself tricky; but, when undertaken in conditions that are equivalent to a blind man crossing the road in Naples during the rush hour, it becomes even more difficult. Anyway, having instructed the woman to follow directly behind him and act as his eyes, Scott somehow managed to haul her husband through the waves – and all three made it back to the launch without being run over by any passing speed boat. Once they had negotiated the precarious business of getting aboard the overloaded boat and Scott stood dripping in front of the steering wheel, Claudia leant over and kissed him on the cheek. Giving him a pat on the back, she said, with a laugh, 'You'll do, I suppose.'

'So will you … for the time being,' countered Scott, as he opened the throttle and they continued on their way through the melee. When they had negotiated the Canale di San Marco and were making their way across Canale della Giudecca, Scott pointed to the right and shouted, 'Look, two big ships have collided just outside the Cruise Terminal. That'll make it even more difficult for people to get to the train station!'

After they had landed their fifteen passengers at San Giorgio, Scott moved away from the landing station. Then he slowed the launch and put it in neutral. As the boat bobbed in the water, he and Claudia looked across at the city. Dense smoke and a fiery blaze were advancing on the historic Piazza San Marco complex – the pink and white Doge's Palace, the five-domed Basilica, the 90-metre high Campanile, Sansovino's Library. All along the Riva degli Schiavoni there were orange and yellow tongues of flame darting from the rooftops, and they could see that their beloved Danieli was on fire. In the sky,

Italian Air Force utility planes and helicopters circled over the eastern islet, dropping great bursts of water on the burning buildings below. Thick clouds of smoke and steam drifted westward in the wind. Claudia and Scott were staring in the same direction the sirocco was blowing, so they could not hear any of the sounds from the city: the sirens, the shouts, the screams, the explosions, the uproar. Such was the terrible impression of the noiseless scene that silent tears of grief poured down Claudia's face, and Scott, who was pale and visibly shaken, put his arm around her to comfort her.

'I know it's wrong, darling,' Claudia said, 'but I'd … I'd like to return to Florence as soon as possible. I say it's wrong because, in my heart of hearts, I feel we should be over there on the other side of the water trying to help.'

'There's nothing useful we can do, honey, you must see that,' said Scott. 'We'd be a liability. We'd be attempting to save dying or injured people without medical assistance or knowledge. We'd be fighting the blaze with our bare hands. And we'd probably lose our lives into the bargain. I agree, we should return to Florence – although getting there's not going to be easy. In a sense we *are* running away – that's true. But there's no way we'll be able to leave behind the memory of this terrible calamity. It will stay with us for the rest of our lives.'

'Man has destroyed his own exquisite creation,' Claudia said quietly, 'a city beyond compare.'

As more tears welled in her eyes, Scott clasped her tightly to his side. 'Honey, let's see if there's any way outta here. I'll call Directory Inquiries and ask them for the airport's number.' He produced his mobile and put it to his ear. 'Hell's bells, the goddamned thing's dead. The network must be down due to the fire. There's no Internet connection either. We better go round to the Cipriani and find out if they have any way of contacting the airport.' Scott shifted into forward and accelerated. The bow rose up and they headed for the Hotel's private harbour.

* * *

That evening, when Mario told Baldini that Venice was on fire, he didn't seem very concerned. 'It was sinking anyway!' he exclaimed. 'Fortunately, even if the whole city burns down, it's not a problem for the 'Ndrangheta. True, they own several buildings in Venice, including three main banks – and maybe those buildings have been damaged beyond repair. But it doesn't matter.'

'Why, boss?' Mario asked.

'Why? Because, due to the astuteness of the family, those buildings are insured for more than the current market value – and the company that insures them is controlled by the family. So they're not going to lose money, are they? They're going to make a substantial profit instead.' After a pause for reflection, he added, 'Of course, Venice was a beautiful place. And its loss will have a damaging effect on the country's economy – and the tourist industry in particular.'

His mobile beeped. 'Hello? Ah, Serge. So what is the position at your end? ... Everything is ready for shipment by train in special containers? ... *Scopami*, that's quick. Right, so I'll go ahead and pay Ouspensky half the money today. When it's confirmed that the shipment has been received at the Natanz plant in Iran, we will pay him the rest. Okay? … Yes, I know. I did say we'd pay all the money when you were ready to make the shipment – but the family won't hear of it. They say they're taking a big enough risk paying 2.5 million before the goods are shipped … Yes, I'm quite sure you're straight-up and a man of your word. I've tried to convince them of that, to no avail … No, I'd be stupid to take it any further. Even when you're a member of the organisation, you don't argue with the family – not unless you want to end up with a bullet in your head!'

* * *

When Scott and Claudia arrived at the Cipriani harbour, they found there were eleven boats already moored there. Scott managed to squeeze their launch in between two other boats.

Inside the Hotel there were people – some with drinks in their hands – running around and voicing their concerns. 'I can't get through. I can't get hold of my daughter. She said she was going to do some shopping in Calle Larga.'

'No, dear, the mobile isn't working, so there's no point in calling for a water taxi.'

'Keep calm, Cyrus darling. There's nothing we can do about it.'

'Well,' said Scott, 'clearly the Hotel doesn't have any network or landline connections. So shall we have a coffee and discuss what we're going to do?' They went into the Gabbiano Bar and ordered a couple of espressos. After considering their various options, they decided the next step should be to head south for Chioggia, which they were assured by the barman was on a different network and would therefore be connected to the Internet and Wi-Fi.

Back in the boat, Scott studied the map he had found in the cabin. 'We have to go round the end of the Lido onto the Lagoon and head south. The distance to Chioggia is between 25 and 30 kilometres, so I reckon the journey's going to take about an hour.' Scott looked at his watch. 'It's now 19:30. Sunset is in half an hour. That means we'll have to travel part of the way in the dark, which, with all these other boats running about on the water, is not ideal. I notice there are a couple of spotlights on the cabin roof. Let's hope they have good penetrating beams.'

'Darling,' Claudia said, 'I know it's only half dark at the moment, but wouldn't it be a good idea to put the lights on now? That way other boats will see where we are, and we'll be able to judge whether the lights are going to be any use in the dark!'

'Good idea, honey.' Scott started the boat and located the appropriate switch for the spotlights, which he turned on. They moved off and picked up speed. 'Honey, I suggest you get some sleep. I'll wake you when we get there or if anything happens.'

'No, I'll keep you company,' Claudia said, moving beside him.

'You realise, with this wind blowing, the Lagoon is going to be a tad choppy. I take it that's not a problem for you.'

'No, not at all.' Pointing up at the sky, she said, 'Look at that huge red glow. It extends much, much further than it did before.'

'Good God, it must have reached Piazza San Marco. What a disaster! Why haven't they been able to control the fire? They should have made firebreaks by blowing up buildings on both sides of the larger canals, thereby creating wide gaps that the fire couldn't traverse. As things stand, though, the flames will shortly reach the Grand Canal, and that will act as a natural firebreak and halt the fire, hopefully. But by then the history, the art, the architecture of one of the most beautiful cities in the world will have been demolished.'

They had been heading out onto the Lagoon for about 20 minutes, when the boat's engine spluttered a couple of times and then died. Scott looked at the dashboard. 'Hell's bells!' he shouted. 'We've run out of gas. I never thought to check the fuel gauge. *Now* what are we going to do? Paddle? We have no way of communicating with anyone. We may be stuck here for hours. We have no water to drink. Nothing to eat. Nobody will see us when the spotlights fail because the battery's gone flat.'

'Please, Scott, don't get stressed. It doesn't help. We're just going to have to stay put until someone rescues us. We can, of course, try attracting people's attention: have you checked to see whether there are any rescue flags on board – or flares?'

'No, I haven't,' Scott said, recovering his equilibrium. 'Shall we look round the boat to see what we can find?'

'Yes,' Claudia replied. 'Just another thought, though: shouldn't we be able to send some kind of emergency radio signal which indicates our position? Presumably it will be controlled from the dashboard.'

They studied the dials and switches on the fascia. 'Nothing relevant there, as far as I can see.' She looked down. 'What's this small cupboard for?' She tried the handle. 'It's locked. Somewhere I saw a bunch of keys? Maybe there's one that fits this lock.'

Scott picked up the keys and waved them in the air. 'The driver left them on the passenger seat. We're lucky nobody noticed them and ran off with the boat. I'll try them one by one until hopefully we find the right key.' About halfway through this process, the key he was trying opened the small door. Inside was a large smartphone, which was held in a charging cradle. It had a small screen and a keyboard. What made it different to a regular mobile was the short round tube sticking out of the top. 'If this is what I think it is, then we're gonna be okay.'

'Why, what is it?'

'It's a satphone, honey. It connects …' he pointed at the tube, '… via this antenna to orbiting satellites, not to cell sites here on earth. With this device one can call anyone practically anywhere. But let's just hope the hotel is – was – up-to-date with its payments for airtime. Otherwise the goddamned thing will be of no use to us at all.' Pointing at the cradle, he said, 'Also, let's hope it's fully charged. Anyway, here goes.' He took the phone, switched it on and put it to his ear. 'It's working. It has a dial tone. I'll go ahead and call the airport.' He pressed the keys and then put the phone to his ear again. 'It's ringing. But no one's answering. Wait a minute, there's a message.' He passed the phone to Claudia.

Claudia translated: '"… unable to answer your call. Due to circumstances beyond our control, Venice

Marco Polo Airport has had to be evacuated. As a consequence, there will be no flights in or out of the airport until further notice. We apologise to our customers for what we hope will only be a temporary inconvenience." But that's ridiculous! The airport isn't on fire. It isn't under threat from the fire. It—'

Scott interrupted, 'If you ask me, the management decided they wouldn't be able to cope with what they expected to be a huge influx of frantic customers without tickets, so they shut down the airport! Anyway, I'll try the railway station.' He went through the same procedure and received much the same response: a message relaying the fact that Venezia Santa Lucia Station had been closed due to an unprecedented demand for tickets. 'There's one other place worth trying: the local Coast Guard.'

'Yes, good idea,' said Claudia. 'Being one of the larger stations, they'll have a utility aircraft for special rescue purposes.'

'Their number's here on the dashboard.' Scott tapped out the figures and waited. '*Ciao* ... do you speak English? Great. We're in a serious emergency situation here. Our boat has run out of fuel. We're on the Lagoon a short distance west of – just a minute, I'll check the map – Poveglia Island. Is there any chance you can help us? ... No? ... All your guys are involved in rescue operations ... and then they will have more rescues to attend to. That means we'll be out here alone all night. What happens if there's a storm or a tidal surge or something? ... Oh right, we'll have to cope with it as best we can. Thanks a lot, pal.' Scott switched off the satphone. 'Well, that's brilliant, isn't it? What are we going to do now? I certainly don't want to stay out here all night.'

'Nor do I,' Claudia said. 'Look, I'm reluctant to suggest it, but, given that no one else is able to help us, it seems to me the only person who *can* possibly assist us in this situation is Laurence.'

Scott nodded in agreement. 'I agree. I'm gonna give him a call now.' Once again he pressed the keys on the satphone. 'Hi Laurence, it's me, Scott. This'll have to be quick because I'm—'

'My god!' Laurence exclaimed. 'I called you at the Danieli and on your mobile, but I couldn't get any response. Are you okay?'

'Yeah. Fine.'

'And Claudia?'

'Yeah, she's fine, too. Look, I'm using a—'

'But what an absolute tragedy, Scott. Venice, *beautiful* Venice. What *have* we done to cause such a terrible disaster? But thank goodness both of you are safe. Were you anywhere near the fire?'

'Yeah, at one stage we were. Look, Laurence I'm using a satphone which has limited talk time. So I need to tell you quickly what our problem is …' Scott then recounted what had happened to them since their departure from the burning city. 'The thing is, Laurence, we're well and truly stymied. That's why I've called you, hoping you with all your good sense will think of some way we can get outta here.'

'Well, I'll certainly do my best to help you. Obviously what we need is somebody in the vicinity who has a boat. Then they can come out to you with some fuel. I have one or two friends who have boats in Venice, so I'll try them first. Do you have any bright lights on board?'

'Yeah, there are two spotlights on the cabin roof.'

'Are they on?'

'Yeah.'

'Then I suggest you turn them off to save battery power. You say you have a satphone. Well, I haven't a clue what that is. So, do I call you back in the usual way or …'

'No, it's quite complicated. It involves a two-stage dialling process. I'll explain.' Scott then gave him the details.

'Yes, I've got that,' said Laurence. 'Now don't you worry, I won't let you down. Just hang on and I'll organise something, I promise. Where exactly are you?'

'We're about one and a half kilometres west of an island on the Lagoon called Poveglia.'

'Okay. I'll get back to you as soon as I can. Bye for now.'

Claudia looked at Scott with a slightly anguished expression on her face. 'Poveglia you say? I thought I heard you say Poveglia a moment ago. Are you sure that's what the island is called?'

'Yes, that's what it says on the map.'

'Well, I don't know whether it's a bad sign or not, but Poveglia is believed to be the most haunted place on earth! It was once a quarantine station for people with infectious diseases and a mass burial ground for plague victims. Ghosts of the terminally ill who died on the island are believed to haunt the place.'

'Now you tell me!' exclaimed Scott. 'What a delightful boat journey this is turning out to be. We're parked off Death Island, we have no gas left, and over there, beyond Giudecca,' he pointed to where a large part of the sky was orange red in colour, 'Venice is burning down!'

* * *

All this while, the fire had continued its relentless path of devastation unchecked. Its next target was St Mark's Square, where, as if by intuition, the notorious mess-making pigeons had long since gone. Also, there was no sign anywhere of the mosquitoes that had harassed the city. They had escaped to the Lagoon islands where they found a new supply of humans to prey on. When the inferno surrounded the Piazza, the temperature at its core was reaching 1,000°C. It ignited everything in its path – except remarkably St Mark's Basilica, which, disfigured only by some charring and superficial damage, rose defiantly and indestructibly above the flames. Opposite the iconic cathedral was the Doge's Palace, where, despite the best efforts of staff to remove priceless works of art, most of the contents had been destroyed. This famous rose-coloured building had been so badly scorched and blackened that it was no longer recognisable. Next, the conflagration swept remorselessly through the St Mark's Square complex. The Campanile was burning internally. The old stairs had caught fire and flames from them licked at the recently installed lift shaft, which was buckling under the heat. People trapped inside the lift itself were slowly oven-baked, and others on the viewing platform at the top of the bell tower shrieked in fearful anticipation of their fate – some choosing to jump off the building and plummet to the ground below rather than be burnt. The buildings on the northern, western and southern sides of the square – including the Old Procuracies, Napoleon's Wing, the Correr Museum, the New Procuracies and the Old Library – were ablaze. The contents of the renowned shops and cafés in the arcades were reduced to ashes. Flames were racing through the offices above the arcades. The rooms beside and above the Clock Tower were blazing so fiercely that the face and mechanism of the famous timepiece melted. Below, flames swept through the archway along the narrow streets of the Mercerie, the main shopping area. From there the conflagration spread out across the southern and central areas of the San Marco district and consumed the houses and shops lining the *calli*. In the south, the blaze encountered the lower curve of the reverse S-shaped Grand Canal and, driven on by the sirocco, it burnt its way through the waterside palazzi – Ca' Dario, Ca' d'Oro, Ca' Rezzonico, Grassi, Mocenigo and Pisani Moretta, among them.

In the centre, in one of the older parts of the city, the flames attacked the Teatro la Fenice and the narrow streets surrounding it. It was part of the city in which there were mainly wooden buildings crowded together in a very small space. The Teatro, which had been burnt down in 1996 and painstakingly rebuilt in the original style, was again destroyed.

Then suddenly the wind dropped and the conflagration lost its driving force. Fireboats were operating successfully on the Grand Canal, where there was more water to draw on. Also the Canal, being from 30 to 90 metres wide, formed a natural firebreak. This stopped the relentless progress of the flames and they began to abate. In their wake, at least 60% of the eastern islet of Venice had been devastated. Celebrated examples of Byzantine, Gothic, Renaissance, Baroque and Neo-classical architecture were now blackened, smouldering, gutted ruins.

It was 23:45. The sky over the burning city was of the same colour as the sun at dusk. 'The wind has died down,' Scott observed. 'While we're waiting to hear from Laurence, let's try and get some sleep.' Scott and Claudia settled down in the launch as best they could and eventually fell asleep in one another's arms.

CHAPTER 10

Shortly before 03:30 the next morning, Scott's mobile buzzed. It was Laurence. 'Scott, I've been calling all and sundry and haven't earned myself popularity points by contacting various people in the middle of the night – because none of them were able to help. That is, no one except, believe it or not, Baldini. Very kindly, he's arranged for one of his associates to send his private jet to the small airport on the Lido – it's called the Nicelli airport. The pilot is expecting to land there at about 04:30.'

'That's great. But how are we going to get to the airport without any gas?'

'That's all dealt with. The same associate has arranged for one of his men to come out to you from Chioggia with some fuel. The chap left at just after 03:00. He's in one of those Riva speedboats, so it shouldn't take him long to reach you. He'll be with you in the next ten minutes or so – that's if he finds you. Don't forget to have your lights on, otherwise he might shoot straight past you. Once you've taken on fuel, you can make your way to the northern end of the Lido. You'll need to dock at the Santa Maria

Elisabetta boat station. From there the airport is about ten minutes' walk. Overall, how long do you think it will take you?'

'I reckon about 25 minutes from here to the boat station. With the walk to the airport, let's say just under three-quarters of an hour.'

'Well, I hope our friend with the speedboat isn't delayed. Let's see, it's just gone 03:35. So you need to set off in the next ten minutes. You'll have to get your skates on, too. Unfortunately, the pilot won't be able to hang around, because Baldini's associate requires his services first thing in the morning at Pisa Airport. That's where he's flying you both – and where Paolo will be waiting to drive you back to Florence.' While Laurence was speaking, a classic Riva Aquarama speedboat appeared in the light of the spots on the launch.

'Laurence,' Scott said, 'the guy with the gas is here. I'd better get on.'

'Right, see you soon. Good luck!' The line went dead.

'Dammit! I forgot to thank him.'

The Aquarama came alongside. A man in a white suit stepped over into the launch carrying two jerrycans. He put them down and shook hands with Scott. 'These are with Mr Baldini's compliments,' he said. He got back into the Aquarama and, without another word, sped off into the dark.

'He was in a hurry! Come to think of it, so are we.' Scott poured the fuel into the tank at the back of the boat. 'Let's hope this is enough to get us there. It says on the side of these jerrys that each contains 20 litres.

That should just about do the trick. Hey, you're very quiet, honey.'

Claudia was looking in the direction of the city. 'Look how much less red the sky is,' she observed. 'The flames must have died down. What we're seeing are the glowing ashes of the smouldering buildings reflected in the night sky.'

'Yeah,' said Scott, looking up. 'They've obviously gotten the fire under control. But what a disaster! How much of the city, I wonder, has been destroyed? It just doesn't bear thinking about.' Scott started the engine and they moved off. The journey to the boat station took 23 minutes and passed without incident, even though Scott was not used to piloting a boat at night.

In the small port, he drew up alongside the harbour wall, got out and secured the boat to a mooring ring. He jumped back in and asked Claudia for a pen and a piece of paper. Quickly he scribbled a message, which he left in the cubbyhole by the steering wheel:

TO WHOM IT MAY CONCERN

I borrowed this launch from the Danieli Hotel at 11:00 yesterday (23 August). I was expected to return it to the S. Zaccaria dock by 19:00. Unfortunately, due to circumstances beyond our control, I have had to leave it here at Lido Santa Maria Elisabetta. Apart from running out of fuel, the boat has operated faultlessly. If you wish to contact me, my mobile no. is 086545973.

[Sgd] Scott Lee

They reached Nicelli airport, which was deserted, at 04:18. Dawn was beginning to break. They sat outside the small arrivals and departures building, each deep in thought. Tired and saddened, Claudia found herself dwelling on the insignificance of man. Over the course of many centuries, he fashioned a city of unparalleled beauty, which, in the space of a few hours, had been laid to waste. It was as if Fate was ridiculing human achievement. And then what about man's relationship with Nature? Humans with their greed, their destructiveness, their selfishness, their thoughtlessness – they have to be kept in check. So from time to time Nature releases the awesome forces at her command – earthquake, volcanic eruption, hurricane, tsunami, flood, avalanche – to remind man who's boss.

Beside her, Scott was reflecting on what a goddamned day it had been. Only that morning he had been reviewing an author's proposal for an illustrated history of Venetian Art. One assumed there were now very few extant paintings or sculptures for him to describe. Quite possibly the author no longer existed, either. However, there was a positive side as far as his company's publications were concerned. Knowing the mentality of the book-buying public, Scott was confident that existing books on Venice would sell well, as mementoes: books such as those his firm published on Titian, Tintoretto, Veronese, Bellini and other masters of the Venetian School.

They were aroused from their thoughts by the sound of a plane coming in. They watched as a small jet landed on the runway and taxied to a standstill. When the side door opened and someone beckoned, Scott and Claudia ran across the tarmac and got on the plane. Shortly afterwards another passenger clambered aboard and made his way to the rear of the plane. It was Gennady Alexandrov. He was holding a large package. Scott and Claudia smiled and nodded at him as he struggled by, but he did not seem to recognise them. Having exchanged looks of surprise with Claudia, Scott unbuckled his seatbelt and went to speak to the man, who in the meantime had sat down. 'Mr Alexandrov? Hi! We met at Signor Baldini's. My name is Lee, Scott Lee.'

Cradling the package in his arms, Alexandrov replied, with a sniff, 'Oh yes, I remember,' and turned and looked out of the window. He was not interested in holding a conversation.

'My pleasure,' said Scott, adding under his breath, 'I don't think,' as he returned to his seat; whereupon Claudia looked at him inquiringly. 'Sure is strange that a guy who was happy to chat to us on Saturday now seems oddly reluctant to acknowledge us! It's as if he wishes we hadn't recognised him.'

The flight took 25 minutes. On disembarking at Pisa's Galileo Galilei Airport, Scott and Claudia noticed that Gennady Alexandrov did not follow them.

At the Airport's meeting point they were pleased to be greeted by the ever affable Paolo, who took their bags and led them to the car. They thanked him for coming at such an early hour. On the way to Florence they made some small talk initially, then they fell silent. Paolo looked in his rear-view mirror and found they had both dozed off.

It was just after 05:40 when Scott and Claudia walked through the front door of her apartment. She sat down at her desk, called her parents' number and left a message: 'Hi! It's Claudia. I've just this minute returned from Venice. It was a truly harrowing experience. But, with the help of friends and people we know, Scott and I managed to escape the fire without injury. Now I'm very tired and need to go to sleep. Hope to speak to you soon. *Ti amo*, c*iao*!' She also left a message for the Institute: 'Hello, this is Claudia. It's 05:43 on Thursday morning. Scott and I have just returned from Venice. You can't imagine what we've experienced. We realise we're lucky to be alive. Anyway, we're both exhausted and need some sleep. I trust you received the specimens I took from the canal pathways and you'll be letting me have your report a.s.a.p. I'm signing off now and going to bed. Please note I'm switching off the phone and will be incommunicado until about 13:00. *Addio*!'

Meanwhile, Scott called Laurence. 'Laurence, hi!' he said, trying to sound calm and unruffled. 'We're back safe and sound!'

'God, am I glad to hear it. So everything went to plan: the chap came out with the fuel, and you were able to make it to the airport on time. Thank goodness!'

'Thanks again for all your assistance. You and Baldini have been unbelievably kind and helpful. If it hadn't been for you two, we would still be stuck on the Lagoon wondering what to do! Mind you, I can't tell you how glad I am we hired a boat early on in the afternoon. When the fire started, you can imagine there was a run on all forms of water transport. If we hadn't had a boat, I doubt we would have got outta there alive!'

'My God, Scott! I've been watching TV and they're

broadcasting an endless stream of reports on what they call the Great Fire of Venice. Films from the air show that most of the eastern islet has been devastated. Nothing much remains intact, apart from the Cannaregio region, which the fire didn't reach. News of the catastrophe has shot round the world, and even people who have never heard of or been to Venice are in shock. Were you anywhere near where the fire started?'

'No. Claudia and I came out of Sant' Antonin just off the Fondamenta dei Furlani, turned the corner and were confronted by an inferno that was blazing as far as the eye could see and enveloping everything in its path. We of course got outta there as quickly as possible. About six hours later, when we were at a standstill out on the Lagoon, we couldn't see the fire. What we did see was a vast vermillion cloud in the sky above the city. From the length and size of the cloud, it appeared that the whole place was in flames. Anyway, we're back. We've survived. Neither of us has been burnt or hurt, thankfully. But understandably we're both pretty traumatised by what we've been through and just want to recover our composure by having a good night's – good day's – sleep.'

'Yes, of course, I understand. You have a good rest. Maybe we can get together tomorrow or the day after. Meanwhile, I'll buy a whole load of newspapers and read up on what will surely be seen as a ... a disaster of the utmost significance to the world. That so many important art treasures and buildings should be ruined – it's impossible to contemplate. It's a terrible tragedy. Whatever can mankind have done to deserve ... well, we'll talk about that another time.

Goodnight, old chap.'

'*Buona notte*. Talk to you soon.' Scott turned off his mobile and went into the bedroom. Claudia had gone out like a light. Scott followed suit as soon as his head hit the pillow. They were both exhausted, overcome by the stress and alarm of the previous twelve hours.

* * *

At 09:30 that morning, just as Baldini was enjoying breakfast by the swimming pool of his villa in Oltrarno near the Forte di Belvedere, he received a phone call that caused him nearly to choke on his cereal. 'Signor Baldini, I have bad news.' It was Francesca Maruichi. 'Gennady has disappeared – *with* the picture.'

'What do you mean, disappeared? *When* did he disappear?'

'At Gorizia. One minute I was talking to him, then our agent asked me something. When I turned round, Gennady had gone!'

'And he had the picture with him?'

'Yes. He was carrying it in a package under his arm.'

'The bastard. He'll be sorry when we catch up with him, believe you me. How about the two shipments? No problems with them, I hope.'

'None so far. The first consignment has been safely delivered to the warehouse in Reggio Calabri. The second consignment has passed through Sheki on its way to Azerbaijan and should be delivered tomorrow evening some time. At the moment, everything seems to be going smoothly. Our friends in border control are once again proving invaluable, and of course transit is facilitated where necessary by use of the diplomatic bag.'

'I'm glad to hear it. But I'm afraid that without the picture we're in deep shit. The whole sodding house of cards collapses. If we reveal that the picture is missing, presumed stolen, or if we say we don't have a buyer for it after all, Ouspensky and his friends are going to think we're time-wasters and complete idiots. Either way the deal falls through ... and all because of that bastard Gennady! I thought he was supposed to be a safe bet.'

'So did I – so did we all. But clearly he's working for somebody else and has taken the picture on their behalf.'

'Well, no one puts one over on me and gets away with it. I'll ask Mario to scan a photo of Gennady to all our agents, at home and abroad. Perhaps you can give him a hand, Francesca. I don't see why Malatesta shouldn't help as well. It's time he *earned* some of the money we pay him and, in any case, he's the one who's supposed to be in charge of the picture's safekeeping. I'll phone him and say that we expect him to involve the police and Interpol in locating Gennady, who I hope, for his own sake, still possesses the picture when we catch up with him.'

* * *

When Claudia woke at 13:30, Scott was still fast asleep, so she got up, had a quick shower and, dressed in a kimono with a towel round her wet hair, went to her desk, switched on the mobiles – his and hers – and started her laptop. She opened the Inbox and up popped a familiar-looking headline:

From: Ettore, Institute of Ecology, Rome

Subject: Mosquitoes

Can't tell U how glad I am U & Scott R back in 1 piece. Have been reading & watching, in absolute horror, n/paper & TV reports about destruction of beautiful Venice. 2 think it was my suggestion U went there & were placed in such danger. Mio Dio! If anything had happened 2 U, I'd never have been able 2 live with myself. Pls, dearest Claudia, forgive me 4 putting U thru such a nightmare. U R the great star of R firmament & yr loss for a few mosquito samples wd have been unbearable. But knowing U as I do, I'm sure U just want 2 get back 2 work asap & R anxious 2 have news of specimens U caught in Venice - specimens so nearly obtained at great cost 2 the Institute. When U've recovered, give me call.

She made the call straightaway. 'Hi, Ettore. Yes, I'm fine. I had eight hours' sleep, which I needed. I'm now keen to get on with things here in Florence. Hopefully, work will put the memory of what happened in Venice out of my mind.'

'I know I've already said this,' said Ettore, 'but I'm *so* glad you're back safe and sound. Of course, ideally, what I'd like is to see you here in Rome. We all miss you. Anyway, let me tell you about the specimen situation! The Venice adults and pupae that we've measured so far are, like the Florence samples, abnormally large. Incidentally, this time there's an increase in different species as well as in the number of specimens.'

'There's no doubt, then, that mosquitoes *are* getting bigger,' Claudia said, and then added portentously,

'The larger a mosquito is, the more blood it can suck out with one bite.'

'Yes, that's right. Not a very nice thought, is it? Among the specimens you caught in Venice, there were six species that were found to be vectors: African Malaria, Asian Tiger, Common Malaria, Floodwater, Pale Marsh and Yellow Fever. Between them, they were carrying Dengue, Encephalitis, West Nile, Zika and, obviously, Malaria and Yellow Fever.'

'Heavens!' exclaimed Claudia. 'I hadn't expected the situation to be so serious. The danger, surely, is that there could be widespread transmission of one or other or all of these diseases, and then we'd have a major emergency on our hands.'

'Exactly. And that's why I've advised the Minister of Health and the Mayor of Rome that strong measures for the elimination of mosquitoes should be taken without delay, under advice from entomologists, immunologists, malariologists and, of course, ecologists. Battle should once again be joined in earnest with man's age-old enemy, and a campaign of spraying from the air—'

'Spraying? I don't think that's the answer, Ettore. There's no point in trying to wipe them out in and around Rome if they're running wild in the rest of the country! They'll come back anyway.'

'No, I'm suggesting a *countrywide* spraying campaign from the air and on the ground – you know, like they carry out once a year in New York's Central Park. We've advised the Minister that the cost of such a campaign, which will have to be borne by the Government, could be in the region of 100,000 euros.

We've also stressed that, for environmental reasons, botanical-based insecticides should be used. I know this is important as far as you're con—'

'Not just important, it's essential. But the truth is, as you know, I'd rather not have any spraying at all.'

'Well, in that regard we have a problem, which you're not going to like. About an hour ago the Minister's Private Secretary called me to say that, although the Treasury had grudgingly agreed to provide adequate funds for the campaign, there's no chance of using a specific up-to-date insecticide. According to Ministry advisers, not enough stock of any one pesticide, botanical- or chemical-based, is available to spray a region with, let alone the whole country. Predictably the insecticide of which there is the most stock is Malathion, which—'

'—which was first used in the mid-1950s and subsequently found to have unfortunate side effects on those humans, especially the young and elderly, who are exposed to the stuff. More important, though, is the fact that mosquitoes have grown resistant to Malathion.'

'I agree Malathion is not as effective as it used to be. But, in the absence of a sufficient amount of one of the new pesticides, there is no alternative. Also, the economics of the project dictate that all the Malathion must be used up, in combination with whatever other pesticides can be obtained quickly and at acceptable prices.' Claudia could hear voices in the background. 'Sorry, Claudia, but I have to go. I hope you'll return to your post here as soon as possible. We need you to direct operations. *Ciao!*'

'*Ciao*, Ettore.'

Claudia was dazed and flabbergasted. Without reference to her, its acknowledged expert on the mosquito, the Institute had decided – indeed, had actually advised the Government – to reinstate hostilities against the insect. She was contemplating the implications of this when Scott came into the drawing room in his dressing gown. 'Oh darling, you're awake!' she said. 'I was just thinking it was time you got up. Did you sleep well?'

'No, not really,' Scott replied. 'I had too many thoughts buzzing around in my head.'

'Me too.' There was a pause for reflection. 'I don't know about you, but I'm not in the least bit hungry.'

'Nor am I.'

'Maybe we can go for a long walk – to clear our heads.' Claudia was in need of distraction. She wanted time to decide how she was going to react to what she considered a very unwise decision by the Institute. Torn between her aversion to chemical spraying and her desire to find a feasible, ecofriendly solution to the mosquito problem, she knew that, regardless of any pressure which might be exerted on her, she must not rush into a decision.

'Yeah, honey!' Scott replied. 'Why not? Let's just hang out. I'll go put some clothes on.'

'It'll be good for us to relax,' Claudia observed, 'after the trauma of the last 24 hours. Maybe we can revisit some of the sights here like the Pitti Palace and the Boboli Gardens. I haven't been to either for years.'

'Come to think of it, nor have I. What a great idea. A Florentine walkabout,' Scott said, as he headed for the bathroom.

* * *

At his villa, Baldini called Serge on his mobile. 'Serge, *come va*? ... Good, good. Look, I'm wondering what the position is with the second shipment ... Yes, I know it's a long haul to Iran ... Yes, I know it had to be loaded into a massive shielded transport container ... Yes, I know you had to obtain a Certificate of Approval for the transport of radioactive material. And it is of course good to hear everything's gone without a hitch. But what I need to know right now is *where* the shipment is. How far away from Natanz is it? ... Two days, you say? *Bene*. Well, let's leave it then that you'll call me when the shipment has been delivered ... Serge, there's something else I wanted to speak to you about. We have a big problem with the painting. We no longer have it, it's been stolen ... Yes, I know, the Bratva won't be amused. Fortunately, we have a pretty good idea who's responsible. He's a compatriot of yours called Gennady Alexandrov ... oh, you've heard of him, have you? Well, there's a possibility he may have been flown from Italy to Russia in a private jet belonging to his accomplice, Jacapo Malavasia. I'll email you pictures of both of them. What I'm hoping is that the Bratva can get someone to find out whether the two men have entered Russia. I'm sure they must have contacts in the Border Service or in the State Civil Aviation Authority, who can be persuaded to check yesterday's flight arrival records. I'll email you details of the type of aircraft they were in and its registration number … Alexandrov and Malavasia may be in Russia or they may not. Either way, let me know what you find out … Thank you, Serge. I'll wait to hear from you. *Caio*!

* * *

In his apartment, Laurence was sitting on the Savonnerie rug surrounded by newspapers with large dramatic headlines filling the front pages: '**IL MONDE PIANGE LA MORTE DI VENEZIA** [WORLD MOURNS DEATH OF VENICE]', '**GRANDE INCENDIO DI VENEZIA** [GREAT FIRE OF VENICE]', '**IL FUOCO DISTRUGGE ARTE VENEZIANA** [FIRE DESTROYS VENETIAN ART]', '**SOLO SAN MARCO SOPRAVVIVE** [ONLY ST MARK'S SURVIVES]', and so on. Inside one paper there was an article listing all the palazzi, churches, galleries and museums thought to have been destroyed. The article went on to declare that 'it is hoped in the next few days we will be able to quantify all the works of art – the paintings, sculptures, carvings, furniture, wall hangings, tapestries, rugs – that have been lost to mankind forever.' According to an article in another paper, '60% of the eastern islet has been ruined beyond repair – with no hope of rebuilding so many properties in architectural style.' It added, rather confusingly, 'Approximately 40% of the entire city has been destroyed.' Estimated casualty figures ranged from: '500-2,500 dead; 3,000-7,500 missing; 10,000-35,000 injured; and 10,000-40,000 homeless.'

Lawrence sat, not moving. Even when Paolo came in with some coffee, he continued to stare vacantly into the distance. *Why Venice?* was the thought uppermost in his mind. *So many artefacts, so much beauty ruined. What have we done to warrant such a catastrophe?* Tears formed in his eyes. *Works by artists of the Venetian School – Bellini, Titian, Tintoretto, Veronese – which had such an influence on the development of painting. Gone. Paintings by Tiepolo, Canaletto and Guardi, the groundbreaking Venetian artists of the eighteenth century. Gone. The architecture of Sansovino and Palladio, the sculptures of Vittoria. Damaged beyond repair.*

Laurence's mobile rang. 'Hello. Signor Baldini, how are you?'

'I am fine, Signor Spencer. I call you because I have a small problem. You know I said we expected to receive the painting next week. Well, that's now unlikely.'

'That's not a problem as far as we're concerned, Signor Baldini! There's no hurry to authenticate the picture. My client is quite happy to—'

'Signor Spencer, to speak the truth – the picture is ... *gone.* It has been stolen! It is possible we'll never get it back.'

'But ...' Laurence didn't know what to say. Already shaken by the situation in Venice, he was now shocked by Baldini's news.

'We think we know who is the thief. But we don't know where the thief is!'

* * *

As she waited for Scott to get ready for their walk together, Claudia reflected upon what was happening. She realised that, due to global warming, Europe had become a happy hunting ground for mosquito species mainly from the subtropics and Americas. But at the same time global warming was surely not responsible for the sudden increases in both sizes and numbers of mosquitoes. Yet what other reason was there? It appeared to be a natural progression. *Is Nature,* she thought, *reacting to deforestation, greenhouse gas emissions, pollution of the sea, ice melt and other man-made acts of destruction? And what about beautiful Venice, a city without equal, which was devastated in a single night? Was the fire man-made? If so, was it by chance a sirocco happened to be blowing when the fire started? Was it coincidental that the same fierce wind drove the flames forward in the most destructive direction? Is it possible that Nature is intent on making man suffer for his insensitive, uncaring misuse of the Earth?*

Scott came into the room and looked at her in her kimono. 'Honey, I think you need to put something else on!'

'Yes, sorry. I forgot all about getting changed. I've been thinking about things. I'll go and get dressed. I won't be long.'

Fifteen minutes later, as they were walking along Via di Mezzo, they passed a newsagent's with a large sign outside: '**DISTRUZIONE DI VENEZIA - ULTIME NOTIZIE** [Destruction of Venice: Latest News].' 'I'll get copies of the main papers,' Scott declared. 'We can go through them later.' When he came back carrying a plastic bag full of newspapers, he glanced at Claudia and said: 'You were staring into space when I got up this morning – or rather this afternoon. And when I came out of the bathroom, you were still staring into space! You obviously had something on your mind. Do you want to tell me about it?'

'No, not really. I had a long conversation with Ettore. We talked about the specimens I sent back from …' knowing that neither of them wanted to awake sad memories, she mouthed the word, 'Venice. And then we discussed what to do about the mosquito problem. Basically, that's it. Now, shall we get a move on? It's quite a walk to the Pitti. When we return to the flat, I'll need to do some serious thinking, so I—'

'I thought you were doing that earlier.'

'Yes, I was. But I still have some things to sort out and come to terms with. I just need time to myself. I suggest you take the opportunity to drop in on Laurence and tell him about our experiences.'

'Okay, honey, fair enough. I'll give him a call and find out if he's free to see me.'

* * *

Claudia sat at her desk. The stress of the previous day's experience and the conflict between her ideology and her job weighed heavily on her mind. The last thing she wanted to do was to reflect upon the distressing plight of Venice. Opening her laptop, she accessed the file entitled, 'My Thoughts on the Mosquito Problem.' The page was blank, apart from the heading. Looking out at the trees in Piazza d' Azeglio, she paused for inspiration. Then she began tapping on the keyboard. 'For me the position is clear. Control, not eradication, is the key. The consequences of man's 135-year war against mosquitoes are there for all to see. In almost every species in each generation, a few mosquitoes develop the ability to adapt to modifications in the outside world and so become immune to the new chemicals that humans choose to spray at them. These atypical mosquitoes carry genes that fit them, and their offspring, to adapt when changes are brought about, either by natural causes or by the intentional or unintentional interference of humans. This resistance is passed onto succeeding generations of mosquitoes, and more and more of them adapt and become immune. My theory is that each time mosquitoes fight off a human attempt to destroy them, they grow stronger and more resilient. They also increase in number and size, with the result that there is a rise in the number of dangerous diseases and viruses transmitted by them, including Malaria, Yellow Fever, West Nile Fever, Zika and Dengue. Mankind, in its headlong hurry to deal with this problem, chooses to overlook the fact that the mosquito fulfils an important role as one of the major pollinators of flowers. In attempting to obliterate the insect, man runs the risk of disordering an essential link in the chain of being. And as man should know by now, a heavy price is paid for interfering in the physical world and tampering with Nature.'

But, she thought, *won't people like Ettore and Giuseppe assume I'm on the side of the mosquitoes? Won't they suspect that, rather than trying to cull mosquitoes with chemical pesticides, I'd prefer that the insects went around spreading Malaria and Dengue and causing maximum disruption and discomfort for human beings? It'll look as if I want to safeguard mosquitoes at a time when they represent such a major danger to mankind. No one, though, will shake me from my belief that human beings must learn to live with mosquitoes, not try to wipe them out.* She continued typing: 'What is needed is an integrated pest management scheme, which regulates the mosquito population by biocontrol. This includes breeding mosquito fish, guppies and three-spined sticklebacks in ponds, sewage pools, chicken ranch ditches, etc. and dispersing soil bacterium (BTi) by hand or helicopter in order to interfere with mosquito larval digestive systems. However, these concepts are at the planning stage and will not be put into practice for several years.

'Behavioural controls are also at the development stage. I have a problem with them, anyway. I'm uncertain about their efficacy, as well as the ethics of their deployment. Take antisense therapy, for example. Its two principal aims are, in the short run, to interfere with the DNA or RNA of a mosquito so that any disease it is carrying is neutralised and, in the long run, to place inside the mosquito's germ cells genetic material that will make its offspring disease-resistant. There is also the proposal to sterilise male mosquitoes so that they are unable to impregnate females. These projects strike me as meddling with Nature in a way that is likely to have unforeseen and disastrous consequences. For instance, it's not beyond the bounds of possibility that something may go wrong and mutations are created – much larger, more dominant mosquitoes that suck increased amounts of blood from their hosts, inflict painful lacerations with the saw-teeth of their stylets, and inject so much histamine with their saliva that their victims in some cases suffer immediate heart failures.'

* * *

'I thought I'd never see you two again,' Laurence declared. 'It's a miracle you got out of there alive. So many people died, yet you survived, thank God.'

'Thanks to *you*, my friend,' said Scott, with

emotion. 'I know we weren't in immediate danger when I called you last night, but we both felt this desperate need to get out of the place as fast as possible. Believe me, it's a helluva painful experience to watch from the sidelines as so much unique beauty is destroyed. Naturally, Claudia felt we should stay in the city and help to save people.'

'If you'd done that,' Laurence said, 'you would almost certainly have been seriously injured or even killed. As you've probably seen in the newspapers, the latest figures are that at least 30,000 inhabitants have lost their homes, some 55,000 people – both inhabitants and visitors – have been injured, and the number of dead is estimated to be 2,500.'

'3,000 according to *Il Tempo*,' Scott said, 'and the death toll is expected to rise. The effects of the disaster will be felt for months, if not years.'

'There are already serious repercussions. Shares have crashed, business confidence has been shattered, and thousands of tourists have cancelled their bookings, principally because there's nowhere for them to stay. Worse still, the Government is so shaken by events that it appears to be on the point of resigning. The country is in crisis. But you're here and in one piece, that's the most important thing! I grieve for the loss of so much of Venice and so many important works of art – but at the same time I feel elated by the knowledge that you and Claudia are alive and well here in Florence.'

'The fact that we are is *entirely* due to you,' said Scott. 'I doubt I could've turned to a better guy for help. We counted on you – and you sure as hell didn't disappoint us. You came up trumps, with Baldini's help, and I guess we owe you a *big* "thank you".'

'No, I did what I could. Any friend would have done the same. Now, can we talk about something other than Venice, something that is nowhere near so depressing – but is nonetheless rather disappointing news?'

'Does it concern the missing Raphael, by any chance?' asked Scott.

'Yes, it does. You won't believe it, but this morning our friend Baldini dropped a bombshell. He rang to tell me the painting has gone. It's been stolen, he said, by one of his own men.'

'Gennady Alexandrov didn't have anything to do with it, did he?' said Scott.

'Yes, as a matter of fact, he did. How did you work that out?'

'Well, after we'd gotten on the airplane at Nicelli airport, another passenger came aboard – which, given that it was 4:20 in the morning and very few folk knew about the flight, was quite a surprise. Anyway, it was Gennady all right.'

'Are you sure?'

'Yeah, 100%. What struck me at the time was that he was holding – or rather clasping – a large rectangular package, about 75 by 55 centimetres in size. In view of what you say, I take it the Raphael portrait must have been inside.'

'So it would seem,' said Laurence. 'Quite how he thinks he's going to get away with it is another matter.'

'Certainly when Baldini tracks him down, he'll have some explaining to do!' said Scott.

'Scott, you said a moment ago that very few people knew about the flight from Nicelli. But according to my reckoning, there were eight people: Baldini, Baldini's associate, the pilot, Gennady, Paolo, you, Claudia and me. Now, unless Baldini is involved in some elaborate fraud and has had the painting stolen to get back at Ouspensky and his Russian friends, my guess is that the theft was organised by Ouspensky. I reckon he paid Gennady a great deal of money to double-cross Baldini. Of course, Baldini doesn't know yet that Gennady flew with you on the plane from Nicelli airport.'

'I'm not so sure,' said Scott. 'It *is* possible, as you've suggested, that this is a put-up job, which Baldini – maybe with the assistance of his associate, who knows? – has masterminded in order to swindle Ouspensky and his contacts out of the proceeds of sale of the painting. After all, he knows a number of people are interested in bidding for the Raphael, and he probably thinks, "Goddamn it, why shouldn't I have the money?" The only way to find out who's cheating whom is to tell Baldini that Gennady was on his associate's plane with a likely looking package in his arms. Either Baldini knows that already and nothing will happen, or he doesn't know and all hell will break loose! Maybe you could ring him tomorrow morning.'

'Yes, I will do,' said Laurence. 'But I bet you Baldini *doesn't* know. Look, if he and his associate are in cahoots, I hardly think Baldini would organise to fly Gennady, with a painting-sized package in his arms, out of Venice on the very same plane he arranged for you and Claudia to fly in, and then turn round a couple of hours later and calmly advise me that the Raphael portrait has been stolen!'

They went on to discuss the consequences – political, economic and cultural – of the Fire of Venice. Laurence was beside himself, as he catalogued the catastrophic loss of art treasures. Clearly he was deeply affected. It occurred to Scott, *This man loves art as other men love women* – but it was only a passing thought.

* * *

On Scott's return to the apartment in Piazza d' Azeglio, Claudia closed her laptop. Kicking off her heels, she swung round and held Scott's face in her hands. 'I feel really down,' she said. 'I need to be taken out of myself. Help me do that, darling. Make love to me … *please.*' They kissed intensely. Pulling clothes off each other, they hurried into the bedroom. Their lovemaking was fiercely passionate. Claudia's appetite was unappeasable. She wanted to hold him inside her forever and willed him to take her repeatedly. Seeking sensation without end, she had climaxes that were frightening in their intensity. It was as if she was trying to scorch the memory of recent events from her mind with the blazing fires of lust.

CHAPTER 11

Saturday 24 August

The next morning, Claudia woke at 09:35. Scott lay on his side, snoring faintly.

She looked at him approvingly, got out of bed and padded into the bathroom. Glancing in the mirror, she noticed the smudges of lipstick round her mouth, the scratch on her shoulder and the passion mark on the side of her neck and smiled. Their lovemaking had done the trick: her slide into depression had been halted. She felt ready to face up to things – Venice, the Institute, mosquitoes, the conflict between her ecological principles and her job. She had a shower, put on her robe, wrapped a towel around her wet hair and went to her desk in the sitting room. She switched on her laptop, found she had email and opened the Inbox.

From: Ettore, Institute of Ecology, Rome

Subject: Mosquitoes – URGENT

U <u>must</u> come back immediately. We need U here as matter of urgency. Hopefully U will have some notion of how 2 deal with situation that worsens by the day. In South, there R reports of mosquito plague of Biblical proportions. Here in Rome even starlings on Via Veneto have been terrorized into silence!

The Govt, which may not B in power 4 much longer, appears 2 B backing away from idea of mass spraying with Malathion. We have major crisis on R hands & frankly just do not know how 2 handle it. We need yr advice & ideas. Pls come back NOW! Yrs, in desperation!

Claudia was on the point of tapping out her answer when her mobile buzzed.

'Hello, Claudia, *mia bella*.'

'Hi, Papa, how *are* you? I missed you at Signor Baldini's lunch party.'

'Yes, I know. I'm sorry. I had no idea you were there – just as I had no idea you would be in Venice. Your mama and I are *so* glad you got back in one piece. We were worried sick. Are you sure you're okay? No bruises, no cuts, no burns?'

Claudia got up and closed the door to the room. 'I'm fine, Papa. Scott saw to it that I came to no harm. He was marvellous. So resourceful, so positive, so … dependable. It was entirely due to his quick-wittedness that we escaped the flames and weren't burnt alive. You should get to know him better, Papa. He means a lot to me.'

'Do you love him?' Roberto asked abruptly.

'No, Papa, I don't. We make love, of course, and he clearly adores me. But from my point of view that's as far as it goes. I'm very fond of him. He's great company. He's amusing. He's kind and considerate. I enjoy being with him, whether we're in bed or out on the town.'

'Well, I'll get to know him better, if that's what you want. Just to check, though: you're not planning to marry him, are you?'

'No, Papa. As I said, I don't love him.'

'I know someone who'll be happy to hear you're not going to marry him – your Mama. As you know, she has set her heart on your partner being a younger man, an Italian preferably. It's because, if you have *bambini*, which we all hope will be the case, she believes the father should be the same age as you and not someone who's old enough to be the children's grandfather. You wouldn't marry without Mama's approval now would you, darling? It would break her heart if you did.'

'No, of course not,' Claudia said resignedly and then, as an afterthought and with just a touch of anger, 'I just won't get married!'

'*Mia bella*, don't say such things! Mama and I want very much for you to get married – to someone who will make you a good husband. Let me meet Scott again, see how we get on and maybe I can persuade Mama to change her view. But don't forget, darling, it's not easy for her now she is confined to bed. You have to make allowances for that.'

'I do, Papa, I do. I love Mama so much, and I would never wish to be a bother to her. She has a heavy enough burden to bear already.'

'I know you're busy, but maybe you could give her a call some time and have a chat with her. She'd love to hear from you.'

'Yes I will, Papa.' A conscience-ridden Claudia realised she had not thought of her bedridden mother for a week or more.

'Now, as far as Scott is concerned, I'm wondering whether he knows Laurence Spencer.'

'Yes, he does, Papa. Laurence is one of Scott's oldest friends. Why do you ask?'

'Well, it's too involved to go into over the phone. Let's just say that I have something important to discuss, and I wonder whether you and Scott can have lunch with me today?'

'I'm sure we're free, so yes, we'll be delighted to. Where would you like us to meet?'

'Trattoria di Salvestro – it's off Piazza Santa Maria Novella in Via Palazzuola. Shall we say at 13:00? Oh, by the way, I'd rather like my associate Giorgio Belori to join us. Would you mind?'

'No, not at all. I heard he was with you at Signor Baldini's last Saturday. I haven't met him before, have I?'

'No, *mia bella*. He's someone I know quite well. He's in the art business, like me. A nice fellow, I'm sure you'll take to him. In fact, I was due to meet him half an hour ago, so I must go. See you at 13:00. *Ciao*!'

'*Ciao*, Papa!' Claudia switched off her mobile and went into the kitchen. She boiled some water and made a cup of tea, which she took into the bedroom to give to Scott. 'Morning, darling,' she said, giving him a kiss. 'How are you feeling?' She took the towel off her head and shook out her hair.

'I feel good,' Scott said, 'albeit a bit exhausted.'

'Exhausted?' said Claudia, sitting on the side of the bed. 'I don't know about that. There's plenty of life in the old man yet, and I bet I can prove it. Let's see what the position is down here.' Claudia slipped her hand under the duvet.

At that point the landline phone rang. Reluctantly, Scott picked up the handset. 'Hi, Scott Lee speaking.'

'Ah, Signor Lee, *buongiorno*.' Claudia pulled back the duvet and leant towards his naked groin. 'It's Gennaro Lombardi.' Scott pulled gently on Claudia's hair to attract her attention. She looked up. He shook his head and put his forefinger to his lips. 'Sorry to disturb your peace, but it's urgent I meet with you. I don't normally work on Saturday, neither do you I suppose, but is it possible you might be able to come here to the Uffizi today?'

'Gee – er – Signor Lombardo, I *was* rather hoping to spend some time relaxing this weekend with my partner. You see, we were in Venice on Thursday and fortunately managed to escape without injury.'

'Oh, Signor Lee, I did not know. Of course you are resting. I'm sorry for disturbing you. Maybe next week we can have a meeting, if you are wishing it.'

Scott thought, *This is a changed man.* 'Hold on, Signor Lombardo, I'll just have a word with my partner.' He cupped his hand over the mouthpiece. 'Honey, Lombardo sounds kinda different. He says it's urgent he meets with me. Is it okay if I go and see him sometime today?'

'Well, I haven't had a chance to tell you yet, but Roberto has asked us to go to lunch with him and Giorgio Belori at 13:00 at the Trattoria in Via

Palazzuolo. So I suggest you see Lombardo this morning, but only for a short while.'

'Right. Hi, Signor Lombardo? If it's of any use, I can see you for half an hour at 11:30 this morning.'

'Thank you, Signor Lee, you are very kind. I am seeing you then. *Ciao*!' Scott replaced the handset. 'Honey, why has Roberto asked us for lunch, I wonder?'

'He says he has something important to discuss with us. It has to do with Laurence.'

'I find all this kinda weird. Lombardo wants to see me, and Roberto has something important to tell us. What *is* going on?'

'Well, we'll soon find out, won't we? Right now, I suggest you have a shower – and,' she added with a wicked smile, 'I'll help you wash!'

* * *

Baldini received two phone calls that morning. The first was from Laurence. 'Signor Baldini, *buongiorno*. I was wondering whether you've had any success in tracking down Gennady and the portrait.'

'*Buongiorno*, Signor Spencer. We are making progress. Why do you ask?'

'You know when your associate arranged for his personal pilot to fly Scott Lee and Claudia Mattioli from Lido di Jesolo to Pisa?'

'*Sì.*'

'Incidentally, what is your associate's name?'

'Jacopo Malavasia.'

'Well, Scott and Claudia were not alone on the plane. There was another passenger carrying a large package. It was—'

'Gennady, of course! *Bastardo ladro*!' cried Baldini. 'Now I see what is happening. Without one word, Malavasia flies from Pisa yesterday in his plane. His passenger is Gennady, who has the painting with him. It's very clear now. *Grazie*, Signor Spencer. I had my suspicions about Jacopo. Now I know what he is. He's a no-good thieving bastard. Worse than that, he's a traitor to the 'Ndrangeta. Signor Spencer, I thank you for this.'

'Tell me,' Laurence asked, 'was Signor Malavasia one of the associates who contributed towards the advance payment of $750,000 that was made to Ouspensky's contacts?'

'No, Signor Spencer, he was not.'

'Good. What will you do now?'

'We are telling our agents everywhere to be on the lookout for Malavasia as well as Alexandrov. We *will* locate them, I assure you. At Aeroporto Marco Polo, it's possible they have a record of the – er – *piano di volo*—'

'The flight plan—'

'—*si*, the flight plan of Malavasia's jet, although I think it's unlikely. It's more probable that Malavasia is taking off in his jet *senza permesso*. If you ask me, he and Alexandrov are in USA.'

As long as they're not in South America, thought Laurence, *trying to sell the ruddy painting to my client!*

'Anyway, Signor Spencer, you'll be the first person

to know when the painting is back here again. I am owing you. If there's anything I can do for you, let me know. Now I must go and do some business. *Ciao!*'

Baldini's other phone call was from Ouspensky, who rang to say that he would like to see him to discuss finalisation of their business transactions, particularly regarding payment arrangements. They agreed to meet at 15:00 that afternoon at the Hotel Belcari.

* * *

At the start of their meeting, Lombardo surprised Scott by asking him whether he was still interested in copublishing the proposed series on the great painters of the Uffizi. 'I thought we covered that question extensively at our last meeting, Signor Lombardo. Anyway, the answer is yeah, I'm interested, so long as we can proceed on the terms I proposed on Monday – and with which I understood you were quite categorically unable to agree.'

'Signor Lee, I think it's possible we agree your terms – if you are making me a small service.'

'What small service?'

Lombardo opened the top right-hand drawer of his desk and took out a small digital voice recorder. 'Please excuse me, but I wish to record this conversation, because what I am saying to you is of the utmost confidence and not for repeating to any other persons.' Lombardo pressed the 'Record' button. 'You promise now not to tell other people what I am saying to you?'

'Yeah, I promise.' *Even though,* thought Scott, *the position you put me in is kinda like the dentist suggesting I need a filling before he looks at my teeth!* 'I'm fascinated to know what it is you have to tell me.'

'What I am telling you is concerning Signor Spencer and the painting assumed to be by Raffaello Santi, the *Portrait of a Young Man*. I know Signor Spencer has a great knowledge of Cinquecento art. If he declares this painting to be genuine, it will be offered for sale in a blind auction. In such event it is understood Signor Spencer will be one of those making a bid on behalf of a client. To prepare for this, I am needing a small service from you.' Lombardo's face was becoming more weaselly by the minute. 'In return, I will be most happy to accept your terms for the publication of a series of books on the Uffizi.'

'And what is it you want me to do?' asked Scott, suspiciously.

'To be blunt, Signor Lee, I am hoping you are finding out from Signor Spencer how much he is bidding and then you are telling me.'

'Am I right in thinking, Signor Lombardo, that you yourself are intending to make a bid for this painting? Alternately, could it be that you're acting on someone else's behalf? If so, whose? I'd like to know.'

'I am acting for someone, *sì*, but I'm sorry, it is secret. I am not telling you the person's name.'

'It makes no difference, anyway. I would not be prepared, under any circumstances, to divulge information given to me in confidence by a friend – or anyone else, come to that. It's my opinion that Signor Spencer, on whose critical assessment of the portrait every interested party is relying, deserves at the very least, if the portrait is genuine, to enter a sealed bid like anyone else who wants to buy it. I certainly wouldn't dream of asking him what that bid might be.'

'It's a pity you are saying this, Signor Lee! Now for sure we have no deal, but I am reminding you of this.' He pointed at the voice recorder. 'What you said is here on the memory. You promised not to tell—'

'You needn't fret yourself. Unlike the majority of business people these days, I believe in keeping my word.'

'I am glad to hear this, Signor Lee. So we are finished, and I am thanking you for coming here, and I am saying *addio*.' They shook hands.

'Goodbye,' Scott said, with a tone of finality.

Lombardo switched off the voice recorder, and Scott left the room.

As it was only 11:55 and he felt stressed and annoyed, he decided to pay what he hoped would be a short, calming visit to the Gallery. He went upstairs to the First Corridor and through to Rooms 10-14 to see the Botticelli exhibit. He was studying *The Birth of Venus* when he felt a tap on his forearm. 'Yes, what is it?' he asked irritably. He turned to find Francesca Maruichi standing beside him and his manner changed immediately. 'Ah, Ms Maruichi, what an unexpected pleasure.'

'Well Mr Lee, we have twice seen each other across a room but have never been introduced,' she said, in perfect English. 'So when I saw you standing here, I thought it was time to say "hello".' Until then she had seemed a rather shadowy figure, who was always in the background of events, so he was surprised to discover close up how attractive she was. She had deep-set dark brown eyes, high cheekbones, pale skin and long raven hair, which she wore in a sleek ponytail. He guessed she must be in her mid-thirties. She had on a red top, a black above-the-knee skirt and high heels. As tall as Scott, she stood, hand on hip, with her weight on one leg and the other leg set apart: it was a provocative stance. Francesca smiled at him, a wide-mouthed, enchanting smile that lit up her face. 'Do you like what you see?' she asked.

'Oh, gee, I … I'm sorry,' Scott stuttered. 'I … I was just thinking how striking you … how strange it is that we … we did not get to speak to one another at Signor Baldini's lunch party last Saturday.'

'Now we can make up for lost opportunity.' She turned and considered Botticelli's masterpiece. 'In my eyes,' Francesca said, 'she would be the dual personification of chastity and sensuality, were it not for her abnormally long neck and awkward, almost malformed left arm,' which seemed as forthright a comment on the painting as Scott had heard.

'You evidently enjoy looking at paintings?'

'It is one of the main passions in my life.'

'Do you have a favourite painter?'

'No, not really. My taste is catholic and embraces all art from cave painting to Damien Hirst. How about you?'

'Basically, I decide what I like on *impulse*, not from any deep knowledge of art. I like to leave the business of critical assessment to experts like my pal Laurence Spencer. I think you met him at Signor Baldini's.'

At this Francesca suddenly took his arm, leant towards him and whispered in his ear, 'Would you like to know something of advantage to your friend?'

'In what connection?' Scott asked, in a low voice.

'His business.'

Scott took a step back and said in his normal voice, 'Isn't it possible for you to relay this information to him direct?'

'No. You will understand why when you know what it is I have to tell you.'

Although bemused by this enigmatic answer, Scott replied, somewhat stiffly, 'If you can't tell him directly, then anything you have to say which is of benefit to my friend is of interest to me *as a go-between only*. You do understand?'

'Yes, I understand. As the information I have is supported by photographs and is of a highly confidential nature, I will have to make arrangements for us to meet somewhere where we will not be recognised – that is most important – and can come and go without causing comment. If you will telephone me tomorrow at the number on this card between 10:45 and 11:00, I will let you know where we can meet. If you do not telephone me, I will assume you are not interested in my information. It has been a pleasure to meet you. I hope to see you again tomorrow. Now I must say goodbye.' She took his hand and kissed him on both cheeks. Then she looked him straight in the eyes and smiled her captivating smile. She turned and walked out of the room.

Scott glanced at his watch and saw that the time was 12:55. He rushed downstairs, passing Francesca with a wave of his hand, out of the Uffizi into the heat of the day and careered down Lungarno degli Acciaiuoli and Lungarno Corsini, along Via dei Fossi, to his destination, Trattoria di Salvestro in Via Palazzuolo. Inside, he was shown to the table, at which Claudia, her father and Belori were already seated. A waiter was telling them that they would not have to pay for the entire three-litre bottle of Tuscan white wine, which he had placed in the middle of the table. They would be charged pro rata for the amount of wine they actually drank. He went on to say that there was no set menu. Instead, he would bring them the day's choice of *crostini*, *antipasti*, *pasta*, *carne*, *formaggi* and *dolci* – all *tipico della Toscana*.

After the waiter had moved away to another table, Scott stooped to kiss Claudia and then he shook hands with Roberto. Roberto indicated the other man and said, 'I don't think you've met Giorgio Belori, have you?' Scott and Belori shook hands. 'Giorgio is an art dealer like me. In fact, we have an unofficial partnership, don't we Giorgio?' Scott sat down at the table.

'Yes, I am grateful to your father,' Giorgio said, ignoring Scott and speaking directly to Claudia. 'He convinced me to pack in my boring clerical job in the Civil Service and join him in the art business.'

'We're sorry we missed you both at Signor Baldini's,' said Roberto. 'Unfortunately, we had to go and see someone about a painting. If we had stayed, I think I might have been surprised to find you there – bearing in mind Baldini's background. Do you know him well?'

'No,' Claudia replied. 'We were taken to the

Castello by Laurence Spencer, but neither he nor we normally associate with the Mafia.'

'I don't quite understand, *mia bella*. None of you normally associate with the Mafia, you say, and yet there you were at a special lunch party laid on by the local Mafia boss. Surely, your friend must have considerable influence to be invited?'

Thinking on his feet, Scott said, 'Heck no, not at all. He knows Baldini because he's selling a painting that Laurence is interested in acquiring for a client. Baldini invited Laurence to the party to discuss the terms of sale, and Laurence asked if we would like to go along as well.'

'This is Laurence Spencer you're talking about?

'Yeah.'

'Well, I've heard of him, of course. He's a leading authority on Cinquecento paintings. His is one of the names that is always cropping up in the art world. I don't actually know him, so I'd certainly be interested to meet him, if it could be arranged.'

'The problem is, Papa,' said Claudia, 'Laurence is quite busy at the moment. He's involved in some important business negotiations. I think it probably makes sense to put off any meeting with him for the time being. What do you think, darling?'

'I agree,' said Scott, wondering why Claudia seemed not to want her father to meet Laurence. 'He works most of the day in his capacity as an art expert. Right now, he's having discussions with Baldini, among others. I'm staying with Laurence and I know by the end of the day he's usually worn out. I doubt he's going to be too keen to see anyone socially at night-time – even you, Roberto.'

'Well, of course, I wouldn't want to tire Signor Spencer. Nonetheless, it's a shame. Apart from meeting him socially, I would have taken the opportunity to ask his advice about a sixteenth-century painting I'm interested in buying. Perhaps you'd mention it to him. If a meeting could be arranged at his home or anywhere else he chooses, I wouldn't take up much of his time, I can assure you, and I'd certainly be most grateful.'

'Okay, I'll see what I can do,' said Scott, looking at Claudia who pulled a face. Inwardly, he wondered why Roberto was so keen to meet Laurence. It was a question he pondered over, while the four of them enjoyed a seemingly endless succession of courses and discussed the political situation, the destruction of Venice, immigration and the pros and cons of conducting a national spraying campaign against mosquitoes.

* * *

A few minutes before 15:00, in a conference room at the Hotel Belcari, Borgo Pinti, Ouspensky asked a waiter to bring him a bottle of Dom Perignon 1996 and some glasses. Shortly afterwards, Baldini was ushered into the room. He was accompanied by Giovanni, who was carrying an attaché case, and Mario. 'Signor Ouspensky,' said Baldini, with his flashing smile, 'I am so glad we're having this meeting. I have various important things to tell you, including the good news that the first consignment has reached our warehouse in Reggio Calabria and been checked and passed for payment. Therefore, I owe you some money. Giovanni!' Giovanni opened the attaché case and held out a bundle of 1,000-dollar bills. 'I think you'll find it's all there: $500,000 as agreed.'

Ouspensky took the bundle and flicked through it to see if the bills were genuine. 'Well, that seems to be all right. I'll take your word for it that it's all there.' He put the bundle in his pocket. 'Of course, a somewhat larger payment is due, as and when the second consignment is delivered. Any idea when that will be?"

'According to my assistant, Francesca, the second consignment has reached Azerbaijan. If all goes well, it should be delivered to Natanz by tomorrow evening.' There was a knock at the door. Giovanni went to the door and, after a brief exchange, let in the waiter who was carrying a bottle of champagne in a chrome bucket on a silver tray. No one spoke again until the waiter had opened and poured out the champagne, handed everyone a glassful and left the room.

'What about the painting?' asked Ouspensky. 'What's happening on that front?'

'Oh, everything's going according to plan. We expect to receive sealed bids from at least four interested parties.'

'I take it, then, that the painting's been authenticated by Signor Spencer.'

'Er, no, not yet. Signor Spencer has been too busy to examine the painting.'

'I find that surprising, I really do. From the little I know of the man, I'd have thought, once he'd realised we had a painting that was worth looking at, he'd have been champing at the bit to see the damned thing. I mean, frankly, Signor Baldini, my contacts aren't going to be too happy about the situation.'

'Well, we're doing our best, believe me. Don't forget we're not auctioneers, we're businessmen. We're not used to handling this art crap!'

'Nor are my contacts! They just want to be shot of the painting and get their money for it, a lot of money. I wonder, has there been any indication of the sort of bids that are likely to be offered?'

'No – and even if there had been, I couldn't possibly tell you. It wouldn't be ethical.' Baldini flashed his smile again. 'What sort of money are your contacts hoping for?'

'About $75,000,000.'

'Hell, that *is* a *lot* of money!'

'They reckon anyone buying the painting at that sort of price will be getting a bargain.'

'Well, I know nothing about this painting business, but all I can say is that, if such a shit picture of some sixteenth-century faggot – and I certainly wouldn't have it hanging anywhere in my house, even in the lavatory – can command that sort of money, then maybe I ought to give up arms dealing and take art lessons!'

Baldini and Ouspensky drank champagne and talked for about an hour and then went their separate ways, each with a different outlook on the meeting: Baldini to his villa, thinking that he had handled the question of the missing painting rather well; Ouspensky to his apartment near the Duomo, believing that Baldini was up to something.

* * *

As the lunch at Trattoria di Salvestro lasted for two and a half hours and afterwards Scott and Claudio went shopping on Via Panzani, they didn't get back to her apartment until 17:20.

On opening her laptop, Claudia found the following email message in the Inbox:

From: Ettore, Institute of Ecology, Rome

Subject: Your return here

I'm surprised & hurt U do not answer my emails. As I've tried 2 make clear, we need U here urgently 2 direct mosquito eradication programme. This is 3rd time I'm asking U: <u>pls come back 2 Rome</u>. Let me know immediately when U plan 2 return. I hope it's 2morrow. U will then be able 2 come in early on Mon a.m. 2 deal with what is now very difficult situation.

'Scott!' Claudia shouted. Scott came in from the bedroom, where he had been watching television. 'Scott, look at this latest email from Ettore.' Scott studied the screen briefly.

'Well, he has a point, you know. I mean, from what I can gather, he's been asking you to go back, and you haven't bothered to answer him!'

'That's right, I haven't,' she exploded, 'and I'll tell you why. I'm going to pack this job in. I'm going to resign from the Institute. I've thought long and hard about it, and there's no way I'll participate in their eradication programme. It's environmentally irresponsible, and I'll have no part in it.'

'But ... but ... honey!' Scott was appalled. 'The goddamned skeeters *have* to be destroyed – otherwise they'll infect *everybody* with their killer diseases. What do you mean, environmentally irresponsible? What's more important than mankind? Mankind has to survive. It's the goddamned skeeters that must die!'

Claudia turned on him. 'Mankind doesn't deserve to survive,' she screamed, beside herself, 'after wreaking so much destruction on the Earth. What we've done in such a short period of time to pollute the land, water and air and degrade the forests, freshwater systems and oceans – it's *appalling*! It's *disgusting*! It's *unforgivable*!'

Scott was surprised by her sudden fury, which he had not encountered before. 'Oh, okay, then. If you feel so strongly, honey, go back to the Institute and kick some arse! Make the jerks see your side of the argument. Don't just jack everything in, for Chrissake, and let all the good work you've done go to waste. *Please*, honey, reconsider. You know all there is to know about these goddamned insects. Nobody else in this beautiful but increasingly disorganised country has a clue! Besides, what the hell will you do with yourself?'

'I'll go and work with Roberto, I suppose. But that's irrelevant! The point is,' she said, in a steely voice, 'if I go back to the Institute, they'll want me to make concessions. Well, I'm *not* prepared to compromise my beliefs.' She sat down at the laptop again.

Scott raised his voice. 'Well, I think you're freakin' crazy! I mean, whaddya think you're trying to do? Play

God or something? For Chrissake, getta grip! There are folk out there who are being attacked and infected and need your help. For fuck's sake do something about it! Don't just abandon them!' There was a brief silence, while he calmed down. He realised that shouting at Claudia would only strengthen her resolve and make her more dismissive of him. 'If I didn't know you better, honey,' he joked, 'I'd begin to suspect that you're on the side of the skeeters. It's almost as if you'd rather they went around spreading *dreadful* diseases—'

'That's absolute *rubbish*,' Claudia cried. 'Now you're just being stupid. You *don't* know how I feel about mos—'

'I don't know how you feel about *me*, never mind the blessed insects,' he said, sarcastically.

'You're becoming more and more fatuous! You haven't a clue what you're talking about.'

'Oh yeah? Well, what I know for sure is that these treacherous mozzies cause maximum disruption and discomfort to human beings, and they should fucking well be zapped with pesticides and, if not eradicated, then at least …' he paused momentarily as he searched for the right word, '… culled.' He couldn't believe that Claudia wanted to safeguard mosquitoes at a time when they represented such a danger to humans and to living creatures generally. 'Mosquitoes or mankind? Which is it to be? Which do you care about most?'

'That's a *silly* question, and you know it,' she said. 'Human beings must learn to live with mosquitoes, not try to wipe them out. Anyway, I've had enough of this inane conversation. I need to write a letter to the Institute. I also want to make some notes. So … can you leave me in peace to deal with these matters? Go back and watch your wretched football or whatever it is.' She turned her attention to her laptop.

'Okay, ruin your career – as if I care,' Scott said, leaving the room. *What the hell! She's obviously made up her mind,* he thought, as he went back into the bedroom, slammed the door behind him and strode about angrily. *If she wants to jack in her job, that's her lookout – but she's got no goddamned right to treat me like a piece of shit. It's true, I don't know much about skeeters, but I'm entitled to an opinion as much as the next guy. Yet, when I say anything that she doesn't agree with, she dismisses me out of hand. She's too fucking clever, that's the trouble. What's worse is she knows she only has to snap her fingers and guys will fall over themselves to take my place. It's just a game to her. She doesn't have any true feeling for me. How can she, if she treats me as she does? No, all she wants me for is my goddamned dick!* He sat down and stared blankly at the TV screen.

* * *

That evening coordinated protest marches took place in Milan, Rome and Turin, and also in Florence, where some 500 people – mainly students – assembled in Piazza della Repubblica. The placards they carried were daubed with assorted anti-authoritarian and pro-environmentalist messages – the most conspicuous being **'GOVERNO FUORI!** (Government Out!)', **'RICONGIUNGERSI ALL' UE** (Rejoin the EU)' and **'FINE CORRUZIONE** (End Corruption)'. Others included ecologically minded exhortations such as **'LASCIA LA NATURE DA SOLA** (Leave Nature Alone)' and, on two boards combined, **'SALVA LA**

TERRA (Save the Earth)' and '**PRIMA CHE SIA TROPPO TARDI** (Before It's Too Late)'. There were also placards in support of equal rights for women, including '**NON MALTRATTARE LE DONNE** (Don't Abuse Women)' and, again on two boards, '**CASTRARE GLI UOMINI** (Castrate Men)' and '**CHE ABUSANO DELLE DONNE** (Who Abuse Women)'.

The march began peacefully enough. As they moved along, some of the young men sang the Italian National Anthem. Others waved their placards, shouting, 'Down with the Government' and 'Imprison the Tax Evaders'. Among their number was a large noisy group of gesticulating, foul-mouthed hoodies who were exhorting protesters to 'get their act together' and 'beat up the fucking pigs'. When the protesters turned south into the Via dei Calzaiuoli, they found themselves confronted by several lines of armour-clad policemen. The hoodies shouted abuse and, with the stolen pickaxes and shovels that some of them had brought with them, started to hack out large cobblestones from the street, which were then hurled at the police. Many of these missiles hit their targets. They also shattered the windows of some of the prestigious shops in the street, with the result that opportunists began looting the well-known products on display. In response, General Malatesta, who was the officer in charge, gave the order for his men to fire tear gas canisters at the protesters and then baton-charge them. The hoodies met this attack with a barrage of smoke bombs and firecrackers, and those who had pickaxes and shovels whirled them round their heads and brought them smashing down on their opponents' blue helmets and black shields.

Frightened non-violent protesters, together with innocent bystanders, ran through the side streets to the Piazza della Signoria. There they were faced with more lines of riot police, who, straightaway, rushed at them and with their batons thwacked their heads, shoulders, backs, midriffs, legs and any other part of their bodies that was accessible.

Law and order was quickly re-established in what Malatesta described as 'an appropriate manner'. Rioters and genuine protesters alike were individually bludgeoned into submission. Hoodies came in for special attention. Some of them were pinioned against the wall of the Palazzo Vecchio and viciously jabbed in the groin with baton ends, as the police involved shouted, '*Siamo fottutamente maiali, siamo noi*? (We're fucking pigs, are we?)' Others who had been the ringleaders of the riot were dealt with in a particularly harsh manner, being repeatedly beaten, punched and kicked and then thrown semiconscious into police vans.

When this uneven conflict ended and the hoodies had been taken to Police Headquarters, the Piazza della Signoria and the Via Calzaiuoli were littered with bleeding, crumpled people, whose only aim had been to protest peacefully. Their spirits broken, their cries of dissent silenced, these unfortunates had one resolution in common: not to take part in any more protest marches. Apart from the sound of their groans and muted whimpers, an eerie stillness descended on the historic centre of Florence.

Then suddenly, seemingly from nowhere, a cloud of mosquitoes pounced, not just on the injured people on the ground, but also on the passers-by and curious onlookers, the ambulance men and women who were trying to help and comfort the distressed, and the remaining riot police who were still making arrests. The speed of the attack was alarming. In the space of a few minutes, insects in their tens of thousands latched onto people, who were already traumatised by the protest march. There was much flailing of arms and cries of *'Vattene da me!* [Get away from me!]'

When they had sucked their fill of blood, the mosquitoes vanished just as quickly as they had arrived.

* * *

Meanwhile, unaware of what was happening in the city's historic centre, Claudia typed out her letter of resignation from the Institute, which she concluded by pointing out that as there were more than four weeks' holiday due to her, she would not be returning to the office to work out her notice. Having read through what she had written, Claudia printed the letter, folded it and inserted it into a self-seal envelope. She also attached a copy of the letter to an email which said quite simply: 'Ettore – herewith copy of letter sent to you in the post today – Claudia.' She clicked on 'Send' and the crucial communication was received shortly afterwards in Rome.

Scott was cool towards Claudia after her outburst, despite a half-hearted attempt on her part to mollify him. At about 21:50, when she had finished working on her report, she went into the bedroom. 'Come on, grumpy,' she said, holding out her hands, 'don't be such a wet blanket. Let's go to bed – and I'll see what I can do to bring a smile back to your face.'

'No,' he said, knowing full well what he was denying himself. 'I'm gonna bunk down on the sofa bed.' He got up and walked from the room, saying as he went through the doorway, 'It's just that I'm kinda pissed off with you at the moment.'

'Okay, suit yourself. You know where the sheets are,' said Claudia, closing the door after him.

CHAPTER 12

On Sunday, unusually, Claudia was late rising, and Scott was up before her because he had found the sofa bed uncomfortable. He took Claudia a cup of tea at 10:30, gave her a perfunctory peck on the cheek and asked, 'Do you remember Francesca Maruichi, the dark-haired woman at Baldini's lunch?'

Claudia mumbled sleepily, 'Yes, I think so. She's quite attractive, isn't she?'

'Oh, I … I don't know about that! The point is she wants to meet with me today to give me some important information relating to Laurence's business. I've arranged to call her between 10:45 and 11:00 to find out where we're supposed to be meeting.'

'Why doesn't she just give the information to Laurence?'

'She said I'll understand why not when I hear what the information is.'

'Oh, come off it, Scott! She's having you on!' Suddenly wide awake, Claudia sat up in bed. 'I reckon she has an ulterior motive. Information, indeed! Honestly, Scott, sometimes you can be so naïve.'

191

'She says we gonna have to meet somewhere where neither of us can be recognised. She has photographs to show me, apparently. Don't forget, she works for Baldini. She runs a considerable risk, if she tells me anything that is confidential to the 'Ndrangheta and is found out.'

'But what if she's persuaded you to meet her under false pretences? What if she has no photographs and nothing of importance to tell you? As you say, she works for Baldini: she could be trying to trap you. Remember what happened on the way back from Poggibonsi. The Mafia are ruthless. They could be planning to incriminate you in some way, in order to discredit Laurence – who knows? I urge you not to see this woman. Cancel the meeting. Tell her the truth. Tell her we've had a row and you want to stay here to sort things out.'

'Heck, I'm sorry, but I think you're overreacting. The way I see it is that, regardless of the potential danger to herself, Francesca wants Laurence to know something that could be to his advantage. I believe it may have something to do with the painting but is too sensitive to relay to him directly.'

'*Why* does she want him to know?'

'I'm not sure. Maybe she has some grudge against Baldini. Or maybe she took a fancy to Laurence when she chatted to him at Castello di Montezano.'

'Or maybe she's has the hots for you, more likely. Scott, tell me in all honesty, if you had received such a bizarre invitation from any person other than this attractive, dark-haired woman, would you really be thinking of accepting? I mean, what if one of Baldini's henchmen had sidled up to you and whispered in your ear, "I have some information that may be useful to your friend!" You'd have thought he was propositioning you, wouldn't you?'

Scott, however, was adamant that he was acting purely in Laurence's best interests. He saw himself as a go-between, nothing more. Claudia said she thought he was making a big mistake and turned away to drink her tea.

He went into the sitting room and rang the number on the card Francesca had given him.

'*Pronto!*'

'Francesca?'

'*Si.*'

'Hi! It's Scott Lee here.'

'Scott? Oh good! I'm so glad you phoned. I've found a suitable place for us to meet – the Hotel Afami in Via Guido Cavalcanti. If it's convenient for you, can you meet me there at about 15:00 this afternoon?'

'Yeah, sure. Via Guido Cavalcanti is in Le Cure, isn't it?'

'Yes, that's right. You'll need to take a taxi. Until 15:00 then. Oh, by the way, the room is booked in the name of Astuzia: that's a-s-t-u-z-i-a. *Ciao!*'

* * *

Having had a further argument with Claudia about his attending the meeting, Scott arrived at the three-star Hotel Afami at 15:10. He was shown to a room on the second floor, where he was welcomed at the door by a kiss on both cheeks from a vibrant Francesca. With her waist-length dark hair cascading around her shoulders and down her back, she was dressed in black high heels and a midnight-blue silk sheath that was split up one side to the thigh.

She ushered him into a small, compactly arranged, air-conditioned room. Soundproof tiles lined the walls and ceiling. Heavy drapes were drawn over the windows, which, considering it was the middle of the afternoon, Scott thought was odd. Illumination was provided by a small spotlight that shone directly on the queen-size double bed and two low-voltage sidelights, one beside the bed and the other on a table between two armchairs in front of the windows. The only other piece of furniture in the room was a small chest of drawers that stood beside the door.

Francesca sat down in one of the armchairs and crossed her long legs which showed through the opening in her skirt. 'Come and sit down,' she said.

Scott sat in the other armchair. Trying hard to focus, he said, 'Okay, I'm longing to hear what it is you have to tell me that will be of use to my friend Laurence.'

'I have two pieces of information for you – one of indirect interest to Signor Spencer, the other of great assistance to him businesswise. Both concern the missing portrait.'

'I thought that might be what this meeting is about.'

'First, I know who the two men are who stole the painting and where they are based. I know they have the painting with them. As I told you yesterday, I can corroborate this with photographs. Secondly, I know

– and this is what should be of direct commercial benefit to Signor Spencer – how one of the interested parties can be dissuaded from entering a bid for the painting. Again, I have the evidence to support this claim.'

'So, please, tell me what you know.'

'Oh no!' said Francesca. 'Not just like that, I'm afraid. There is a price for this information.'

'Oh, I see,' said Scott. 'I thought all this was too good to be true. What *is* the price?'

The tone of her reply was matter-of-fact. 'I am prepared to give you the information on two conditions. One, it is agreed that I am owed 25,000 euros. You will sign an IOU to that effect. Two, you and I ...' she paused as she fixed on him with her bewitching dark eyes, 'make love ... here and now. To ensure your cooperation as a willing partner, I shall give you snippets of information after each sexual act we engage in, until such time as you know all there is to know.'

Momentarily, Scott wondered how many acts she had in mind and whether, as with his all-night experiences with Claudia, he had sufficient stamina not to disappoint. Otherwise he was dumbfounded by her proposal. His mind was in a whirl. *I certainly fancy her,* he thought, *and I'd love to make out with her. How's the saying go? Don't look a gift-horse in the mouth? Yeah, but what if Claudia – beautiful, insatiate, clever, strong-minded Claudia – were to find out? That would spell disaster for our relationship. Then again, she won't find out – so long as Francesca and I remain mum about our meeting. Conversely, there are also Laurence's interests to consider. I want to be of use to him. And who knows? What Francesca has to divulge may possibly help him to realise his dream of establishing an Art Foundation. On the negative side, there's the money issue. I'm not so well-heeled that I can afford to dish out 25 grand for information which is of no direct benefit to me. And it's not as if I need to have sex with a woman I know hardly anything about, even if she is attractive and sexy. After all, I have the lovely amorous Claudia to go to bed with!*

Sensing his indecision, Francesca stood up and reached behind her back to undo the fastening of her dress. The tight-fitting sheath slid caressingly down her body to form a circle of dark-blue silk round her ankles, which she stepped out of wearing only her high heels and black silk panties and bra. She looked at him with those wide dark eyes and said, 'Well, do we have a deal?'

In a state of confusion, Scott rose from the chair. 'I'm afraid I can't do this. I have obligations to other people. If they—'

'When you say other people, I take it you're including your lovely partner. If so, she'll never know from *me* the things we get up to. What I'm offering you is a secret one-off, which will be pleasurable for you and of benefit to your friend.'

'No, no. I can't risk deceiving any of my friends. I can't cheat on Claudia. The temptation … the weakness of the flesh … I would if I could, but I can't. Jeez, I've gotta get out of here.' Having hurried to the door, Scott stopped in his tracks and turned. 'I … I don't want to forgo the undoubted pleasure of … Look, I'll go for a wander and think about what's involved. I'll come back later and let you know what I decide – whether to take you up on your offer or go back to Claudia.' And with that he left.

Francesca, having laid her dress on the bed with the comment, 'I'm pretty sure I'll be needing this later,' went into the bathroom.

Scott took the ten-minute walk to Ventaglio Park by way of Viale Alessandro Volta and the long avenue of Via Giovanni Aldini. In the park, with its views of Florence and unusual hedgehog maze, he found the peace to organise his thoughts. He fancied Francesca. She was a highly desirable woman, who he was sure would be mind-blowing to make out with. But one can't always have what one wants, and he knew he shouldn't be considering Francesca's proposal at all.

Then there was Laurence. If he found out what happened in the Hotel Afami and under what circumstances Francesca's information had been obtained, how would he react? Laurence trusted him. So did his other friends, his authors and his suppliers. He had established himself as a man of his word. How could he successfully hide from these people the fact that he had deceived Claudia, someone else who trusted him, and fucked another woman, who he hardly knew, ostensibly to obtain some unspecified information, but basically to satisfy his lust and sexual curiosity.

There was only one decision for him to make. Under *no* circumstances was he going to get involved with Francesca. He was *not* going to let anyone down, least of all Claudia and Laurence.

He returned to the Hotel Afami, fully prepared to reject Francesca's offer. When she opened the door, he found she was dressed in the dark-blue sheath dress as before. 'Welcome back,' she said, ushering him in. 'Come in and sit down,' she pointed at one of the chairs, 'and tell me what—'

'No, I'm not staying,' Scott said determinedly. 'I'm not interested in taking you up on your offer. I'm going back to my partner's flat.'

'Oh, what a pity,' Francesca said. 'I'd been so looking forward to … are you sure?' She moved towards him, with her mouth slightly open.

'Yes. I don't want to. I … I …' Francesca once again released the fastening on her dress, so that it slid down her body. The difference this time was that she was naked.

'Are you sure?' she repeated. She paraded before him, flaunting herself. 'You're excited at the prospect, I can see.' She reached out and fondled the bulge inside his trousers. 'The plans I have for you this afternoon are not to be missed. You'll experience an erotic sequence of increasing excitement and release.' Kneeling in front of him, she murmured, 'First, I think we should do something about—'

'No, please don't,' cried Scott. 'You mustn't. I … I …' He thought of Claudia once more. Then his resistance crumbled. The temptation was too much for him. Aroused beyond control and no longer having any thought to the consequences he said breathlessly, 'Yeah … yeah … do it to me. Give me head!'

Disappointingly, Francesca got up and walked over to the chest of drawers. 'You've forgotten. The sexual experiences you're going to enjoy this afternoon don't come free.' She opened a drawer and took out a pen and a piece of paper, which she brought back and handed to Scott. Typed on the paper were the following words:

For services rendered, I owe Signorina Francesca Maruichi of Via Santa Monaca, San Frediano, Firenze, the sum of 25,000 euros, this sum to be payable on demand.

Sgd _____ dtd 24 August

Jeez! Let's hope nobody else gets to see this, thought Scott as, with a shaking hand, he signed the IOU. Having put the pen and paper back in the drawer, Francesca took out a folder from which she extracted a photograph. She handed it to Scott.

On the right-hand side of the photograph there was a painting of a long-haired youth in a bonnet and fur-lined cloak, which Scott recognised as being the same as the one in the tatty photograph that Ouspensky had showed Laurence at the meeting in the Badia. On the left-hand side, there was a folded copy of a newspaper entitled *El Mercurio*, on which the date, *jueves el 22 de agosto*, was clearly visible. 'That's the missing portrait, isn't it?' Scott asked.

'Yes,' said Francesca, as she retrieved the photograph and put it back into the folder. Returning to Scott, she loosened his tie, unbuttoned his shirt and stroked his chest.

'You're not ... say ... saying much,' he murmured, nervously.

'There's not a lot to say,' Francesca answered. 'In a situation like this, action speaks louder than words.' She unbuckled his belt and pulled down his zipper.

Kneeling before him again, Francesca tugged his trousers down around his ankles. 'Oh dear, you seem to be less enthusiastic than you were a few moments ago! We can't have that now, can we?'

'The thing is I ... I'm not sure ... I ...' Scott's guilty conscience had resurfaced.

'You're not sure? Well, let me see what I can do to stiffen your resolve,' she said, taking him in her mouth.

Some ten minutes later, as Francesca went over to the chest of drawers again, a dazzled Scott, in the afterglow of orgasm, thought, *Jeez! That was fantastic! Such an intense sensation, it almost hurt. It felt like she was drawing my insides out through my dick.* Francesca came back and passed him another photograph. It was of Alexandrov and a short, dark-haired, moustached man in a silk suit walking from the large porch of an ultra-modern Holiday Inn. 'I recognise Alexandrov, but I don't know who that guy is,' said Scott, pointing at the short man.

'That's the man in whose plane you flew from Venice to Pisa. His name is Jacopo Malavasia. Do you happen to know where they are in this photograph?'

'They appear to be at a Holiday Inn, presumably in Spain or South America. I say that because in the first photograph there was a Spanish newspaper alongside the Raphael, and you said the painting is where Alexandrov and Malavasia are – but I've no idea, really.'

'Well, you'll know the answer in a short while, because that'll be your next snippet – *if* you give me as much pleasure with your mouth as I've just given you with mine,' Francesca said, and, having taken the photograph and put it back in the folder, she went to the bed, removed the counterpane and, sitting on the edge, lay back with her legs slightly apart. Having stepped out of his trousers and pants, removed his shoes and socks and thrown off his shirt, Scott knelt in front of her and with his tongue slowly and rhythmically worked her up to a prolonged, moaning, convulsive climax. When she had recovered, Francesca swung her legs up onto the bed and lay back on the pillows. 'That ... that was quite something,' she said. 'You certainly have the knack, unlike most of the men I've known!' Scott lay on the bed beside her and stroked her hair. 'Anyway,' she said softly, 'to get back to Messrs Alexandrov and Malavasia: they *are* staying at a Holiday Inn, as you observed. It's situated in Chile, at a place called Temuco, which is about 650 kilometres south of Santiago.'

'If you don't mind me asking, Francesca, how do you know?'

'I overheard Signor Baldini talking about it.'

'And the photographs: how did you get hold of them?'

'They're copies I made on Signor Baldini's colour printer.'

'That must have been kinda risky.'

'Not particularly. He, Giovanni and Mario were out on a job at the time, and I had been left in charge of the office.'

'Presumably, Signor Baldini has taken steps to get the painting back.'

'Yes, he has. Signor Spencer will be pleased to hear

the news – no?'

'He will indeed. He'll be delighted to hear that he now has a painting to examine and authenticate. Any idea what will happen to Alexandrov and Malavasia?'

'No. And if I knew, it would be as much as my life's worth to tell you.'

'Yeah, I can see that. We don't want you ending up dead by the roadside, do we?'

'Definitely not, darling ...' Scott winced at the word. 'You don't mind me calling you darling, do you?'

'No, no, of course not,' he lied. It was after all the term of endearment Claudia always used.

Francesca leant forward and kissed him on the mouth. 'It's time,' she said in a low provocative voice, 'for you to ... fuck me.'

She again lay back on the bed. 'Darling, I need you – *now*!' she cried. Their lovemaking was strenuous and sustained. Twice she was gripped by shuddering climaxes, before Scott made one final, deep-reaching thrust into her, and they joined in an ecstatic simultaneous orgasm. Post coitus, Francesca, resting with her head in the crook of Scott's arm, whispered, 'That was some fuck, darling!' Scott himself was reflecting upon the fact that he had just enjoyed one of the more satisfying sexual experiences of his life. For a while they lay there, quietly basking in the afterglow of extreme excitement and its resolution. Then, emerging as from a trance, she said, 'Before we try to go one better, if that's possible, and in case you've forgotten why you're here, I must give you your next snippet.' Stroking Scott's arm, she continued, 'You remember I spoke of someone who can be persuaded not to bid for the painting. Well, the person in question is Signor Pennington.'

'What, you mean Signor Hyram G. Pennington the Third?'

'Yes, he of the ridiculous name.'

'But *how* can he be persuaded?'

'Well, for the moment, let's just say there's some incriminating evidence against him, which, if revealed, would certainly cause him considerable professional and personal embarrassment.'

'What is the evidence? Can I see it?'

'I think you're jumping the gun a little, darling. I haven't finished with you yet. There are a couple of other activities I'd like us to take part in before you leave here. When we next have a pause, I'll tell you what the evidence is. Then, when we've completed the course, so to speak, and if I'm not too sore and still able to walk,' she smiled, 'I'll give you the evidence.'

'Not too sore? I don't understand. Whaddya mean?'

'You'll find out – that's if you're still game for what I have in mind.'

'Also, you said you'd tell me about the evidence. What evidence?'

'It's evidence that's been captured on film – very useful evidence. And I suggest a copy of it is sent to HG anonymously, together with a note advising him that, if he doesn't immediately withdraw as a bidder for the painting, further copies of the film will be sent to his clients, his wife and the newspapers. But first, we have further pleasure to indulge in with a variation I hope you'll enjoy as much as I do. Let me tell you what I have in mind.' She leant towards him and whispered in his ear.

Scott could hardly believe what he was hearing. 'But I've ... I've never done that before and ... I'm afraid it ... it just *doesn't* appeal.'

'You'll love it, believe me. It's something no man should miss out on.'

'No, no, Francesca, anything else – but *not* that!'

'Okay. We'll leave it, then,' she said unsympathetically, getting off the bed and collecting her dress from the floor. 'I thought I was dealing with a real man, not a wimp with weak-minded susceptibilities.' Her tone was hard-edged. 'I'm going to take a shower now, and when I come back, I don't expect to find you still here.'

'Just wait ... wait a moment,' Scott spluttered. 'Heck, I'm sorry. I really am. You took me by surprise.' He got up and went over and embraced her. 'It's been really awesome so far. I'm sure, as you say, it's an experience worth having, especially with you. After all, there's a first time for everything.' They kissed ardently, and Scott became aroused again. Francesca reached for a jar of lubricant, which was on the bedside table. 'I'll put some of this on. It'll make things easier.' When he was sufficiently slippery, she got down on all fours on the carpet and said urgently, 'Take me ... take me *now*!' As Scott knelt behind her, he noticed there were yellowed bruises on her bottom and the backs of her legs.

'What are these marks?' he asked.

'I'll tell you later. Do it please, darling: take me.'

Although what followed was initially off-putting to Scott, he gradually established a rhythm which, increasing his stimulation and sensual pleasure, took control of his body. Involuntary reflexes followed one another at a quicker and a more forceful rate, until quite suddenly he attained the acme of pleasure. His orgasm was so intense he collapsed on top of Francesca, pressing her to the floor. They lay like that, breathing heavily, for several minutes. On recovering, they uncoupled and Scott sat in one of the armchairs and Francesca lay on the bed.

'Wow!' Scott exclaimed. 'That was awesome! But Jeez, I'm really whacked out!'

'You better not be *whacked out*!' She smiled. 'Such an apt phrase, given what we're going do as a finale – that's if you still want the film.'

'Ah yeah, the film. Tell me, what *is* this incriminating evidence that you have against Pennington?'

'Well, let me fill you in a bit on the background. Until quite recently, he and I had what for want of a better word was a relationship – but I broke it off. I couldn't stand the obnoxious bastard any longer!'

'What, dear old Hyram G the Third?'

'Yes, Hyram G. It would be more appropriate to call him hideous Hyram the brute, believe you me. He paid me to have sex with him. Unfortunately money is my weakness, and I found it impossible to refuse the substantial amounts of cash he was offering me. Anyway, the sex was quite normal to begin with – you know, nothing overtly kinky. But it was not long before he introduced me to his bestial side. I found he was into anal sex in a big way. He didn't just want to do it occasionally. He *always* wanted to do it. That's why I now enjoy being buggered by someone I fancy. He also liked hitting me, with whatever came to hand – hairbrush, belt, riding crop, nylon rope, you name it. Latterly, he used to thrash me with a cane. He got hold of a supply of thin bamboos, so that if he hit me too hard and the cane broke, which was frequently the case, he always had a replacement available. The problem is, after a while, I found I *liked* being hit. That's why I had to pack him in. I realised I didn't need the money that badly – not at the cost of turning myself into a complete masochist. I can't tell you how much I despise him, anyway. He's the most disgusting, vile man I've ever had the misfortune to meet – and what's worse he smells absolutely foul!'

'So that's what those marks are. Jeez, Francesca, how goddamned awful for you! I mean, what can I say? For someone so attractive to end up with a freakin' sadist like that: it doesn't bear thinking about! I tell you, I'd like to give the slimeball a taste of his own medicine.'

'Well, in a manner of speaking, you will be doing just that, if you send him this film.'

'Why? What's on the film?'

'Two hours of him viciously beating and buggering me on three separate occasions.'

'God, what a despicable pervert! Obviously how HG carries on is going to be of great interest to Signor Baldini, isn't it? But as far as Laurence is concerned: I suspect he's too sensitive, too unworldly a soul to view such depraved carryings-on. So what is it that I have to do to obtain this film?'

Francesca got up and went into the bathroom. A few moments later, she re-emerged carrying a handful of thin bamboo canes, each about a metre in length. 'Beat me,' she said.

* * *

A kilometre away in the Stadio Communale 'Artemio Franchi', where Fiorentina had just gone one-nil up against Bari in the first game of the new football season, the team's fanatical supporters were beside themselves with exultation. They were cheering, hooting and letting off firecrackers. Their hero, the striker Giovanni Mastroberardino, had scored the goal, and members of the Fiorentina side were jumping on top of him, in time-honoured fashion. The celebrations, both on and off the pitch, were protracted and, despite repeatedly blowing his whistle, the referee was unable to restore order for quite some time. When the game did get under way again, relative silence gripped the spectators as the ball was passed around from one player to another. On such a hot, bright afternoon, it was therefore surprising when a large shadow began to spread across the ground. There was also a noise, a spine-chilling high-pitched whine like a dentist's drill. It grew in intensity. Some of the players, who were not immediately involved in the game, looked upwards and pointed. Others stopped kicking or intercepting the ball and stared in disbelief at the sky. One or two broke into a run and headed for the players' tunnel. Spectators on the western side and at the southern end of the stadium took one look at the approaching ominous cloud and rushed from their seats. The people on the other side and at the northern end could see nothing, because the cause of the distraction lay in the east and therefore behind the covered stands in which they were sitting.

Soon, there was consternation everywhere, as a vast, darkening, amorphous mass descended out of the sky into the stadium. Millions of voracious mosquitoes suddenly enveloped the 40,000 spectators. Chaos ensued. People panicked, pushing and shoving each other in their efforts to flee from the whirlwind of insects. It was as if a fire had started in one of the stands, such was the rush for the exits. The ensuing stampede claimed many victims, mainly children and old people, who fell and were trampled underfoot. The turnstiles and other exits were so choked up that the emergency services were unable to get in to attend to the injured and dying. To add to the turmoil, fights broke out between gangs of rival supporters. All the while, a dense whirlwind of mosquitoes harried and terrorised the unfortunate would-be runaways.

The terrifying aerial bombardment was not confined to the stadium. Further afield, in Piazza della Repubblica, clients of Caffè Gilli and passers-by, who were being entertained by a juggling unicyclist, suddenly found themselves at the mercy of the mosquitoes, as did people window-shopping or sightseeing in nearby streets. In Piazza della Signoria, the heart of the city, no one was invulnerable, neither visitor nor resident. There were tourists who were intent on taking selfies or sitting down on the steps of the Loggia to eat baguettes filled with mozzarella and tomato. There were those who walked round and round the copy of Michelangelo's *David* or went in and out of the Palazzo Vecchio. There were others who surveyed the city from the top of the Palace Tower or stood and stared at the beautiful Fountain of Neptune. There were the cake-eaters and the coffee-drinkers outside Rivoire's, who were watching the world go by; the scattered groups of youths, who talked and argued about football, hairstyles, girls, the best make of scooter; the cabbies who sat in their carriages and waited for fares; the horses who chewed on the feed in their nosebags. All were suddenly set upon by multitudes of vicious-biting Alaskans, Gallinippers, Spears, Tigers and other highly aggressive species. Anyone in striking distance of the river became a target for wave after wave of marauding swarms.

* * *

Meanwhile, inside the soundproofed room in the Hotel Afami, Francesca's bottom and the backs of her thighs were a mass of vivid red weals. Three canes and thirty-six strokes later, Scott was still beating her, though no longer so forcefully. As he plied the cane with his right hand, he slowly masturbated with his left hand, while Francesca, with her hands rubbing spasmodically in between her legs, had attained a state of almost continuous ecstasy. Upon hitting her for the fortieth time, Scott, whose left hand was now a blur, dropped the cane. Reaching over Francesca's bent form, he pulled her back by her hair and twisted her round, so that she was confronting his groin. He moaned and ejaculated over her face and hair. Then he pushed her roughly to the floor. No longer himself, he bellowed, 'Gimme that fucking film, you slut, or I'll thrash you all over again on your front side!' Francesca wiped some of the mess from her face and rose shakily to her feet. As she went to the chest of drawers, it was noticeable that several of the weals on her bottom were bleeding. She produced a USB Flash Drive from the drawer and handed it to Scott.

'I suggest,' she said in a low expressionless voice, 'you look at this, while I go and clean up. There's a small laptop in the cupboard of my bedside table. It doesn't have a password. HG's address is shown at the beginning.' She walked unsteadily into the bathroom and locked the door. Scott took out the laptop and went and sat at the table, where he connected the Flash Drive. The film opened with the words 'Pennington's Address' in large type with a four-line address printed below in smaller type. The scene that followed revealed a stark naked Francesca bent almost double over a triangular wooden frame, to which a partially clothed Pennington was busily tying her by her wrists and ankles. Having secured her to his satisfaction, he reached for a cane, which he bent a couple of times, as if to test its strength and durability. 'All righty, you filthy tramp!' he said, shifting his erection in his pants. 'I'll teach yer to be so goddamned sassy. You're gonna get it big time!' Taking the bamboo, which he held in an interlocked double-handed grip, as far back behind his head as possible, he paused for a moment before whipping the flexible stem down onto her pale exposed buttocks with a swish and a crack that sounded like a rifle shot in a wood. Scott clicked 'Fast Forward' and the same image, of Pennington thrashing Francesca's striped upturned bottom, seemed to speed endlessly across the screen. Then suddenly the picture changed, and Scott clicked 'Play'. Francesca was on all fours on a bed, and behind her a nude, flabby, sweating Pennington was pulling her head back by the hair while brutishly sodomising her with violent jerks of his body. Scott felt sick. For he himself to have buggered and beaten Francesca as he had put him on a par with the nauseating HG. He could not have sunk lower. Why, oh why had he accepted Francesca's invitation to have sex? The film and the information she had doled out to him would be useful, there was no denying that; but had it been worth obtaining at the cost of betraying Claudia and shaming himself? He closed the laptop and removed the Flash Drive. He quickly put his clothes on and pocketed the device. He left without saying a word and went downstairs.

Waiting outside the Hotel for the taxi he had asked the porter to order for him, Scott looked at his watch and was horrified to find the time was 18:50. *Ah Jeez!* he thought. *What am I gonna say to Claudia? Tell her, maybe, that I met someone on the way back from Francesca. Who, though? How about Filippo Casti? She doesn't know him and is unlikely ever to encounter him. I'll have to stop on the way somewhere and have a few drinks. If she smells alcohol on my breath, she may believe me.*

The porter came running out to tell him there had been some sort of panic in the city centre, and Radio Taxis were so busy that it would be at least three-quarters of an hour before anyone could collect him.

'That's okay,' said Scott, handing the man a ten euro note. 'I'll walk. It'll do me good!' He made his way along the Viale Alessandro Volta, where he stopped at a bar to have a couple of bourbons on the rocks. He then turned into Via Antonio Pacinotti, crossed the bridge over the railway line and stopped for another couple of bourbons in Piazza Georgio Vasari. On leaving this second bar, he walked into a cluster of mosquitoes that was hovering in the small square at head height. He felt feathery touches on his face and neck and, flicking agitatedly at the insects with his hands, he broke into a run. It was twenty metres or more before he shook off their unwanted attentions and, at walking pace, he continued on down the Via degli Artisti, past the Cimitero della Misericordia, into Borgo Pinti, where he turned left into Via della Colonna and so arrived in Piazza d' Azeglio.

When he entered Claudia's apartment, he found her working at her laptop. Having finished writing a report about the previous night's incident, she was studying the brief notes she had taken from the TV news about the attack at the Stadium. 'I've been bitten,' Scott remarked in a matter-of-fact manner.

'What, by the female of the species?' asked Claudia, acidly. She looked at her watch. 'And if you don't me mind asking, what on earth have you been doing all this time?'

'Er, on the way back from my meeting, I – erm – bumped into Filippo Casti and we went and had a few drinks.'

'And who's he?'

'Oh, he's Trace-Art's agent in Florence. I was introduced to him at Laurence's. He was the guy who took us to the Badia to meet with Baldini.'

'And how was your rendezvous with the lovely, long-haired Francesca?'

'Just fine. The information I've gotten from her will,

I'm sure, prove invaluable to Baldini and Laurence.'

'And what *is* the information?'

'It concerns the Raphael portrait, as I told you I thought it might. She knows how one of the people who plans to put in a bid for the painting can be persuaded not to do so. Francesca has given me the means,' he said, tapping the Flash Drive in his jacket pocket, 'to achieve that end.'

'So you were with her only a short while, and then you spent the rest of the time drinking with this Filippo Crasti, Casti or whatever his name is?'

'Yes, that's right. But why the third degree?'

'Well, just look at yourself in the mirror, Scott! You're a mess. Your hair's all ruffled, your clothes are rumpled, and you look washed out!'

'Well, heck, it *is* quite a long walk, over a mile, from La Cure.'

Claudia got up and went over to him. 'You know, I've really missed you,' she said sweetly and, taking his face in her hands, she kissed him on the mouth. 'Pooh! You smell like a distillery! I hope you haven't had *so* much to drink,' she said, placing her hand on his groin, 'that you're unable to have sex.' She dropped to her knees and started to undo his belt. Scott grabbed at her hands.

'No, no, honey. After I've had a bath and something to eat, maybe I'll feel in the mood. But not right now.' Claudia rose and stepped back.

'You weren't drinking with Casti, were you? You had those drinks to provide yourself with an excuse for being so long with Francesca. You've been all afternoon with her, haven't you?' she asked, her dark eyes flashing. 'I could taste her when I kissed you, and I can smell her perfume on your clothes. There's only one way to establish how much you've been enjoying her company. Go on, take down your trousers and pants: I want to examine the main evidence!'

'No!' Scott shouted. 'I'm *not* going to take anything off – and I *haven't* been screwing her, if that's what you're implying!'

'How many times, Scott, how many times did you fuck her? It's no good denying it. You look as guilty as hell, you *bastard*!'

'Chrissake, honey, you're … you're being neurotic. I—'

'Pack up your things,' she said quietly, 'and leave.'

'Oh, now you're just being goddamned crass!' he yelled. 'I haven't *done* anything. Can't you understand that? I don't deserve to be treated like this, and you fucking well know it!'

'Go! Just *go*!'

'I'm *not* going to go, so shut the fuck up!' Scott was beside himself with anger. 'You're always trying to be clever at my expense. I'm sick of it! What you need is to be taught a fucking lesson, you spiteful bitch. And I'm going to teach you it right now. What you need,' he yelled, starting to unbuckle his belt, 'is a goddamned good thra …'

'What, teach me a lesson, you unfaithful piece of shit?' she screamed. 'I'd like to see you try! If you so much as touch me ever again, I'll tear your face to ribbons with these,' Claudia shaped her hands, the fingers of which were topped with long pointed ivory-painted nails, like claws, 'and while you're attending to the damage, I'll use them to rip your bollocks off! And for good measure, I'll ask my father and his friend Giorgio to come round here and smash in your already ruined face! They'll enjoy the experience, I can tell you. Now get out, you treacherous creep! And don't *ever* come back!'

Faced with such a furious onslaught, Scott said resignedly, 'I'll get my things.'

'Yes, get your things, and then ... get the fuck OUT!'

* * *

Twenty minutes later, in Piazza della Santissima Annunziata, Scott, with suitcase in hand, was ringing Laurence's doorbell. 'Yes, hello? Who is it?' Laurence's voice crackled on the answer phone.

'Oh, hi, Laurence, it's Scott. If you're free, I'd like to see you.'

'Yes, sure, old boy, come on in.' The buzzer sounded and, pushing open the heavy oak door, Scott went on in and up the marble stairs. Laurence was waiting at the top. 'I say, you look down in the mouth! And why are you carrying your suitcase?' he asked, as he guided Scott in through the entrance door of the apartment.

'Well, I got kissed off, didn't I?'

'Kissed off? You mean *kicked out*? What, by Claudia?' Laurence asked, incredulously.

'Yeah. We had the most humongous row. I'll tell you about it – but first, if it's not too much hassle, I'd like to freshen up. I feel mucky.'

'Sure. Have the green room, as usual. Stay the night. Stay as long as you like. Fancy a drink to take with you?'

'Yeah, please.'

'Bourbon as usual?'

'Fine, thanks.'

Half an hour later, Scott, feeling refreshed and more relaxed, with a second bourbon on the rocks in his hand, gave Laurence a heavily doctored version of the afternoon's events. Laurence was pleased to hear that the whereabouts of the portrait had been established. However, he was not so happy about the proposed use of the film of Pennington.

'You say it's highly compromising. In what way?'

'Well, it shows him indulging in – er – kinky sex. I won't bore you with the details, but let's just say that his antics on film are hardly gonna impress his sweet wife or his wealthy client: which is why I'm suggesting a copy should be sent to HG anonymously with a note to the effect that, if he knows what's best for him, he won't be entering a bid for the painting, and—'

'But that's blackmail, a criminal offence!'

'Do you seriously *want* the painting to go to Pennington? Apparently his client is one of the richest men in the States. He may well outbid you. *Then* what's gonna happen to your Spencer Art Foundation? Listen, you don't have to get involved. I'll do what's necessary. You just rest easy in the knowledge that your main rival for the Raphael has been, or is gonna be, eliminated from the proceedings.'

'Look, old boy, I appreciate you have my best interests at heart, but do we really have to stoop to blackmail? I mean, when eventually I examine the Raphael and, if I then decide it's authentic, I'll be in a better position than any other interested party to assess the painting's worth. I'll know how much I should offer for it on behalf of my client, who has given me carte blanche in the matter. Pennington won't have that advantage and, in any case, he's probably been told by his client exactly what figure to bid. The point is, even if the painting is genuine, it may have faults that detract from its value. For instance, it may have been largely executed by one of Raphael's pupils. Alternately, it may have been altered or coloured in or retouched. Anything that points to there being less original work by Raphael and more participation by a pupil or some third party will have a deflationary effect on the offer I make for the painting. If Pennington outbids me when I've discovered that, say, 40% of the painting is by a pupil, I shan't be too upset for my client.'

'Well, I think it's gotta make life simpler and easier for you, if Pennington is out of contention. Then you can still put in a high bid for the painting, even if it *is* 40% by a pupil. After all,' he said with a sly grin, 'your client isn't going to know, is he? And what's more important is that you'll have the benefit of a higher commission, which will leave you with more money to invest in your Art Foundation.'

'I'm wondering what's got into you, Scott? This isn't like you. I can't believe you're seriously suggesting I should put in an inflated bid for the Raphael. There's no way I'd pull a fast one like that on my client.'

'Well, that's up to you, isn't it? I just don't wanna see you miss the opportunity of realising your dream of setting up the Foundation. Enough said?'

'Yes, sure. I'll see how things work out first, before making any major decisions.'

'There's something else I'd like to discuss with you, anyway.'

'What, your row with Claudia?'

'No, although I'd certainly value your advice in that respect. No, it concerns her father, Roberto. When Claudia and I went out to lunch with him yesterday, he made it known that he's rather anxious to meet you. But we said we didn't think that was going to be possible, because you work all day and prefer not to see people socially in the evening. However, I did promise—'

'Oh no, I don't mind meeting him, as long as he can come here, to the apartment. Any idea what he wants to see me about? I mean, what does he do?'

'He's an art dealer, and he wants to consult you about a sixteenth-century painting he's interested in buying.'

'He is Claudia's dad, after all. I can hardly refuse him. I'll see him here tomorrow at 18:00, if he's free. Can you find out?'

'Yeah, sure thing. I'll call him in a minute. I think I have his number.'

'Good. Now, tell me what the problem is between you and—'

'Actually, old pal, I was just wondering whether you have any antihistamine tablets or cream. A couple of bites I must have gotten on my way back from Signorina Maruichi are beginning to itch like crazy.'

'Yes, I can see you have a nasty-looking one on your forehead. Apparently, this afternoon a whole horde of mosquitoes invaded the Football Stadium. People watching the game were set upon. There was panic and several people were killed, including two policemen, and a lot more were injured. Like many of the spectators, Paolo's uncle was bitten quite badly. That's why Paolo isn't here: he's at the Santa Maria Nuova Hospital. I take it Claudia, when she's not arguing with you, is hard at work trying to find a way to deal with these attacks.'

'Well, I think she spends a lotta time writing reports for the Institute in Rome,' Scott said. 'As to whether she's trying to find a solution to the skeeter problem: I know she believes the best way of reducing the number of mosquitoes is by biological controls – but that's unlikely to be a fully functional option for several years to come. So she's obviously figuring out what to do in the meantime. Anyway, after what's happened today, I doubt I'll be privy to her thoughts on the subject any longer, will I?'

'No, I suppose not,' said Laurence. 'But knowing how determined Claudia is, I'm sure she'll find a way of ridding us of this menace. Now, shall we go to my bathroom and have a look in the medicine cabinet, where there's a veritable chemist's array of tablets and creams? I'm sure I have some antihistamine. Then I suggest we go and eat. We can pop round to Trattoria Atmosphera in Via Faenza. It's about ten minutes' walk. On second thoughts, we'd better go by car. You don't want any more bites, do you?'

Over dinner, the two friends discussed Scott's enforced departure from Claudia's apartment. However, because Scott did not describe what really happened in the afternoon, but declared instead that, having argued with Claudia about something quite insignificant, she had lost her temper and ordered him to leave, Laurence was not able to offer any meaningful advice. As he had no way of telling whether the two had had anything other than a lovers' tiff, he said Scott should grit his teeth, give Claudia a call in the morning and apologise for all he was worth. He certainly didn't want to lose someone as beautiful and talented as Claudia.

* * *

That Sunday night in Florence certain people were restless, and not just because of the intense humidity.

In her flat in San Frediano, Francesca was too sore to lie on her back and could not sleep, so she got up and went into the bathroom. She lifted up her nightie, turned her back towards the mirror and looked over her shoulder. The dark red stripes on her bottom and the backs of her legs were tinged with grey-blue bruising and blotches of congealed blood. She rubbed some soothing cream into the discoloured skin and let her nightie fall back into place. She went into the sitting room and sat down gingerly at the table, on which there was now a camera as well as her laptop. She attached the camera to the laptop and then tapped the keyboard a couple of times. Onto the screen came a low-angled view of a dimly lit room, in which there was a double bed, a chest of drawers, two armchairs and a small table. A woman with long dark hair was walking away from the camera to the door, which she opened. In the doorway, stood a man, who she kissed on both cheeks. She turned and came back into the room. It was Francesca. The man who followed her was Scott.

In her apartment in Piazza d' Azeglio, although she had gone to bed early, Claudia spent most of the night wide awake and gripped by a dull pain in her chest. She reflected sadly that in the space of fifteen hours she had rejected both her job and her lover, because she no longer had faith in either. Destroying mosquitoes en masse and Scott and Francesca in bed together were two notions she found equally repulsive. She was determined that, under no circumstances, would she take back her job or Scott. A picture of her mother lying helpless in her bed came into her mind, and her eyes filled with tears. She knew she should do what Mama asked and try to find, and fall in love with, an Italian who would idolise her and prove to be a faithful husband and a good father to her children. But who? Disconcertingly and fleetingly, she thought of Giuseppe Corti at the Institute, who was three years younger than her.

Tossing and turning in his bed in the green room of Laurence's first-floor apartment, Scott intermittently scratched at the bites on his neck and forehead. Tormented by visions of naked bottoms and hands held like claws, he wrestled with the idea of phoning Claudia and asking her forgiveness, as Laurence had suggested. In his heart of hearts, though, he knew he had no hope of persuading her to accept him back. Switching his thoughts to Francesca, her sexy body, her beautiful hair and the possibility of caning her already heavily bruised bottom, he became, by degrees, aroused and disgusted.

Close by, Laurence wasn't sleeping either. He was worried about his friend. It had been out of character for Scott to suggest that Laurence should dupe his client. Also, why had Scott and Claudia fallen out? It was unlike Scott to argue about something insignificant, and Claudia would surely not chuck him out unless she had exceptional justification. Maybe he had been cheating on her and Claudia had found out. Laurence began to think there must be another side to Scott that he knew nothing about.

CHAPTER 13

Monday 26 August

On Monday morning, despite having had very little sleep, Claudia woke at 06:30 and went into the bathroom to have a shower. Although oppressed by the hurt and the disappointment of Scott's betrayal, she knew what she was going to do. In the short term, she proposed to establish a free Mosquito Advisory Centre. She would suggest the idea to the Commune di Firenze and hope that they would want to set her up in suitable premises. If not, she would seek her father's help. As for her financial status: she had substantial savings at the bank, and she could always earn money by writing articles for scientific journals and newspapers. Also, among the documents on her computer, there was the outline and sample chapter, in English, of her projected book on the environmental issues of the day, which she could refine and submit to an academic press, with the expectation of receiving an offer of publication, together with an advance on royalties.

The one dilemma she did not have an answer for was how she was going to adjust to life without Scott. She needed male companionship. She thrived on the stimulation, both intellectual and physical, that a man could give her. As she was aware, she had no difficulty in attracting the opposite sex. The trick was to find someone who was interested in her mind as well as her body. In time, she would find the right man. Meanwhile, she was in no hurry to hitch her horse to another wagon.

Claudia sat down at her desk and opened her laptop. Finding she had an email, she clicked on the Inbox:

From: Institute of Ecology, Rome

Subject: Your resignation

Since receiving yr resignation letter, I've sat around house this weekend in state of incredulity. Can't believe U have turned yr back on what wd have been glittering career in ecology. IMO U wd have ended up as DG of Institute & world's leading authority on mosquitoes, I'm sure of that. Nevertheless at same time I have sneaking admiration for strength of yr convictions & yr standpoint on environmental issues. There is, I know, no way I can persuade U 2 take yr job back, & I'm writing really 2 wish U well in whatever U decide 2 do. Don't forget, we're at yr beck & call, if U need R advice, assistance or research facilities.

My regards 2 Scott. He's a lucky man.

When U're next in Rome, pls do look us up.

All best,

Ettore

P.S. I have favour 2 ask U. Disheartened by yr loss, Giuseppe gave in his notice yesterday. I wonder if U cd possibly ring him & try 2 persuade him 2 reconsider. He's only been with us for short while, & with such limited work experience, he's not going 2 find it easy 2 land another job in ecology. Anyway, I'd appreciate it if U cd talk 2 him. He listens 2 what U say. Thx.

* * *

Scott got up late. When he looked in the bathroom mirror, he hardly recognised himself. Pale-faced, except for the red bump on his forehead and the dark rings under his eyes, he had a haunted look. *Jeez!* he thought. *Why did I have to be so weak-minded? At the first opportunity, I couldn't wait to plumb the depths of depravity. How could I have submitted to such primal urges? I disgust myself. Little wonder I disgust Claudia. However badly she thinks of me now, though, imagine how much worse her opinion would be, if she knew precisely what I got up to yesterday afternoon.*

Scott bathed, shaved, dressed and went through to the drawing room, where he found Paolo dusting. 'Is Signor Spencer up yet?'

'No, signore. He's in his bed. He says he slept not well.'

'He's not the only one. Paolo, do you have such a thing as a jiffy bag – *busta imbottita* I think it is in Italian – or, failing that, some cardboard and a piece of wrapping paper? I have something I need to post.'

* * *

In the conservatory of Castello di Montezano, Baldini was enjoying his usual breakfast of raw oats, sliced banana and raisins, buttered toasted, wholemeal muffin and an Americano with hot milk, when Mario came in holding a mobile phone with his hand over the mouthpiece. 'Boss, we had a call earlier from José, your contact in Buenos Aires. He said everything's arranged for this morning. They're going to do a special, just for you. Also, he expects the painting to be on its way to us tomorrow.' He passed the phone to Baldini. 'It's Signorina Maruichi. She wants to speak to you.'

'*Buongiorno*, Francesca. Did our friend cooperate?'

'Yes. It's all on film. You may possibly have to edit it in one or two places.'

'Did he indulge in anything – er – unusual?'

'Yes, and he seemed to enjoy it.'

'Did he hurt you?'

'Erm, a bit. But you know me. I'm used to it. HG saw to that.'

'Well, Francesca, you've done an excellent job. If you hand over the film to Mario later this morning at the Hotel, he'll have a well-earned bonus for you. *Ciao*!' He handed the phone back to Mario. 'Can you go to the Hotel and get this film. Then waste her, will you? If she hadn't let Gennady out of her sight, all this trouble we've been put to wouldn't have been necessary. Also, she knows too much for her own good. If she were to reveal anything about us in an unguarded moment, we'd be in deep shit. Waste her and dump her body somewhere in the countryside. Oh, and make it look as if she was indulging in her peculiar pleasures with a person or persons unknown, who went too far.'

'Okay, boss. Sure thing. I'll take Giovanni and

Primo with me to make sure she enjoys our company before she snuffs it.' Mario left the room, as Baldini's mistress, Caterina, came in wearing a negligée.

'I missed you last night, baby. Where were you?"

'I was out with the girls,' she replied. 'We went to the cinema and then had dinner together.'

'Well, I wanted you,' said Baldini, pushing his chair back from the table and opening the folds of his dressing gown. 'I still want you. So lock the door, baby, take your gown off and come over here.'

* * *

Claudia made two phone calls that morning. The first was to the Commune di Firenze to arrange a meeting with the Environmental Officer on Tuesday afternoon. The second call was to Giuseppe in Rome.

'Giuseppe?'

'*Sì*.'

'It's Claudia.'

'Claudia? Oh, I'm glad to hear your voice again. Without you in the office, it was chaotic. Nobody seemed to be able to cope. Everybody argued. No one, including Ettore, who just shuts himself away, had a clue what to do about the mosquitoes. Anyway, I couldn't stand it any longer, so I resigned on Friday.'

'I'm not sure that was such a good idea,' Claudia said.

'Well, to be honest, and I know it's a bit much to ask, I'd rather work with you, if possible. I'd like things to be as they were and I was able to consult you when it was necessary to do so. I admire your stance on the environment – and I know I can learn a great deal from you.'

'Giuseppe, you're thinking only about what *you* want!' Claudia said, with surprising forcefulness. 'You're not thinking about other people and what they need. My advice is go back to the Institute. It's the best chance you have of making a successful career for yourself. Do the sensible thing: ring Ettore and ask him to …' She stopped, because she realised what she was saying applied to herself.

'No, Claudia. It's no use! I'm *not* going back to the Institute. I'd rather join the Voluntary Service Overseas and go to Namibia or Ethiopia.' He paused for effect. There was silence at the other end. Claudia was thinking. She had done what Ettore had asked her to do, without success, but maybe she could work the situation to her advantage. 'Claudia? Are you still there?'

'Yes. I was just giving the matter some thought. Look, Giuseppe, I can't promise anything, but there is a *slim* chance that you may be able to work for me for a while. It all depends on the outcome of a meeting I'm having tomorrow afternoon. I'll let you know what happens in the evening. Okay?'

'That sounds great, but can't … can't you give me some idea of what you have in mind?'

'No!' she said, emphatically. 'It may not work out, so don't get your hopes up. We'll speak tomorrow evening. Until then, *ciao*!'

* * *

Deep in the southern hemisphere at Temuco, Chile, it is dark in August at midday. The sun rises at 16:00 in the afternoon and sets at 03:00 in the morning. In the brightly lit porch of the Holiday Inn Express, Jacopo Malavasia and Alexandrov were waiting, with their two bodyguards, for their driver to collect them. Suddenly a large van came charging into the driveway and screeched to a halt. Six men wearing balaclavas and armed with pump shotguns jumped from the back of the van. 'Get in!' one of them shouted, with his gun at the ready. Malavasia and his three companions were searched, deprived of their weapons and shoved into the back of the van. The armed men jumped in after them, two into the front and four into the back – and the van drove off at speed.

* * *

As arranged by Scott, Roberto called at Laurence's apartment promptly at 18:00. Scott, who had spent the afternoon absent-mindedly looking at art books in the nearby Biblioteca delle Oblate, greeted him and showed him into the drawing room. 'Claudia and I have split up,' he announced, almost casually.

'Split up? Why, for heaven's sake?'

'We had a row and she told me to get out.'

'Oh, my poor bambino! I must give her a call. She'll be upset.'

'She's packed her job in, too.'

'What? Has she gone crazy?'

'Nope. She's just very strong-minded, as you should know.'

Laurence came into the room, accompanied by Paolo. 'Good evening, gentlemen. Sit yourselves down. Paolo, can you pour us some Prosecco, please?' He turned to Roberto. 'Signor Mattioli, I'm delighted to meet you. Your daughter's vitality and expertise have brightened my drab life. I shall be pleased to help you in any way I can.' Paolo handed out flutes of Prosecco and then left the room.

'Scott,' Roberto said, 'I hope you'll understand, but what I have to say is for Signor Spencer's ears only.'

'Sure,' said Scott, getting up from the chesterfield. 'I'll take this excellent fizz with me, if I may.' He smiled at Laurence and left the room.

Roberto leaned forward, with an intense look on his face. 'Signor Spencer, I hope you won't mind, but I have to stress that what I'm about to reveal to you is highly confidential. If it goes beyond these four walls, I shall be in considerable danger.'

Laurence nodded. 'You have my word. I won't repeat our conversation to anyone.'

'I expect Scott has told you I am an art dealer. That is what he, my daughter, my wife, my friends and my clients believe. And it *is* true: I *do* buy and sell paintings. So does my partner, Giorgio Belori. But it's just a front. In reality, we both work undercover for the Italian intelligence agencies, AISI and AISE. We specialise in recovering stolen works of art. Have you heard of Rudolfo Siviero?'

'Yes. He was a connoisseur who lived in Florence. I believe his house is open to the public. After the last war, he spent many years tracking down and bringing back to Italy stolen works of art. In the 1970s he drew up a catalogue of some 2,000 missing statues, paintings, etc., which was not published until twelve years after his death in 1983. It was thought that if the list had been published earlier, it would have offended Germany and Russia, the two countries from where most of the art stealers emanated.'

'That's right. The Siviero catalogue is normally our main point of reference. However, currently we are in pursuit of a work that is not listed in the catalogue, the *Portrait of a Young Man* by Raphael. Forgive me, but I believe you know about this painting.'

'I do indeed.' Laurence shifted uneasily in his chair.

'You are acquainted with its recent provenance?' asked Roberto.

'Yes. In 1915 it was loaned by the Czartoryski Museum in Krakow to the Gemäldegalerie Alte Meister in Dresden, and was returned to the Czartoryski after the end of the First World War. Prior to the start of the Second World War, the Czartoryski family hid the painting at their country house in Sieniawa, but by October 1939 it had been <quote> presented <unquote> to Hermann Göring, no less, who put it on show in the Kaiser Friedrich Museum in Berlin. However, the Governor General of South Central Poland, Hans Frank, organised for the portrait to be brought back to Krakow, so that it could adorn his apartments in Wawel Castle. A year and a half later, when Germany was about to invade Russia, it was thought prudent to return the painting to the relative safety of Berlin. Late in 1942, when the bombing of the Reich capital intensified, Raphael's *Young Man* was on its way east again, to Krakow. Then, at some point during the next two years, the picture vanished and has never been seen since. Whether Frank sold it or someone pinched it is anyone's guess. Anyway, it disappeared into thin air.'

'You certainly know a lot more about it than I do. Have you any idea where it disappeared to?'

'I presume Russia, because that's where the as yet unauthenticated painting has come to light. Maybe some time in 1944 it was stolen from Wawel Castle and ended up in the hands of Stalin's Trophy Brigade, who knows?'

'Well, whatever the case, the painting, as you know, is now on its way from Russia to Florence, where it will be—'

'Look, Signor Mattioli, I'm not sure where all this is leading, but there's one point about your position in this matter that needs clarification. You say that, as an undercover agent in the Italian intelligence organisation, you track down works of art which are listed in the Siviero catalogue and therefore were stolen from Italy. Raphael's *Portrait of a Young Man* was *not* stolen from Italy. Why, therefore, does it interest you?'

'I hope you don't mind me answering your question with a question of my own. Do you know what happened with another stolen Raphael painting, *Madonna of the Hay*?'

Recalling his conversation with Frances Morley, Laurence replied, 'Yes. It was offered by the Mafia to some of your people, who were posing as buyers of nuclear materials. I believe one or two of the minor individuals involved were arrested.'

'That's right. What we'd like to try – with your help, if possible – is to engineer a similar scenario, this time incriminating the big fish as well. We know the Mafia has asked you to examine the *Young Man* picture with a view to authenticating it and, if and when you are satisfied it is genuine, sealed bids will be invited from bona fide would-be purchasers. As Giorgio and I have managed to convince Signor Baldini that we're acting on behalf of a wealthy client, we shall be entering a bid, too. Now, this is where it gets tricky and we need your cooperation. In order for our "sting" operation to succeed, Giorgio and I *must* enter the best bid. The only person who can advise us as to the sort of figure—'

'Excuse me for interrupting you again, Signor Mattioli,' there was a note of irritation in Laurence's voice, 'but if the painting is genuine, I intend to secure it for my *actual* client, who trusts and expects me to do no less.'

'I am aware of your commission, Signor Spencer. I didn't—'

'I must say, you seem to be remarkably well-informed about what is going on.'

'Yes, we have someone working for us inside the Mafia here in Florence. I didn't say we proposed to *buy* the painting. There's no way we could, if we wanted to. The new Minister of Cultural Heritage was not prepared to provide the necessary funds, despite professing to be keen to save the painting for the nation by slapping an export order on it. Fortunately, he relented when our Director pointed out that, if he did such a thing, he would not only alert the media and the world generally – not to mention the Czartoryski and the Polish Government – to the whereabouts of the portrait and the fact that the Italian Government was blatantly harbouring stolen works of art. He would also succeed in putting off prospective buyers of the painting, who mostly seem to be foreigners. Anyway, if Giorgio and I put in the winning bid, Baldini has to phone or meet us in order to tell us the good news. In so doing, he will implicate himself and his organisation – and *that's* what we want to achieve!'

'Before that happens, though,' said Laurence, 'the Russians for whom the 'Ndrangheta are selling the painting will want evidence that you and Giorgio have the money, i.e. they'll check out your bank account. How are you going to get round that?'

'Oh, that's taken care of. The Minister and the Bank of Italy have organised a fake account in our names, which has fictitious funds in it of almost one billion dollars.'

'Right then,' said Laurence, who was amazed by what he was hearing. 'After I've vetted the picture and if it's the real McCoy, how do I contact you with a suggested bid? I mean, Baldini is a clever little sod. He's probably keeping me under surveillance until the whole business is over.'

'I've thought of that. Rather conveniently, I've been retained by a client to purchase a small "Madonna and Child" painting which is believed to be by Giovanni Bezzi. So, when you've decided what the Raphael is worth, I suggest you email me at this address,' Roberto stood up, handed Laurence his business card and sat down again, 'with one of those "Without Prejudice, in my considered opinion" letters, in which you state the value of the Bezzi as being, say, $60,000. I will interpret this to mean that we should bid $60,000,000 for the Raphael – or $75,000,000, say, if you put $75,000. Do you see what I'm getting at?'

'Yes, I understand,' Laurence said, stifling a yawn.

'I can see I'm tiring you, Signor Spencer. I'm sorry about that, but I do have a couple of requests to make of you, and then I'll leave you in peace. First, I wonder, would it still be possible to implement this plan, should the Raphael portrait turn out to be a fake or the work of a pupil? You see, the priority as far as we're concerned is to apprehend Baldini, come what may, and hopefully have him put away for a very long time.'

'You mean, you're asking me to act as if the painting *is* by Raphael, even if it isn't? I don't think that'll do a lot for my professional reputation!' *But why should that bother me?* he wondered. *Life's too short. Anyway, I'd be helping them to put Baldini behind bars.* 'So who cares about my reputation? I'd like to help you if I can. Just tell me what you have in mind.'

'The position as we see it, Signor Spencer, is if you say the picture is fake, no one is going to want to buy it! On the other hand, if you say it's genuine but know it to be fake, you obviously enter a bid which you know will *not* be high enough to be successful. The others, of course, will put in their highest bids. Which is why we will still need you to suggest a bid that *is* going to be successful. Conversely, should you discover the painting is genuine, then you will enter a bid which hopefully *will* be the highest — except, of course, for the bid that you recommend *we* put in.'

'In either event,' Laurence said, 'I will be most happy to advise you as you suggest.'

'Thank you. Your offer of help is much appreciated. As regards my other request: if at all possible, can you please try to find out more about the much larger transaction in which the portrait plays only a small part? We know it involves stolen arms and nuclear materials. Any information you can pass onto us will, I'm sure, be most useful.'

'I've made it clear to Baldini,' Laurence declared, 'that I insist on being told about the exact nature of the entire transaction and the people involved, before I go ahead and examine the Raphael. He's promised me that once the painting is in Florence, he will tell me what I want to know. Presumably, if I could record my conversation with him, it would be helpful.'

'Yes, yes, it would indeed, but how – ?'

'I have a digital watch which has a 'Just Press and Record' app on it. The watch was given to me a couple of years ago by a Swiss art collector. If Baldini's henchmen search me, I doubt they'll realise the watch is anything other than (if you'll forgive the pun) an up-to-the-minute timepiece.'

Roberto smiled. 'Any sort of admission you can extract from Baldini and record will strengthen our hand against him – but *please* be careful! Don't arouse his suspicions by asking *too* many questions.'

'No, I'll be careful, believe me. With his teeth set in that maleficent grin of his, Baldini reminds me of a great white shark moving in for the kill.' Roberto nodded his head and chuckled. 'What will happen about the painting?'

'We'll only make a move against Baldini and his mob, once the Raphael is in our possession. Then I've agreed with the Minister that we'll hand the portrait over to whoever puts in the second highest bid, which, if the portrait is genuine, we trust will be you. By that stage, the Russians will have discovered the money we paid them doesn't exist and will probably be only too pleased to negotiate the sale of the painting to you privately at a special price.' *Or,* thought Laurence, *they're more likely to want to kill me.* Roberto got to his feet. 'Signor Spencer, there's no need for me to keep you any longer. You have been very patient, and I'm sorry if I've tired you with my talking.' He offered his hand, which Laurence shook rather wearily. 'My sincere thanks to you, sir. It has been a pleasure meeting you. Hopefully, with your help, we can nail this scumbag Baldini once and for all!'

CHAPTER 14

Tuesday 27 August

Next morning, in the national media, there were worrying reports of further increases in the numbers of people suffering from Malaria, Dengue, Yellow Fever, Filariasis and other mosquito-borne diseases. The death toll, especially among the young and the old, was mounting inexorably.

In *La Nazione*, the daily newspaper of Florence, a grim picture was painted of a changing and vulnerable city:

ZANZARE PERICOLOSE NEL CONTROLLO DELLA NOSTRA CITTÀ

[DANGEROUS MOSQUITOES IN CONTROL OF OUR CITY]

Since the massed mosquito attacks on Sunday, there are noticeably fewer people out and about. Residents and tourists alike are reluctant to venture forth. They prefer to stay indoors with the windows shut, even in oppressively hot rooms without air conditioning.

Streets that are usually teeming with mopeds and scooters

are strangely quiet and inactive. Occasionally a lone, putt-putting Piaggio or Vespa disturbs the uncanny tranquillity. This has resulted in a reduction in the petrol and diesel fumes that hang in the air.

The city's notable gardens and parks, such as Bardini, Boboli and Cascine, where mosquitoes persistently harass passers-by and breed prolifically in the ponds, pools and grottoes, are no longer visited or tended.

Camping sites in and around the city, which are normally overflowing with backpackers and caravan owners, are deserted, except for a few people who are brave or reckless enough to spend the night under canvas with hundreds of mosquitoes for company!

In the countryside, farmers and their livestock, market gardeners and winegrowers are all under such sustained attack that supplies of meat, milk, fresh vegetables and local wines are erratic and unreliable. There has been panic buying by the public and as a result stocks in food shops are running low.

Graffiti on the trains in Stazione S.M.N. capture the prevailing mood of mordant pessimism, with such examples as: 'Give blood and get the shakes'; 'See Florence and live (if you're lucky)'; 'Nature is the very devil'; 'Mosquitoes are true communists: they make no distinction between rich and poor'; and 'What's biting you today?'

Florence's many renowned churches are no longer filled with admiring sightseers, but with people praying. Devout Italians are joined on their knees by Catholics from other countries, who, despite the risks, have opted to remain in the city …

* * *

After breakfast, Scott asked Paolo to tell Laurence, who was still upstairs, that he was going out for the day and would not be back until the early evening.

Not wishing to run into any more mosquitoes, Scott went by taxi to his destination – the Uffizi Library. Once there, he sat at a reading desk and opened the file he had brought with him. His aim was to compile a cash flow forecast for his business. However, as he started to calculate what its income was likely to be for the next twelve months, his mind wandered.

He thought of the dilemma he was in. What should he do? He had two choices: go back to New York and get on with his job – or remain where he was. He knew it made sense for him to return home. Now that the projected joint venture with the Uffizi had fallen through, there was no commercial reason for him to stay in Florence. If his independent publishing company was to continue to set the high standards of book production which other art publishers followed, he needed to find new and important titles to take the place of the projected Uffizi series. He was more likely to do this in New York than in Florence.

On the other hand, he knew he'd left the business in the capable hands of its editor-in-chief, who was as good at finding the right books as he was. There wasn't any *immediate* need for him to return. In any case, he had some booksellers and authors still to see in Florence, and several more in Milan and Rome. He'd like, if possible, to continue to stay in Florence with Laurence – but should his friend not be keen on the idea, he would book into a hotel or find himself a small short-stay apartment instead.

Then there was Claudia. He must admit his own weaknesses and shortcomings to her and tell her the truth. He understood well enough that, by doing so, he had no chance of ever winning her back. He had burnt his bridges as far as their relationship was concerned the moment he had signed Francesca's IOU. He realised that. Even so, he wanted Claudia to know what a despicable and two-timing bastard he was. He wanted to confess to her his inexcusable failings. But his admission of guilt would be deficient in one respect. It would omit the fact that, despite acknowledging how abjectly he had let down such an incomparable partner, he was nevertheless unable to dismiss from his mind the titillating image of Francesca, naked and prostrate, waiting to be caned. Indeed he was positively salivating at the prospect. With Claudia no longer available to him, he would be able to use Francesca as a willing sex slave, on whom he could take out his pent-up frustrations.

Jeez, goddamnit! What nasty, perverse devil had possessed his soul and made his dick govern his brain?

* * *

Shortly before 15:00, Claudia called at the City Administration building in Via del Leone for her meeting with the Environmental Officer.

Enrico Pallucchini, a short harassed-looking man, was agreeably surprised when she was shown into his office. For some reason, he had imagined he would be dealing with a plain, spinsterish academic. The vision of beauty he saw before him prompted him to spring to his feet and welcome her with his hand extended. 'Signorina Mattioli, how delightful!' They shook hands. 'It's a pleasure to meet you. Please,' he made an expansive gesture, 'take a seat.' He watched as Claudia sat down and crossed her legs, then he returned to his desk. 'Signorina, our phone conversation yesterday was, of necessity, rather brief, because I was otherwise occupied at the time. Just explain to me again why you decided to resign from the Institute.'

'Basically, Signor Pallucchini,' she said, putting on her spectacles, 'because I disagree with the mosquito eradication programme which the Institute wishes to pursue. I am against the idea of a national spraying campaign. Man's overuse of pesticides has contributed to the unbalancing of the Earth's ecology. I—'

'But, signorina, are you aware that the Commune may decide to permit spraying here in Florence and the surrounding areas?'

'No, I didn't know that. What do they intend to use?'

'Malathion. It's the only chemical available in sufficient quantity.'

'You do know that it can cause children to have headaches, runny eyes, sore throats, nausea, and so on. Also, it can be environmentally destructive if sprayed on top of other pesticides that are already in use.'

'Yes, signorina, I do know – but what other action can we take? The Commune must be seen to be taking steps to protect the public.'

'Well, I do have one or two ideas. However, before I get involved, I'd like to establish the basis on which I'd be prepared to proceed. Whilst I am temporarily unemployed, I'm happy to offer my services free to the Commune, with the object of setting up a Mosquito Advisory Centre, preferably in the very heart of the city. In return, I'd expect all the expenses of the operation – rent, city tax, services, cost of computers, printers, photocopiers, office furniture, etc. – to be met by the Commune. I'd also need some administrative assistance. Maybe one or two of the Commune's employees, who are currently dealing with the mosquito problem, could be delegated to help me. There may be a chance, too, that a former colleague of mine at the Institute can be persuaded to join the venture. If so, he will probably have to be paid a modest wage.'

'What is your plan of action?'

Claudia passed him some sheets of paper. 'I've drawn up a schedule of the day-to-day activities of, and services offered by, the Centre, together with a list of eventualities that it may be called upon to handle. For your convenience, I've also prepared an estimate of the likely costs involved.'

'Thank you, signorina. That's most helpful. What I'll do is read these, and then I'll ask one or two of the other City officers whether they think I can give you the go-ahead – without having to have the matter considered by the next full meeting of the Commune, which doesn't take place for another ten days. At the same time, I'll find out if we can set you up in the offices the Commune owns beside the Misericordia Museum in Piazza del Duomo. As soon as I have some answers, I'll phone you.'

* * *

In Chile, shortly before 21:00 on the same day, a Mapuche couple were walking their Magellan sheep dog along an unmade road near Boyeco, a small settlement 13km northeast of Temuco. The huge landfill site for which Boyeco was best known had been filled in, although piles of household waste indicated that fly-tipping was still prevalent. There was an unpleasant smell in the air. Suddenly they heard horrifying screams. These were so disturbing that the dog lay down on the ground whimpering and the woman, with an agonised expression on her face, put her hands to her ears to cut out the dreadful sound. The man shouted in Mapudungun, 'Quick! It is the Wekufe. We must escape or we will be possessed!' The couple ran away as fast as they could, dragging the whining dog after them.

* * *

That evening Enrico Pallucchini rang Claudia to tell her that he was delighted to give her the go-ahead for the Mosquito Advisory Centre and to be able to let her use the office at No. 21 Piazza del Duomo, where he suggested they meet the following day at 11:00 to discuss her requirements.

Claudia called Giuseppe.

'Claudia! I've been waiting to hear from you. I—'

'Giuseppe, listen. I've something important to ask you. With the backing of the Commune di Firenze, I'm setting up a free Mosquito Advisory Centre here in Florence. The offices are likely to be in Piazza del Duomo, opposite the Campanile. Some of the Commune's environmental workers are going to help me, but I need a right-hand man. Are you interested? The pay won't be all that good, and I'll expect you to work quite long hours.'

'Oh yes, Claudia, I *am* interested. I'd work for you

for peanuts. The only thing is, will I get accommodation easily and cheaply enough?'

'Giuseppe, if you promise to be self-dependent and tidy, you can stay in my flat. I have a spare room.'

'Really? That's fantastic – but won't I get in the way? I mean, I'll be an annoyance to Signor Lee, surely?'

'Signor Lee and I have split up. That's why I don't want you to misconstrue the situation or my motives. I am inviting you as a lodger, *not* as a prospective partner. If you try to make a pass at me, I'll ask you to leave. Do I make myself clear?' She sounded neurotic and knew it.

'I'm sorry, I didn't know about you and Signor Lee,' Giuseppe said calmly. 'Of course, I understand your position, and I'll be as unobtrusive as possible, I promise you. I'm very grateful for the offer of accommodation, and I'm pleased you want me to help you.'

'Well, that's good,' she said. 'Just *don't* disappoint me, all right? Now, when do you think you'll be able to move in?'

'I reckon I'll be there at about 10:00 tomorrow. I'll pack my things this evening and drive up first thing in the morning. Yes, roundabout 10:00. Is that too early for you?'

'No, that's fine. Just don't drive too fast! I'll see you—'

'The address, Claudia, I need to know the address – and how to get there. I don't have a satnav unfortunately.'

'Of course. Sorry. It's Flat 10, No. 49 Piazza d' Azeglio.' Speaking more slowly, she continued: 'Follow the signs for the city centre – I suggest you write this down – and opposite Ponte San Niccolò … turn right into Viale Amendola … which leads into Piazza Beccaria … where you take the *fourth* turning off the roundabout … for Via Manzoni and Via Niccolini, which lead into Piazza d' Azeglio. Did you get that?'

'Yes, thanks. See you tomorrow morning. *Ciao*!'

* * *

'Mario,' Baldini shouted from his study. 'I have something important to ask you.'

Mario hurried into the room. 'Yes, boss. What is it?'

'Mario, is it safe to assume that Alexandrov and Malavasia sleep with the fishes?'

'Yes, boss. Though their end wasn't very pleasant, I must admit. And, as you know boss, I've had a fair amount of experience in this type of thing.'

'Not pleasant, you say? Why? What sort of end did José arrange for the thieving shits?'

'Well, as instructed by José, Arsenio, my friend in the Chilean organisation, and his pals abducted Alexandrov and Malavasia from their hotel in Temuco and took them to a small farm at a place nearby called Boyeco.'

'Yes, and what happened then?'

'They stripped the two men naked, pinioned them and with small serrated knives proceeded to make short, shallow cuts all over their flesh. By the time they had finished, the two bodies were slick with blood and

Alexandrov and Malavasia were gasping and quivering with pain. But they had far worse to come.'

'Good. The more pain the better, treacherous bastards!'

'The Chileans carried the bleeding men, struggling and face upwards, into a fenced compound with a shed at one end, from where the sound of loud snorts and grunts could be heard. The two men were stretched out on the muddy ground and roped tightly by their wrists and ankles to the metal fences on either side of the compound. The gate to the shed was opened and out came four large piglike creatures ...'

'Pigs, you say?'

'No, boss, not pigs as we understand them. Arsenio said they were giant peccaries. They come from Brazil. The thing is they hadn't been fed for four days, so they were ravenous. Apparently they have razor-sharp tusks, crushing jaws and interlocking canine teeth.'

'A-hah! I sense retribution must have been a most painful and messy business!'

'So it proved to be, boss. According to Arsenio, these peccaries snuffled around the bodies, smelling the fresh blood. Then the biggest of them thrust and twisted his tusks into the side of one of the men, ripped out some flesh and gobbled it up. And that was the sign. They all tore into the bloody bodies and set about devouring the human flesh and crushing and eating the bones. Alexandrov and Malavasia screamed and screamed as they were eaten alive. Arsenio said it was so satisfying to hear them scream. *"Mierda!"* he said to me. "Could they scream! They made *such* a commotion, shrieking and screeching. It was a noise like none of us had ever heard before." For most of their terrible ordeal the two men were semi-conscious, but eventually they were silenced as the peccaries gulped down their innards and internal organs. When the peccaries had sated their appetites, there was hardly anything left: just two skulls and a hip bone.'

* * *

'Hi Claudia, it's me.'

'Yes? What are you ringing for?' she asked irritably.

'I ... I just wanna say that I'm sorry to have been such a disappointment to you. Since I—'

'Look, you slimy bastard, I've got much better things to do than listen to you make excuses for yourself—'

'Please, Claudia, hear me out. Since we started going out together in the spring, I've not so much as glanced at another woman – that is, not until Sunday. Why should I? You're amazing – wonderful company, gorgeous, fascinating, caring. You are *pure* woman, almost too good to be—'

'For God's sake, cut the platitudes, you grovelling shit!'

'Please, Claudia. I'm not trying to absolve myself. I'm trying to tell you how and why I managed to let you down so badly. The fact is I never thought I'd need anyone else but you. But on Sunday, I discovered otherwise. I found—'

'You mean, faced with temptation, you were easy meat. You put pleasuring your dick before common sense and loyalty!'

'Yes, I'm … I'm *so* sorry. On Sunday I found I'm easy prey for a much less pure type of woman: the artful temptress. You warned me, of course, and I took no notice. I fell for her seductive charms without regard to the consequences. Egged on – and I hesitate to put this in words – egged on by sheer lust for her, I discovered a bestial side to me that I never imagined existed, and I did things I never thought I'd be able to do, and … and …' His voice began to crack. 'I … I had anal intercourse with her, something I've never attempted to have with anyone else, and … and then I thrashed her bare backside with a cane … and … do you … do you know … I *enjoyed* it!'

'Good for you, Scott! No doubt, you feel you have to make a clean breast to someone about your perverted carryings-on with Francesca, but quite why you have to pick me, I don't know. If you think that by admitting now what you denied on Sunday you are going to wheedle your way back into my affections, think again. You say that when you were with this woman you discovered you have a bestial side to you and you enjoyed beating her. But it appears you'd like to beat *other* women as well – because don't forget, just before I chucked you out, you wanted to give *me* a good belting. No, there's no way I'd *ever* want someone living with me who, by his own admission, gets a kick out of brutalising women. Go back to Francesca, you sick creep! Get her to satisfy your disgusting predilections!' Claudia pressed the 'End call' icon on her mobile.

CHAPTER 15

Wednesday 28 August

Early in the morning, in the Church of San Frediano in Cestello alongside the river in the Oltrarno district, some 150 people were at Mass. The server intoned the words, '*Confiteor Deo omnipoténti, beátæ Mariæ semper Virgini, beáto Michaéli Archángelo, beáto Joanni Baptistæ, sanctis Apóstolis Petro et Paulo, ómnibus Sanctis, et tibi, Pater: quia peccávi nimis cogitatióne, verbo et ópere,*' and struck his breast three times, saying, '*mea culpa, mea culpa, mea máxima culpa.*' At that point, thousands of mosquitoes, which overnight had infiltrated the church through air vents, cracks in windows and other openings and were resting on the underside of the frescoed dome, took off as one and swooped down on the unsuspecting congregation. Esurient insects, thirsting for blood, environed the faithful, who, with love of the Lamb of God in their hearts, were preparing to celebrate the Eucharist. Belief and expectation were abruptly displaced by fear and desperation. The officiating priest, who was constrained to wave away hundreds of insects that were seeking to turn his face into a bloody pincushion, dropped the chalice and so spilt the blood-red Communion wine over the white marble chancel steps. Having grabbed the ciborium from the altar, the server staggered into the sacristy with a ring of ferocious Asian Tigers and Spears round his head. Members of the congregation stumbled into one another, dropping missals and knocking over chairs, as hordes of large Alaskans and Bandeds and even larger Gallinippers alighted on arms, faces, legs, necks and scalps and pierced the proffered skin with their fascicles. A balding English man, with insects in his ears and nose and on his head and eyelids, was careering about like a wounded bull. A young French woman, who wore a maternity dress but, because the weather was so hot, no underwear, lay sprawling and screaming on the floor as marauding Dawn-and-Dusks and Brown Saltmarshes dived under the loose flaps of her garment and bit her all over her lower body. A Spanish couple, whose faces were covered with blood-filling Inland Floodwaters, were whacking each other's cheeks in a vain attempt to deflect their attackers, with the result that they soon looked as if they had both been in a bare-knuckle fight, so bloody and puffy were their appearances. Bitten or not, most of the churchgoers were hurt in the mad rush to get out of the building. 37 people sustained injuries such as cuts, heavy bruising, crushed fingers and broken bones, two elderly women were suffocated and one portly, middle-aged man died of a heart attack.

As those who had been bitten but not otherwise injured retreated, with relief, to their homes and hotels, they little realised that most of their number had been infected with highly unpleasant and, in some cases, life-threatening viruses.

* * *

At 09:30 on the same morning, at the Comando

Legione Carabinieri 'Toscana', a high-ranking officer of the national paramilitary police force was ushered into General Malatesta's office. 'Colonel Guiliano Botta reporting, sir,' he said, with a click of his heels.

'Good morning, Botta. Take a seat.'

'Thank you, sir.'

'What can I do for you?'

'Sir, I believe you know Signorina Francesca Maruichi.'

'Yes, socially.'

'Well, I'm sorry to have to tell you that her body has been found in a grove near Arcetri.'

'Her body? How did she die? She was only in her thirties, surely?'

'I'm afraid she met a ghastly end, sir. She must have suffered terribly, before finding relief in death. She was subjected to a beating that was as savage and remorseless as any I've seen in fifteen years' service. According to the pathologist's report, approximately two to three hundred blows were dealt all over her body with a variety of implements, which may have included electric flex, bamboo canes, birch rods, leather belts and nylon cord. As you know, sir, she was a lovely lady and remarkably her head and face, although blood-bespattered, were completely free of injury, almost as if her tormentors respected her beauty.'

'Or just wanted to watch her agonised expressions and hear her scream, more likely,' said the General.

'*Mio Dio*, sir! To think what that poor lady must have gone through! She was just a mass of contusions, lacerated skin and pulped flesh. But that's not all, sir. Before she was beaten to death, she was raped by her attackers. According to the pathologist, several men's discharges are involved, so it's a pointless exercise to attempt DNA profiling.'

'Do you have any leads?'

'Well, sir, we are aware Signorina Maruichi was involved with the Mafia, so at some stage we will be seeking an interview with the organisation's local area boss, Signor Luca Baldini.'

'I don't think that'll be necessary, Botta,' said the General. 'Signorina Maruichi's murder, as you have described it, bears none of the hallmarks of a classic Mafia killing, which is swift, calculated, clinical and execution-like. You may not be aware of this, but the police in this city, particularly the Carabinieri, are indebted to Signor Baldini for a number of reasons, the chief of which is that, due to Signor Baldini's personal cooperation and the strong links we've forged with his representatives, organised crime in Florence is much less active than practically anywhere else in the country. It would therefore be inappropriate and non-productive, at this time, to involve Signor Baldini in a murder inquiry, particularly one that relates to the vicious rape and beating to death of an attractive local woman. My advice to you is: forget Signorina Maruichi's connection with the Mafia, go through the usual steps of holding an inquiry and an inquest and so on, but in as low-key a manner as possible, and then shelve the matter. It goes without saying, that if you act on these suggestions successfully and without arousing undue media interest, I will have no hesitation in recommending you for promotion and a substantial increase in your pension.

Do I make myself clear, Colonel?'

'Yes, sir, perfectly.'

'Good. I look forward to receiving your further and *final* report in due course. Now, if you'll excuse me ...'

* * *

Bringing with him three suitcases, four cardboard boxes and a sports bag, Giuseppe turned up at Claudia's apartment at 10:40.

A tall, good-looking young man, he had the blue eyes and fair hair of his native Piedmont. 'I'm so glad to see you again,' he said, making as if to kiss Claudia on both cheeks – but she reached for his hand and shook it gently. 'You look *amazing*!' he exclaimed. Claudia was wearing a bustier, a mid-thigh length linen skirt and strappy sandals. 'I'm a bit late because there was an accident on the A1. Also I drove slowly, as you asked. By the way, those,' he indicated the four boxes, 'are your belongings from the Institute.'

'Thank you, Giuseppe. That's really thoughtful of you. Look, I'm sorry, but I have to rush off. I'm meeting the Environmental Officer at 11:00. I also have to find out more about what happened at the Church of San Frediano this morning. I heard on the news that mosquitoes attacked the congregation. Did you hear about it?'

'Yes. On the car radio.'

'Anyway, while I'm out, I suggest you unpack your things and take the opportunity to settle in. I'll show you your room.'

'Oh, can't I come with you?'

'No,' she said firmly. She opened the door to a small single bedroom, with a view of the green copper dome of the Great Synagogue. 'I'm afraid the room's not very big, but there's plenty of storage space.' She opened some cupboard doors. 'Anyway, I'll let you get on. I'm off to the Palazzo Vecchio to see Signor Pallucchini. I also have some shopping to do. When I'm finished, maybe we can have lunch together. Why don't you meet me at Trattoria di Michelozzi – it's in in Via della Condotta – at, say, 12:30? We can talk things over and make plans. See you then, okay? *Ciao*!'

* * *

After another restless night, Scott got up late. He decided not to call Francesca's number – fortuitously, as it happened, because her mobile was by that stage in Colonel Botta's possession.

Scott had come to the conclusion that his excessive carnality was a legacy of his relationship with Claudia. In being so physically demanding, she had spurred him on to such heights of sensuality that he could not now do without sex on a regular basis, which had not been the case before he met her. So, notwithstanding his urgent need to have a subservient Francesca expertly ministering to him while he grasped her beautiful hair in his hands, he must henceforth concentrate his energies on publishing, not sex. His priority was to meet with publishing and printing companies in northern Italy, with a view to acquiring English language volume rights of important Italian art books and arranging for their translation.

* * *

Hyram G. Pennington the Third was highly regarded as the Big Daddy of American art dealers. Having recently received a letter bomb, which failed to go off properly – fortunately for him only the fuse exploded – he had become obsessive about his own safety. Before opening any of his mail, his live-in secretary, Arnoldo, had to pass all items received in the day's post through a small X-ray scanner. On Wednesday morning, Arnoldo called out, 'HG, there's what feels like one of those flash-drive things in this packet that's just arrived.'

Pennington came into the room. 'Gimme it!' Pennington seized the packet, tore it open and took out a USB Flash Drive and a piece of paper. Having read what was on the paper, he turned white. Clutching his chest, he collapsed into a chair. 'Gemme ma pills!' he yelled. The piece of paper fluttered to the floor. It bore the following printed note:

DO _NOT_ BID FOR THE RAPHAEL PORTRAIT, YOU DISGUSTING DEVIANT, OTHERWISE COPIES OF THIS FILMED RECORD OF YOU VICIOUSLY THRASHING AND BUGGERING SIGNORINA MARUICHI WILL BE SENT TO YOUR WIFE, YOUR PARTNERS, YOUR MAIN CLIENTS, OTHER ART DEALERS, THE AAADA,[6] THE PRESS AND ANYBODY ELSE WHO CURRENTLY VALUES AND/OR PERPETUATES YOUR MISCONCEIVED REPUTATION.

* * *

About an hour after he had seen Botta, Malatesta

---

[6] The American Art & Antique Dealers' Association

received a call from Baldini. 'Bruno, I'm glad to tell you the painting is arriving this afternoon. Thank you, by the way, for helping us to locate Alexandrov and Malavasia. It's good that we were able to find them so quickly. It's also satisfying to hear that such thieving swine ended up most fittingly as pigswill, thanks to our friends in Chile! Anyhow, the painting is being flown over from South America in Malavasia's jet, which we've commandeered for our own use. ETA is 14:45 hours at Aeroporto Vespucci. Can you arrange for it to be collected and transferred to the Castello, where I suggest you leave at least four of your men on guard duty?'

'I'll organise it immediately, Signor Baldini. Incidentally, Francesca Maruichi's body has been found. I've suggested to the officer in charge that he will benefit personally if the inquest and inquiry are pushed through expeditiously, with the minimum of fuss.'

'Good. No point in disturbing the status quo, is there? You've done well, Bruno. I think you'll be pleased with your Christmas bonus this year.' Baldini hung up. 'Mario, get me Signor Spencer.'

'Sure, boss.' Baldini basked in self-adulation. *What a clever fellow I am,* he thought. *I hold everything and everybody in the palm of my hand. La vita è bella.* 'Boss, he's on line two.'

'Okay.' Baldini picked up the handset. 'Signor Spencer, *buongiorno.* It's truly a wonderful day,' he said. 'We are expecting the painting here this afternoon. So it is time we are having our meeting, as you requested. Is it possible tomorrow?'

'Signor Baldini, that's very good news! I'm delighted to hear the painting will finally be with us. I'm also delighted, too, to hear that you want us to meet, as promised. Can we possibly do that tomorrow afternoon? I leave it to you to suggest a suitable venue.'

'Is it convenient for you if we meet at the Hotel Belcari in Borgo Pinti?'

'Yes, very convenient. Thank you.'

'Shall we say 15:00?'

'Yes. I look forward to seeing you then.'

* * *

When Claudia arrived at the fashionable Trattoria di Michelozzi restaurant, which is renowned for its Tuscan cuisine, she found Giuseppe sitting at a table in the garden under a weeping willow. 'Oh, didn't you get yourself a drink?' she asked.

'No, I thought I should wait for you,' he answered, getting up and holding her chair for her.

'Thank you, Giuseppe. I'd like some wine. Shall we have a bottle of Vernaccia? How about some *crostini*, as well? Can you organise it?'

Giuseppe signalled to a passing waiter, who came over and took their order. 'Are you pleased with the offices in the Piazza del Duomo?' he asked.

'Oh, they're absolutely ideal. You'll see for yourself. We'll go there later. They comprise four rooms arranged on the first and second floors of a beautiful sixteenth-century building. There's a large staircase serving the two floors, and on the ground floor there's an office which is used, on and off, by the Misericordia Museum. Not only are we in the centre of things, we're also right beside the Ambulance Service!'

'When do you think you'll be able to move in?'

'Well, Signor Pallucchini has promised that my order for computers, copiers, desks, et cetera will be delivered on Monday. So, all things being equal, we should be able to start up on Tuesday.'

'What about the mosquito attack in San Frediano?'

'It was bad. Apparently, there were some 150 people in the church, and most were bitten, several were injured in the panic and three died. We must go there this afternoon and get some samples. We must also decide what we're going to do about the increasing frequency of these attacks. But first, let's eat something. I'm famished. What do you fancy? I can tell you, the pasta here is *fantastico*!'

* * *

After Claudia had shown Giuseppe the offices in Piazza del Duomo, she walked with him across the river to San Frediano. In the church, they found that the interior had been fumigated with pesticide. There were no live mosquitoes left and they had to content themselves with collecting dead samples. It was painstaking work and they did not return to Piazza d' Azeglio until the late afternoon. Apart from a short break for coffee and sandwiches, they spent the evening examining and classifying the specimens and making plans for the Centre. They discussed how they could best promote the service they were offering the public. They designed and printed out flyers and posters. They drew up a list of guidelines, which was similar to the one issued by the Mayor of Rome, on the avoidance and elimination of mosquitoes. They decided on their agenda in the event of a large-scale insect attack: how to mobilise the emergency services and put local hospitals on the alert; which doctors to call; where to set up temporary treatment and isolation centres; and what to do if there was a widespread panic. It was after midnight when Claudia said, 'It's late. We ought to turn in. It's going to be a busy day tomorrow. Giuseppe, you've been really helpful. Thank you. I think we're going to be a great team together.' She took his hand, reached up on tiptoe and kissed him on both cheeks. 'I'll see you in the morning. *Buonanotte*!' Smiling, she turned, went into her bedroom and closed the door.

Giuseppe flopped back on the sofa, in a daze. His emotions were churning inside him. His chest ached. If only … but that was wishful thinking. He was bound to disappoint her. She probably had had lovers by the score. What did the sum of his experience amount to? Various girls in Turin, one of whom spent the entire time listening to heavy metal on her headphones, and another who smelt of cheap scent, chewed gum with her mouth open and had bobbed up and down on him in such a rough and perfunctory manner that, embarrassingly, his erection had wilted. Then there was the older woman who liked to suck his dick in between taking drags on her foul-smelling cigarillo.

Dejectedly, Giuseppe got up and went to his room, there to sleep fitfully as thoughts of kissing Claudia and holding her close, together with visions of her wide smile, her long legs and her curvaceous figure, drifted through his mind.

CHAPTER 16

Thursday 29 August

The following day in the afternoon, Laurence went to the Hotel Belcari, where he and Baldini met alone in a small reception room. To ensure they were not disturbed, the entrance doors were closed and Mario and Giovanni stood guard outside the room.

'*Buongiorno*, Signor Spencer. It's good we have this picture at last.'

'Indeed it is, Signor Baldini.' Surreptitiously he pressed the 'Record' icon on his watch. 'I very much look forward to examining and hopefully authenticating the painting, always assuming, of course, that you can …'

'*Sì*, Signor Spencer. Last time we met, you asked me for details of the deal I've made with Signor Ouspensky. Well, the painting is – how do you say – the ice on the cake? What the deal concerns mostly is arms.'

'No nuclear materials?'

'*Sì*, there's some plutonium-239.'

'Where does that come from?'

'From contacts of Signor Ouspensky. Who they are I don't know. I've never met any of them.'

'What about the arms? How many and what sort of arms are involved, and where do they come from?'

'It's a big consignment of – erm – *mitragliatrici*. How do you …?'

'Machine guns.'

'There are automatic rifles, too. They are also coming from Ouspensky's contacts.'

'When you say big, how big?'

'It isn't possible to tell you that, Signor Spencer.'

'What sort of sums of money are we talking about?'

'Signor Spencer, this is confidential as well. Now you're asking me too many questions.' Baldini was beginning to sound edgy. 'I don't like this third degree. I've already told you what you said you wanted to know. You've asked me: What is the big deal about? Who is the big deal with? And I've answered you on both counts.'

From his prior experience of talking to Baldini, Laurence knew that it would be difficult to extract any further information from the man, but he decided to have one more try. 'Signor Ouspensky's contacts in Russia are hoping that the painting will fetch a great deal of money, aren't they? It's *not* the icing on the cake at all, is it? It's the main item in the transaction. They expect it to raise more money than the arms and the plutonium put together, don't they? That's why you're so keen that I should authenticate the Raphael portrait. But what if I decide *not* to play ball? What if I decide not to examine the painting or, if I do, I declare it's a fake? Signor Ouspensky's contacts aren't going to be too pleased, are they? Well, we can avoid any unnecessary bad feeling between us, *if* you give me just a little bit more detail about the overall transaction. Because, as things stand, I'm not happy—'

'*Che peccato*! I had hoped we wouldn't reach the point in our discussion where I have to threaten you, Signor Spencer. But I'm afraid you *do* have to play ball, to use your expression, otherwise we will *ruin* your friend Signor Lee!' Baldini said, bluntly.

'*Ruin* Scott? How? How do you mean, *ruin* him?'

'Have you heard of Signorina Francesca Maruichi?'

'Yes, the name rings a bell. Wasn't she at your lunch party?'

'She was indeed. On Sunday, Signor Lee met her and they went to a hotel together. They were there for more than three hours and in that time Signor Lee did some bad things to Francesca.'

'Bad things?' Laurence asked, apprehensively. 'What do you mean, bad things?'

'I will show you. When you see these pictures, you will be as surprised as I am that he treated Francesca so badly. I thought he was a gentleman, but he deals with her like some animal, not like a signorina. Anyway, we filmed the proceedings and here, Signor Spencer, here are some screenshots we took from the film. Also *this,*' he waved a piece of paper, 'will be of interest to you, I'm sure.'

Like a man clinging to a lifebuoy in a freezing sea, Laurence felt numbness encroaching upon his body.

His vision was misted. His head was spinning. Disbelief and dismay overpowered him. 'On Sunday, you say?' He tried to focus on the first photo. When the clouds lifted from his eyes, he found he was staring at an image of a man having anal intercourse with a long-haired woman, who was on all fours on the floor beside a bed. There could be no mistake: the man was Scott. In the second photograph, Scott with his right hand was whipping the blurred outline of a cane down towards the long-haired woman's inflamed bottom, while with his left hand he was masturbating. In the third photograph, Scott was holding the kneeling woman in front of him by her hair, as he ejaculated over her face. Then there was the piece of paper: 'For services rendered, I owe ...' Stunned, Laurence handed the photographs back to Baldini.

'It's not nice, eh?' Baldini said. 'You should not see this film. Nobody should see this film. Nobody *is* seeing this film, unless ...'

'Point taken, Signor Baldini.' Laurence shook his head. He thought of Claudia and his eyes watered. 'Just ... just tell me where and when you want me to examine the painting, and I'll be there.'

'Please take note,' said Baldini, 'that the film is my insurance policy. It is necessary for my peace of mind. If the painting is a forgery or sells to someone other than you, then I will claim on my insurance. Which means I shall expect your client to refund the downpayment of 750,000 dollars, and if he doesn't – well, need I spell out the consequences to your friend? *È chiaro?* I'm personally sorry I am having to do any of this, because I like you, Signor Spencer.' *Bloody bastard,* thought Laurence. 'Is it possible for you to examine the painting tomorrow?'

'Yes.'

'*Buono*. The painting is at Castello di Montezano, so may I suggest you drive there early in the morning with an ETA of approximately 09:30. Is that okay for you?'

'Yes, that's fine by me. By the way, Signor Baldini, I haven't told you this before, but I won't be able to authenticate the picture single-handedly. It will be necessary to carry out certain ageing and verification tests, for which I don't have the equipment or the know-how. I will therefore need to bring a professional authenticator with me. The man I have in mind is Filippo Casti. He was with us at the Badia. I don't think you were introduced. Do you have any objection to his coming along as well?'

'No. If you need Signor Casti, then bring him. But please make sure he keeps his mouth shut.'

As if from a long way off, Laurence heard himself say, 'Signor Baldini, one thing still troubles me. When we were returning from your lunch party, we encountered some unpleasant people on the hillside, who seemed keen to shove us off the road into the valley below. I wonder, was that little escapade your responsibility, by any chance?'

'No, Signor Spencer, of course not. Why would I want to do such a thing? I *need* you. It's a ridiculous suggestion! No, I believe the people responsible were my former colleagues, Gennady Alexandrov and Jacopi Malavasia. It was their handiwork. They tried to kill you, because you want to buy the painting. They also tried to kill Signor Pennington for the same reason. Then, when they failed on both counts, they stole the painting!'

'What has become of them?'

'I don't know,' said Baldini, lying through his glittering teeth. 'What is important is that the painting is here, and you are examining it tomorrow.'

* * *

When he got back to his apartment, Laurence wanted to tell Claudia that he was always there, if she needed his help or a shoulder to cry on. He rang her number, but there was no answer. He then rang Roberto at his office and, taking care to be unspecific, told him he had been to the meeting they had talked about on Monday, but he did not think anything of use had come of it. Even so, Roberto was welcome to drop by later to hear what had been discussed. Roberto thanked him and said he would call round at 18:30.

At just after 18:15, Laurence went through from his bedroom to the drawing room, where he sat down to await Roberto's arrival. Paolo came in and asked him if he wanted anything – tea, coffee, drink.

'No thank you, Paolo. I'll have something when Signor Mattioli is here.' As Paolo was on the point of leaving the room, Scott's voice could be heard in the passage outside. He was asking where Signor Spencer was.

'He's in here, signore,' Paolo said and stood aside to let Scott enter. 'Signore, you like a drink?'

'Er, yeah, please, Paolo. I'll have a bour—'

'Scott,' Laurence said brusquely, looking up from the magazine he was reading, 'I'm expecting Roberto

Mattioli here any minute. Would you mind taking your drink to the study and reading a newspaper or something for about twenty minutes? We can talk after Roberto has gone.'

'Yeah, sure.' *Laurence's frosty this evening,* thought Scott. *Maybe he's getting fed up with having me around.* The thought that Laurence might know about his perverted carryings-on with Francesca hadn't occurred to him.

'Bourbon on the rocks, signore?' asked Paolo.

'*Sì, grazie.*' The doorbell rang. Paolo handed Scott his drink and they went out of the room together. A few moments later, Paolo showed Roberto in.

'Ah, Roberto!' said Laurence. 'Fancy a drink?'

'Yes, thank you. I'll have an Aperol Spritz.'

'Sit down, old chap. I'll have my usual G & T please, Paolo.' Roberto and Laurence made small talk, while Paolo prepared and dispensed their drinks. When he had left the room, Laurence unbuckled a large smart watch from his wrist and said to Roberto, 'I've told you about this thing before. It doesn't just tell you the time and what your heart rate is. It has a "Record and Playback" facility as well. Sound reproduction is excellent, but volume level is rather low. If I put it in the centre of this table, we should both be able to hear what's going on. If you can't hear something and want me to replay part of the recording, just let me know.' Laurence touched the face of the watch. Baldini's tone of voice was unmistakeable. '*Buongiorno,* Signor Spencer. It's good we have this painting ...' Roberto listened intently. He did not ask Laurence to replay anything. When they came to the point where Baldini said, 'I had hoped we wouldn't reach this point,' Laurence paused the recording. 'What Baldini is about to say concerns my friend, Scott, who you know, and amounts to blackmail. It also indirectly involves your daughter, who I admire greatly. I would have preferred to delete this bit, but unfortunately, if I had done so, what follows wouldn't have made much sense. So I must insist on your assurance that you will *not* repeat what you're about to hear to *any*body.' Laurence said this with all the forcefulness he could muster.

'Signor Spencer, I'm in your debt for all the help you are giving us in this matter. I am not about to dishonour your wishes. I promise, therefore, on my daughter's life, that I will *not* repeat what I am about to hear.'

Laurence touched the watch face again.

'… you have to play ball – otherwise we will *ruin* your friend … On Sunday … Signor Lee did some bad things with Francesca … You will be as surprised as I am that he treated her so badly … Anyway, we filmed the proceedings and here are some screenshots from the film … Nobody should see this film … Nobody *is* seeing this film, unless … The film is my insurance policy …'

As he listened, Roberto was having difficulty containing his emotions. Alternately, he would clasp his hands to the sides of his neck and drop his head or sit bolt upright with his hands on the table and his mouth open. At the conclusion of Laurence's recording, he burst out, *'Madre di Dio*, Signor Spencer! This Scott, your friend, who my daughter said she was fond of and wanted me and my wife to get to know better, he's *un bastardo completo*!'

'Signor Mattioli! Really! I understand your feelings, but—'

'Okay, I'm sorry. I respect your position. But tell me, Signor Spencer, tell me about the photos from this film. Do they show Scott – how do you say – *abusing* this woman?'

'Yes. The woman by the way is Francesca Maruichi. She was at Signor Baldini's lunch party.'

'Yes, I know. I was introduced to her. Do any of the pictures show Scott ... *beating* her?'

'Yes, one of them shows him caning her. Why ... why do you ask?'

'You are not aware, Signor Spencer, that Signorina Maruichi is dead? She was *beaten* to death. It was in today's paper.'

You cannot possibly be suggesting that Scott—'

'No, I'm not. The report said she was *very* severely thrashed and battered and that several people were involved. Obviously, Scott was set up. Even so, I'm wondering why, when he had a partner that most men would give their eyeteeth for, he found it necessary to go with another woman, particularly one who he must have known was connected to the Mafia, and then to use her for his own warped pleasure. One can only question his judgement, his sense of priority, his ... his morality. Now we know he has feet of clay, I'm *glad* that Claudia has got rid of him, although I have to say I'm worried he may persuade her to see him again, so that he can deal out the same rough treatment to her. I am trusting in you, Signor Spencer, not only to make sure he doesn't bother her, but also to persuade him to return without delay to New York where he belongs. He would certainly be wise to go, because he was with Francesca Maruichi on Sunday and she died, according to the pathologist, on Monday afternoon.' Looking tired and dejected, Laurence remained silent. 'I see you're as upset as I am, Signor Spencer, and I regret having to speak as I have done. I ... I am anxious not to get things out of perspective here and to sound ungrateful. Your recording helps us immensely. It adds to our case against Baldini and his cronies, because, although such recordings are not accepted as permissible evidence in court, we can confront Baldini with the tape at the optimum moment and hopefully extract a confession from him. You have done a fantastic job so far. It's just a pity that our concerted effort to entrap Baldini has had the side effect of revealing Scott in his true colours. Anyway, enough of that. You're seeing the portrait tomorrow, so can I expect you to email me with a suggested bid price sometime in the evening?'

'Yes, *if* we reach a decision about the painting's authenticity. Do you want to take this recording with you? I have another more traditional watch I can use instead.'

'No, no, you hang onto to it, for the time being.' Roberto got to his feet. 'Well, Signor Spencer, I'll be going. I apologise if I've distressed you by expressing strong views about Scott. He and Claudia were together for five months and my daughter was quite taken with him. Everything I've said about him must be viewed in that context. Don't bother to get up. I'll find my own way out.' Roberto left. Shortly afterwards, Paolo came in and asked a tired-looking Laurence whether he was all right.

'Yes, thank you, Paolo, everything's fine. Do you think you can let Signor Lee know that I'm free to talk to him now?' Paolo went out and a few minutes later Scott appeared.

'Okay if I grab myself another drink? I've just been into the kitchen and Paolo's busy cooking us a great-smelling *tagliatelle bolognese*.'

'Yes, a real Italian *bolognese*.'

'Another G & T for you?'

'No thanks. Scott, there's something I have to have a word with you about, so I think you'd better sit down and hear me out.'

'My, this sounds vaguely ominous.' Scott, with bourbon in hand, lay back on the chesterfield. 'I feel as I used to at college,' he drawled, 'when, having gotten into some scrape or other, I was ordered to report to the principal's study.'

'Did the head man still beat students in your day?'

'Yeah, sometimes. Why do you ask?'

'Do you *agree* with beating?'

Sitting upright, Scott looked askance and turned pale. 'B ... beating? Do I agree with ...? No, no. Again, why d' you ask?'

'Well, for good reason. Your meeting with Signorina Maruichi last Sunday was caught on camera.' Scott gasped. 'I've seen some of the stills from the film. In one of them, you were filmed caning the wretched woman, while ...' Laurence's voice trailed off.

'I … I don't know what to say. I … I'm totally ashamed of what happened. I just can't understand what came over me. It's as if I lost all reason and became a … a brute. You see, I went to the meeting ostensibly to help you. Francesca said she knew something that could be of use to you in your business, and I … I told you what that was on Sunday evening. The problem was that she would only give me the details, if (a) I signed an IOU—'

'For $25,000, yes, I know – Baldini showed it to me.'

'—and (b) I had sex with her, not just once but several times. Each time, after we had finished, I received an additional piece of information. I should have left at the outset, I know that. I should *never* have gotten involved, I realise that now, but I was too … too weak-minded. The truth is, I rather fancied her. I wanted to—'

'Scott, I'm not interested in hearing how or why you failed those who once had a high regard for you. What I am concerned about is the diabolical situation you now find yourself in. Signorina Maruichi, as you know, worked for the Mafia, so it's hardly surprising to find that the video of your assignation with her is in Baldini's possession. It could not be in worse hands.'

'Yeah, but what is he up to? Why did he show you the IOU and the screenshots as well? Why didn't he show them to me? What does my regrettable liaison with Francesca have to do with *you*? If he wants to blackmail anyone, it's *me* he should be aiming his sights at, surely?'

'No, he's used your wretched indiscretion to get at me. As I've told you, the Raphael portrait is not the only item for sale in the transaction between Ouspensky and Baldini. When, in a vain attempt to find out more about the arms and plutonium that are involved, I unwisely threatened not to examine the portrait or otherwise to declare it a fake, Signor Baldini hit me, so to speak, with the video of you and Signorina Maruichi. After that, there was no question but that I had to toe the line. I'm just hoping the painting isn't really a fake!'

'Gee, Laurence, I'm so sorry. I've been such a fool. I mean, if there's any way I can make it up to you ... I feel so wretched. I just really wanted to help you. That, as I've said, was my motive for going to Francesca in the first place. Can't I—?'

'My best advice to you, Scott, is to get out of Florence while the going's good. I'll be all right, don't you worry! It's good of you to consider me, but I have Paolo to look after me. You must get back to your business in New York.'

'Why can't I stay on for a while and try to be some sort of assistance to you?'

'You're obviously not aware that Signorina Maruichi is *dead*, are you?' Scott looked at him in disbelief. 'Yes, she's dead. She was *beaten* to death. Apparently, she died on Monday afternoon – and you saw her the day before. If the police find that out, you'll have a lot of explaining to do and be put in a very embarrassing position. I think the best thing you can do is get on a plane for New York tomorrow.'

There was a knock on the door, and Paolo entered. 'Signori, it is dinner. You prefer I bring it in here?'

'No, Paolo, thank you. We'll have it in the dining room. Incidentally, Paolo, Signor Lee will be returning home tomorrow.'

CHAPTER 17

Friday 30 August

Before departing for Baldini's on Friday morning, Laurence left a note for Scott, who was still in his room.

Scott, I've gone off to examine the Raphael portrait. Paolo has left you some croissants and coffee in the kitchen. I'll ring you in New York this evening and let you know how I get on. Please don't think I'm chucking you out. For you to go back now is the best course, I'm sure of that.

Kind regards,

Laurence

Setting off at 08:30, Paolo drove Laurence to Castello di Montezano. There were no delays on the way, and they arrived at 09:15. Parked in the driveway was a black van with the words *'Filippo Casti, Autenticatore e Restauratore'* painted in gold on the side.

An effusive and smiling Baldini met them under the pillared entrance porch and, having taken Paolo to the kitchen and asked the cook to serve him some breakfast, he showed Laurence through to the study, where the *Portrait of a Young Man* was displayed on an easel. In the room, there were three Carabinieri, each with a black submachine gun dangling by his side. Beyond the French windows, two more similarly armed Carabinieri were patrolling. Filippo was sitting in one of the red velvet armchairs, with an assortment of carrying cases and containers ranged about him on the carpet. Mario and Giovanni were on guard beside the door, with pump guns at the ready. 'I am leaving you now. I will make sure nobody disturbs you. If you want anything, just ask Mario or Giovanni. They'll be waiting outside. Signori, I wish you *buona fortuna*!' He, Mario and Giovanni left the room, closing the doors behind them.

'Is not easy working beneath pressure,' remarked Filippo, as he knelt down to open a case.

Laurence, who had become energised by the challenge that lay ahead, smiled. *This man,* he thought, *has a way with English!* 'I'll look the painting over,' Laurence said, 'then I'll leave it to you to carry out the usual tests.' Laurence's task was to determine the work's authenticity by evaluating its appearance, content and style. While Filippo unpacked various items of equipment, including a worktable, a laptop, a high-powered camera microscope, a laser pump-probe microscope and an infrared camera, Laurence studied the portrait from about two metres away. His initial impression was that it needed cleaning, due to the discoloration of the varnishing, but was otherwise in good condition. The painting was a masterpiece of chromatic as well as plastic symmetry. Remarkably, the removal of part of the sitter's right hand, which had resulted from the cutting off of a centimetre-wide strip from the left-hand side of the painting, had not ruined the proportionality of the composition. Noticeable, too, was the use of sfumato, the smooth and almost imperceptible transition between one colour and another that Raphael had learnt from studying Leonardo's paintings. Laurence thought, *There's also a particular kinship to the Mona Lisa: in each case the sitter is portrayed in a relaxed three-quarter length pose and appears calm, elegant, graceful, self-assured; the eyes are swivelled leftwards, following the observer as he moves about the room, and the smile is fascinatingly enigmatic. I wonder, did Raphael the convivial, courteous, good-humoured lover of women purposely paint a feminine-looking man to contrast with Leonardo's ostensibly masculine-looking woman?*

However, there was no Leonardesque chiaroscuro in the portrait. Instead, as in many of his later paintings, Raphael had covered large areas of the picture plane with saturated colours. There was also the heavier impasto in the flesh areas that he used from about 1510 onwards. The luminosity of the sitter's face and hands kept them in balance with the vivid surrounding hues, creating a pure and uniform tonal harmony. There were some small cracks and minor paint losses in the impasto, but the remainder of the paint layer was in near perfect condition.

Laurence was in seventh heaven. There were so many facets to marvel at: the subtle hatching in the shadows in the nostrils and between the thumb and forefinger of the left hand; the deep-cut nails of the thumbs, which had been painted very precisely, probably as a finishing touch; the brilliantly executed billowing sleeves of the white chemise; the richness of the gold and brown ocelot-like cloak, which had the appearance of being thrown over the left shoulder on impulse; the diagonals formed by glimpses of the cloak's dark blue lining; the gorgeous green-gold of the table covering; the long, wavy, slightly frizzy hair breaking away from the temples and streaming down onto the shoulders; the right forearm and hand resting nonchalantly on the edge of a table; the smooth round face that seemed to gleam in the light; and the lifelike womanish eyebrows and soft brown eyes.

In comparison with these achievements, there were one or two parts of the painting that seemed less distinguished. The view of a pale blue sky and sparse landscape through the window and the border on the right-hand side – indeed, the background generally – had probably been executed by an assistant, possibly Giovan 'Il Fattore' Penni. In the last years of his life, Raphael accepted so many commissions that he had to delegate work to members of his busy workshop.

Who had sat for the painting? Clearly, by his appearance, an Italian but not a professional man. Was he a friend of the painter? Was he a poet, perhaps? Alternately, could it have been one of Raphael's girlfriends, who he mischievously dressed up as a man? There was, after all, the tiniest hint of a bosom under that cloak.

Laurence approached the easel, gently took hold of the painting and turned it round. As some warping had occurred, the panel had a slight convex curve. Although darkened with age, the back, which had a rough surface, did not appear to have been damaged or restored. However, the right-hand edge looked newer than the other three edges, which indicated that, at some stage, the portrait had been cut down on that side. In addition, three strips of wood of more recent vintage had been secured horizontally across the back, in order presumably to prevent any further warping.

Intense excitement overtook Laurence. He felt in his bones that this was an original work by the artist, who, more than anyone else, epitomised the High Renaissance style. Laurence was aware that objective and scientific authentication tests had yet to be carried out; even so, he needed no convincing that what he held in his hands was a largely autograph work, which was painted some three or four years before Raphael died on Good Friday 1520, worn out from overwork. He turned the painting round to the front again and put it on the easel. 'Filippo!' he said, delightedly. 'I've finished. Your turn now!' Filippo, who had by this stage assembled an impressive array of machinery, looked up from the computer he was busily programming. 'Signor, you are looking like a little boy who is having big surprise in his Christmas sock! I believe you are thinking picture is genuine – I am right, no?'

'Let's say, I shall be surprised if it's not. Anyway, I leave it to you with your equipment to prove the case, one way or the other. Elated I may be, but I also feel quite tired – I didn't sleep much last night – so I'm going to sit down over here and take a breather. Give me a shout if you want any help.'

'Okay, I'm doing the business.' While Laurence removed his jacket, flopped into an armchair and tried to relax, Filippo took the portrait from the easel and went over to his worktable. As a first step, he briefly considered the panel. Solid and weighty, it measured 72 centimetres high by 56 centimetres wide by three centimetres thick and was made from a single piece of wood, which had been sawn tangentially from the tree trunk. From experience, Filippo judged that the panel was made of poplar wood, which was often used as a support by sixteenth-century Italian artists, including Raphael. As tree-ring growth in poplars is erratic and therefore an unreliable guide to age – in dry years new rings are not often formed, whereas in years when there are late frosts or fungal outbreaks two rings may be formed – Filippo did not attempt to date the panel.

Next, having placed the painting on his worktable, Filippo opened a case and took out a hand-held, high-powered UV lamp, which he plugged into the mains. Sitting upright and watching his every move, Laurence may have been tired, but he was too excited to rest. Filippo asked one of the Carabinieri to close the curtains and another to turn off the lights. While they were doing this, he put on a pair of protective goggles. When the room was dark, he switched on the lamp, and the ultraviolet fluorescent tubes gave off an eerie blue light. Filippo passed the lamp methodically over the surface of the painting. The appearance of dark spots would have indicated that a restorer had recently filled in areas of paint loss. However, as there were no such spots, clearly the painting had not been the subject of retouching for at least 75 years, which meant that for most of that time it must have been kept in store rather than hung on a wall. Instead of dark spots, Filippo was pleased to see a brownish green tinge, which signified that old paint and varnish were fluorescing, a phenomenon that cannot be faked. The portrait was not a forgery, of that he was almost certain.

At Filippo's request, the lights were turned on again. His next objective was to make an X-radiograph of the painting, and with that end in mind he went through various steps. From one of the boxes that surrounded him, he produced a sizable piece of foam rubber and two sealed golden-coloured envelopes, which each contained a top-quality X-ray plate. He spread the foam rubber on the floor at the far end of the library. He placed the envelopes end to end on top of the foam rubber. With great care, he laid the painting face down over the envelopes. Alongside the painting, he positioned a device consisting of a metal tube with an arm that could be moved up and down a large black pole on a stand. Attached horizontally to the arm was a green cylinder, inside which was an X-ray tube. Having set the tube laterally over the painting at a distance of about three-quarters of a metre, he flicked a switch on the side of the tube and a column of light shone around the painting. Twisting the tube slightly and manipulating the shutters inside, Filippo transformed the diffuse beam into a rectangle which matched the shape of the painting almost exactly. Satisfied that the X-ray tube was lined up correctly, he switched off the light. He positioned a large mobile screen behind the X-ray machine. Having stood well back from the screen and signalled to the Carabinieri to do likewise, Filippo pressed the operating switch at the end of a cable that was attached to the machine, and there was a muffled buzzing sound of about three to four seconds in duration. Pushing the frame and the machine to one side, he gently picked up the portrait and put it back on the easel. He collected the golden-coloured envelopes and took them to his worktable, where he turned on a low-intensity red light. He made another signal and the main lights were switched off. Casting a monstrous shadow as he stood at the table, Filippo opened one of the envelopes, took out the plate and inserted it in a state-of-the-art high-speed processor, which he switched on. Forty seconds later, he took out the developed radiograph and put it on one side. Having repeated the operation with the other X-ray plate, he called for the lights to be turned on. He held the two plates, one above the other, up to the chandelier in the centre of the ceiling. The impression he received was of a greyish white haze, in which it was just possible to discern the faint, ghostlike outline of Raphael's sitter; a stronger white showed in streaks and blotches in the areas of the face, the neck, the arms and the hands. One or two darkish spots indicated paint losses in areas where the paint layer was thick, such as the face and table cover. The radiograph was not particularly revealing, because the painting had been primed with a consistent layer of lead white, which absorbs X-rays and blocks the blackening of the film. However, this was not the disaster it might seem.

It was Raphael's practice to spread over the bare surface of a panel a preparation consisting of a compact gesso ground, which, when dried, would be covered with four or five coats of the smoothest size available, with each coat being allowed to dry before the next was laid. He applied the layers of glue plentifully, so that they were not completely soaked up by the ground but formed thin films on its surface. He would then have overlaid the ground with a priming of lead white and a little oil, which he would have beaten with the palm of his hand, until it was thinly and evenly distributed.

Filippo was confident that a priming layer of the sort that Raphael would have used had been applied to the panel support of the portrait. To make sure, he took out a large ring-file, in which there were plastic wallets containing radiographs of other works by Raphael, including *La Belle Jardinière*, *La Donna Velata*, *Canigiani Holy Family*, *Small Cowper Madonna* and *Madonna of the Meadow*. He compared these with his radiograph and noticed how uncannily similar and consistent was the way in which the artist had used lead white to highlight the flesh areas in all the paintings. The affinity of the misty images was such that Filippo felt he was well on the way to acknowledging that the painting was by 'Raffaello Urbino'.

He inserted each of the new radiographs into a wallet and closed the file. He went over to the easel again, took the portrait and laid it on his worktable beside a powerful (x50 magnification) digital microscope with a long arm that reached out over the painting. He proceeded to scrutinise the paint surface centimetre by centimetre and found, as expected, azurite or copper carbonate both in the green or verdigris pigment of the table cover and the landscape and in the blue or ultramarine of the sky. Tiny specks of azurite were also present in the cloak, where the brown colour in places probably resulted from a mixture of verdigris, brown ochre, lead-tin yellow, lead white and a little carbon black. On examining the areas where paint losses had shown up on the radiograph, Filippo found that tiny flakes had peeled from the impasto on the face and neck and the thick paint on the table cover: a minor problem that could be easily remedied by some expert retouching.

Filippo replaced the digital microscope, which he switched off and packed away, with a polarising microscope. He was on the point of using this instrument when Baldini came into the room. He was accompanied by Mario and Giovanni, who were carrying heavily laden trays. 'I am thinking you may be hungry,' Baldini enthused, 'so chef is making you *una pranzo leggero*, something nice. There's a little *affettati misti*, some *linguine con salsa di spinaci*, and – er – what's this, Mario? I've forgotten.'

'*Saltimbocca alla Romana*, boss.'

'*Sì*, this is good. Chef is also giving you *Gorgonzola Montagna*. This is good, too. To drink you have Vernaccia and Chianti, or, if you prefer water, there is Acqua Panna and San Pellegrino. Mario, Giovanni, please put everything over here, on this table.' He indicated a rococo Louis Quinze escritoire. 'Signori,' he said, turning towards Laurence and Filippo, 'we will leave you, so you can have your meal in peace. Also, you no doubt have things to discuss between you. *Buon appetito!*'

'Thank you, signore,' said Laurence. 'It's kind of you to think of us.'

'It's my pleasure,' Baldini said, with his customary smile. He and his sidekicks left the room. Filippo and Laurence sat down and, as the former tucked into his meal and the latter ate without much enthusiasm, they discussed how the morning's work had gone, although at times Laurence found it difficult to understand the drift of some of Filippo's comments.

Sure in his own mind that the portrait was genuine, Laurence was pleased to learn that Filippo so far had no reason to doubt that they were dealing with a sixteenth-century work of art, which could quite possibly be by Raphael.

After about half an hour, Mario and Giovanni came in to clear the dishes. Filippo and Laurence got up from the escritoire. 'Better I am 'aving my nose in the sharpener again,' Filippo announced.

Forbearing to smile, Laurence asked, 'How much longer do you think you'll be?'

Filippo looked at his watch. 'I am thinking maybe is possible we are finishing here at 16:00.'

'Well, in that case, I'll let you get on with it. Don't forget: let me know if you need a hand. I'm going to write some letters.' Each sat down: Filippo at his worktable, Laurence at a writing desk near one of the French windows.

Filippo turned on the polarising microscope and, looking into the eyepieces, delicately scraped a tiny sliver of paint from the right-hand top edge of the portrait with a scalpel. He placed the sliver with a pair of tweezers in a drop of Canada balsam on a slide, which he overlaid with a cover slip. Analysis of the cross-section revealed, from the bottom upwards: a gesso ground; a fine brownish band of animal glue; a thin priming of lead white mixed with a little oil; a delicate pink underpaint consisting of lead white and red lake pigment; a blue paint containing, beside lead white, azurite in the lower part and ultramarine in the upper part; and a layer of discoloured varnish. He took a photomicrograph, which he developed in the processor. He referred to a file containing copy photomicrographs of cross-sections taken from skies in other paintings on panel by Raphael and compared the photomicrograph of the cross-section from *Portrait of a Young Man*: there was no doubting the similarities.

Buoyed up by ever-increasing conviction, Filippo set about his final and lengthiest task, which was to discover if there was an underdrawing on the priming layer of the panel. He packed the polarising microscope away and from another case brought out an infrared scanner, which he positioned so that the scanning arm was at the right-hand edge, and spanned the length of the portrait. He switched the machine on, and a motorised optical head consisting of a lens, a photodiode and an illumination system began to move at a snail's pace from the bottom to the top of the arm. When the head eventually reached the top, it moved to the left a couple of centimetres and then made its laborious way down the arm, and so the scanning progressed painstakingly. Meanwhile, signals from the photodiode were being received by an analogue-digital converter and assembled by Filippo's software into a high-quality digital reflectogram on the computer monitor. When the scanning was completed some three hours later, a photo-plotter produced, on transparent film, a 1:1 scale copy of the reflectogram, which Filippo scrutinised carefully.

Raphael often drew a full-scale preparatory sketch or cartoon of his chosen subject, which he or one of his assistants subsequently transferred to the priming layer of a canvas or panel by one of two methods: a stylus was pressed heavily along the lines or else pricks were made at intervals and charcoal tapped or rubbed through the resulting perforations. On other occasions, he tended to draw directly onto the priming layer. No incised lines or punch marks were revealed by the reflectogram of the portrait. Instead, it was clear that the underdrawing had been sketched, in an arbitrary yet confident manner, directly onto the priming layer, without the aid of a cartoon. The fine, precise lines of the eyes, nose, mouth and thumbnails, which were probably executed with pencil or charcoal, and likewise the elements of spherical drawing in the head, contrasted with the relatively broad and thick lines of the cloak, the cap and the sleeves, which appeared to have been sketched by brush with raw umber. The impression gained was of a fluid, even casual, almost shorthand style, which mingled angular, rather awkward brushstrokes with quick-spirited, sketchy lines. A few alterations, or *pentimenti*, could be observed. The angle of the right arm, the positioning of the eyebrows and of the left thumb and forefinger, the shape and extent of the fur cloak on the left shoulder: these the painter had obviously had second thoughts about and changed slightly. Otherwise, there were no major modifications and the final painted forms were closely based on the underdrawing.

Filippo took out a file of wallets containing reflectograms of paintings by Raphael, one of which was of particular interest: that of *The Ecstasy of Santa Cecilia*, which, on completion in 1517, was originally set up as an altarpiece in the chapel dedicated to the patron saint of music in the Church of San Giovanni in Monte, Bologna.[7] The style of the underdrawing

---

[7] Now in the Pinacoteca Nazionale, Bologna.

bore a striking resemblance to that of *Portrait of a Young Man*. There was the same mixture of thin, precise lines with thick, broad brushstrokes. There was a comparable freedom and fluidity about the preliminary outlines. Unquestionably, the same artist sketched both underdrawings.

'Signor Spencer,' Filippo called out, 'is finished. Normally, I am wanting to take many photos and test samples *in laboratorio*. But here I am being very happy with position.' Laurence had come over to the worktable. 'Signore, I am having certainty, like egg is egg, Raffaello Sanzio is designing and painting this picture, though is possible some minor details are being completed by *assistenti*.'

Laurence smiled and extended his hand. 'Jolly good job, Filippo, under,' he looked round at the Caribinieri, 'difficult circumstances!' They shook hands. 'So we have a real Raphael on our hands.'

'*Sì,* signore. Is missing dis picture for 75 years. No person is seeing it *in galleria* for 80 years.' Filippo could hardly contain himself. 'Is *fantastico*! Never am I touching painting like this. Is beautiful, is *molto importante*!' He put his forefinger up to his lip and whispered, 'Is incredibly valuable, signore! But we are keeping this under the hat, no?'

Laurence nodded. 'I think we should tell Signor Baldini the good news, don't you?' He strode over to the door, waving aside the Carabiniere who was in his way. He opened the door and said, 'Would you kindly tell Signor Baldini that we'd like to speak to him? Thank you.'

A few minutes later, Baldini came into the room

with Mario and Giovanni, who were again armed with pump guns. '*Si,* signori, you want to see me?'

'Yes, Signor Baldini,' said Laurence. 'I'm pleased to tell you that Signor Casti has successfully completed the usual authentication tests, and both he and I agree that the portrait is a genuine work which was designed and almost entirely executed by Raphael. There are one or two minor background details which were probably painted by one of his assistants.'

'This is good news. *Very* good news. I am happy for you, Signor Spencer, because, assuming yours is the highest bid for the painting, I will no longer need my insurance cover. Next week, I shall get the item that concerns your friend Signor Lee from the bank and give it to you, I promise.'

'I'm glad to hear it. But, Signor Baldini, what guarantee have I that you will keep your word? If I give you my sealed bid now, how do I know that next week you may not change your mind and decide to keep the film?'

'Because I always keep my word. Isn't that so, Mario?'

'Yes, boss.'

Mario's brief acknowledgement was hardly the ringing endorsement Laurence was looking for. The problem was that if he insisted on withholding his bid until he received the film, he would be stopped from leaving the building. He'd probably be placed under lock and key. In the process, he wouldn't exactly endear himself to Baldini and his gang.

'Well,' he announced, 'I will take your word for it, Signor Baldini. So, all that remains is for me to give you my sealed bid.' Laurence sat down at the escritoire, produced a pen from his inside pocket, took a sheet of writing paper from a red-leather papeterie, and wrote:

TO WHOM IT MAY CONCERN

I, Laurence Spencer, of Spencer Galleries, Mayfair, London, hereby confirm and certify that, on behalf of my client, I am empowered by him to offer the sum of $85,000,000 (eighty-five million US dollars) for the painting Portrait of a Young Man by Raffaello Sanzio, as seen and authenticated by Signor Filippo Casti and myself at Castello di Montezano, Poggibonsi, today, Friday the 30th of August.

[Sgd] Laurence Spencer

He folded the sheet and was on the point of putting it in an envelope, when Baldini said, 'Signore, you have given the bank details of your client?'

'Oh no, I forgot!' Laurence opened his attaché case, which was on the writing desk, and took out a small diary. Referring to a particular page, he unfolded the sheet of writing paper and wrote down the relevant details. 'Incidentally, the account is under a fictitious name. My client is a recluse and doesn't want anyone to know his name,' he said. He refolded the paper and inserted it in the envelope, which he then licked and sealed and handed to Baldini. As he stood up, a sudden wave of dizziness came over him and, staggering slightly, he put the palms of his hands on the desktop for support.

'Are you not feeling well?' asked Baldini, anxiously.

'Shall I send for some water?'

'No, no, thank you. I'll be fine. I'm just a bit tired, that's all. It's been a long day and I really need to go back home and get some rest. Can you please call my driver?' While Mario left the room to fetch Paolo, Laurence spoke to Filippo. 'Old boy, you've been fantastic. I can't thank you enough for all your hard graft and the time you've put in on this today. Don't forget to let me know what I owe you. Better still, come round and see me and we'll have dinner together. I'll speak to you next week, and we'll arrange a time. Goodbye, dear friend, and thank you again.' They shook hands. 'I'm sorry Paolo can't stop to help you load this stuff onto your van. I ... I *have* to get back. I hope you understand.'

'I am understanding perfectly, signore, and I am hoping soon you are straight as rain.'

* * *

When, weary but jubilant, Laurence got back to his apartment, he found that his note for Scott was exactly where he had left it, on the small boulle table in the hall. He went to the green room and knocked on the closed door. 'Scott, are you in there?'

'Yes, c ... come in.' Laurence entered the room and found Scott in bed. He looked flushed. 'Sorry, I ... I realise you were expecting me to be outta here by now, but I'm afraid ... I'm afraid I woke this morning with one helluva headache and a pain behind the eyes, both of which I've still got, and I reckon I'm running a temperature. When I got up to go to the john, I didn't feel right – a bit muzzy and unsteady on my feet. I think I may have gotten the flu.'

'Do you want me to call a doctor?'

'No, no. Waste of time and money. He'll probably put me on antibiotics, which'll cost a lot and do nothing to help. No, let me rest up and who knows, I may be okay tomorrow. If you have anything for a headache, like aspirin or paracetamol, I'd be glad if you'd—'

'Yes, of course dear chap. I'll go and find you something straightaway.'

Later that evening, after he had barely touched the dinner Paolo had prepared for him, Laurence sat down, switched on his computer, clicked on 'Outbox' and typed the following email:

From: Laurence Spencer

To: Roberto Mattioli

Subject: Licinio Madonna & Child

Without Prejudice

Dear Mr Mattioli,

Having now had an opportunity to examine the Madonna and Child, as requested, I am writing to advise you that in my considered opinion it is an autograph painting by Giovanni Francesca Bezzi (known as Il Nosadella), which it should be possible to secure, at auction, with a maximum bid of $90,000.

Yours truly,

Laurence Spencer

Laurence clicked on 'Send', shut down the computer,

got to his feet and again staggered. He felt dizzy and uncoordinated. *I do hope I'm not going down with something. Maybe I've caught the same bug as Scott has,* were his thoughts.

CHAPTER 18

Saturday 31 August

The next morning Laurence woke short of breath and with a bad headache. On getting out of bed, he felt faint and nauseous. Also, his leg and abdominal muscles ached. He called Paolo.

'*Sì*, signore?'

'Oh Paolo, I'm going to stay in bed today. I think I may have caught the same bug as Signor Lee has. Do you think you can get me the paracetamol? I gave it to Signor Lee yesterday, so it should be in his room.'

'*Sì*, signore. When Signor Lee is up, I'll ask him for it.'

'If that doesn't do the trick, we'll have to go and see the doctor.'

'Signore, if you want me to take you, just say so. Now would you like me to bring you some breakfast?'

'Just coffee and hot milk please Paolo. And some mineral water. Thanks.'

* * *

Claudia woke early, as usual, and went and had a bath. As she lay soaking, she realised she had not had sex for a whole week. When she got out of the bath, she stood naked with her legs slightly apart in front of the full-length wall mirror, her brunette hair falling onto her shoulders. She ran her hands across her wet breasts and stomach, down her sides, over and around her buttocks and hips to rest on the soft dark-haired mound between the tops of her thighs. As she surveyed herself, a mischievous thought occurred to her. What about looking in on Giuseppe and, if he's awake, offering to make him some tea – but if he's asleep …? She quickly dried herself, put on her silk kimono and went from the bathroom to the door of Giuseppe's room. Charily, she turned the door handle and peeped in. Giuseppe was lying on his side facing the door, with one leg sticking out from under the single sheet that covered him. Unknown to her, he had only just fallen into a deep sleep, after tossing and turning for most of the night. Claudia went and knelt by the bedside. She lifted the sheet. A half-smile came to her face, as she focused on his genitals. She leant forwards – but then she thought better of what she had in mind. There was always the risk that he might wake, and she certainly didn't want that. In view of her stern admonition that Giuseppe should not try to make a pass at her, it would be too embarrassing for words if he awoke to find her with his prick in her mouth. She did not want to give him the idea that she was easy. No, *he* had to make the first move. He had to seduce *her*, not the other way round. Then, only then, would she discover whether he had the sexual drive to satisfy her … over and over again.

As far as men were concerned, Claudia remained resentful and angry. Scott's betrayal still rankled, so much so that she wanted to take out her irritation on the male species. Giuseppe happened to be there, ripe for the picking. She would *use* him for her own ends. She would avail herself of his body, until he dropped. Then she would find other men and drain them, too.

She got to her feet and quietly left the room.

* * *

Overnight, the paracetamol that Scott had taken eased his fever and his headache. Consequently, when he woke up, he thought he was feeling better, but on going to the bathroom he became dizzy. He felt nauseous and his joints and muscles ached. After urinating and washing his face and hands, he became disorientated and had difficulty in finding his bed.

A few minutes later, there was a knock at his door. 'Come in,' he said.

The door opened and Paolo appeared carrying breakfast on a tray stand. 'Signore, *buongiorno*! I thought you might like some coffee and croissants,' he said, placing the stand on the bed in front of Scott. 'Signor Spencer needs to take some paracetamol. Can I help myself to some tablets?'

'Yeah, sure. But why? What's the problem with Signor Spencer?'

'He has the flu like you.'

'And he's in bed, as well?'

'*Sì,* signore. It is strange you and Signor Spencer are not feeling well at the same time.'

'Yeah, it is. Paolo, just take the paracetamol. It's in the bathroom. And tell Signor Spencer I'm hoping to get together with him today some time. It's not as if it's very far to go. Then we can have a chat and a laugh and commiserate with one another about our being laid-up. The only problem is I … I'm not feeling too healthy …' He attempted to get up, but dizziness overcame him and he fell back onto the bed, narrowly missing the tray stand. 'Paolo, about my seeing Signor Spencer today, I'm not sure I'm going to make it.' He got back into the bed.

'Signore, you like I call the *dottore*?'

'No, Paolo, thanks,' Scott said, pulling the duvet up to his neck. 'I'm going to get some shut-eye. I need to rest. With any luck this goddamned bug is the 24-hour variety and will be history by tomorrow.'

* * *

With Laurence's sealed offer safely to hand, Baldini spent half an hour on Saturday morning calling the other likely bidders.

'Signor Mattioli?'

'*Si, pronto.*'

'It's Luca Baldini here, with some exciting news. The Raphael portrait has been authenticated by Signori Spencer and Casti. They confirm that the main part of the painting is by Raphael's own hand. The background and one or two minor details were evidently completed by a pupil. Anyway, Signor Spencer has given me his sealed bid, and I am wondering whether you are still an interested party and, if so, when you will be able to let me have your bid. I should add that I'll be coming into Florence this morning. I'll be at the Hotel Belcari in Borgo Pinti from 11:00 to 14:00.'

'I'll bring my bid round to you personally.'

'Good. I look forward to seeing you later. Don't forget to bring your client's bank details. *Ciao!*'

Baldini made three further calls. The first was to Lombardo, who also said he would bring his bid round to the Hotel Belcari. The second was to Vincenzo Carducci, whom Mafia associates in Rome had introduced to Baldini as a likely bidder for the painting on behalf of a Swiss client. As Carducci had meetings to attend all day in Milan, he said his sealed bid would be delivered by his colleague, Manfredo, who with any luck should arrive at the Hotel Belcari before 14:00. Failing that, Manfredo would drive on to Castello di Montezano, if Baldini could kindly provide directions on how to get there.

Baldini's third call was to Pennington. Arnoldo answered the phone.

'*Pronto!*'

'May I speak to Signor Pennington, please.'

'Who is it?'

'Luca Baldini.'

'Ah, Signor Baldini, I'm afraid HG has had a death in the family and is not speaking to anyone on the phone at the moment. He did say to me, though, that if you rang, I was to tell you he's no longer interested in bidding for the painting.'

'Well, that *is* a disappointment, particularly as I was calling him to tell him the painting has now been authenticated, and I'm inviting people to let me have their bids today. Do you know *why* he is no longer interested?'

'No, I haven't a clue,' lied Arnoldo.

'May I suggest you tell him what I've just told you. If he changes his mind, he can bring along his offer today to the Hotel Belcari in Borgo Pinti, where I'll be from 11:00 to 14:00. Otherwise, he must get the offer to me at Castello di Montezano by 17:00 at the latest, when bidding closes. Is that understood?'

'Yes, but I'm quite certain HG won't change his mind.'

'You know, it seems odd to me that at the last minute he – or rather his client – should have this extraordinary change of heart. All along, Signor Pennington's involvement has been most enthusiastic. It makes no sense that he should drop out now – unless his client has gone bust or something.'

'As I said, I don't know anything about it. I'm not privy to his clients' decisions.'

'Never mind, I'll find out the reason in due course, don't you worry. Incidentally, what's your name?'

'Arnoldo. I'm HG's secretary.'

'Okay, Arnoldo. Do be sure to give HG my best regards. *Ciao!*'

He put down the phone and turned to Mario. 'You know where Pennington lives?'

'Yeah, boss, I do.'

'Well, after you've dropped me off at the Belcari, I want you to go round to his place and say that you have a gift from me. HG is for some reason keeping out of our way, and I wonder what his motives are. His secretary, Arnoldo, will probably answer the door. If he does, grab him, take him somewhere – I suggest the Amafi – and beat the shit out of him, until he tells you why HG is no longer interested in bidding for the painting. I noticed this Arnoldo guy has a funny way of speaking – he *sounds* like a filthy faggot – so establish whether he and HG are buggering each other. That sort of information always comes in handy. Depending on what you find out, you either dump Arnoldo back at HG's or whack him. I mean, if the lowdown he gives you puts HG in our pocket, shoot him up the arse! It'll only be poetic justice, after all.'

'Okay, boss, whatever you say. Now hadn't we better get started, otherwise you're never going to make it to the Belcari by 11:00.'

'Shit, yes,' said Baldini, looking at his watch, 'you're right. We need to make a move. Better ask Giovanni to get the Maserati out. I'll be with you in a minute. I have to go upstairs to get my case and say goodbye to Caterina. Tell Giovanni we haven't time for one of his sightseeing trips, so I'll be driving.'

Mario's eyes looked heavenwards. He recalled that when Signor Baldini last took the wheel, he narrowly avoided causing the mother of all autostrada accidents *and* was caught on camera travelling at over 225km/h. 'Okay, boss.'

Thirty-two minutes later, after a drive that scared his two minders out of their wits but otherwise passed without incident, Baldini parked his white Maserati Quattroporte in Via della Colonna. It was 10:55. 'In another life I would have made a successful racing driver, don't you think?' Ashen-faced and white knuckled, Mario and Giovanni nodded without much enthusiasm. Baldini took his attaché case from the boot and locked the car with the remote control. 'See me into the Hotel, both of you – then, Mario, you and a couple of the boys go round to HG's place, as discussed. Giovanni, you stay with me.' The three men crossed over the road, turned into Borgo Pinti and made for the Hotel Belcari.

* * *

At about the same time, in Piazza d' Azeglio, Claudia was working at her computer, when Giuseppe came into the room wearing a towelling robe. Looking embarrassed, he mumbled, 'Sorry, I overslept.' Claudia looked up and, allowing herself the momentary thought of what was under that robe, smiled and said, 'You had a busy day yesterday. You must have been tired.'

'I was, but I had a restless night and didn't go to sleep for hours. Anyway, I'll get dressed and come and help you. I won't be a minute.'

'There's no need to rush, Giuseppe. Take it easy. It's Saturday. We can do some work this afternoon. You'll find coffee and croissants in the kitchen, butter, milk and jam in the fridge. Just help yourself.'

'Thanks. In that case, I'll grab a cup of coffee – can I get you one, too? –' Claudia smiled again and shook her head, 'and then take a quick shower.'

Later, when she heard the sound of the shower, Claudia visualised the steaming water running down the tall, lean, fair-skinned body and its succulent appendage. If only … *What* has *got into you?* she asked herself. *You're behaving like a besotted schoolgirl. Pull yourself together! Why, only a week ago you were having sex with a man old enough to be Giuseppe's father. Now you're mooning around, because this young fellow has a big dick! You really should grow up!* Madre di Dio, *you have many more important things to think about than Giuseppe's bits and pieces. Get on with your work and leave it to him to make the first move — if he wants to, that is, and isn't too reticent. Just to ensure he does show some interest …*

Claudia got up from the desk and went into her bedroom. She removed her kimono and put on a pair of silk panties, a red silk mini dress and high-heel sandals. She leant forwards and brushed out her long hair, which, when she stood upright again, she flicked behind her shoulders. She paraded in front of the full-length mirror, turning from side to side. *That should whet his appetite,* she thought. *By the end of the day, he'll be positively panting for it!*

* * *

After a late lunch and before setting out for Poggibonsi, Baldini made a telephone call from his car. 'Signor Ouspensky, it's Baldini … Just to let you know we've received four sealed bids for the painting and, although bidding doesn't close until 17:00, I think it's unlikely there'll be any more bids. If you come over at about 18:00, we can consider the offers, decide how to proceed and then maybe have some dinner. The second shipment has arrived safely, so I'll have some more money for you as well … See you later then. *Ciao!*' Mario slid in beside Baldini in the back seat. Giovanni was in the driver's seat. 'Okay,' Baldini said, tapping the big man's shoulder, 'let's go!' He turned to Mario. 'So, what did you find out about HG and his little faggot?'

'Quite a bit, boss. When this Arnoldo guy saw us three standing at the door, I can tell you he was fit to shit in his pants. I mean, he was unbelievably cooperative. I just had to suggest to him that if he valued his miserable existence, he'd better tell us why HG's no longer interested in bidding for the painting – and, damn me, if he didn't spill the beans there and then.' There was a pause. Mario said nothing more.

'Well?' asked Baldini. 'What *did* he have to say?'

'Nothing very useful, as it happens, boss. Basically, HG is being blackmailed. He was sent a copy of a video showing him doing nasty things to the late lamented Francesca Maruichi. There was a note attached that advised him to withdraw from the bidding for the painting, otherwise copies of the film would be mailed to his wife, his partners, his main clients, and anybody else who is likely to take a dim view of his weird behaviour.' Mario paused again.

'So … have HG and his poofter friend any idea who the blackmailer is?'

'They thought it was *you,* boss. Maruichi worked for you, so they assumed you must have had the idea of filming her and HG together.'

'That's fucking stupid! I want HG—'

'I already told him, boss. You want HG to bid for the painting. Why on earth would you blackmail him into doing the opposite? It doesn't make sense.'

'The Maruichi woman probably made the film herself. I gave her a handycam – it must have been about nine months ago – because I wanted her on the odd occasion to seduce a business associate or a Commune official, who I needed to put the squeeze on, and film them screwing. However, I never asked her to film HG indulging in his nasty habits. No, *she* must have decided to film the two of them together – why I have no idea. When … when did HG actually receive the odious video?'

'Wednesday morning, boss.'

'Well it's possible, I suppose, that she mailed the film to HG early on Monday morning, before she had the pleasure of meeting you and the boys. But why, if she decided to blackmail HG after all this time, didn't she take him for some big ones?'

'Maybe she wanted to get back at you in some way, boss.'

'No, no, I don't think that's it. *She* wouldn't have sent HG the video and the blackmail note. She must have given them to someone, who has a personal stake in seeing that HG doesn't enter a bid for the painting. There's only one person I can think of who not only had contact with Signorina Maruichi immediately prior to her unfortunate demise, but also knows about the sale of the Raphael – and that's Signor Lee.'

'Of course, boss. It must be him. But why?'

'He probably wants to narrow the odds in favour of his friend, Signor Spencer, who, as you know, *is* a bidder. Lee no doubt has a copy of the video – he's presumably put it in a safe place – and there's not much we can do about it. I mean, there's no point in beating the shit out of Lee, because that would upset Signor Spencer – and I like Signor Spencer.'

'We could always kidnap Lee's woman, boss,' Giovanni interjected. 'She's so hot, we'd *love* to bang *her* brains out. Primo would be in his element!'

'What, and upset another bidder, her father, Signor Mattioli? Don't be so *fucking* idiotic! No, we'll just bide our time. When this business with the painting is over, I'll ask our friends in New York to pay a call on Signor Lee – and I can tell you, when that mob's finished with him, he'll wish he'd never been born!'

'By the way, boss, just for good measure we bashed the poofter to a pulp and left him there in the apartment. We thought it might be difficult for HG to explain why his little friend's body was lying drenched in blood in the middle of his floor.'

* * *

By the afternoon, the temperature had climbed to 40°C and the sun blazed in a clear blue sky. North east of Florence, among the dark trees on the hillside below Fiesole, a wedding reception was in full swing at the Hotel Landini, which had been booked for the day by the bride's wealthy American parents. Normally, in the summer months, such functions are held in the Hotel's terraced gardens, where guests can enjoy an astounding view of Florence. However, the American couple, whose daughter had been married at midday to an Italian computer analyst in the Church of San Martino in nearby Maiano, were mindful of the mosquito menace. Sensibly, as they thought, they had decided that the reception for 150 people should be held inside the former fifteenth-century monastery, specifically in the Barzagli Bar, which in ancient times had been the monks' refectory, and in the adjoining Etruscan Sala da Pranzo, a long, corridor-like room overlooking the gardens. It had also been decided that all the windows in the Hotel should be closed. On such a hot day this decision proved to be a heavy imposition on the male guests, who wore morning dress, and the female guests in their suits and hats. With so many people crammed into such a confined space, it was not long before condensation appeared on the windowpanes and the air conditioning system began to malfunction. Perspiring guests took off their coats, and eventually, to general acclaim, a plump red-faced man with a sodden shirt and wet, straggly hair opened the six tall arched windows that lined one side of the Dining Room. To more cries of approval, someone else opened the windows in the Barzagli Bar. A slight but refreshing breeze rippled through the two rooms, and people returned to their meal of Beluga caviar on buckwheat blinis, *linguine con salsa di aragosta*, *costata alla fiorentina,* and assorted desserts and fine cheeses.

The bride's father was on the point of rising to make his speech of welcome, when the brightness outside faded, and there was a shrill, piercing, scalp-tingling sound that grew louder and came closer and closer. Suddenly, darkness descended upon the Hotel, and in through the open windows of the Dining Room and the Barzagli Bar burst millions upon millions of different species of whining, ravening mosquitoes: so many, in fact, that millions more were unable to gain access and formed a huge cloud outside. The rooms filled with a dark, swirling, predatory mass of insects. Incredulous and horrified guests rose and flailed their arms about their heads. The plump red-faced man, who had got up too late to shut the windows, was engulfed by a swarm of wolfish Banded Foul Waters and Woodland Pools. Overwhelmed, he fell back onto one of the tables, which split in two and, emitting dreadful choking sounds, was simultaneously suffocated and bitten and within eight minutes sucked dry of his blood. What had been a happy group of friends and acquaintances was transformed into a heaving throng of frightened, panicking humanity. The amity, cordiality and laughter were replaced by ill will, boorishness and foul language. In their effort to leave the Dining Room, either through the doorway or by the windows, insect-smothered people yelled at one another to get out of the way, men pushed whimpering women to one side, confused old ladies and children were shoved onto the floor and trampled underfoot, and the bridesmaids had their white chiffon dresses torn and bloodied. Those who managed to elbow their way outside were inundated by a tidal wave of mosquitoes, which the scent of blood issuing from the Hotel had made even more murderous. Person after person fell, forced to the ground by the onslaught of overpowering assailants.

Inside, the bridegroom's sweet, inoffensive, 78-year-old grandfather, whose face and balding head were being scythed into by a thousand stylets, careered about blindly until he collided with the wedding cake and fell face first into a pyramid of unfilled champagne glasses. The bride had her long train stamped on by several guests at once, and the jolting effect was such that her flimsy white silk-organza dress was ripped from her body, and she stood alone in a corner, in her veil and white silk bra, panties and stockings, attempting to ward off the ever-increasing attentions of large, sharp-set Alaskans and Southern Salt Marshes. Her struggle did not last long: overcome by the sheer weight of numbers, she collapsed onto the floor, where soon her white undergarments turned red with her own blood. The bridegroom, having been swept from the room on a human tide, managed to fight his way back in. When he found his wife of three hours, he knelt in tears beside her body and did not attempt to protect himself against the insects, which, squirming all over his body, lanced him so viciously that, when they had finished and moved onto another victim, his copper-toned skin was perspiring blood.

Despite having to run the gauntlet of the huge cloud of mosquitoes outside the building, some twenty of the guests, including the best man, and three members of staff managed to dive into the swimming pool that had been built into the hillside above the Hotel gardens. In the Dining Room and Barzagli Bar, thirteen other people survived by being covered by the dead or dying. Here and there legs and arms twitched as bodies were slowly drained of lifeblood. When there were no more accessible humans to assail, the invasion force gradually disbanded, and an unearthly silence encompassed the desolate building.

* * *

In the mid-afternoon, Laurence woke from a restless two-hour sleep. Feverish and weak, he had a feeling he was going to be sick. He got out of bed, tried to walk, but was unable to do so. His muscles were so seized up he had to crawl on his elbows into the bathroom. There he managed to make it to the lavatory bowl before throwing up several thick globs of yellowy slime. When he had finished, he dragged himself back into the bedroom. On the small table beside the bed was an intercom. He pressed the call button.

'*Si,* signore. You have a problem?'

'Yes, Paolo. I'm not feeling at all well. I need to go

to the doctor.'

Later, having been driven to and from the local surgery by Paolo, Laurence went back to bed. According to the doctor, he had influenza B and should stay in bed, get plenty of rest, drink lots of fluids and take aspirin and/or ibuprofen.

* * *

At 18:25 Ouspensky was shown into the Library at Castello di Montezano by Mario. 'The boss will be with you shortly. He's asked me to offer you something to drink. We have champagne on ice, if you'd like some?'

'Thank you, Mario. That would be most agreeable.' Mario left the room, and while he was gone, Ouspensky examined a fine, early calfskin-bound edition of Dante's *La Vita Nuova*, which he found in one of the bookcases.

'Ah, Signor Ouspensky, I see you're interested in books.' Baldini had come into the room with Mario, who was carrying a bottle of champagne in an ice bucket. 'I'm interested in them, too – purely as an investment. I don't read them and, of course, I don't buy them myself. I – er – "borrow" them from clients.'

'Which, of course,' said Ouspensky, 'is infinitely preferable to having to pay for them! After all, book collecting is an expensive pastime – particularly if, as I do, one collects first editions of Russian writers such as Tolstoy, Dostoevsky, Turgenev, Solzhenitsyn, etc.' He returned the *Vita Nuova* volume to the bookshelf. 'Well, Signor Baldini, talking of things Russian, I'm longing to know how much my contacts in Moscow have been offered for this Raphael portrait.'

'Yes, so am I.' Baldini pulled out a chair from the escritoire and beckoned Ouspensky to sit down. 'Have a glass of champagne, and we'll find out.' Baldini sat down opposite Ouspensky, unlocked a drawer in the desk and took out a folder, from which he removed four white C5 envelopes. Meanwhile, Mario poured the champagne. 'Your health, Signor Ouspensky.' They touched glasses and each took a sip of the Louis Roederer Cristal Brut 2002. Ouspensky approved. 'That's good. Very silky and fresh. The Russian stuff doesn't begin to compare!'

Baldini opened one of the envelopes. "'I, Laurence Spencer, of ... blah-blah-blah ... hereby certify that ... blah-blah ... I am empowered by him to offer the sum of ..." How much did you say your contacts were hoping for?'

'About 75,000,000 dollars.'

'Well, your contacts have no cause for complaint. Signor Spencer has offered *85*,000,000 dollars – and as he clearly knows his business and represents an extremely rich client, who has given him a free hand in the matter, I would guess he has put in the highest bid.'

'85,000,000, yes, that should bring a smile to their faces!'

Baldini opened a second envelope. "'I confirm that I am authorised ... blah-blah-blah ... my client has funds at ... blah-blah ... and is prepared to offer 50,000,000 dollars ... blah-blah-blah ... signed G.S. Lombardo." Well, we can certainly rule *him* out!'

'Lombardo? Isn't he the person connected with the Uffizi?'

'Yes, he's the manager of their publishing division.'

'Who's he bidding on behalf of?'

'Cavatini, you know, the fellow who was tried for stashing away millions of taxpayers' money while he was Prime Minister.'

'But wasn't he acquitted?'

'Yes, but members of the jury – how shall I put it? – knowingly enriched themselves by finding him not guilty! Apparently, temptation was thrown in their path by some of Signor Cavatini's friends. Disgusting, isn't it?' With a bigger and more dazzling smile than usual, Baldini opened a third envelope. 'Now, who do we have here? "This is to confirm that I, Manfredo Carducci, of... blah-blah-blah ... am acting in this matter on behalf of ... blah-blah ... who authorises me to offer the sum of 80,000,000 dollars", etc., etc. A strong offer, but not strong enough, I fear.'

'Made on whose behalf?'

'A Swiss banker, who wishes to remain anonymous, probably because he's using the bank's profits to buy himself an interesting painting – or he thinks the Raphael portrait will make a useful addition to the bank's collection of art stolen by the Nazis in the last war! Anyway, let's see what's in the last envelope.' This time Baldini read the contents quickly to himself, looked up in amazement and said, 'Well fuck me! Signori Mattioli and Belori have *outbid* Signor Spencer! They've offered *90,000,000*! That's incredible!'

'*90,000,000*? *Blin!* They're the two who were briefly at your lunch party, am I right?'

'Yes. They recently set up in business together, and are acting for a Munich businessman called Günther Engel.'

'Do we know whether this Engel has the money to make such an offer?'

'Well, Signor Mattioli confirms here that the necessary funds are held in a special foreign currency account at Banca Nazionale. Of course, we'll check out the bank references. Mario?'

'Yes, boss.'

'I believe we have passwords and access codes for Banca Nazionale in Rome, don't we?'

'Yes, boss.'

'Well, do a spot of hacking, will you, and find out whether these references are genuine?' Baldini handed Mario the letter from Roberto Mattioli. Mario glanced at it.

'It'll take me a couple of minutes, boss.' Mario left the room.

'Useful chap,' Ouspensky observed.

'I wouldn't know what to do without him,' said Baldini, truthfully. 'Incidentally, while he's busy and before we get round to discussing the second shipment, I wonder if I can just raise the question of my commission. When we first discussed the matter, I believe we agreed that in respect of the total amounts paid for the two shipments and the portrait, I should receive 2.5% and 7.5% respectively.'

'That's correct.'

'Well, I'm happy about the commission payable for the shipments, which, after all, the organisation will be selling on at a profit. However, when you and I agreed these terms, I had no idea it was going to be such a hassle arranging the sale of the portrait. I mean, we had to chase halfway round the world to get the bloody thing back from Malavasia and—'

'Yes, but you *were* supposed to be looking after the paint—'

'Not personally. I entrusted that job to others, who unfortunately made a botch of it! Besides, I've had sweeteners to pay out. There have been unlooked-for expenses, as I've said, and obviously I'm going to have to give Malatesta something – and Mario and Giovanni.'

'What new terms do you have in mind?'

'I want 10% of the sale price of the portrait.'

'So how much are we talking about altogether?'

'Commission of 9,750,000 dollars on the sale of the painting and the plutonium, i.e. 2,250,000 more than originally agreed. I'm happy to settle for a flat 9,000,000. Are you in agreement?'

'My contacts will *kill* me!'

Baldini smiled. 'Then you're in a quandary, my friend, because if you don't agree to pay me 9,000,000, *I'll* get someone to kill you!' Mario came back into the room. 'Ah, Mario! Did you—?'

'Yes, boss. This Engel man is good for 120,000,000 dollars. An instruction attached to the account says, "Possibility all or part funds will be withdrawn shortly by banker's draft."'

'When was the account set up?'

'Two weeks ago.'

'Signor Ouspensky, are you happy?'

'Yes, sure. Of course, it's a pity that, with so much money in the Engel account, Signor Mattioli didn't bid more for the picture! It's interesting, isn't it, that he offered just 5,000,000 more than Signor Spencer? Do you suppose the two of them were in cahoots?'

'No, no way. Signor Spencer wanted his own client to have the portrait, once he had proved its authenticity, so he would hardly have advised Signor Mattioli to put in a higher bid than his own, now would he?'

'No, I suppose you're right. It *is* extraordinary, though, how close their bids are.'

'The point is the winning bid, on behalf of a client who we know has the wherewithal, was put in by Signor Mattioli, so I'll ring him later and arrange a time for him to come here to hand over his banker's draft and collect the painting. Now, if we might deal with the shipment of the plutonium critical mass, which was checked into our warehouse yesterday: Mario, could you get the 1,000,000, please!' Mario left the room.

'*1,000,000*? We agreed a price of 10,000,000 dollars for the plutonium, surely?'

'Yes, but I'm taking my commission on the sale of the painting as well as on the plutonium.'

'But what if for some reason Signor Mattioli doesn't pay up?' Ouspensky had begun to sweat.

'Too bad!' Mario came back into the room carrying a large holdall. 'Now, do you want the 1,000,000 or not?'

Later, when Ouspensky, to his relief, had driven

away intact from the Castello with the holdall, Baldini took Mario by the arm. 'I'd like to reward you and the boys for the help you've been giving me. But tell me something: you're not all still worn out after your exertions with the Maruichi woman on Monday, are you?'

'No, boss. I think we've all recovered from that by now. Primo, I know, is raring to have some more fun. He believes it's a shame we had to waste Maruichi so soon. He'd much rather we'd been able to keep her around for a couple more days, so that we – or ideally he – could get to know her better! You know, boss, he's a fucking sexual athlete, that man, nothing less.'

'As I say, I have a little treat in store for you, so I suggest you, Giovanni, Primo and the others go now to the stables – you know, the brick building that stands to one side of the large meadow.'

'Okay, boss.'

'By the way, how many of you are there all together?'

'Seven, boss – not including the *soldati*.'

'No, I don't want the *soldati* involved. Just you seven go to the stables and wait for me.'

'Sure, boss.'

Baldini's enforcers had been standing around on the straw-strewn floor of the derelict stable block for about quarter of an hour, when they heard a voice outside saying, 'Baby, you won't believe the stallion I've got in here for you.' The main door opened and Baldini entered with his arm wrapped around the diminutive Caterina, who was barefoot and wearing only her nightie. 'Gentleman, I think most of you already know Signorina Ricci. Well, I promised to give her a stallion for her birthday. Primo, come and introduce yourself!' A dark-suited giant of a man stepped forward. 'Caterina, baby, I think you'll find Primo's *hung* like a stallion. That'll have to do!' He thrust her at Primo, who caught her in his huge hands. He was more than half a metre taller than her. Baldini turned and started to walk towards the door.

Her brown eyes wide with fear, Caterina said, 'Darling, I don't understand. Why are you doing this? What have I done wrong? Please, *please*, don't leave me here with these ... brutes!'

Ignoring her and before going out through the door, Baldini said, over his shoulder, 'Guys, she's an informant. She's been passing vital information to the AISE. Give her the Maruichi treatment, will you!'

* * *

'I'm beat, and my feet are killing me,' exclaimed Claudia, throwing herself onto the sofa.

Having enjoyed a leisurely dinner at Il Leone Dilagante, she and Giuseppe had returned to her flat at 22:15. Before going out, they had worked, for about six hours, on their plans for setting up the Centre. Claudia had been pleased and impressed by Giuseppe's dedication – despite the distraction of her short dress. He, for his part, had endeavoured to concentrate on the promotional material he was preparing, but he could not help taking the odd surreptitious peek at Claudia's long legs as she walked about the room or, when she leant over the table and the top of her dress fell forwards, the soft skin of her full, firm breasts. When they looked at each other as they talked, he imagined how it would feel to kiss those soft moist lips and slide his tongue past the flawless teeth that lit up her frequent smiles.

Claudia plonked her calves on the arm of the chair in which Giuseppe was seated. As she did so, her dress rode up and revealed her silk panties. 'Can you be a darling and undo my shoes. I can't wait to get them off.' Giuseppe had never before been confronted at close quarters by a woman's bare feet. Nervously, he undid the buckles and removed her sandals. 'Can you rub my feet? They're sore.' Giuseppe kneaded the balls and arches gently enough, but in a detached, embarrassed way. Claudia wondered whether she might not be wasting her time. 'That's ... that's fine,' she said, swinging her legs back onto the floor. 'You're not very talkative tonight, Giuseppe.'

'Yes sorry, I'm quite tired,' he said. 'I ... I haven't been sleeping too well. Would you mind if I went to bed?'

'No, no, not at all. I think I'll go as well.'

She was on her way out of the room when he said, plaintively, 'Are ... are we not going to wish each other "goodnight"?'

Claudia turned. 'Yes, of course we are.' She came over to him and was stretching up, as if to peck him on the cheeks, when he grabbed her by the back of the neck and kissed her hungrily on the mouth. Claudia tried to push him away, but he was too strong. Gradually, she succumbed to the insistent pressure of his lips and was on the point of responding, when he broke off as suddenly as he had begun.

'All day I've been fantasising about kissing you,' he exclaimed. Then he put his hands to his forehead. 'I'm sorry. I know I shouldn't have done that. It's just ... it's just that my feelings for you ... they're difficult to control. I find you *so* attractive, *so* clever! And I ... I can't stop thinking about you. And there's ... nothing I can do to change the way I feel. Please forgive me. I've let you down, badly. Tomorrow, I'll ... find somewhere else to stay ... I'll ...'

Claudia held his face in her hands. 'Shush, silly boy! I don't want you to leave. You're much too good a worker, and besides, I think we should make the most of a golden opportunity, don't you?' She reached for his mouth and they kissed passionately. Then she dropped to her knees. Passing her hand over his crotch and the thickening ridge in the front of his trousers, she looked up at him, her eyes shining, and smiled the smile of a girl who knows that, on unwrapping her present, she'll find just what she wants.

CHAPTER 19

Sunday 1 September

Laurence had an appalling night: alternately shivering with cold and burning with fever, he was racked by nightmarish visions of a Raphaelesque portrait of Baldini grinning from ear to ear with blood dripping from his razor-sharp teeth. Taking short and irregular breaths, Laurence began to cough – a hacking, rasping cough. Reaching for a glass of water, he knocked over the lamp on his bedside table. He called out, in between coughs, 'Paolo!' He called again. 'Pao – lo!'

Paolo came running into the room. '*Sì*, signore. You're having problems?'

'I'm not at all well, Paolo. Call 118. I need ... to go ... to hospital.'

Paolo rang the Health Emergency number, and a few minutes later Misericordia di Firenze were outside the building. Having been placed on a stretcher and carried from the apartment to the waiting ambulance, Laurence was driven to the Ospedale di Santa Maria Nuova, where he was rushed into the Emergency Department. It was 04:40 in the morning.

* * *

As news of the terrible attack on Hotel Landini in Fiesole filtered through, people from all walks of life poured into Florence's many churches to seek guidance and reassurance. In the open, beyond the security of their houses, flats, hotels and guesthouses, the residents and the tourists scurried along streets that no longer interested them, with their heads down. They dared not linger, for fear of inviting sudden and vengeful attack from the azure sky.

Among the few people not joining in the church-going frenzy was Roberto Mattioli. His and Bellori's bid for the Raphael portrait, he learnt from Baldini the previous evening, had been successful. Baldini confirmed that their client's bank references checked out. He also inquired when Mattioli and his partner proposed to visit Castello di Montezano to hand over their payment and collect the painting. Mattioli's suggestion that they call on him the next day at 18:00 met with Baldini's approval.

During the morning Mattioli made three telephone calls. First, he rang Bellori to say that Baldini was expecting them the following afternoon – but not, he joked, the surprise they were laying on for him. Next, he called the police, the *Polizia di Stato* – not the Carabinieri, whose senior officers he knew included Baldini's contact, General Bruno Malatesta – to request them to provide backup the next day in the form of armed riot police. His instructions were that they should be assembled by no later than 18:45 just outside Castello di Montezano on the road going south to Poggibonsi. Then he called Laurence Spencer's number. Paolo answered, '*Si, pronto.*'

'Can I speak to Signor Spencer, please? It's

Roberto Mattioli here.'

'Ah, signore, I regret to have to tell you that Signor Spencer is in hospital. He was taken ill yesterday morning.'

'Is that Paolo?'

'Yes, signore.'

'Well, I'm extremely sorry to hear about Signor Spencer. Is he very ill?'

'Yes, signore. He is in Intensive Care.'

'*Oh, Santo Cielo*, poor man! I must go and see him. Is it possible to visit him, do you know?'

'Yes, signore, between the hours of 08:00 to 10:00 and 17:00 to 19:00.'

'I'll go to see him today. Thank you, Paolo. I am only too conscious of the enormous help that Signor Spencer has given me, so if there's anything I can do for him or you, please let me know. *Ciao!*'

* * *

Not a churchgoer and normally never conscience-stricken, Baldini awoke in a troubled frame of mind. He had been fond of Caterina, in his fashion. She had catered to his physical needs and been a lively and entertaining companion. He would miss her warmth and her energy, particularly in his bed. However, Malatesta had been told laughingly by a friend of his, who was in the Secret Service and well oiled at the time, that Caterina was passing on important information about Mafia operations to the AISE. There could be no doubt about it.

What discomfited Baldini was that he had not dealt

with her himself.

Instead, he had handed her over to the boys, because he had wanted her to suffer for her disloyalty, the backstabbing whore! But it was he who should have rubbed her out: it would have been kinder. He knew that. After all, she had been his mistress for nearly two years.

As Baldini was eating, without much relish, his usual fibre-rich breakfast, Mario came into the dining room. He looked like a man who had been on a three-day bender. 'Boss, I hope you're okay about what you asked us to do last night, and haven't had second thoughts, or anything like that.'

'Why? Didn't you have a good time?'

'Oh *yes*, boss, but I can tell you, I'm completely knackered! She sure was a feisty little thing. I mean, I had her—'

'Spare me the details! Just tell me the snitching bitch snuffed it.'

'Yes, boss. She sure did. It was Primo who—'

'I don't want to know,' said Baldini, raising his voice.

'Sorry, boss.'

'What've you done with her?'

'Nothing – except cover her body with straw. We're awaiting your instructions, boss.'

'Right, take her in a body bag to Aeroporto Vespucci. Put heavy weights in the bag and get Stefano, or whatever his name is – you know, the fellow who was Malavasia's pilot and now works for us

– to fly you out to sea. Then just dump her into the drink.'

* * *

Feeling better, Scott got up, had a shower, dressed and went downstairs to have breakfast, which Paolo, who had gone out shopping, had left in the kitchen for him.

Taking a taxi to travel the short distance from Piazza della Santissima Annunziata, Scott arrived at Ospedale di Santa Maria Nuova just as the morning visiting hour began. Passing through the swing doors to the emergency area before climbing the bare stone steps that led to the main concourse of the Hospital, Scott had a fleeting premonition of himself being wheeled through the very same entrance on a trolley.

On being shown into Laurence's room, Scott, who had been given a face mask to wear, was shocked to find his friend attached to an intravenous drip, with a tube coming out of his nostril and beside his bed a row of monitors displaying his vital signs. 'Hi there, pal. How you doing?'

Laurence, very pale, raised his eyelids and looked puzzled. 'You … still … here?' he asked, breathing heavily and irregularly.

'Yeah, I'm afraid so. Yesterday, as I trust Paolo explained to you, I was not feeling well enough to visit you. Today I feel better, so I've come to see you before I go back to New York. I'll try for a flight tomorrow. Meanwhile, is there anything I can do for you? Laurence, are you with me?'

During their conversation, Laurence's eyes frequently closed and opened, as he drifted in and out of consciousness. 'Yes,' he said, breathing in rapid bursts. '… I need … to see … Roberto. Can you … can you ask him to drop by?'

'Sure, I'll give him a call – although whether he'll wanna speak to me is another matter.' Scott pointed at the vital signs indicators. 'What's all this about? What's wrong with you, my friend?'

'Waiting … for results … of … blood tests. Did you … manage … to speak to … Claudia?'

'Yeah. I called her on Tuesday evening. I told her how sorry I was to have let her down so badly and tried to explain my loathsome behaviour.'

'And?'

'Not surprisingly, she didn't want to know. She just told me to stay the hell away and never come back.'

'So you see … there really isn't … anything here … for you now. You might as well … leave Florence without further delay.' Laurence's eyes closed and he stopped talking.

'Laurence are you okay?' Scott asked. After waiting a few minutes, he was on the point of ringing for the nurse when Laurence came to. 'Would you like me to call someone?'

'No … no. I … I black out … from time to time. Wha … what was I … saying?'

'That it's time for me to go back to New York.'

'Yes, I'm worried … the police … will cotton on … to your connection with Signorina Maruichi … and suspect you … of … of being implicated in her death.'

Scott touched Laurence's hand. 'But what about you, old buddy? I can't leave you like this. I mean, this may be the last time—'

'Don't … be ridiculous! I … I'm not done for … yet. Stop worrying … about me … and save your own neck.' The effort to speak was making Laurence feel weak. 'I … I'll be … as right as rain … in no time. Now, please … leave! I … I can't abide … protracted … farewells.'

Scott stood up, his eyes watering. '*Addio*, my friend. I'll mi … You're the best pal a man could have, do you know that? I'm not likely to find another like you, that's for sure.' Scott turned on his heel and left the room, with a backward wave of his hand.

On the stone stairs he met Roberto Mattioli, who was just on his way up to see Laurence. '*Mio Dio!*' said Mattioli. 'You're *still* in Florence? Why haven't you gone back to New York?'

'I've been ill.'

'That doesn't surprise me. You've certainly got a *sick* mind.'

'Thanks a bunch. Are you calling on Signor Spencer?'

'Yes.'

'Good. He just told me he wants to see you. But be warned. He's not at all well. You'll find him in Room 31.' Scott continued on down the stairs. Roberto looked after him for a moment, shook his head sadly and then went up to Laurence's room.

'Ah, Signor Spencer! I see they have you all wired up.'

'Yes,' Laurence said, smiling with difficulty. 'I'm what ... you might call ... switched on.'

'But what's all this for? You're ill – but do you know why?'

'No, not yet. Waiting ... for results ... of blood tests. How ... how ... did you ... get here ... so quickly? I only ... just told ... Scott ... a few ...'

'I know. I met him on the stairs. In any case, I had decided to come and see you, because I need to ask you something. Signor Spencer?' Laurence had passed out. At the same time, the vital signs monitor began beeping. Two nurses came hurrying into the room. "I'm afraid you must leave, signore,' one of them said.

'But I have something important to ask Signor Spencer.'

'Well, write it down and, if need be, one of us will read it to him.' And with that she ushered Roberto out of the room, adding, 'Don't forget, we have access to Signor Spencer's mobile, so when someone rings, we ask him if he wants to speak to the caller. If he does, we hold the mobile to his ear or we select the speakerphone.'

Roberto went to Reception and asked for a piece of Hospital paper. He then sat down in the corridor, took out a pen and wrote:

Dear Laurence,

I'm sorry we couldn't continue our conversation today. I look forward to speaking to you again when you are feeling better.

However, there are one or two important things I need to

ask you about, so I trust you won't mind if I write to you in the first instance and then call you later.

A certain person, having accepted our offer and verified our bank references, has agreed to see us at his home tomorrow evening, so that he can receive our payment and hand over the item that is of particular interest to you. We will make sure this item is put in a secure and protected place. Then we will return to a certain person's house with *our* friends, whose intention will be to escort him and *his* friends to a place of safekeeping as well.

What I need to know from you is how I get hold of the item I left with you on Thursday. I assume Paolo is aware of where it's kept. In which case, please can you arrange for him to let me have the item. At the same time, I suggest he lets us know what you want us to do with *your* item.

It remains for me to thank you for everything you've done on our behalf. Without your help, we would not be calling on a certain person tomorrow.

Wishing you a speedy return to good health,

Yours,

Roberto

* * *

After a night of prolonged lovemaking, Claudia awoke at an uncharacteristically late hour. She got up and, as was her habit, switched on her laptop. Her intention was to consult the website of the World Health Organisation for an update on the current number of cases of Dengue, Malaria and other mosquito-borne diseases. Checking first on the emails she had received, Claudia found the following:

From: Ettore, Institute of Ecology, Rome

Subject: Mosquitoes

I think U should check out Fiesole. Something happened there yesterday at Hotel Landini. There's a news embargo in force, but we've heard on grapevine some sort of mosquito attack took place. We've got someone going there 2 investigate. As U're so near, it makes sense U should go 2. Good luck with Advisory Centre, which I hear (again on grapevine!) U're setting up with G's help. (N.B. No hard feelings at this end.) The 2 of U should make a formidable team. I miss U both. Kind regards.

Claudia went into the bedroom. 'Giuseppe, darling,' she said, kissing him on the temple, 'wake up! We have to go to Fiesole, where there was a major mosquito attack yesterday. Can you get up, please, darling, and get ready to go out?'

'Oh, what a pity! I was having such a fabulous dream. It was quite incredible! It felt like it was really happening. I dreamt you were—'

'Tell me later, darling. I look forward to hearing all about it, when we've been to Fiesole. Right now, I'm going to get dressed, and I'd like you to make a move, too.'

'Okay, boss,' he said, springing out of bed, 'no sooner said than done!'

Claudia smiled as she watched his lean, tanned, well-muscled body head for the bathroom. *Last night I certainly taught him a thing or two about sex,* she thought, *but I wonder how much will sink in* – and she chuckled at the unintentional pun.

Giuseppe drove Claudia to Fiesole in his open-top Alfa Romeo. When they arrived at the Hotel Landini, the grounds were cordoned off by police, because there had been some looting of the premises, and they were stopped at the entrance gates. 'Signore and Signorina, I regret the Hotel is closed. No one is allowed in.'

Smiling sweetly, Claudia slid herself out of the low-slung sports car, swept her ruffled hair away from her face and approached the Carabiniere. She handed him a card, which she produced from her handbag. 'Officer, I think my colleague and I may be of some use here.' The Carabiniere looked at the card and then at Claudia, who was wearing a stunning short, figure-hugging emerald-green chiffon dress and matching high-heeled sandals.

'Of course, *Dottore*.' He gave her back her card. 'Please proceed. I hope you find some solution to this dreadful mosquito problem.'

'We'll try, believe me. Thank you, officer.' Claudia slid back into the passenger seat, and they motored through the open gates and along the short driveway to the hotel car park, where, sadly, there were automobiles that would never again be driven by their former owners. Outside the Hotel, there was frenzied activity. Paramedics were stretchering bodies to waiting ambulances. Television cameramen and news reporters from all over the world were busy recording the scene and recounting the story of the bride and bridegroom whose nuptials ended in such tragedy. Relatives of guests at the wedding were rushing from one group of people to another trying to establish what had happened to their loved ones. Harassed policemen were endeavouring, without much success, to keep the situation under control.

The distressing process of dealing with the dead had been going on since late Saturday afternoon. The task of identifying each body, once it had been photographed in situ, was not made any easier by the fact that there was no wedding guest list available. Most of the people staying at the Hotel were identified from photographs in passports that had been left at the front desk or by their identity and credit cards. In respect of wedding guests who lived locally and members of staff, identification was a matter of course. Such was not the case with wedding guests who had no form of identification on them and came from abroad or from outside Florence. Once identification *was* established, relatives had to be contacted, commiserated with, advised that the deceased was being taken to the Cimitero della Misericordia on the other side of Florence, and asked what their instructions were for the disposal of the body. The procedure of transferring corpses in two ambulances from the Hotel to the Cemetery – a ten-kilometre journey – was laborious. By the time Claudia and Giuseppe arrived, all the bodies outside, which were at the mercy of the heat and the flies, and some 40 of the bodies inside had been cleared.

Giuseppe opened the car boot, took out Claudia's sports bag and slung it over his shoulder. They walked, hand in hand, into the Hotel and presented themselves at the reception desk, which was manned by three policemen. 'Hello, I am *Dottore* Claudia Mattioli of the Mosquito Advisory Centre in Florence, which is sponsored by the Commune di Firenze.'

Putting on her spectacles, she continued, 'This is my colleague, Signor Giuseppe Corti. We're here because we assume there must be a great many dead mosquitoes around, both on the remaining bodies and in the rooms where the attack took place. We would like permission to take specimens to establish which species were involved, whether there were any that had abnormal features and, if possible, why they carried out this attack.'

'Please, go ahead, *Dottore*,' said one of the policemen. 'By all means, see what you can find out.' As Claudia and Giuseppe made their way to the dining room, the policeman added, 'By the way, *Dottore*, there's already somebody here carrying out the same sort of examination: Zorro or Zorba I think he said his name was.'

'That must be Professor Zobi,' Claudia said to Giuseppe, 'the Institute's northern representative. I've never met him before.' In the dining room, they were stunned by the sight that greeted them. The floor, the windowsills, the mantelpiece, the tables that had not been upturned and the serving trolleys were covered in dead mosquitoes, many of which had been squashed messily. Scattered about the floor in pools of dried blood were some 25 human bodies, most of which had been identified and examined. In one corner, however, seemingly ignored by everybody, lay the bride and bridegroom where they had fallen. Although the police were keen to investigate the circumstances surrounding their deaths, no one so far had disturbed their tragic union. The fact that the bride had on her veil, bra, panties, stockings, shoes and nothing else was the subject of considerable speculation. For instance, the story going the rounds amongst foreign journalists was that the bridegroom, a red-blooded Italian, had, in a fit of unrestrained lust, ripped off the beautiful American bride's dress with the intention of consummating their marriage there and then, but unfortunately the mosquitoes intervened.

'Giuseppe, can you collect as many specimens that haven't been squashed as you can find, while I have a look at the bride and try to discover the extent to which she was attacked by the mosquitoes.'

Giuseppe removed a pipette and a specimen jar from the sports bag and began to crawl around on the floor. Claudia took out a large 40x magnifying glass, went over to the corner of the room and crouched, as decorously as her short dress allowed, beside the bride's heavily bloodsoaked body. Peering through the glass, she found the girl's blood had issued from deep pinhole lacerations that had been made not only where the skin was bare, but also where it was covered by her underwear and stockings. All over her torso, there were squashed mosquitoes, many with their fascicles still inserted in the skin, and hundreds of red weals. Lifting the bridal veil, Claudia found that the once pretty face underneath was puffed and blotchy, and set in an expression of pained desperation. Protruding from the inner corners of the wide-open and anguished pale blue eyes were the body parts of several large insects. In between the swollen lips and the parted rows of perfect white teeth was a mouthful of Alaskans. The tongue was red and bloated. There were other species sticking out of her blood-spattered nostrils and her swollen ears.

What if this had been me on my wedding day? thought Claudia, her eyes watering.

'Excuse me, signorina, but I hope you're not disturbing the body in any way.' Claudia looked up to find a senior officer of the Polizia di Stato standing beside her. She got to her feet.

'No, officer, I haven't touched it at all.'

'May I ask you to identify yourself and to tell me, please, why you're examining the body.'

Claudia showed him her identity card, told him what she was doing and added, 'I wanted to establish whether the mosquitoes that attacked this poor lady caused her to bleed so much.'

'And what have you found out, *Dottore*?'

'That she was literally a living pincushion. Thousands upon thousands of mosquitoes pierced deeply with their mouthparts into her blood vessels *without* – and this is the most unusual feature – sucking her blood. They did not feed on her. They let her *bleed*! In other words, she was pricked to death, and her attackers seem predominantly to have been members of the Alaskan species, some of which look as if they were at least a centimetre-and-a-half long.'

Giuseppe came over to them. 'Claudia, can I borrow that for a moment?'

He pointed at the magnifying glass, which she handed to him. 'I think I've spotted something important. I'm just going to have a closer look at one or two of the specimens, and then maybe, when you're free, we can have a word.' He looked at her meaningfully and walked away.

'Sorry, *Dottore*,' said the policeman, 'I'm keeping you from your work. What you were telling me, though, is appalling. I mean, if I understand you correctly, you believe the mosquitoes that carried out this attack intended to kill these people.'

'Yes, that's correct. Mosquitoes are the deadliest enemy we face in the world today – and it seems they have embarked upon a full-scale war against mankind.'

'But why?'

'I have my theories, but they're not for public consumption – at least, not for the time being. Let's just say that climactic changes caused by global warming have upset the natural course of things. Now, officer, if you'll excuse me ...'

'Of course, *Dottore*. Thank you for your time.' The policeman went out of the room.

Claudia walked to where Giuseppe was poring over a collection of specimens that he had arranged on a white table napkin. 'Take a look at these,' he said.

Claudia looked through the magnifying glass. 'Well, there are several different species. I can see an Alaskan, an Inland Floodwater, a Banded Foulwater, a Southern Saltmarsh, an Asian Tiger ... what, is this some kind of test? Oh, hang on! They're all males, aren't they? But wait a minute! That's odd! If I'm not mistaken, they have female stylets.'

'Yes, that's ... that's what I noticed. In fact, nearly *all* the dead mosquitoes I've looked at in this room are males with female-type stylets. Only about one in every 50 or so is a true female.'

'*Mio Dio*, Giuseppe, the overwhelming majority are gynandromorphs!' she said, lowering her voice. 'What *is* going on? We know males don't normally bite, because they don't need blood. Yet these males have the facility and the propensity to bite. Is it possible that we're dealing here with a huge swarm of *males with proboscises*, which wilfully attacked and bit to death 126 people? The bride was bitten all over her body – so much so that thousands of capillaries beneath her skin were pierced – but the insects that attacked her didn't feed on her blood. They bit her – or perforated her, if you like – and then withdrew, and she bled to death. Is it reasonable to assume that the same fate befell the other dead people in the room, in view of the fact they too have bloodstained clothes and are lying in pools of dried blood? We must find out what the prevailing medical view is.' Claudia approached a group of people who were surrounding one of the remaining bodies, that of a bridesmaid in a torn and bloodstained dress. 'I'm sorry to interrupt you,' she said. 'I know how busy you must be. The thing is, as an ecologist studying the behaviour of mosquitoes, I'm anxious to establish whether all the bodies here suffered the same injuries.'

'You mean, signorina, were the bodies literally riddled with pinpricks, as if they had received millions of short stabs from hypodermic needles? And in each case did the lifeblood of the person in question seep away through all those skin punctures? The answer to both questions is "Yes". I know, because I've been here since yesterday evening and have seen most of the bodies. I'm Camillo Calieri, by the way – a consultant physician, at your service. I'm Senior Consultant of the Infectious and Tropical Diseases

Department at Santa Maria Nuovo.'

Having talked briefly to Dr Calieri and his aides, Claudia and Giuseppe were on the point of going into the bar, when a man in a white coat with grizzled frizzy hair approached them. 'Excuse me,' he said, addressing Claudia, 'but I am myself an ecologist, and I couldn't help overhearing what you said a few moments ago. Forgive me if I'm mistaken, but I know of only one ecologist with an interest in mosquitoes who, how shall I say, looks – er – like you do: Dr Claudia Mattioli.'

Claudia smiled. 'I am she. And you are?'

'Antonio Zobi of the Institute of Ecology, an organisation with which I understand you are no longer associated.'

'Yes, that's right. I'm afraid I didn't see eye to eye with Doctor Ravegnani on how to deal with the mosquito crisis. Anyway, it's a pleasure to meet you, Professor Zobi.' They shook hands. 'May I introduce another ex-employee of the Institute, Signor Giuseppe Corti.' Giuseppe and the Professor shook hands.

'Ah yes, Signor Corti. Are you and Dr Mattioli together?'

'Working together, yes,' he replied. He didn't think he should elaborate. Instead, he continued, 'What happened here yesterday is incredible, isn't it?'

'It is, indeed. But …' Beckoning to Giuseppe and taking Claudia by the arm, Professor Zobi led them away from Dr Calieri's group to a quiet corner of the room. 'There have been a number of attacks elsewhere in Italy that have eclipsed even this terrible tragedy, but they've been hushed up. In the last week, mosquito activity has intensified massively throughout the country, but freedom to report on the situation has been severely restricted by the Government's emergency measures, which were introduced earlier this week in the hope of forestalling public hysteria. Dr Ravegnani told me yesterday that the Institute's current computer projection, which is based on his own conservative estimate of the number of mosquitoes per square kilometre in and around Rome, is that there are currently in the order of sixty *billion* mosquitoes in Italy – i.e. one million per capita!'

'But it's a figure, surely, that could be wildly inaccurate, one way or the other. It's just speculation,' said Claudia. 'I mean, what about the unborn mosquitoes?'

'The figure is an approximation, of course, and relates only to the number of adult insects. How many instars and pupae there are is anyone's guess.'

'You mentioned unreported attacks. Do you know whether anything's happened in the Florence area that's been hushed up?' asked Giuseppe.

'Yes, I'm afraid I do. About 35 kilometres to the southeast of Florence, in the Arno valley, where it's low-lying, just off the A1 before you get to San Giovanni Valdarno, there's a large campsite by a lake, in which the water is stagnant and at a low level. Now as you know it's the sort of area that people have been advised to avoid. Nevertheless, despite the warning, last Tuesday several hundred people – adults and children – were camping there. Unbelievably, just before dusk, they were preparing their evening meals out in the open on barbecues and suchlike. Suddenly there was a mass launch or breakout from the lake of newly moulted adults that rose as one into the air and then swooped down on the campers like some gigantic arched cloud. They struck so suddenly and with such ferocity that people had no chance. It's not known how many died or survived. Within 25 minutes of the attack, the whole area was sealed off and no one was allowed in or out. The little I know about what happened at the campsite I gleaned from my nephew, who is in the Rapid Response Division of the State Police.'

'If mosquitoes are breeding on that sort of scale,' said Giuseppe, 'surely widespread preventative measures should be taken as a matter of urgency.'

'Such as poisoning the lakes,' said Claudia, in a matter-of-fact voice. She smiled at Giuseppe.

Professor Zobi looked at them both inquiringly. 'You know about the national spraying campaign, I presume.'

'No,' said Claudia. 'I thought the Government was in such a weak position politically that it had decided not to go ahead with the idea.'

'Quite to the contrary: spraying began five days ago in the south, where the situation was considered more serious than in the north. There are problems, of course. Logistically, it is a huge undertaking and, although the Air Force is helping, there are currently only a few planes and helicopters that have been specially adapted for spraying. Also, this being Italy, the project isn't very well organised! As a result, progress is painfully slow.'

'When do they expect to spray in the Florence

area?' asked Giuseppe.

'Not for at least another month.'

Claudia refrained from airing her views on the wisdom of mass spraying. 'Professor Zobi, it has been a pleasure meeting you,' she said, extending her hand. 'I hope you'll excuse us, but there are one or two things we need to check before they remove all the bodies.'

He shook her hand gently. 'Of course, I understand. I'll let you get on.' He turned to Giuseppe. 'Very nice to meet you.' They shook hands, and Professor Zobi turned and went out of the room. Claudia and Giuseppe remained in the Hotel, collecting specimens and information, for about an hour, and then, depressed by what they had seen, they decided to go home.

On the road down to Florence, Claudia suddenly called out, 'Darling, can we stop! I'd like to get out and walk in these fields.' She sensed that they both needed to relax after the tenseness of their visit to the Hotel.

Giuseppe parked the car on the verge. 'A bit risky, don't you think? There may be Alaskans lurking in the grass.'

'No, no, they won't bother us,' she said, emphatically, taking her glasses off. 'Come on, let's go!' She extricated herself from the passenger seat, while he leapt over the side. They went through a swing gate and, holding hands, skipped and danced through the wildflowers, stopping occasionally to kiss one other.

* * *

Sitting on the steps of the Duomo with his mobile to his ear, Roberto discussed with Giorgio the arrangements for their afternoon visit to Castello di Montezano. A buzz indicated that Roberto had an incoming call on hold. He saw that it was from the Hospital. 'Sorry, Giorgio,' he said. 'I've got the Hospital on the line. I must answer. I'll speak to you later … Hello.'

'Signor Mattioli, it's Sister Gabriela here. When Signor Spencer had a brief period of consciousness this morning, he managed to read your note. Then he requested me to put his mobile on speakerphone and call his home number. Somebody called Paolo answered. Signor Spencer asked him whether he remembered anything about an envelope he'd put in his bureau and Paolo said "yes". Signor Spencer said he'd like Paolo to give you the envelope today. He said he thought you would be calling at the apartment roundabout midday. Their conversation then ended, and just before Signor Spencer drifted off again, he said he wished your venture this afternoon every success.'

'Is it known yet what's wrong with him?' asked Roberto.

'Not definitively. He's had the relevant blood tests, but there are other investigations – scans, X-rays, etc. – that need to be carried out before anyone can give a definite diagnosis. I can't tell you any more at the moment.'

'Well, give him my best wishes, will you? And say I'll be round to see him again when he's better.'

'Signor Mattioli, there's one other thing: Signor

Spencer said, if possible, he'd like to see your daughter, Signorina Claudia. He has something to ask her.'

'Okay, I'll let her know. *Ciao,* Sister Gabriela. Thank you for your help.'

CHAPTER 20

Having bought his plane ticket and taken a last look at some of the sights of Florence, Scott went to bed feeling better in himself and more relaxed than he had done for several days. However, during the night, he developed a throbbing headache and a raging fever, much worse than the temperature he had had on Friday. In between fitful snatches of sleep, he was terrorised by a recurring nightmare of frightening intensity. Huge cockerels with razor-sharp combs and talons chased him to the summit of a frozen mountain, where he was rammed anally onto a pinnacle of ice and then lifted up and thrown into space. Tumbling over and over, he fell among Bosch-like demons, which attacked him with severed legs and arms, before dragging him towards a huge fiery furnace. Covered in sweat and trembling with fear, he half woke to a sensation of being roasted alive. He reached out for the sidelight at quite the wrong angle and fell onto the floor. Rolling himself into the foetal position, he shivered and whimpered. Then, sitting up abruptly, he stared wide-eyed, as half-discerned objects in the darkness grew monstrously top-heavy and lunged towards him. He screamed with terror, once, twice, then flopped semiconscious onto the floor.

Roused from a deep slumber, Paolo staggered out of bed and, in his dazed state, proceeded to go into Laurence's bedroom. Realising his mistake and gathering his thoughts, he went into the green room and turned on the lights. He rushed over to the prostrate body and felt Scott's wrist. The pulse was erratic. Paolo lifted Scott up and put him back into bed, making sure he was well covered.

'Paolo,' Scott murmured, 'can you please bring me a bucket or something? I feel I'm going to be sick.'

Having provided Scott with a plastic washing-up bowl, Paolo went out of the room and rang the doctor.

* * *

Claudia had intended that Giuseppe should satisfy her prodigious sexual appetite all night long, if need be, but Nature interposed. After a long, slow session of lovemaking, during which each explored the other's body and sensuality to the full, they fell asleep.

Some seven hours later, Giuseppe woke. He looked at the clock: it was 06:25. He turned off the alarm, which was set for 06:45. Claudia was lying on her side facing him. Gently he stroked the long strands of her luxuriant hair. He leant over and kissed her ear. 'Darling,' she murmured sleepily, 'what time is it?'

'Time to get up!' he replied, getting out of bed and ambling naked into the kitchen. 'I'll make us some coffee.'

Three-quarters of an hour later, Claudia and Giuseppe left the apartment and walked, hand in hand, to Piazza del Duomo. Another dazzlingly hot day was in prospect. At No. 21 they discovered that the computers, printers and office furniture had been delivered. '*Bene*,' said Claudia. 'Now we can get on with some work.'

With the help of members of the Commune staff, she and Giuseppe arranged the placement of the desks, chairs, tables, sofas and cabinets in the Centre's offices. There was so much to be done – allocating workspace and jobs, networking the computers, downloading software, deciding how to deal with inquiries from members of the public, printing out information sheets and leaflets – that Claudia and Giuseppe had scarcely an opportunity to acknowledge, let alone embrace, one another. For lunch someone brought in pizza, which they both ate heartily at their separate desks; otherwise, they were wholly engaged, under difficult working conditions – it was a sweltering hot day and there was no air conditioning in the offices – in preparing for the opening of the Centre the next day.

* * *

In his office at Ospedale di Santa Maria Nuovo, Dr Calieri sat down with members of his department to discuss the latest and most serious cases of Malaria which had been admitted to the Hospital. 'The main concern,' he said, 'is there's been such a run on anti-malarial drugs recently that we have very few left in stock. More are on order – but the manufacturers are hard-pressed to meet the increased demand throughout the country.'

One of the consultants spoke. 'Currently we have two patients with Cerebral Malaria,' he said, 'and they're both on chemo. How long can we expect the atovaquone/proguanil to last? Another week, maybe? So if we don't get any more supplies by the end of the week, we'll have to put them on quinine. Do we have enough of that, I wonder?'

'Yes,' said another consultant, 'we've got bottles of the stuff, fortunately.'

The internal phone rang and one of the doctors took the call. 'Yes? ... Yes, I see ... He stopped taking it ... Also there was a delay ... Right ... And now he's on chemo. Good ... Yes, I'll tell Dr Calieri ... Yes, I'll be down when the meeting is over. *Ciao.*' He looked at the others. 'I'm afraid we have a third patient who has contracted Cerebral Malaria: Mr Spencer in Room 31. Apparently he went to Ghana in mid-July and was taking a/p. But he suffered from side effects – nausea, vomiting, diarrhoea, etc. – so he stopped taking the tablets. To exacerbate matters, there was a delay in dealing with the onset of the disease. So he was already seriously infected by the time he was brought in here.'

* * *

'*Buongiorno?* This line is bad, it's crackling ... I am not hearing you very well ... Are you hearing me? It's Luca Baldini here ... *Sì*, I am confirming your order has arrived in our Reggio warehouse ... As soon as you transfer the money to our account, we'll send you the goods by our distribution network. You have details of our account already, no? *Buono* ... Sorry? I am not hearing what you say. This line is ... You are transferring money today. *Buono.* I am waiting for confirmation from our bank ... Yes, then I am giving the go-ahead for delivery ... It's a pleasure doing business with you, Mohammed, my friend. You are

giving my best regards to Signor al-Barnawi please …
I'm wishing you well, too. *Ciao*!' said Baldini ending
the call. Attired in a silk dressing gown, he was sitting
at the escritoire in the Library. 'Mario.'

'Yes, boss.'

'Our Boko Haram contacts in Maidugari are
paying us today – so keep an eye on the bank account.
As soon as the money – 340,000 dollars – is received,
let me know, will you?'

'Okay, boss.'

'Did you manage to fly out to sea yesterday
afternoon?'

'No, boss. Stefano wasn't available. He had to go
to a family funeral.'

'Oh, did he? Well, tell him he works for us now,
and if we want him to do something, he does it –
otherwise next time he'll be going to his *own* funeral!'

'I'll tell him, boss.'

'He *is* going to fly you today, I take it.'

'Yes, boss, but not until tonight. He says – and I
think he's right – it'll be easier to load and drop the
cargo under cover of darkness. Anyway, he'll be
calling for me here at 20:00.'

'Where is … you know?'

'Bagged up, boss, and ready to go.'

'Good.'

Giovanni came into the room. 'Boss, there's a
Papak Kazimi calling from Iran. He's on line one.'

Baldini picked up the handset. '*Buongiorno*, Papak

my friend. You are keeping well, yes? … Oh, I am –
how d'you say? – surviving. It's all work, no play –
that's the only problem … I am needing a little fun,
for sure … You have a decision, that's good news …
How many kilograms are you needing? … Yes, we
have enough … How much are you prepared to—?
… Yes, it's acceptable. You are transferring money to
our account in Switzerland? … When the bank is
telling us your money is received, we are sending you
the 239 by special container … Good, then we have a
deal … I am giving you my best wishes too, Papak.
Ciao!' He replaced the handset. 'Well, boys, what price
war in the Middle East? I can tell you. 30,000,000
dollars for 10kg of pu-239 – that's the price. I reckon
it's only a matter of months now before Iran nukes
the shit out of Israel – and "bang" go all those
bothersome Yids!'

'Have you sold all the stuff you bought from
Ouspensky, boss?'

'No, not quite. But that's nothing to worry about.
As things stand, we've made a load of money.
20,000,000 profit from the sale of the isotopes, plus
commission of 2.5% of the selling price. Then there's
90,000 profit from the one half of the weapons we've
sold. Add on the commission of 9,000,000 on the sale
of the painting. That makes a total of almost
30,000,000 – which should raise a few smiles in
Calabria.'

'You never know, boss. Ouspensky may not come
and get his money. I mean, you scared the shit out of
him the other night.'

'No, he'll come running for his money all right.
He's more frightened by his Russian friends than he is

by me. Anyway, forget Ouspensky: where was I? Oh yes, if, as I hope, I sell the rest of the guns for 450,000, there will be a further profit of 200,000. So, at the next family meeting, the Don should be pleased that I've made so much money. Talking of which ... shit, I nearly forgot! I must ring Signor Spencer.' Baldini picked up the handset again and dialled Laurence's mobile number. '*Buongiorno*! ... This is Luca Baldini here. Who am I speaking to? ... Sister Gabriella at the Santa Maria Nuovo Hospital. Well Sister, if possible, I'd like to speak to Signor Spencer please.' There was a long pause. 'Hello? ... Is anybody there? ... You are putting Signor Spencer's mobile on loudspeaker ... I understand ... Ah, Signor Spencer, how are you? ... I'm sorry to hear you're in hospital? What is the trouble? ... Malaria? Oh shit! ... Well, I am hoping this as well ... No, I'm afraid the bid you made was not successful ... Your bid was the second highest. The bid of Signori Mattioli and Belori was the highest ... They are collecting the picture this afternoon ... I'm sorry about this, because now I am having to remind you about the money you owe us. We agreed that if your client's bid for the Raphael proved not to be the highest bid, then your client would repay the deposit of 750,000 dollars, no? ... I'm sorry, but that is what we agreed, Signor Spencer ... Good, you are contacting your client ... Yes, a cheque is acceptable ... Next week will be fine ... In the meantime, I hope you are getting better ... *Ciao*!' Baldini replaced the handset. 'I am going to get dressed. Boys, if an Abu Mansoor from Somalia rings, let me know immediately. I'm hoping he's going to buy the rest of the guns.'

* * *

Promptly at 18:00, Roberto Mattioli and Giorgio Belori arrived at Castello di Montezano and were shown into the Library by Giovanni. Mario was standing by one of the windows. Baldini was sitting at the escritoire. Beside him, on an easel, was the *Portrait of a Young Man*. '*Buongiorno*, Signor Mattioli. How nice to see you again.'

'May I introduce my partner, Giorgio Bellori.'

'Signor Bellori, what a pleasure.' Baldini smiled his smile. 'I am glad,' he gushed, 'that you and Signor Mattioli are the successful bidders. I trust Signor Engel will show his appreciation of your efforts by paying you an appropriately handsome commission. Now, signori, to complete the formalities, I think you may have a piece of paper for me.'

'Signor Baldini, if we may first look at the painting—'

'Of course, Signor Mattioli. You must make sure it is the real painting and not a cleverly substituted forgery, I understand that. Please, go ahead. Look as long as you like.'

Mattioli took the painting carefully from the easel and went over to the window. Bellori joined him and, turning the panel this way and that, they scrutinised the paint surface. When they were satisfied, Mattioli returned the painting to the easel. 'Signor Baldini, in the car we have some packing materials. Is it okay if my partner goes and gets them?'

'Of course. Mario go with Signor Bellori in case he needs some help.'

From the inside pocket of his jacket, Mattioli produced a piece of paper, which he handed to

Baldini. 'A cashier's cheque for 90,000,000 dollars. It's made out to you personally.'

'Good. Thank you.' Baldini studied the cheque for a moment. 'Yes, that seems to be in order.'

'I trust Signor Ouspensky and his contacts are happy with the large amount that's been paid for the painting?' *Particularly,* he thought to himself, *as it probably cost them nothing in the first place!*

'Oh yes, I'm sure they are – more than happy. Personally speaking, I can't imagine why your client is prepared to pay so much for, well, such an *ordinary* picture. I mean I realise the painting is by Raffaello Santi, but even so, I can't see why it's worth so much. At any rate, it's not something I'd want to hang on my wall.'

'*Chacun à son goût,* Signor Baldini. I think it's a superb portrait by one of history's supreme artists at the height of his very considerable powers. As such, it has great rarity value and is therefore an extremely good investment.'

'Well, I'll take your word for it, Signor Mattioli. If it was me and I had that sort of money, I think I'd buy a biochemical company or shares in Amazon or buy up as many Chianti vineyards as I could! I wouldn't want—'

Bellori and Mario reappeared, each carrying a roll of bubble wrap and some cardboard sheets. 'Is it all right to wrap the painting?' asked Bellori.

'Yes, Signor Bellori, go ahead. You have tape and scissors, I take it?'

'Yes, thank you.' Bellori unrolled a sheet of bubble

wrap and spread it on top of the writing desk. Mattioli took the Raphael off the easel and placed it in the centre of the bubble wrap. While they were packing up the painting, Mario took Baldini to one side and whispered something in his ear, whereat Baldini looked at the two men at the writing desk and shook his head. He gave Mario a few mumbled instructions, the last of which was audible: '... tell the others to be on their guard.' Mario went out of the room. Bellori and Mattioli glanced at each other. 'Signori, have you nearly finished? I don't mean to rush you, but I have something else to attend to.'

'Yes, Signor Baldini,' said Mattioli, picking up the heavily wrapped painting, 'we've finished, so we'll be on our way. Thank you, signor, it has been a pleasure.' He shook hands with Baldini, as did Bellori.

'It has been a pleasure for me too, signori. My best wishes to you both. *Ciao*!'

'Incidentally, whose bid did we beat? I mean, who was the underbidder?'

'Signor Spencer. He bid just 5,000,000 less than you did.' Mario came back into the room. '*Ciao*, signori. Mario, I need to speak to you.'

Mattioli and Bellori found their own way out, got into their car and drove slowly down the drive and through the gates, which were opened for them by a big man with a machine gun tucked under his arm. Some two kilometres along the road to Castellina, they encountered a squad of riot police, who were standing alongside three armoured vans. They wore black battle dress, black shields and blue helmets with black-tinted visors and were armed with sub-machine guns and grenades.

Before getting out of the car, Mattioli turned to Bellori and said, 'Giorgio, I want you to stay with the painting.'

'You mean you don't want me to help you arrest Baldini?'

'That's right. I want you to take the painting into one of those vans and guard the damn thing with your life. I'll ask whoever's in charge to leave a couple of armed policemen with you, for extra security.'

'Why into one of the vans?'

'Because I need the car. Wait here for a moment, until I've checked that everyone knows what's going on.' He got out of the car. 'Who's your Commander?' he asked.

'I am,' said a tall, dark-haired, moustachioed man, who was holding his helmet in one hand. 'Colonel Leon Cortellazzo of the Arma del Carabinieri, at your service.' He clicked his heels.

'I'm Roberto Mattioli. How do you do?' They shook hands. 'If I could just have a word with you, Colonel.' They walked up the road in the half-light side by side. 'I take it you know I had a meeting with the Commissioner last week.' The Colonel nodded. 'Have you been briefed on what we discussed?'

'No, not fully. I've been away in Puglia and I only came back yesterday.'

'Well, in that case I'll recap the main details. The target is a member of the Mafia. His name is Baldini and he has a suite here in the hotel. We have someone working for us on the inside, and her last report, which we received three days ago, was that there are normally eight to ten men who protect him and they have access to a considerable cache of arms. She—'

'What sort of arms?' the Colonel asked.

'Assault rifles, semi-automatic shotguns, sub-machine guns, maybe even rocket launchers.'

'*Mio Dio!*'

'Hopefully, we can surprise them, before they utilise the full range of their weaponry and ammunition. Anyway, as I was about to say, our informant drew up this plan of the Castello,' he handed a piece of paper to the Colonel, 'from which you can see that a stone wall surrounds the property, and here,' he pointed a finger at the plan, 'there are electronic entrance gates. The room in which Baldini spends most of his time is the Library, here. Now my idea is first of all that you fire a gun, just once, then you send in most of your men over the wall – warn them there's razor wire on top – and have them spread out around the Castello. I'll wait until you tell me they're in position, and then I'll drive up to the gates, hopefully gain entrance and make my way to the front door. For reasons that are too long-winded to go into here, I should be able to entice the target and at least two or three of his entourage to come outside, ostensibly to look at something in my car. If that happens, then I trust your men will move quickly to secure the target and whoever else comes out of the house with him. If nobody comes out and I have to go in, then you'll have to storm the place and I'll have to take my chances. I suggest the men that you keep back should position themselves at intervals on the outside of the perimeter wall, in case any of the target's merry men try to escape. Incidentally, my partner has a valuable object to look after and, as I obviously have to turn up in the same car as I left in, I've suggested he stays here in one of your vans. If you could leave a couple of men to keep him company, I'm sure he'd appreciate it. One important consideration: the building *is* a hotel. And even though the guests and staff have been evacuated discreetly to a place of safety, the owners would like us to do as little damage to the property as possible.

'Right. I'll get on and organise things. How far up the road is this place?'

'About a kilometre.'

'Well, it'll take me about five minutes to tell the men what's involved, then another seven minutes, say, to walk to the property, so by the time we get there, it'll be dark – which means it'll be easier for us to scale the wall without being seen. I reckon I'll be calling you on this,' he handed Mattioli a walkie talkie, 'at about 18:50. Shall we synchronise watches? It'll be 18:26 in ... five ... four ... three ... two ... one ... zero. By the way, what happens if they don't let you through the gates?'

'Well, I think they will. After all, ostensibly I've just paid the target a great deal of money for said valuable object. If I can't gain access, I'll let you know, and leave it to you to do the necessary. I suggest, incidentally, that you make any forced entry through the Library French windows. *Buona fortuna*, Colonel.' They shook hands, and the Colonel went over to his men, while Mattioli got back into his car. 'Giorgio, the man I was talking to, Colonel Cortellazzo, will show you which van to get into. Can you go to him now, with the painting? I'll see you later.'

Quarter of an hour later, there was a buzz on the walkie talkie that Mattioli was holding. 'Yes?'

'We're in position. I'll wait for you to arrive at the front of the house or to radio me, if you're barred entrance. Good luck. Over and out.'

Mattioli put the walkie talkie down on the passenger seat, started the car and drove off down the road to Castello di Montezano. At the entrance gates, he got out and walked in full view of the security camera. 'Hello!' he shouted.

Primo came out of the lodge house. 'Yes?'

'I am Roberto Mattioli. I was here earlier this evening. I came at 18:00. I need to see Signor Baldini. I need to see him about the painting that Signor Ouspensky and his contacts sold me through Signor Baldini. I have something important to show him.'

'Wait here a moment.' Primo went back into the lodge house, called the main house on the intercom and explained the situation. Moments later, he called to Mattioli, 'Okay, you can come on through.'

Mattioli got back into his car, put it in gear and waited as the gates opened. He drove along the driveway to the front of the house. Standing in the light of the front door was Giovanni. Mattioli wound down the window. 'I need to see Signor Baldini urgently.'

'Okay, come in.'

'No ... no, you don't understand,' he shouted hysterically, getting out of the car. 'My partner, Giorgio, he's ... he's been SHOT. I've left him ... by the roadside. I don't know … wh-what to do. Please … PLEASE, I need Signor Baldini's help.'

'Okay, keep your hair on! I'll go tell the boss.' Giovanni, who, fortunately for Mattioli, was not the brightest of men, went into the house, scratching his head. Mattioli turned towards the trees facing the house and raised both his thumbs. As he did so, an image flashed before his eyes of his bedridden wife and his beautiful daughter both weeping inconsolably. *Mio Dio*, he thought, *I must be crazy to be doing this job!*

Moments later, Baldini came out onto the front steps with Giovanni and Mario, both of whom were carrying pump-action shotguns. 'Signor Mattioli, what is this I hear? Signor Belori has been shot?'

'Signor Baldini,' said Mattioli, producing a .44 Magnum and pointing it at the Mafia boss, 'you're under arrest on suspicion of dealing in arms, stolen paintings and coercion. I must advise you that anything you say …' As he recited the mandatory caution, about half the riot police who were in the vicinity stepped out of their hiding places. They were armed with sub-machine guns, which were aimed at the three men in the doorway. Simultaneously, windows in the upper floors of the building opened and gun barrels of various different calibres appeared in the apertures.

If Baldini was fazed by the turn in events, he didn't show it. 'So Signor Not-What-You-Seem Mattioli,' he said, 'we appear to have something of a standoff. What, pray, do you suggest we do?'

'Tell your men to lay down their weapons. You three disarm as well.' Mattioli gripped the big revolver in both hands and aimed at Baldini's chest. 'Do as I say. There's no point in resisting arrest. You're heavily outnumbered.'

Shrieking, 'NOW!' Baldini backflipped through the doorway with the agility of a martial arts expert. In the split second that it took Mattioli to adjust his aim, Giovanni and Mario fired several shots in his direction, one of which hit him in the right shoulder and spun him round and backwards onto the gravel in front of his car. All hell broke out. Spurts of flame lit up the house and grounds as a relentless salvo from the upper windows was met by withering sub-machine gunfire from behind the trees, ornaments and walls in the garden where the police were located.

Baldini and Mario scrabbled unharmed into the house and slammed the door behind them. 'No point in hanging around here,' Baldini said. 'While the men upstairs are keeping the pigs busy, we can exit across the lawn and over the wall. Bring that rug with you. We'll need something to cover the razor wire with.'

Giovanni was not so fortunate: bleeding profusely after being shot several times, he slithered face down in his own blood on the steps, like a wounded marooned whale. The fusillade that the police aimed at the first floor shattered the windows, and in the shower of broken glass a jagged piece the shape and size of a warning triangle plunged into Giovanni's kidneys.

Without being noticed by Baldini's gunmen, who were locked in battle with the police, Mattioli managed to crawl one-handed out of their sight behind his car. His shirt was sodden with blood, and he was light-headed as if he was going to faint. There was no sensation in the right-hand side of his upper torso. Gingerly, he laid his left hand on the wounded shoulder. All he could feel were strips of flesh, ripped muscle, broken bits of bone and blood pumping from his torn subclavian artery. *If someone doesn't help me,* he thought, *I'm a goner.*

There was a brief lull in the shooting, as each side weighed up their position. From behind a large urn pedestal, Colonel Cortellazzo, who could see that Mattioli was badly wounded, spoke into his walkie talkie. 'Hello, Signor Mattioli, can you hear me? Over. Hello, Signor Mattioli. I need you to acknowledge that you can hear me. Over.'

Mattioli responded, in a faltering voice. 'Ye … es. I … hear … you. Over.'

'Good. Listen carefully. I'm going to send two of my men to collect you. How badly are you injured? Over.'

Another pause. 'Shoulder … blown apart … gunshot wound. Losing lot of blood. Getting cold. Over.'

'Okay. Try to stay awake. Rescue party on its way to you now. Over and out.' Having passed the word along to his men that, on his signal, every damned weapon they had – sub-machine gun, revolver, rifle – was to be fired at the house, Cortellazzo delegated two experienced sergeants to retrieve Mattioli. He produced another walkie talkie, which he used to contact the men who were guarding Belori. He asked them to phone from the van for a helicopter ambulance.

On the gravel beside the car, a shivering Mattioli imagined himself to be in a tiny, freezing cold room, in which the only source of light, a small window, was slowly being covered by a heavy curtain.

Cortellazzo gave the signal. The gunfire was deafening, as bursts of flame from a hundred barrels lit up the surroundings. Hundreds of rounds of ammunition ripped into the external and internal walls of the house. So penetrative and overwhelming was the police onslaught that hardly a shot was fired in return. Seizing their opportunity, the two sergeants ran out to the car and were on the point of lifting Mattioli by his legs and under his back, when a spray of exploding bullets shattered the gravel around them. One of the sergeants covered Mattioli with his body, as the other peered down the drive. In the flashes of light, he made out the approaching figure of an abnormally large man, who was firing a MG-3 machine gun from his hip. It was the last thing the sergeant saw, as a volley of bullets hit him in the chest and head. All the while shooting bullets in bursts, the large man continued to advance until he was on a line with the police in their hiding places. Many of Cortellazzo's men fell. Others fired back, but Primo went on blazing away. Cortellazzo's men were going down like ninepins. 'He must have a bulletproof vest on,' shouted the Colonel. 'Shoot him in the balls!' Instantly Primo was seen to collapse on his knees, as bullets tore into his upper thighs and groin. But still he continued to send devastating bursts of bullets in their direction. Cortellazzo took a dumdum bullet from his pocket and loaded it into the magazine of his Beretta revolver. Taking careful aim at the centre of the outsized head, he squeezed the trigger. By that stage, Primo was so close that Cortellazzo and the remaining policemen could clearly see the dark cloud of blood and fragments of brain and bone as the back of the big man's head exploded.

While Cortellazzo and his men were preoccupied in dealing with Primo, the five Mafiosi who were left on the first floor of the house decided to make a run for it. They rushed downstairs, into the Library, out through the open French windows and across the side lawn. When they reached the perimeter wall, one of them, Gonzalo, pointed at the razor wire and took off his jacket. The others were about to take their jackets off, when Gonzalo drew their attention to where the rug that Baldini and Mario had used for their escape was still covering the razor wire. Gonzalo put his jacket back on, and the five of them walked to the section of wall he had indicated. Having whispered that the tallest member of the group should crouch down, Gonzalo slung his sub-machine gun over his shoulder and assumed a piggyback position on the man's back. The tall man stood up, and Gonzalo hauled himself over the rug and dropped onto the road on the other side of the wall. The other four followed suit, except that the third man pulled the tall man to the top of the wall. They were all safely over when ten policemen with sub-machine guns in their hands appeared from behind the bushes on the opposite side of the road. 'Drop your weapons!' one of the policemen yelled. There was a clatter as their guns hit the tarmac. '*All* your weapons!' There was another clatter, as they threw down knives, hand grenades and knuckledusters. The five men were body searched, handcuffed, chained together by the ankles and marched off down the road to the waiting police vans, where they found Baldini and Mario had already been detained.

Seeing Primo fall and noticing that there was no longer any firing from the house, the sergeant sprang into action. Having opened the car door and checked to see that the key was in the ignition, he picked up Mattioli and laid him on the back seat. He then jumped into the driver's seat, started up the car and, spinning the wheels on the gravel, drove off at speed. He screeched to a halt at the gates, which were shut. He got out, tried to open the gates and, having no success, went, with revolver in hand, into the lodge house. No one was there and, after an extensive search, he found the remote control unit, which he operated. Through the window, he could see the gates opening. As he got back into the car, he heard the nearby whirring of a helicopter.

The sergeant drove down the road to where the police vans were parked. On arriving, he could see that two paramedics were alighting from the helicopter ambulance, which had landed in the nearest field. He jumped out of the car and waved franticly at the paramedics. Within minutes, they were rushing a barely breathing, ashen-faced Mattioli on a stretcher to the helicopter, which, shortly afterwards, received special dispensation from the authorities to land in Piazza della Signoria, near the spot where Savonarola was hanged and burnt, even as people in the square were being herded away by police. With its siren blaring, an ambulance rushed Mattioli to the Ospedale di Santa Maria Nuova, where he arrived at 20:10 and was taken to the Emergency Room.

At about the same time, Stefano the pilot drew up at the Castello entrance gates, got out of his car and walked over to the intercom on the wall. 'Hi! Stefano here. I've come to collect Mario, as arranged.' Hardly had he spoken the words when an armed policeman appeared, told him he was under arrest, read him his rights, handcuffed him and marched him off in the direction of the police vans.

Meanwhile, as there was no longer anyone shooting at them, Colonel Castellazzo and the remnants of his squad stormed the Castello. Having established that the only Mafiosi who were still there were dead, the Colonel ordered his men to conduct a thorough but non-destructive search of Baldini's suite. Apart from a vast array of weapons, they found sixteen kilos of heroin, a stash of forged banknotes, a Canova sculpture, three old masters and, in one of the downstairs cupboards, an abnormally heavy body bag, which contained the decomposing remains of Caterina Ricci and several large blocks of cement.

* * *

It was 19:45 and dark when Claudia and Giuseppe left the offices in Piazza del Duomo and set off for Piazza d' Azeglio. On the way, they encountered people walking along the pavements under the streetlights and a group of children, who were carrying papier-mâché lanterns on sticks and running somewhat furtively in and out of courtyards. As the children proceeded in this manner along the Via della Colonna, they sang:

> *Ona, ona, ona,*
> *O che bella rificolona.*
> *La mia l'è co' fiocchi,*
> *La tua l'è co' pidocchi!*

E l'è più bella la mia
Di quella della zia.[8]

'I'm surprised,' said Giuseppe, 'that, given the potential risks, children are allowed to wander around the streets unaccompanied at this hour, aren't you?'

'No, not really. People are obviously beginning to venture out of their houses again. They probably don't feel so threatened as they did. After all, there hasn't been any sort of mosquito activity in Florence, since the attack on the congregation in San Frediano last Wednesday. Suddenly, there seem to be fewer mosquitoes about, far fewer than there normally are at this time of year.'

'Isn't that strange?'

'Yes, very strange,' Claudia said. 'The mosquitoes are still breeding here, but when they emerge as adults, they fly off somewhere else.'

'Well, in that case, why are we opening a Mosquito Advisory Centre?'

'Because they'll be back, of that I'm sure.'

Giuseppe stopped and turned. 'What were those children singing about? Something to do with a beautiful stick. That isn't a euphemism, is it, by any chance?' he asked, with a chuckle.

'No it isn't! Honestly, Giuseppe, you have a one-track mind. As I'm sure you must have noticed, each

---

[8] Ona, ona, ona,/What a beautiful stick./Mine is with the flakes,/Yours is with the lice!/And more beautiful is mine/Than that of Auntie.

child carried a lantern. The stick in question is the one to which the child attaches the lantern. *Rificolona* also has a secondary meaning for Florentines: it's what they call an over made-up and overdressed woman.'

'Not a word that could possibly be applied to you, *bellissima*,' said Giuseppe, stepping back to gaze at Claudia, who wore the shortest of dresses and just a hint of make-up about her eyes. He took her hand and they began walking again. 'But why are the children carrying lanterns?'

'They always do in the first week of September. It's part of the build-up to the *Festa della Rificolona* on the seventh of September, along with parties in the piazzas, street theatre and entertainers, and other amusements – although I imagine there won't be too much merrymaking out in the open this year. On the sixth and seventh of September, a big fair for mainly organic food producers is held in Piazza della Santissima Annunziata, and usually on the night of the seventh the festival ends with a procession led by the Archbishop of Florence from Piazza Santa Croce to Piazza della Santissima Annunziata.'

Claudia and Giuseppe had reached the entrance door to the apartment block in Piazza d' Azeglio. 'What's the origin of the festival, does anyone know?' Giuseppe asked.

'No one's sure when or why the festival started,' Claudia said, as they entered the building. 'Some believe it commemorates the entry into Siena in the 1500s of victorious Florentine troops, who tied lanterns to their pikes. It's more likely, though, that the festival grew out of the annual autumn market, which was held in Piazza della Santissima Annunziata on the eve of the Nativity of the Virgin, i.e. the seventh of September.'

'But why do the children sing about an overdressed woman?'

'Well, long before dawn on the seventh of September, farmers and their families made their way from the countryside to the city for the most important market of the year. To light their way, they carried lanterns, which were suspended by string from the ends of thin sticks and constructed of candles in tissue paper surrounds. They wore their Sunday best, but their crude attempts at elegance were ridiculed by the city people, who, amongst other things, hailed any elaborately dressed countrywoman as a *Rificolona*. To add to the discomfiture of these simple folk, Florentine children would whistle and jeer at them and try to knock over the candles in their lanterns.' Giuseppe unlocked the door to her apartment and stood aside to let Claudia enter.

'Right, *bellissima*,' he said, closing the door behind him, 'how about we have some scrambled eggs and a glass of wine and then take a shower together?' Claudia recalled momentarily that Scott used to suggest the same thing.

'No, not yet,' she replied. 'There are two things we must do. First, finalise our plans for the Centre. And secondly, decide what to do about the mosquito problem as a matter of urgency.'

CHAPTER 21

It was 00:25 and not for the first time that night were the occupants of Flat 10, No. 49 Piazza d' Azeglio, locked in sexual embrace. Claudia was straddling his crotch and enjoying the intensifying sensation of sliding up and down on his erection. They were so occupied in giving each other pleasure that they paid no attention when the landline phone in the drawing room rang.

After four rings, the answering machine cut in and played Claudia's recorded message, but the caller redialled and the phone rang again, until the message ended and the machine cut in once more. It was a process that was repeated at least twenty times.

The raising and lowering of Claudia's body quickened, her movements became jerky and spasmodic. She gasped and moaned, as Giuseppe pushed up with his pelvis and she pushed down with hers. In the back of his mind was the image of a hammer repeatedly hitting the pad of a fairground strength-tester mechanism and the peg hitting the bell time and time again. Whimpering and shuddering, Claudia was overpowered by a sensation of rising and

366

falling on a thick, fibrous rope and drowning in the sound of bells. Lifting his behind up off the mattress, Giuseppe tried to force all of himself into her. The dam burst and they were both gripped by the convulsions of orgasm.

As Claudia descended from the heights of ecstasy, she murmured, 'That was *so* breathtaking, darling, my head is ringing!'

'It was fantastic,' he said, and then after a pause he added, 'As for the ringing: I think you'll find that's coming from the landline phone in the drawing room. Shall I answer it?'

'Yes, could you, darling? Thank you.' Giuseppe got out of bed and went through to the drawing room. She could hear him talking and then he came back into the room, looking concerned.

'Claudia, it's the hospital on the phone. It's to do with your father ... they've been trying to get hold of you for some time.'

Claudia jumped out of bed, put on her gown and hurried into the drawing room. She sat on the revolving leather chair at her desk and picked up the handset. 'Hello, it's Claudia Mattioli here.'

'Ah, Signorina Mattioli, at last! My name is Maria Merisi. I'm Assistant Registrar at the Ospedale di Santa Maria Nuova. We've been trying to reach you on your phone for quarter of an hour or more.'

'Yes, sorry, I ... I've been – er – busy. My colleague says your call has something to do with my father. What's happened? He's all right, isn't he?'

'No, I'm afraid not, signorina. He's in a critical

condition. He has had to have a transfusion, and now he's being operated on.'

'But why? What's wrong with him?'

'He was shot in the right shoulder, apparently from close range.'

'Heavens! Poor Papa!'

'We don't know why or where. We're awaiting a police report on the incident. It's a gunshot wound.'

'Gunshot wound?' Claudia repeated, shaking her head in disbelief.

'Yes. Tissue damage is extensive. A main artery was ruptured, and your father lost a great deal of blood. He may have only limited use of his right arm in future. He was very weak before he went under the anaesthetic, but we asked him who his next of kin was and he gave us your name and telephone number.'

'When can I come and see him? Can I come rightaway?'

'No, I'm afraid not, signora. Signor Mattioli will probably be in the operating theatre for at least another hour, and after that he'll be given something to help him sleep. I suggest, if it's convenient, you come in here tomorrow at 08:00 and find out what the position is. I have some papers for you to sign, anyway.'

'Right, I'll call in on my way to work. Thank you for taking so much trouble to contact me. I'll see you in the morning. *Buone notte*.'

* * *

Unknown to Laurence an extraordinary repeat

performance took place in his apartment. Suffering from a headache, pain behind the eyes, and sore muscles and joints as well a high temperature, Scott was diagnosed by the local doctor, who he went to see the previous day, as having type B flu. The doctor prescribed ibuprofen and plenty of rest and fluids.

His symptoms abated somewhat, and Scott slept fitfully for about twelve hours. He woke up on eight separate occasions, each time because he was thirsty and had to have a drink of water and every other time because he needed to urinate. However, in the early hours of the morning, his fever returned with a vengeance, and he was caught up in a series of nightmares of such intensity that he awoke whimpering with terror. Delirious, shaking, gasping for breath, soaked in perspiration, racked by aching joints, excessively thirsty, he could no longer rationalise who or where he was, what was happening to him or whether the world he inhabited was real or hallucinatory. His body hurt, his mind was clouded, and there was a searing pain in his head. Suddenly, there appeared before him – seemingly in Ultra High Definition – four fiery horsemen, each of whom attached a rope to one of his limbs and rode off in different directions. His arms and legs were pulled further and further apart, and the resultant ripping of his muscles and ligaments was excruciating. Then, from nowhere, a huge circular saw appeared: it came spinning towards the midpoint of his parted legs, closer and closer. It barely touched his genitals – and pop! His abdomen burst open and his bowels poured forth like a string of extruded sausages. His chest cavity ruptured and his heart sprung out, squirting blood everywhere. His head split in two. His brains overflowed. His eyes sprung out on stalks and exploded messily.

Scott was riveted to the bed. He could not move. He could not speak. He was catatonic, and remained so for about five-and-a-half hours. At just after 07:00, the rigidity in his body passed. He sat up and leant against the headboard. He flexed his arms and clenched and unclenched his fists. Eventually he got out of bed, walked unsteadily into the bathroom and relieved himself. On turning to wash his hands in the basin, he caught sight of himself in the mirror. He hardly recognised his own face. He had puffy eyelids, red and mattery eyes, a swollen nose, and cheeks that were a livid purple colour. He looked for all the world like a man who had been drinking vintage port every day of his life since he was 12. The only difference was that he also had deep purple patches and spots on his chest and abdomen. As he stood, hands on basin, staring at himself in despair, his nose began to bleed. He put his head back, so that the blood streamed down his throat. When the flow stopped, he straightened up and immediately felt dizzy and nauseous. He wheeled round, slumped over the lavatory bowl and retched violently for several minutes. When he had finished, he rose shakily to his feet and staggered out of the bathroom and over to the entrance to the bedroom. Opening the door, he called out, 'Paolo! Can you ... come ... here, please!' The effort of speaking seemed to make him even dizzier. He lurched backwards and collapsed on the bed.

Paolo came in through the open door. 'Signore, you are not feeling well?' He went over to the bed. *Madre di Dio*, your face, signore! I will call 118, yes?'

'Please,' Scott gasped.

Paolo went out of the room and phoned for an ambulance. Five minutes later, for the second time in three days, Misericordia di Firenze called at the building opposite the Palazzo Grifoni. Scott was stretchered downstairs to the waiting vehicle and rushed to the Ospedale di Santa Maria Nuova.

* * *

After she had showered, Claudia went into the bedroom and shook Giuseppe by the shoulder. 'Darling, time to wake up. It's nearly 07:00.' Giuseppe stirred. 'I'll go and make some coffee.'

Forty-five minutes later, they left the apartment and walked along Via della Colonna and through Piazza della Santissima Annunziata, where stalls were being erected and there was activity on all sides. 'They're getting ready for the *Festa*,' Claudia explained. 'Clearly, the Commune has decided that it's safe to hold the Fair.' They walked down the Via dei Servi and, on the corner by the Palazzo Pucci, they kissed each other and parted company. She crossed over into Via Maurizio Bufalini and he continued down the Via dei Servi to Piazza del Duomo.

As Claudia arrived outside the Hospital, an ambulance pulled up into the parking bay by the entrance to the Emergency Department. The back doors of the ambulance were thrown open, and two paramedics emerged and pulled out a stretcher. Claudia was sufficiently close to observe that the patient was a middle-aged man, who would have looked quite like Scott but for the fact that his bloated face was further disfigured by what she took to be large purple birthmarks. Claudia walked on and up the stone steps to the first-floor Reception area.

Having said that she had an appointment to see Signora Merisi, Claudia was shown to an office in the Registrar's Department. A large, beaming woman jumped up from behind the desk. 'Ah, Signorina Mattioli, how nice to meet you! I hope you have excused my persistence last night, but I thought it was important you should know what had happened.'

'I'm glad you were able to get hold of me. How is my father?'

'He had a restful night and, considering he had a three-hour operation yesterday, is surprisingly lively this morning. Your father is, how shall I say, quite a character, isn't he?'

'He is indeed,' said Claudia, with a smile. 'But be warned. He's a terrible fidget, and he likes to hold forth to anybody who'll listen about the state of the country! Is it all right if I go and see him now?'

'Yes, sure. I'll take you to his room in a moment.' She turned to some papers on her desk. 'First, can you possibly sign these on his behalf? This is a contract with the Hospital for the supply of his private room, and this, belatedly, authorises the Hospital to carry out the operation on his shoulder.' Claudia signed the two forms. 'Right, thank you. Now let's go and find your father.' They went out of the office and up the stairs to the next floor. They walked halfway along a corridor that smelt of phenol and stopped outside Room 39. 'He's in here,' Signora Merisi said. 'If you need to ask me anything before you leave, I'll be downstairs in my office.' She walked back down the corridor.

Claudia opened the slide in the small observation window in the door to the room. Her father was lying on a bed. He was talking to someone she couldn't see. His dark, hairy chest was uncovered, he had a heavily strapped and bandaged shoulder, and he was connected to a drip. She walked in. In the corner on her right, a pretty blonde nurse was adjusting the television set. 'Papa! I see there's not much wrong with you!' She stood beside his undamaged shoulder, leant over and kissed him on the forehead. He took her hand in his.

'Oh, darling bambino! For an instant last night, I thought I'd never see you or Mama again.' Claudia leant over and kissed him again.

'Nurse, if you wouldn't mind ...'

'Of course, signorina,' said the nurse. 'I'll come back and give the signore a blanket bath later.' She smiled and went out of the room.

'Papa, what happened?'

'It was an accident, bambino. Giorgio and I were cleaning our guns, when – boom – his gun went off and I was hit in the shoulder.'

'But you don't have a gun, Papa.'

'Yes, I do. I use it to go hunting.'

'To go hunting?'

'Yes, Giorgio and I quite often go hunting.'

'Does Mama know this?'

'Yes, I always tell her when we're going hunting. I told her yesterday morning we were going hunting, and I arranged for her friend Bettina to stay with her until my return.'

'Shall I ring Mama and let her know what's happened?'

'Yes, but I don't want you to alarm her unnecessarily. Just say that it was an unfortunate accident. She won't be too pleased, I know. She hates it when I go shooting.'

'I'm not surprised. Playing with guns, indeed! Honestly, Papa, you could have been killed.' Claudia gripped his hand. She was relieved to find that his injuries had not incapacitated him to any serious degree and he himself was in such good spirits.

'I know, bambino, I should stick to buying and selling works of art – which reminds me: Signor Spencer wants to see you. He asked me on Sunday and I forgot to let you know.'

"Well, I'll ring him when I'm at the office and try to fix up a meeting. The problem is my new venture gets under way today, and I'm going to be pretty busy.'

'Can't you see him now?'

'No, I ... I must go to the office. They're expecting me.'

'But Signor Spencer's here in the Hospital. Didn't you know that?'

'No.'

'Well, he is. I don't remember which room, but you can find out downstairs. You mentioned you were starting a new venture. What new venture?'

'A Mosquito Advisory Centre.'

'Well, the way things are, we could certainly do with something like that in Florence. Good luck to you, bambino. Anyway, you'd better be going, but I hope you'll be able to come and see me again. The doctor tells me I'll be in here probably for another four or five days.'

'Yes, of course, Papa. I'll try to come in this evening or, failing that, tomorrow morning. *Ciao*, Papa.' Having leant down and kissed him goodbye, Claudia went to the door and, before going out, turned and said, with a smile, 'Enjoy your bath!'

Outside in the corridor, she came across the sister-in-charge. 'Sister, I believe Signor Spencer would like to see me. I am Signor Mattioli's daughter, Claudia. I'm actually starting a new business venture today, so I'd appreciate it if I could see him now before I go to the office – if that's convenient, of course.'

'Well, signorina, I have to tell you that Signor Spencer is *very* ill. He has an extremely high fever – over 40°C, he has muscle spasms and he slips in and out of consciousness. I'm not sure he'll necessarily realise who you are or what you're saying to him.'

'Why, what's wrong with him?'

'He has Cerebral Malaria.'

'*O mio Dio!* So he's been infected with the *falciparum* parasite?'

'I'm afraid so.'

'Are you sure? Has he had all the tests?'

'Yes.'

'And what other symptoms does he have? I mean, has he had convulsions?'

'Yes, twice so far.'

'What about low glucose level? Anaemia?'

'Yes, he has both. Anyway, I'll find out if he's awake and aware of what's going on.' The sister went into one of the rooms off the corridor. A few moments later, she re-emerged. 'Yes, signorina, Signor Spencer is awake and he's able to see you. He remembers who you are. But please try not to tire him.'

The sister held the door open. Claudia went into the room, Room 31, and was shocked to find Laurence so thin, his face yellowy and puffy, his arms attached to intravenous drips. *Heavens,* she thought, *how he's changed in a couple of days.* She sat on the chair beside the bed and gently placed her hand on his. 'I had no idea you were in here. My father just told me. He's a patient in the Hospital as well – Room 39. He's …'

Breathing heavily, Laurence muttered, 'Roberto … in … the Hospital? Why?'

'Of course, I've forgotten. You've met my father, haven't you? Well, he was shot in the shoulder. It was an accident.'

'Is … he … all right?' Laurence wheezed.

'They had to operate on him, but he's fine. Something else he told me, when I was speaking to him a few minutes ago, is that you want to see me.'

'Yes, yes … that's right.' Laurence's eyes closed and for a moment Claudia thought he might be passing out. But his eyes opened again and, with difficulty, he continued: 'You know … the Raphael portrait?'

Claudia nodded. 'Yes,' she said. She recollected that Scott had been the last person to mention the painting to her, just before she had thrown him out of her flat.

'Well, I believe I've ... successfully acquired it ... for my client in South America, which means ...' he paused to take some short, sharp breaths, 'I'm hoping to be paid ... a substantial commission.' He wheezed and took some more short breaths. 'Getting tired.' His eye closed again. There was a pause. Claudia reflected upon how unjust it was that such a kind, sensitive and interesting man should be bitten by the most deadly of all mosquitoes. Laurence's eyes flickered, then opened. 'I'm not sure ... but did Scott ever tell you ... I intend to ... use the commission to set up ... an Art Foundation?'

'No, he never told me that. But I know he was in some way trying to help you acquire the portrait. Indeed, the excuse he gave for his ill-judged liaison with the Maruichi woman, which caused our break-up, was that she was offering him advantageous information about the portrait.'

'Yes, that was ... a disappointing business. Although I believe Scott ... had my best interests at heart ...' Laurence's voice was almost inaudible and he was gasping for breath. 'He behaved ... he ... unbelievable stupidity ...' The alarm on the respiratory wireless transceiver sounded.

A nurse came running in. 'I'm sorry, signorina, but you'll have to leave.'

'Can you please let me know when he recovers? I'll be in the waiting room.' Claudia went out into the corridor. She put her mobile to her ear. 'Hi, darling, it's me,' she said, leaving a message. 'I'm delayed here at the Hospital. I'm not sure when I'll be back. I'll give you a call when I know. *Ciao*.' She went to the waiting room, sat down and looked through her emails on her mobile.

* * *

Along the corridor, in Room 41, Dr Calieri was examining Scott, who he found to have a sore throat, bleeding gums, conjunctivitis and swollen lymph nodes. Scott, on being asked by Dr Calieri how he felt, said he had pains in his muscles, joints and stomach. He also had a throbbing headache and was nauseous to the point of vomiting five or six times so far. Having looked at Scott's record sheet and noted that his temperature had been fluctuating between 38° and 40°C, the doctor asked the nurse to take a blood specimen and to organise an X-ray of the patient's lumbar region. He prescribed acetaminophen to bring the fever down. 'Have you had any mosquito bites recently?' he asked Scott.

'Yeah. About eight days ago, I was bitten on the forehead and neck. Why, what's wrong with me, doc? The little red spots on my arms and the purplish patches on my face – what do they signify?'

Dr Calieri paused, before continuing in an emotionless manner. 'The spots and patches and your other symptoms point to the likelihood – we shall know for certain when we receive the results of your blood test and the X-ray – that you have DHF.'

'DHF, what the hell's that?'

'Dengue Haemorrhagic Fever.'

* * *

At 11:10, there was a knock on the door to Room 39. 'Come in,' said Mattioli. The door opened and in walked Belori, carrying a basket of fruit. 'Giorgio, how nice!'

'Hope you like fruit.'

'Yes, I do. Thank you.'

Belori put the basket on the bedside table. 'How's the wound?'

'It hurts a bit, and apparently it'll be some time before I can use my left hand again. But I suppose I'm lucky to be alive.'

'Well, Colonel Cortellazzo reckons what you did was "courageous but crazy". It was quite something to trick Baldini and his bodyguards into coming outside, but to try to arrest them single-handedly was, you have to admit, taking things a bit far.'

'Well, I had hoped they might see sense and save us all a lot of trouble.'

'How are you going to explain away your injury? I mean, what are you intending to tell people when they ask how you were wounded in the shoulder?'

'That it was an accident. Claudia has been to see me already this morning, and I told her you and I go shooting occasionally, and that we were cleaning our shotguns prior to going on a shoot when yours went off and hit me in the shoulder. Whenever I've had to go away from home on agency business, I've always told my wife that I'm going shooting, either with you or with someone else.'

'So, let me get this straight: I'm sitting opposite you and cleaning my gun, which stupidly I haven't realised is loaded, when damn me if the thing doesn't go off and shoot your shoulder to bits! Talk about my being made to look a prize idiot!'

'Yes, I'm sorry, but ... but it was the only reason I could think of that would tie in with what I had been telling my wife. Obviously I didn't want her or Claudia to know I'm a spy working for the AISI. Look, I know you think you should have been involved in the action yesterday evening and were none too pleased to be left behind to look after the painting, but I couldn't trust anyone else to do the job. Incidentally, where is the Raphael?'

'In the vault at the Criminal Pool Forensic Department in Piazza dell' Indipendenza. What do you want me to do with it?'

'Well, it's agreed that the portrait should go to the underbidder, i.e. Signor Spencer, so I suggest you ask him how he plans to proceed. You can see him here in the hospital. He's a patient. Ask them at Reception for his room number.'

'Okay, I'll pop downstairs in a minute. Before I go, though, I thought you'd like to know how things worked out at the Castello, after you'd been whisked away in the helicopter ambulance.'

'Yes, but ... but please, whatever else may have happened, just *don't* tell me that bastard Baldini got away.'

'No, far from it. Baldini and one of his sidekicks, Mario, were arrested, as were six other members of his gang. Six more members were killed in the gunfight. Cortellazzo's men searched the house and found many incriminating items, including most unfortunately the mutilated dead body of our informant, Signorina Ricci. All told, the evidence we've assembled against Baldini is incontrovertible. Even so, there's a smart lawyer on the scene already, and he's arguing that Baldini should be let out on payment of a bail of 5,000,000 euros. Of course, the last thing anyone wants is for Baldini to be released from custody and then to disappear. However, we are advised by our lawyers that there is very little chance of bail being granted.'

'That must be avoided at all costs. He has to be locked away for a long time. He's a menace to society. Talking of which, I trust you've found out where he's selling his stolen arms and nuclear materials.'

'No, we haven't yet. Of the four or five members of Baldini's organisation who were party to the sales arrangements, only one survives, Mario, so our Director is thinking of offering the little creep a reduced sentence, on the understanding that he will spill the beans. By the way, you'll be glad to know that Malatesta has also been arrested, and there's a good chance he may turn state's evidence. I see I've made you smile, but I think you probably need to rest now, so I'll leave you in peace. How long are you likely to be in here for?'

'At least another four or five days.'

'I'll come back, then, in a couple of days to let you know if there have been any interesting developments.' Belori took Mattioli's good hand and shook it gently. '*Ciao*, Roberto. See you soon.'

* * *

After waiting for half an hour, Claudia was taken back

to Laurence's room. 'I'm lucid again,' he said to her. 'Very good of you to wait for me to recover my wits. Now what were we discussing?'

'Scott, a subject that I find tiresome!' Claudia answered. 'More interestingly, you mentioned you were hoping to set up an Art Foundation.'

'Oh yes. The thing is if Scott had lived up to our expectations, I would now be speaking to him as well as to you.' His eyes closed briefly. 'Claudia, please listen carefully. I ... I don't want to have to repeat myself. Talking tires me.' He then spoke so softly that Claudia had to lean forward to hear him. 'As I may have already said, I want to use the commission from the sale of the portrait ... to establish a Spencer Art Foundation. When I die ... the major part of my estate will be sold ... and ... and the proceeds gifted to the Foundation... Under its articles of association, the Foundation will aim ... amongst other things ... to endow ... a scholarship at the Royal College of Art in London, ... finance art exhibitions, ... sponsor an annual art prize ... and generally encourage ... stimulating artistic enterprises.' Growing wearier, Laurence paused. He was taking short, rasping breaths again.

'Which is marvellous,' said Claudia, 'but I can't quite see where I fit in – or where Scott would have fitted in had he and I still been together.'

'I want *you* to run the Foundation.' His voice was beginning to tail away. 'I reckon that ... with your energy and drive ... you'll be able ... to do the job ... part-time ... and fit it in with your research on ... mos ... mosquitoes. The pay will be good, too – at least 85,000 euros a year – and will ... subsidise your work as an ecologist.'

'But I don't know enough about art!'

'You won't be required ... to buy or sell works of art.' Laurence sounded tetchy. 'When you have to make ... some sort of critical assessment ... you can seek advice from people in the art business ... such as your father or my colleague, Filippo ... who will I'm sure ... be only too pleased to act ... in a consultant capacity. No ... to successfully accom ... accomplish ... the aims of the Foundation ... the Director will need to ... have common sense ... rather than ... an appraising eye.' Laurence struggled to stay awake.

'It sounds like quite a challenge,' Claudia said. 'Look, can I think about it and let you know? I can see you're worn out and I'd better go. I think it's amazing you should have such faith in me. I don't deserve it.' She leant over him and kissed his forehead. 'When I next come to see my father, I'll visit you, too. Until then,' she moved over to the door, '*ciao*! And please get better.'

When Claudia arrived at No. 21 Piazza del Duomo, she found it difficult to enter the building and make her way upstairs to the offices, because there were so many people massed outside and thronging the staircase. 'Excuse me, I work here,' she reiterated, as she pushed her way through the crowd.

'You work here?' asked a red-faced farmer's wife of a woman. 'Tell me, have the wretched mosquitoes gone for good?' It was a question that was to be repeated a hundred times during the day.

'They don't appear to be active in the city at the moment,' Claudia answered cautiously, 'but I recommend that everybody remains vigilant and continues to take all necessary avoidance measures.'

Inside the stifling offices, any pretence of marshalling people into queues and taking inquiries one by one had been given up. Instead, there was confusion and uproar. The advisers at their desks were under siege. Everyone was talking at the same time. Some people stank of garlic and others of alcohol. There was much pushing and shoving. All available leaflets – on subjects such as the effectiveness and cost of anti-malarial drugs, how to recognise the symptoms of Dengue, and what to do if bitten by mosquitoes – had been seized upon and snatched from their wall-mounted holders. Claudia made her way to within a few feet of the desk in the corner of the front room, where Giuseppe was dealing calmly with the encircling band of questioners. Unable to get any closer, she managed to attract his attention and indicated that she needed to speak to him. Giuseppe stood up. 'Can you let the Director of the Centre through, please?' Magically, the way cleared and Claudia went up to Giuseppe. He leant down and she shouted in his ear, 'This is ridiculous. We *have* to get some sort of order into this place! Don't forget we're expecting the press to turn up, and if they find us in this state of chaos, they'll lampoon the Centre in tomorrow's papers.'

'Okay, make an announcement.' Taking hold of Claudia's waist, he lifted her onto the desk and then jumped up beside her. He clapped his hands and yelled as loudly as he could, 'Can you *listen*, please!' The hubbub subsided. 'The Director of the Centre,' he said, indicating Claudia, 'has something important to say to you.'

'What I have to say is quite straightforward. My staff cannot *possibly* be expected to deal sensibly with so many people all asking questions at the same time. Now, either you arrange yourselves into orderly and *quiet* queues for each desk or I'll ask the police to clear the premises. We very much want to help people with their inquiries, but we are not prepared to do so unless there is *peace* and *quiet* and *order* in these rooms. I hope I've made myself clear.'

As Giuseppe jumped off the table and helped Claudia down, men in the crowd, both old and young, clapped, and there was a noticeable enthusiasm among their ranks to do what the 'lovely girl in the dark dress' asked. Although some of the women muttered sullenly about being given orders by a 'flashy whippersnapper' who was showing too much leg, there was an effort to form queues and for each person to wait patiently for his or her turn with the relevant adviser. Giuseppe whispered in Claudia's ear, 'You're incredible! And I'm mad about you,' and sat down at his desk. Claudia went into the next-door office and said to the Commune helper, who was sitting at her desk, that she had some work to do and would he kindly go and photocopy some more leaflets.

* * *

Early that afternoon, Laurence received a third call – from Ouspensky. Again the conversation was conducted on speakerphone. Ouspensky said he was unhappy to hear about Baldini's arrest. He was even more unhappy to learn from Baldini's lawyer that Signori Belori and Mattioli, the successful bidders for the portrait, weren't just art dealers; they were also

Government agents. They had fooled Baldini into believing they were acting for a wealthy German businessman. Ouspensky asked Laurence whether he was aware of the deception. Laurence, metaphorically crossing his fingers, said he didn't know anything about it. Ouspensky said he thought it remarkably well judged that Belori and Mattioli should offer only five million dollars more than Laurence's bid. To which Laurence replied that five million dollars was a lot of money. As professional art dealers, Belori and Mattioli had done their homework prior to making a bid for the portrait, the same way as he had done. In other words, they had consulted the critical catalogues and monologues by Raphael scholars, researched into the provenance of *Portrait of a Young Man*, looked up recent prices paid for Raphael portraits, and so on. It wasn't the first time he had been outbid. Abruptly Laurence lost interest in the topic of conversation. He felt tired and his headache had returned. He said he hoped Signor Ouspensky would forgive him, but he needed to sleep. Wishing him 'goodbye and all the best', Laurence handed the mobile back to the nurse.

* * *

The activity at No. 21 Piazza del Duomo had been nonstop all day and, having slept very little the night before, Claudia and Giuseppe were exhausted when they left the offices at 18:45. On the way home, they stopped in Piazza della Santissima Annunziata to admire the produce on sale on the newly erected stalls, to laugh at the juggling clowns, and to listen to the itinerant musicians, who were dressed in sixteenth-century costume and playing courtly dances on the fife, dulcimer, sackbut and tabor. Under the arcade of the Ospedale degli Innocenti, there were displays of dried fruit and mushrooms and locally made wicker baskets and embroidered fabrics. Twinkling Chinese lanterns and torches covered with coloured paper hung in the air, as did the delicious smell of food and freshly made espresso. People sauntered among the stalls, laughing and chatting. In the corner between the Palazzo Grifoni and the Hotel Loggiato dei Serviti, where there was a large and beautifully made Puppet Theatre, young children were entranced by the timeless antics of Punchinello, Harlequin and Columbine. Casting an eye over the square, Claudia noticed that on top of each display stand there was rolled-up netting, which had been so arranged that it could be pulled down quickly to offer customers protection against any sudden mosquito attack. Scattered here and there were strange awning-like constructions. Each had a canvas roof and sides made of netting that were supported on a wooden frame, and according to the accompanying sign functioned as an 'Air Raid Shelter'.

Claudia and Giuseppe, who had not had any lunch, were hungry, so they left the piazza and called in on a small trattoria in Borgo Pinti, where they enjoyed a hearty meal of *cacciucco*, *tagliatelle con tartufo*, *insalata misto*, *Scaloppine Milanese* and a bottle of Sauvignon Isonzo. They arrived back at the flat at 20:50, refreshed and revitalised. After they had embraced lingeringly in the hallway, Claudia said, 'I'm going to have a shower.'

'Let's have one together,' he said, taking her hand.

'H'm,' she said, 'what a good idea!'

CHAPTER 22

Wednesday 4 September

On its front page, *La Nazione* ran the following article, accompanied by a colour photograph of a 50x magnification of a blood-filled anopheline thrusting its fascicle into human skin:

È LA MINACCIA DELLE ZANZARE FINITA?
[IS THE MOSQUITO MENACE OVER?]

Although we were appalled to have to record the dreadful events that took place at the Hotel Landini in Fiesole on Saturday, we wish tentatively to suggest that the mosquito menace in Florence may now have passed. There have been no reports of any insect attacks in the city, since the blitz on the congregation in the Church of San Frediano in Cestello last Wednesday. Indeed, suddenly, there is very little mosquito activity, certainly far less than is normal at this time of year. According to Professor Zobi, local representative of the Institute of Ecology, mosquitoes are still breeding here, but, contrary to their established behavioural patterns, once they emerge as adults they are flying elsewhere to settle and, in the case of the females, to locate their first blood hosts.

Can it be that the renowned good sense and stolidity of the people of Florence have turned the insects away? Or is it just a case of Florentines being less appetizing than other Italians? Whatever the reason for the flight of the mosquito, citizens and visitors are out and about on the streets again, and the majority of those we interviewed yesterday were in favour of a return to normality. There were one or two dissenters, including an elderly lady from Pignone, who declared, 'It is foolish to think we're out of danger! The mosquitoes are a punishment sent from God. They'll be back! Those who venture out do so at their own peril.'

The Commune has no such doubts. A spokesman told us, 'We believe that, so long as everyone takes the necessary precautions, it is safe for Florentines to go about their daily business and for sightseers to walk around our historic streets. Otherwise, we would not have agreed to give the go-ahead for the Fair in Piazza della Santissima Annunziata and its associated *Festa della Rificolona* or for the traditional procession on the evening of the 7th. We do now have, of course, the added safeguard of the Mosquito Advisory Centre at 21 Piazza del Duomo, which has just been opened by Signorina Claudia Mattioli, one of the country's leading experts on mosquitoes. People who have any problems or inquiries regarding these potentially dangerous insects are urged to seek advice from the Centre.

* * *

Having enjoyed a good night's rest, Claudia and Giuseppe rose early, showered, had breakfast and left the apartment at 07:40. As on the previous morning, Giuseppe went to the offices while Claudia made her way to the Hospital, where she arrived just before 08:00. Her first wish being to let Laurence know the decision she had reached about the Foundation, Claudia asked the Sister-in-Charge, 'Sister, can you find out please if Signor Spencer is able to see me for a few minutes?'

'Oh no, signorina, I'm sorry. During the night,

Signor Spencer took a turn for the worse and had to be moved to Intensive Care. He was having such difficulty with his breathing he had to be put in an oxygen tent. I'm afraid that, for the time being, it's not possible for anyone to visit him.'

'For the time being, you say – so he will come out of Intensive Care, won't he? And I will be able to see him again. I do hope so, because I have something important to tell him.'

The Sister-in-Charge took Claudia by the arm. 'Signorina, please, we'll go and see Dr Calieri. He'll explain to you what the position is.'

As they made their way along the passageway, the Sister asked Claudia, 'How long have you known Signor Spencer?'

'Only about six months,' Claudia replied. 'I was introduced to him by my partner at the time – since when Signor Spencer has been a good friend, for whom I've developed the greatest respect. I would hate to lose him.'

They entered Dr Calieri's consulting room. 'Signorina, I am pleased to meet you again – even if it is under trying circumstances.' Claudia shook his hand.

'Doctor,' she said, 'I know Signor Spencer has Cerebral Malaria. But I don't know what his prognosis is. I mean, what are his chances of making a full recovery? And please, Doctor, tell it to me straight.'

'Well, signorina, unfortunately Signor Spencer has quite a few things wrong with him. Many of his blood cells have ruptured. His blood pressure, his blood glucose, his level of haemoglobin – all are dangerously low. He has developed focal neurologic deficit, which in his case means there is an impairment of various parts of his body – his left arm, his right leg, his neck. To make matters worse, he has acute kidney injury. That means the kidneys lose the ability to filter water and waste from the blood. This results in a build-up of salt and chemicals in the body, which prevents other organs from working properly. As for his level of consciousness: today he is in a coma, but *not* too deeply. I stress this, because the deeper the coma, the greater the danger. The sad fact is that his treatment was begun too late, and it's possible the intense chemotherapy he is undergoing will not save him. So, signorina, I suggest you prepare yourself for—'

'*Mio Dio, Dottore!*' cried Claudia. 'I can't believe it. His deterioration has been so … so sudden.'

'That, I'm afraid, is the nature of the virus.'

'So you mean I'm unlikely to have another opportunity to speak to him … to tell him how much I appreciate his company and … his … gener … generosity.' Claudia began to sob.

The Sister-in-Charge took hold of her hand. 'Signorina, come with me. Let's go and see your father. We need your help as far as he's concerned. He's driving my nurses mad. He tells them he's perfectly well and says he wants to go back to work! But he's deluding himself. He *must* rest, if he wants to use his right arm again. Please, signorina, have a word with him. He'll listen to you, I'm sure.' Claudia wiped the tears from her cheeks, and the Sister-in-Charge led her to and through the door to Room 39.

As Claudia pacified her father, she little knew that a few rooms away the man, who until recently had been her lover, was fighting for his life. Fate had decreed that, on returning from his unfortunate meeting with Francesca Maruichi, Scott should be bitten by an Asian Tiger mosquito, which had been carrying a highly virulent form of Dengue. Overnight his temperature dropped and for a few hours he was strangely lethargic. However, by dawn, he had become restless and was tormented by acute abdominal pain, and there was a bluish-purple discoloration of his skin, which was cold and clammy to the touch. His blood pressure was low. He had a rapid but weakening pulse. There were increasing signs of circulatory failure, so he was removed to an Intensive Care unit and placed in an oxygen tent. In the early afternoon, although conscious, he passed into a state of profound shock.

Extraordinarily, two men, who had been close friends for a quarter of a century, were at death's door not far away from one another in the same hospital, and yet neither was conscious of the fact.

* * *

It was glorious and memorable that Wednesday. The sun shone fiercely in a brilliant blue sky. The city was cheerfully noisy and boisterous as of old. A thin veil of pollution hung over the clamorous traffic. There was much wandering around the squares, especially the Piazza della Santissima Annunziata, where the Fair was in full swing. Children rushed excitedly through the streets, singing, '*Ona, ona, ona*'. People sat at tables on the pavements outside bars and cafés, eating sundaes and drinking espressos. Mimes, jugglers and strolling musicians entertained the crowds. Fun, laughter and merrymaking were uppermost in mind – not disaster, death and sadness, as had been the case a week before.

In Piazza del Duomo, outside No. 21, in response to the instruction given on a large notice, 'Please form an *orderly* queue', visitors to the Centre had lined themselves up from the top of the stairs outside the offices almost to the corner of the square that leads into Via del Proconsolo. Mostly these were people from outside the city, who had come to Florence to attend the Festival and were taking the opportunity to seek advice on how to deal with the mounting mosquito problem they faced in the countryside.

Harrowing experiences were recounted. There was the old, childless couple who had a farm near Campi Bisenzio. They told of how they had put boards and netting over the fireplace and all the windows and air vents inside their house, and had hung curtains and netting from a curtain pole over the front door. Their prize possession was a Friesian cow, called Sylvia, which, despite the obvious hygiene problems, they kept in the kitchen all night and most of the day. One evening, when the old couple had gone to bed early, Sylvia nosed her way out through the front-door curtains and netting and the door itself, which had been left slightly ajar. The old man and his wife, who were both partially deaf, did not hear Sylvia's terrible bellows as she was overwhelmed by a storm cloud of mosquitoes. The next morning they found her body. Sylvia had no blood left in her, which meant she must have been feasted on by at least three million mosquitoes – or so one of the Commune employees calculated.

A good-looking man of about 30 tearfully described the horrifying loss of his young family. One hot day, when he was at work, his beautiful young wife, Daniela, had put their 18-month-old twin daughters, Cosima and Perlita, in the playpen under a sycamore tree and had gone into the house they lived in near Impruneta to make herself a cup of coffee. Hearing strange muffled cries coming from the garden, she ran outside to find a mass of mosquitoes swirling around in the playpen. She rushed over to save her babies, who were being eaten alive, but was herself engulfed by insects. When the husband returned to the house at lunchtime, he was the first to discover the three blood-drained bodies lying in the shade of the sycamore.

A weeping middle-aged woman from the countryside to the southwest of Florence, near a town called Monterappoli, told how she was taking lunch to her husband, a farmer, who was harvesting their 20-hectare field, when she suddenly saw him jump from the cab of the combine, which was still moving, roll over, spring to his feet and rush about madly in the wheat. At a distance, it appeared that a dark, fuzzy corona had surrounded his head and he was unable to see where he was going. She watched horrified as, with flailing arms, he turned and headed blindly straight into the path of the enormous machine. Breaking into a run, she screamed, '*Attento*, Vittorio, *attento*!' It was too late. Launched by the blades of the pickup onto the elevator, his body disappeared from view as it was dragged into the threshing cylinder. She heard Vittorio scream just once, most horribly. A few moments later, she reached the combine and found that, along with the chaff, it was discarding bloody shreds of her husband's flesh onto the stubble like bits of offal from the back of a shark-fishing boat.

* * *

At 16:45 that afternoon, Signor Ouspensky called at Reception in the Ospedale di Santa Maria Nuova, gave his name and asked whether it was possible for him to see Signor Spencer.

'I'm sorry, signor,' said the young nurse behind the desk, 'but for the time being Signor Spencer is not receiving visitors.'

'Not receiving visitors! Why?'

'Because, unfortunately, he's in a critical condition in the Intensive Care unit. If you'd like to leave a message, I'll—'

'Leave a message? You don't understand. I need to see Signor Spencer urgently. I've come to discuss an important matter with him. He spoke to me yesterday afternoon, so why can't he today? There must be some mistake. How can he have become so ill that he's unable to see me?'

'Well, I'm afraid he has. As I said, if you'd like to—'

'No, I *don't* want to leave a message.' Ouspensky turned as if to go out and then suddenly swung round with a gun in his hand. 'Take me to him, now! And don't try anything clever, because I'll be right behind you with this.' He put the gun in the right-hand pocket of his jacket and pointed it at her under the material. Nervously the nurse led him upstairs and along the passageway to the Intensive Care unit. Inside, there were eight beds, each covered by an oxygen tent and surrounded by life support machinery. The nurse went over to one of the beds, removed the clipboard that was hanging on the end and passed it to Ouspensky.

At the top of the medical record sheet were the words, 'Sig. L. Spencer, ex Room 31. Diagnosis: Cerebral Malaria. Treatment: Intravenous Quinine.' Ouspensky handed the clipboard back to the nurse and went and stood beside the bed. He gazed for a few moments at the pained but recognisable features that were on view through the transparent plastic material of the tent. He turned towards the nurse and reached for his pocket. She flinched as he produced the gun and waved it around. 'It's only a toy. Look, see for yourself.' He put the gun in her hand. 'Now can you please help me communicate with Signor Spencer? As I said, I have something important to discuss with him.'

There was a sound from the bed. 'It's Signor Spencer,' said the nurse. 'I think he's trying to say something.' She leant beside the bed. 'Yes, he's asking … whether you know … what's happening … about the painting.'

'Well,' replied Ouspensky, 'that rather depends on him and whether he is prepared to stand by the bid he made on behalf of his client.'

'No, I'm not,' replied Laurence, an answer that Ouspensky heard quite clearly.

In total surprise, Ouspensky cried out, 'WHAT?'

'Please, Signor Ouspensky,' the nurse said, 'think of the patients.'

'Fuck the patients! If he doesn't pay up as he said he would, I'll go to his apartment and take the painting back. Then I'll sell it to the underbidder.'

The nurse put her finger to her lips. 'I can't hear what he's saying …' She moved even closer to the tent-like enclosure. Signor Spencer says … no you won't, because the painting is held by the State Police … It will remain in their safekeeping … until arrangements can be made … to deliver the painting to its rightful owners … the Czar … Czartor … yski Museum in Krakow.'

'That's it!' shouted Ouspensky, taking hold of the nurse. 'Time for you to get out of my way, nursie!' So saying, he shoved her through the swing doors. 'Go and look after somebody else.'

He turned, shaking with anger, or was it fear, and advanced on Laurence's bed. 'You absolute bastard! You've condemned me to death. Thanks to you, the Bratva will eliminate me for certain. So, tit for tat, I'm going to eliminate *you*.' Laurence tried to cry out for help. 'What are these tubes and machines for, I wonder.' Ouspensky yanked the tubes from Lawrence's body and turned off the life-support machines. As he was on the point of leaving, he spotted a syringe in a kidney dish. 'Just to make certain, how about if I inject a syringe full of air into one of your veins?' He picked the syringe up and pulled the plunger back as far as it would go. He returned to Laurence's bed, thrust the plastic curtains aside and grabbed Laurence's arm. He was about to slide the needle into the vein in the crook of his elbow, when the door opened and Dr Calieri came in, accompanied by a junior doctor. Ouspensky dropped the syringe and, pushing past the two men, rushed off down the passageway.

'Quick!' cried Dr Calieri. 'Help me reconnect him.'

* * *

Glancing periodically behind him as he ran to his

hotel, Ouspensky thought, *Der'mo! I've had it. I'm fucked. The Bratva will torture me to death.* He imagined himself with his tongue nailed to a table and men applying electric shocks to his genitals and beating him with rubber truncheons.

When he got back to his room, he pulled some pill bottles out of his suitcase. They contained Aspirin and two brands of acetaminophen: Tylenol and Paracetamol. He poured himself a large glass of vodka, into which he emptied the pills from the three bottles. After several moments of reflection, he flung his head back and emptied the contents of the glass down his throat. If he thought he'd have a quick peaceful death, he was wrong. About quarter of an hour later, he felt nauseous and had diarrhoea. He broke out in a sweat and, shouting swear words, he kicked and hit objects in the room. He became disorientated. His head started aching. His vision was yellowy and blurred. He had a sudden sharp pain in his upper abdomen. His brain was swelling, his liver failing. Bit by bit, his other organs shut down. Finally, he died.

CHAPTER 23

The next morning, having enjoyed another night of intimacy, Claudia woke to the realisation that she had met her match physically. As a lover, Giuseppe was gentle and forceful by turns. He was also inventive. More remarkably, he was multi-orgasmic, something she had never encountered before in a man. His stamina knew no bounds. He adored her and would do anything for her. He was entertaining. He was kind. He was *simpatico*. He was also Italian. (She imagined the delight in her mother's eyes.) But was she in love with him? She didn't think so. She *fancied* him, yes – but had no deep feeling for him. Nor had she had for Scott – foolish, misguided, weak-willed Scott. Her first boyfriend, Dino, had been the love of her life so far, even though, paradoxically, he had been too intent on fulfilling his own sexual pleasure to be much good at satisfying hers. Fond as she had been of all the men she subsequently took as lovers, she treated them essentially as 'bed fodder', and in that capacity Giuseppe was clearly in a class of his own. She might not love him, but she certainly intended to avail herself of his prowess in bed.

Following the pattern of the previous morning, she and Giuseppe got up, showered, breakfasted and, at 07:40, set off down the Via della Colonna.

About 40 minutes later, after she had been to visit her father, who, despite wearing a shoulder abduction sling, was feeling much better and itching to get back to work, Claudia met Paolo on the stone entrance steps of the Hospital. '*Buongiorno*, signorina.'

'Paolo, how are you?'

'Sad, signorina.'

'Because of Signor Spencer? Yes, I know. It's a terrible, terrible waste. Such a good man.'

'He has been wonderfully kind to me, signorina. There's no chance, signorina, that he will …?'

'No, I'm afraid not, Paolo.'

'I shall miss him greatly.'

'So shall I.'

'I'm sad, too, for Signor Lee.'

'Signor Lee? Why, what's happened to him?'

'You haven't heard? Excuse me for saying this, signorina, but I understood you and Signor Lee were close.'

'No, not any more. I haven't seen him or spoken to him for at least ten days.'

'Oh, signorina, then the news will be a shock for you. Signor Lee is seriously ill. Apparently he may die.'

'*Die?*' Claudia clutched the stone handrail. 'Why?'

'He has some virus, which he got from a mosquito.'

'From a mosquito? I must … I must find out what it is. I'll go inside with you. Are you on your way to see Signor Spencer?'

'Yes, signorina. I just wanted to look at him one more time and – you know.'

Accompanied by Paolo, Claudia went back into the Hospital. At the Reception desk, Paolo took her hand and kissed it, and they said goodbye. He went upstairs to the Intensive Care unit. She asked to see Signora Merisi.

'Signorina Mattioli, *buongiorno*!' cried the large jolly woman, as she came along the corridor. 'Your father, he's a one! We have no idea how we're going to keep him here until he's well enough to leave! Do you know what the nurses call him? Signor "Ants-in-his-Pants"!'

'I don't envy you, I must say. He's a born fidget. I asked him again this morning to try to rest and relax and to have some thought for your poor nurses, who have the dubious pleasure of looking after him. I don't suppose he'll take any notice. He does seem to be a lot better today, though, doesn't he?'

'Yes, considering how dreadful his wound was, he's made a remarkable recovery.'

'Signora, I wonder if you could tell me about Signor Lee. Until quite recently, he and I were partners. We split up only ten days ago. Deep down, I feel I treated him very harshly, even though I had good reason to do so – and now I hear he … he's a patient here in the Hospital.' Claudia took a grip of herself. 'What is wrong with him?'

'Signor Lee is very poorly. Do you know what

Dengue is?' Claudia nodded. 'Well, Signor Lee has the haemorrhagic form. Which means, among other complications, he has hypotension, a weak rapid pulse, low blood oxygen and liquid on his lungs and chest. Unfortunately, he hasn't responded to treatment so far, and if that remains the case, he will suffer severe plasma loss followed by circulatory failure.'

'Is he likely to die?'

'At this moment in time, I'd say he has a slim chance of recovery.'

Claudia left the Hospital in a daze. She walked, without much enthusiasm, to Piazza del Duomo, where she found fewer people waiting outside the Centre than on the previous two days. She went upstairs and towards Giuseppe's desk, but found he was talking to a man and woman, so she wandered into the other office and sat down at her desk. Someone asked her if she was feeling all right. 'I'm fine,' she said and, without much interest, proceeded to go through various notes and queries that had been marked for her attention.

In the mid-afternoon, Claudia received a phone call from the Hospital.

'Signorina Mattioli, it's Signora Merisi here.'

'Yes, hello.'

'I'm afraid I have some bad news for you. I understand from Sister Gabriela that you know Signor Spencer. Well, I'm sorry to have to tell you that Signor Spencer passed away earlier this afternoon. He didn't suffer. His lungs gave up. It was a blessed release. If it's any comfort to you, Signor Spencer told Sister Gabriela that he thought very highly of you.' Claudia gave out a slow, pained sigh. 'Signorina, I understand you also know Signor Lee, who is a patient here. Well, I'm glad to say he has suddenly begun to respond to treatment, so much so that Dr Calieri expects him to make a slow but steady recovery.'

'Well, I'm glad to hear it,' Claudia said, as the uncharitable thought crossed her mind that she would have preferred kind-hearted Laurence to have lived, not weak-willed Scott. 'What about my father?' Claudia asked anxiously. 'I hope he hasn't had a setback or anything like that.'

'No, signorina, your father continues to make remarkable progress. So much so that he'll be able to go home tomorrow. I can't say he's been the easiest of patients. He's been very demanding and had everyone running around after him, but we'll miss him you know. Anyway, signorina, I'll leave you to your thoughts. Remember, I'm always here if …'

'Thank you. That's very kind of you,' said Claudia. She thought for a moment and then said, 'Signora, there is one thing: have you any idea who will be handling the arrangements for Signor Spencer?'

'Yes, Signor Paolo Scalvini, who I believe worked for Signor Spencer. He's coming here later this afternoon to discuss that side of things with me. You know Signor Scalvini?'

'Paolo? Yes, I do. I'll give him a call. Thank you, signora. You have been most considerate. I plan to come and give my father a hand when he leaves, so perhaps I'll see you tomorrow. *Ciao!*'

'*Ciao*, signorina!'

* * *

In Piazza Santa Croce, in the fifteenth century, San Bernardino of Siena preached his homely Lenten sermons, the Medicis held spectacular jousts and wild animal fights, and frequent bonfires were made of heretics and heretical literature. Paradoxically, the surrounding area was not only the neighbourhood where Michelangelo lived as a boy. It was also, at one time, the red-light district of the city. Nowadays mainly used as a parking lot, this large rectangular space is dominated by the Basilica di Santa Croce, an essentially thirteenth-century building with a neo-Gothic, heavily ornamented, white and green marble façade.

From about 19:00 onwards, as it grew dark, people began to collect in the square. They came through the narrow streets, where formerly Renaissance artists lived and had their studios, but which today teem with trattorias, picture framers, carpenters and antique dealers. Children, mostly accompanied by adults, were much in evidence. So were tourists with their cameras, iPads and mobiles. Peddlers of *rificolona* lanterns plied their trade, as did stalls selling a variety of goods, including gelato, fancy hats and baguettes filled with salami, tomato and cheese. There was much laughter and gaiety. High spirits abounded. In time-honoured tradition, children with lanterns found themselves under attack from children with blowpipes, who attempted to dislodge the candles inside the lanterns and so cause the flimsy paper of which they were constructed to ignite. Beyond the square, on the banks of the Arno, other children were engaged in the same 'war'.

To introduce a suitably religious tone to the proceedings, priests, monks and nuns mingled with the crowds. At just before 20:00, the septuagenarian Archbishop of Florence, who was resplendent in his cardinal's red biretta and magnificent archiepiscopal white and gold cope, arrived with an impressive retinue, which included a guard of honour dressed in fifteenth-century Florentine costume. Shortly afterwards, the procession got under way and headed into Via Giuseppe Verdi, which, together with the other two streets en route to Piazza della Santissima Annunziata, Borgo Pinti and Via della Colonna, had been closed to traffic by the police.

Claudia was too upset to join in the festivities, so she and Giuseppe went back to her flat. She lay with her head on his shoulder, while he stroked her hair. Weighed down by the anxiety and sadness of recent events, Claudia was disconsolate. Tears streamed down her cheeks and splashed onto his jacket and trouser leg. Neither said a word; and so they remained – she in silent melancholy, he in tacit sympathy – until they heard the sirens far and near, many sirens all over the city.

Her face shining with wetness, Claudia sat up. 'What on earth is going on?'

Giuseppe went over to the window and parted the curtains. *'Santa merda!'* he cried. 'There are mosquitoes all over the outside of the window. They're getting in through the cracks! Quick, we need spray – DEET, permethrin, citriodiol – and also mosquitocides, whatever you have!'

Claudia jumped up and ran into the kitchen. She came back moments later laden with aerosols, bottles, bags, tubes and electrical devices. Giuseppe grabbed some extra strong repellent and proceeded, not only to spray behind the curtains that were drawn across the two windows in the room, but also all round the room itself. Claudia, meanwhile, bent down and plugged in a liquid mosquito killer on either side of the room. 'Oh, God!' she said, jumping to her feet. 'I think I've left the window open in the bedroom!'

'Don't worry. I'll deal with it.'

'No, it's all right. Leave it to me. I'll plug in these,' she picked up a plastic bag that contained four electric mosquitocide killer mats, 'and hopefully the little pests will clear off. Then, after a decent pause, we can go in and shut the window.'

As she went towards the bedroom door, Giuseppe cried, 'Heh gorgeous, you can't go in there unprotected! You *must* put repellent on and cover your hair!'

'Yes, okay, you're right. I'll get something to put on my head.' Claudia rushed into the bathroom and reappeared moments later, tucking her hair up into a large shower cap that she had put on her head. 'You'll need to spray in there, too. They're getting in through the air vent,' she said. She took a can of repellent and was on the point of spraying herself, when a thought occurred to her. 'I don't want to ruin my outfit.' So saying, she took off her top and skirt and, standing in matching white silk bra and panties, proceeded to spray her arms, legs, and front.

'Can you spray my back?' Giuseppe applied the extra strong repellent to the cap on her head and to her neck, her back and the backs of her legs. Meanwhile, Claudia applied a roll on repellent to her face, ears and throat and sprayed the rest of the front of her body. 'You'd better have an aerosol in each hand, so that when I open the door and turn on the light, you can spray any mosquitoes that escape.' Claudia approached the bedroom door with Giuseppe following directly behind her. Standing there in her underwear, high-heels and voluminous shower cap, she looked strangely vulnerable as well as desirable. Holding the aerosol at the ready in her left hand, she turned the doorknob with the thumb and forefinger of her right hand while gripping the plastic bag with her three remaining fingers. She nudged the door slightly ajar and flicked the light switch on with her forefinger. Spraying the aerosol from side to side, she pushed the door fully open. Giuseppe followed her, spraying his aerosols into the air.

An intimidating sight met their eyes. Swirling backwards and forwards across the room was a dark vortex of such opacity that it obscured the bed and other furnishings from view. The light from the chandelier in the centre of the ceiling was a blurred, brown glow. The mosquitoes were so involved in their swarming dance that only a few on the periphery made exploratory passes in the direction of the doorway. Any that flew into the passageway were instantly obliterated by Giuseppe.

'Well, here goes,' said Claudia. Unflinchingly, she walked into the vortex. As she made her way to the socket on the left-hand side of the bed, the mosquitoes veered away from her. She felt the occasional brush of an insect against her arms or face, but none alighted on her skin. She knelt down and plugged in a mosquitocide killer mat. When she looked up, the mosquitoes were spiralling en masse through the large half-open sash window.

'My word!' exclaimed Giuseppe, who had come into the room. 'That repellent you're wearing is remarkably effective!'

'Odd, isn't it? I've never seen them react collectively like that before. They didn't show any sign of aggression towards me at all. What's even odder is there aren't any left in the room. At least, I can't see any. Anyway, I'll plug in another couple of mats, just in case.'

'I'll close the window.' As Giuseppe pushed the lower sash down and locked the window, he cried out, 'Look! It's absolute mayhem out there!' Claudia went over to join him. Indistinctly, through the mass of insects, she could make out in the clouded light of the streetlamps sporadic images of people under attack: a man kneeling with his forearms over his head; two women rushing madly to and fro and waving their arms about; an abandoned baby in a pushchair being attacked pitilessly; a passing dog which was so tormented it was biting its legs, flanks and tail; a small child staggering with its hands over its eyes into a lamppost and falling backwards onto the pavement. Even with the window closed, Claudia and Giuseppe could hear not only the agonised cries of the people they could see, but also the heart-rending screams of other tortured beings that emanated from beneath the plane trees in the square.

'We *have* to do something to help them,' Claudia said. 'We can't just stay here. I'm going to put my clothes on.'

Giuseppe grabbed her arm. 'No! Have some sense,

Claudia! If we go out there, we'll be eaten alive! What good will all your expertise be to the people of Florence, if you're dead?'

She fell against him, beating his chest with her fists. 'I'm useless!' she cried. 'Everywhere I turn, I find people dead or dying from mosquito bites. What's expert about that? I've done nothing to stop these attacks. I've not managed to help anyone. I'm pathetic. My life is a pretence. I want ... I want ...' she started to sob spasmodically, 'to be ... to be with ... *Laurence.*' The name came forth as an extended cry of desolation.

'What you need,' Giuseppe said, taking her hand and folding his arm around her, 'is a good night's sleep. You'll feel much better for it in the morning.' He led her into her bedroom and sat her on the dressing table stool. 'Do you have anything to help you relax?'

Claudia nodded her head. 'There are some sleeping pills in the bathroom cabinet.'

Giuseppe went into the bathroom and returned with a pill and a glass of water, which he handed to Claudia. She took the pill and handed him back the glass. Having put the glass on the bedside table, he pulled the counterpane from the bed. He turned back the top sheet, smoothed out the bottom sheet and plumped up the pillows. He turned to Claudia, removed the shower cap from her head and arranged her long hair on her shoulders. He took off her shoes. He picked her up in his arms and gently laid her on the bed. He covered her with the sheet. He kissed her on the cheek. 'Goodnight, *bellissima*. Sleep tight.' He turned off the light, closed the door after him and went to his own room.

* * *

Earlier that evening, at about 20:15, when Giuseppe had been trying to comfort Claudia, children with lanterns and accompanying adults were happily progressing between the two bridges, Ponte alle Grazie and Ponte Vecchio, either along Lungarno Generale Diaz or, on the Oltrarno, along Lungarno Torrigiani. At first, all that happened was one or two of the merrymakers felt infinitesimally feathery touches against their cheeks and hands. They thought nothing of it and continued on their way, laughing and joking and singing, *'Ona, ona, ona'*. They were not prepared for the onslaught that followed moments later. The air was suddenly thick with millions of mosquitoes, so thick that it was almost impossible to see. *'Babbo!'*, *'Mamma!'*, *'Zio!'*, *'Zia!'*, *'Nonno!'*, *'Nonna!'*, *'ZANZARE!'* yelled the children, as they and their relatives were pounced upon and covered from head to foot by frenzied insects. Passers-by, motorists and lorry drivers with their windows open, cyclists, scooter riders, ice cream vendors, sightseers, students handing out flyers, traffic police, street waste pickers, patrons of alfresco cafés and trattorias: all were beset by bloodthirsty mosquitoes.

In Piazza di Santa Maria Soprarno, a young girl lay on her back, screaming and kicking her legs in the air, while her father tried to brush mosquitoes off her body as well as his own. Her hands and the sweet innocent face they sought to protect were overspread by ravenous insects. Some wormed their way under her hands and bit deeply into the soft clenched eyelids. Others crawled up her nose or flew into her mouth as she screamed.

On the Ponte Vecchio, there was fear and chaos. Those being harried by mosquitoes pushed, shoved and barged into one another, as they sought refuge from the unremitting attack. Like commuters on the Japanese subway during rush hour, they tried to squeeze themselves into the jewellery shops, which were already full to overflowing. The pressure of numbers and the panic in some of the shops grew so great that people were thrust through the riverside windows and into the almost dried-up Arno.

Regardless of all the violent shaking of heads, flailing of arms, kicking of legs, slapping of hands, waving of bags and other forms of evasive action, the mosquitoes preyed on all without exception. Human beings happily installed in the comfort and security of a man-made environment were helpless against such a belligerent force of Nature. The main '*Ona, ona, ona*' procession, which was winding leftwards into Via della Colonna from Borgo Pinti, came under merciless attack. No one escaped the constant bombardment. Anyone who managed somehow to stagger inside, in the hope of finding respite from the horror outside, would be so covered in mosquitoes that his or her life and the lives of the other occupants of the building were immediately imperilled.

Police cars and ambulances, with sirens blaring and lights flashing, rushed onto the streets. Hospitals were on red alert. But bringing the victims in for treatment proved difficult. When paramedics and police stopped to rescue the dying and injured, they themselves became targets of the insects.

For two hours the relentless assault continued. Then, just as suddenly as it had started, it stopped. As if upon some preordained signal, the mosquitoes flew away. They left behind them grief, carnage and confusion. Corpses – some anaemic, others steeped in blood – were strewn haphazardly on the pavements and in the streets and squares. Inside buildings, more people lay dead or dying. There were bodies that had plunged headlong into the thick mud of the riverbed. Barely alive, some of the last people to be attacked were moaning horribly. Others were whimpering or crying as they wandered about aimlessly. To these pitiful sounds were added the tolling tenor bell of Giotto's Campanile, the occasional siren and engine noise of a scooter or car. Otherwise, an unearthly stillness enveloped the once vibrant city.

CHAPTER 24

Overtired and disturbed by distressing memories of the day's events, Claudia slept fitfully. She woke at 05:30, feeling heavy at heart. What she needed, she decided, was some time on her own for reflection, so she got out of bed, threw on some clothes, left the apartment and went downstairs. In the piazza, there was no outward manifestation of what had happened there nine hours earlier. There was no sign of life either, except for a sole cab driver, who was leaning against his car and reading a newspaper. Claudia walked over to him. 'Piazzale Michelangelo, please.'

'Sure, signorina.' He opened the back door of the car for her and she got in. On the way, he talked ceaselessly about how Florence was damned and had been singled out for retribution. 'It all goes back to Savonarola, signorina. He foresaw our fate. "Repent, O Florence," he said, "repent while there is still time!" We've taken no notice, have we? The rich have become richer and the poor poorer than ever. We've deliberately polluted the atmosphere. We've forsaken Our Holy Mother. We've put greed and envy before generosity and love. Selfishly and unwisely we've promoted a get-rich-quick, I'm-all-right-Jack society. We all deserve to die.'

Claudia was heartily relieved when the journey came to an end and she was able to press a 10-euro note into the driver's hand, jump out of the cab, which drove off, and walk across the square. Alone at last, she stood at the edge of the square and watched the sunrise. Edging its way up into the sky from behind Mount Secchieta and the Pratomagno to her right, the orange-red sun cast a corresponding hue, together with long shadows, across the towers, the domes and the terracotta roofs.

It's going to be another beautiful day, she thought, *though I don't suppose Giuseppe or I will see much of it. As for Laurence: he will never see the sun again. I wonder, would he not still be alive, if I had been more forceful in presenting my ideas and beliefs about mosquitoes, and if current research into and experimentation with biocontrol had been begun two or three years earlier? Would such ideas and research have been necessary, had man not overindulged the petrol and the diesel engine, had he not destroyed the rainforests and built the massive dams that force microbes to relocate, had he not overused pesticides, antibiotics and CFCs and – in a nutshell – unbalanced the Earth's microecology and altered its climactic conditions?*

Feeling ill at ease and in need of inspiration, Claudia looked down on the City of Flowers, whose inhabitants had, ironically, been terrorised and tormented by one of Nature's pollinators. As the sun climbed gently into the clear blue sky, it cast an increasingly bright light on the familiar edifices. Raising her eyes, she noticed something moving in the distance. A spiral-shaped haze was rising from behind the Fiesolean hills opposite. Growing darker and larger, it funnelled upwards, spread out and arched towards Florence. Moments later, the sun went in. Claudia turned to the east and saw that another spiral had emerged from somewhere between Pontassieve and Rignano sull' Arno and was also advancing on the city: it was so vast, dense and widespread that it had obscured the light of the sun. Two further thick, black spirals had formed and were heading relentlessly towards her: one in the west, from the direction of the Montalbino mountains, behind which is the small town where Leonardo da Vinci was born, and the other in the south, from Impruneta and the vineyards of Chianti. The light of day dimmed, as the spirals radiated from the four points of the compass, like the ribs in some gigantic celestial fan vaulting, and merged above Florence. From above there was a noise beyond forbearance – a deafening, high-pitched, piercing scream. With her hands to her ears, Claudia looked up. Over her head, as dark as night, was an overarching canopy of trillions and trillions of seething mosquitoes. It hung there for an age. The insects went on massing until they had blacked out every inch of space from horizon to horizon. Then, suddenly, they swooped ...

* * *

In the bar on Via Maggio, there was a subdued feeling – as if people had something on their minds. There wasn't the customary hilarity and good fellowship. Robert Mattioli and Giorgio Belori sat at their usual table sipping cocktails. 'It's hard to believe,' said Giorgio, 'it was nine months ago that the day turned into night. So many people killed, so many infected with disease, so many mentally disturbed. And on the same day, there were mosquito attacks in all the major cities of Europe, combined with violent storms, hurricanes and earthquakes elsewhere in the world. Why?'

'Ask Claudia when she's here. She said she has a theory about what happened – or so she told me when we last spoke on the phone. I haven't seen her since she got married.'

'But that was five months ago!'

'Yes, I know. She's been busy with her book and setting up Laurence's Foundation. And, as you know, you and I have been involved in giving evidence in four – or is it five? – court cases—'

'Six, actually. Baldini, Mario, Malatesta and the three *soldati*.'

'You're right. We played our part in making sure they all ended up in prison, murderous bunch of bastards! After that, we spent our time scouring the area for antique furniture, while,' he lowered his voice, 'covertly tracking down villains and radical Islamists.'

'Papa, Giorgio – how *are* you?' asked Claudia, as she and Giuseppe approached the table wreathed in smiles and holding hands.

'*Mia bella*, it's so good to see you.' Roberto kissed Claudia on both cheeks. 'Giuseppe!' They high-fived and then shook hands. 'You remember my partner Giorgio.' Giorgio stepped forward to kiss Claudia and shake Giuseppe's hand. 'Come and sit down and have a drink. What would you like?' They chose what they wanted and Giorgio went to the bar to fetch their order.

Claudia took Roberto's hand. 'There's something I want to tell you, Papa. I'm … pregnant. The baby, a boy, is due in December.'

Roberto cried out, 'That's marvellous news.' He again kissed Claudia on both cheeks and shook hands with Giuseppe. 'Well done. I'm delighted for you both.' He paused for a second to reflect. 'Mama was so happy when you two married. It made her life – or what was left of it – worth living. Imagine how ecstatic she would be now to find out she was going to be a grandmother!'

'She had a rotten time,' Claudia said, her eyes watering. 'I should have gone to see her more often … I should have talked to her and held her hand … I should have been with her at the end.' Giuseppe did his best to comfort her.

'*Mio caro*, she was so proud of you. You were the apple of her eye. She loved you beyond words.' Roberto moved to the seat beside her and put his arm round her. 'You know, hearing that you were going to get married made her discomfort almost bearable for a brief interval. But there was no avoiding the pain, until the end came for her and she was thankfully and finally released.' Father and daughter stared into the distance.

Sensing that a change of subject was needed, Giuseppe said quietly, '*Bellissima*, tell Roberto what you've been doing.'

Roberto snapped out of his sad reverie and looked at Claudia. 'Yes, bambino, tell me about the Foundation. Have you registered it, yet?'

Claudia was relieved to talk about something else. 'Yes. And I've submitted draft Statutes to the

Regional Council and applied to them for legal recognition. Giuseppe and I are still trying to find suitable premises, so what I've done is ask the City Council whether we can use the same premises as we did for the Mosquito Advisory Centre at 21 Piazza Duomo. It has two floors, four large rooms, a kitchen and a lavatory. It'll do for the time being – that's if the Council approves the idea.'

'And what do you plan to exhibit?'

'Laurence's collection of mainly Renaissance paintings and sculptures, which, unknown to any of us, he kept at the bank. There are some forty works of art in all. There is also his collection of art books and DVDs. Laurence's instructions as to what the Foundation's structure and aims should be are very clear. It is to be established for non-commercial purposes. Any donations made by patrons and visitors will go to charity.'

'But what about capital funding?' asked Roberto. 'Where's that coming from?'

'From Laurence. His endowment is for a considerable sum of money, which includes his life assurance benefits, pension savings and his receipts from the paintings he bought and sold. There is also, of course, the massive commission he earned – much larger than we had anticipated – on the purchase of the Raphael portrait.'

'The fact,' said Roberto, 'that the commission was so large is because Laurence's client in South America didn't have to pay anything for the portrait. We sent him a message saying the portrait was in our possession and there was no way we – the State Police

– were going to pay the Bratva any money, let alone $85,000,000! So far as we were concerned the painting was his and he didn't have to pay a penny for it. We told him, too, that because Laurence had been such a great help to us, we would gladly arrange transportation of the painting, at no cost to him, from Florence to the Czartoryski Museum in Krakow. In reply we received a secure message saying he was delighted with the outcome – so delighted, in fact, that he wanted to give $25,000,000 towards the setting up of Laurence's Foundation.'

'Marvellous!' said Claudia. 'It's great to know there are rich people in the world who are prepared to use their money for other people's benefit, not just their own. The interest earned will be more than enough to meet our annual costs – rental, wages, fees and taxes – and to buy the occasional work of art. Otherwise, the acquisition of exhibits will depend on any bequests we receive and how much sponsorship we raise.'

'We also plan to borrow appropriate works of art from other galleries,' Giuseppe added.

'What happened to Scott?' asked Giorgio out of the blue.

'Yes,' said Roberto, 'that disloyal bastard! Didn't he go back to the States?'

'No,' said Claudia. 'He was actually in the Santa Maria Nuova at the same time as you were. He was infected by a mosquito with a potentially lethal form of Dengue. But he survived and was on the way to recovery when the mass attack occurred. Connected to tubes and suffering from fatigue and low blood flow, he was unable to defend himself and, subjected to thousands of bites and lacerations, he bled to death.'

'What about the Sister-in-Charge and Nurses Merisi and Gabriela. They were so caring and attentive. What happened to them?'

'I'm afraid they were killed too.'

'*Mio Dio*! That's awful! But how did it happen? I mean, how did the wretched mosquitoes get in?' asked Roberto.

'The usual ways,' Giuseppe replied. 'Through bathroom and toilet vents, grilles and ducts, out-of-order air conditioning units, open window screens. Most of the staff and nearly all the patients were bitten to death or succumbed later to the life-threatening viruses they had been infected with.'

'All I can say,' said Roberto, 'is I'm glad I got out of bed and left when I did. I just couldn't lie around there anymore. I wanted to get back to the shop and join Giorgio. When the mass attack came the next morning, he and I managed to avoid the attentions of our little friends by hiding in the shop basement where, following Claudia's instructions, we had blocked up every hole, vent, crack and duct that we could find. The downside was that with no air coming in, we suffered from heat exhaustion. But better that than being bitten to death!'

'What happened to you and Claudia?' Giorgio asked Giuseppe.

Giuseppe replied, 'I took refuge in the loo, which had a sealed door and like your basement had every hole blocked, including the lavatory vent pipe. I also had very little air and what there was didn't smell very nice!'

'And you, bambino? Where were you if you weren't in the loo with Giuseppe?' Robert asked.

'I think you'll find this quite remarkable,' said Giuseppe. 'Tell them, *mia bello.*'

'I was in Piazzale Michelangelo, where I had gone to think things over,' said Claudia. 'As I stood there, I saw the sky turn black with mosquitoes. When they struck, I thought, *You're going to be killed by the very creature you've been trying your best to protect from extermination.* But the strange thing is that, even though millions swept past me, not one of them touched me. It was as if they ... respected me.'

'How extraordinary!' said Roberto. Remembering that his daughter had told him how some people attract mosquitoes and others don't, he continued, *'Mio caro*, I wonder, could it be they were put off by the way you smell?' They all laughed. 'While we're on the subject, maybe you can explain the cause of the mosquito attacks on the city last August and September. But first, do you know what happened to Laurence's charming valet Paolo?'

'I'm afraid he was killed. Sadly, he was on his way to see me. I had suggested he might like to help us at the Mosquito Advisory Centre. He was walking along the Via dei Servi when the mass attack took place. There was no escape and, like Scott, the man he had so often served with bourbon on the rocks, Paolo was bitten and drained of blood.'

'Colonel Cortellazzo, who helped us arrest Baldini,' observed Roberto, 'was also killed in the attack. I liked him. He was a no-nonsense military type. He'll be sorely missed. Now, bambino, how about explaining why the attacks took place. I'm sure you and Giuseppe have discussed the matter many times – so can you please tell us who or what motivated so many mosquitoes to turn on the inhabitants of one of the most beautiful cities in the world?'

'Mother Nature. It's as simple as that. She sent the mosquitoes as a warning. She's likely to send further warnings – in the shape of insectile killers such as African bees, Asian hornets, wasps, tsetse flies, and *more* mosquitoes. What people should realise is that the Earth won't be obliterated by a meteorite strike or a collision of matter and anti-matter. It won't be hurled unto the Sun or sucked into a black hole. In fact, it's not the Earth that'll be destroyed. It's mankind. That's why Nature is warning us. She creates and controls all living things. The Earth is her domain. We humans are her subjects. She is an omnipotent force that has the capacity to feel anger and pity and to distinguish right from wrong.'

'What if we choose to ignore her warning?' asked Giorgio. 'What if humans carry on—'

'If humans carry on polluting the atmosphere, chain-sawing the forests, damaging the coral reefs, acidifying the oceans, wiping out ecosystems and species, and generally trashing the natural world; if, for the purposes of making money and living for themselves, they continue to act as if they own the planet and do as they like with it, never mind the consequences; if they persist in having no consideration for other living things – the animals, reptiles, birds, fish, plants, trees: Nature will lose patience with us as a species. Then she will deploy the terrifying weapons she has at her disposal. Man won't stand a chance. Imagine if, over a short period of time in heavily populated areas of the world, there was a series of eight magnitude-10 earthquakes, each with the destructive power of 25 hydrogen bombs. That means overall there would be a release of energy equivalent to 200 hydrogen bombs. After the earthquakes there would be 500-metre high tsunamis and violent volcanic eruptions. The worldwide devastation and loss of life is inconceivable.'

'What about *super*volcanoes?' asked Giorgio. 'Do they actually exist and, if so, are there any that are likely to explode in the near future?'

'Yes. There are at least two that have become active again. One, the Phlegraean Fields Caldera just west of Naples, is huge. It consists of no less than 24 craters. The other, the Yellowstone Caldera in Wyoming, has a magma chamber measuring 20 by 80 kilometres. An eruption of either of these would be 25,000 times more powerful than a magnitude-10 volcano. Lava and burning rock would cover and demolish everything for hundreds of miles. Vast clouds of ash and exploding CO_2 would encircle the Earth and plunge it into volcanic winter and complete darkness. These are horrendous catastrophes waiting to happen. Nature has only to press the red button. Then there will be a final reckoning, an apocalypse. Whether or not that happens is up to man.'

APPENDIX 1

MOSQUITO AWARENESS RECOMMENDATIONS

Most mosquitoes are at their hungriest at dawn and dusk. They are also active during late evening, night and early morning.

AT THESE TIMES, TRY TO RESTRICT YOUR OUTDOOR ACTIVITIES – OR, IF YOU MUST GO OUTSIDE, WEAR <u>LIGHT</u>-COLOURED LONG-SLEEVED SHIRTS OR BLOUSES AND <u>LIGHT</u>-COLOURED LONG TROUSERS THAT ARE THICK ENOUGH TO PREVENT MOSQUITOES BITING THROUGH TO YOUR SKIN.

Before you go outside, spray repellent containing not more than 30% DEET on exposed parts of your body. When you apply repellent to children, it is recommended that the DEET content should not be more than 10%. Do not spray repellent directly in the eyes. It is an added protection to spray your clothes, as well.

When you are indoors, try to keep mosquitoes OUTSIDE – by fitting screens over doors and windows or making sure existing screens are in good repair. Also, hang netting that has been sprayed with repellent over your bed and use a mosquito killer plug-in or mosquito mat heater in the room.

ELIMINATION: How You Can Help

Mosquitoes lay their eggs practically anywhere where there is standing water.

IF YOU HAVE ANY OF THE FOLLOWING ITEMS IN YOUR GARDEN OR BACKYARD OR ON YOUR PATIO, BALCONY OR VERANDA, GET RID OF THEM OR PUT THEM IN STORE:

NON-DEGRADABLE PLASTIC PACKAGING

TIN CANS

DISCARDED RUBBER TYRES

JAM JARS

BUCKETS

ANYTHING ELSE THAT CAN HOLD WATER UNNECESSARILY

REGULARLY CHANGE THE WATER IN:

BIRDBATHS

WADING POOLS

PET WATER BOWLS

ORNAMENTAL PONDS

REPAIR LEAKY PIPES AND OUTSIDE FAUCETS, SO THAT WATER DOES NOT COLLECT NEARBY.

FILL IN OR DRAIN LOW SPOTS IN THE GROUND WHICH CONTAIN WATER, E.G. PUDDLES, RUTS AND FOOTPRINTS.

FILL IN TREE ROT HOLES AND HOLLOW STUMPS WITH CONCRETE.

KEEP RAIN GUTTERS, DRAINS, DITCHES AND CULVERTS CLEAR OF WEEDS AND TRASH OR ANY OTHER BLOCKAGES, SO THAT WATER DRAINS PROPERLY.

ENSURE THAT CESSPOOLS, CISTERNS, FIRE BUCKETS, RUBBISH BINS, RAIN BARRELS AND SEPTIC TANKS ARE TIGHTLY COVERED.

EXAMINE FLAT ROOFS AFTER RAINSTORMS TO SEE THAT NO STANDING WATER HAS COLLECTED.

LOOK OUT FOR MOSQUITO LARVAE, WHICH ARE COMMA-SHAPED, IN THE WATER IN FLOWER VASES. LOOK OUT FOR THEM ALSO IN THE WATER THAT COLLECTS IN SAUCERS OR DRIP TRAYS UNDER POTTED PLANTS. IN ALL CASES, REPLACE STAGNANT WATER WITH FRESH WATER.

EXAMINE FISHBOWLS AND AQUARIUMS FOR LARVAE. SOME KINDS OF FISH EAT THE LARVAE, OTHERS DO NOT. BUY SOME FISH THAT DO.

MOSQUITOES HIDE IN GRASS, WEEDS AND SHRUBBERY DURING THE DAYTIME. KEEP GRASS SHORT, CUT DOWN WEEDS AND TRIM SHRUBBERY.

WHAT TO DO IF YOU ARE BITTEN

IF YOU ARE BITTEN AND THE BITE ITCHES, TAKE ORAL ANTIHISTAMINES OR RUB ON CALAMINE LOTION OR CORTISONE CREAM. IF THE BITE BECOMES INFECTED AND DISCHARGES PUS, SEE A DOCTOR. WITH REGARD TO BITES TO CHILDREN, PARTICULARLY ON THE BODY: ANY SECONDARY INFECTION SHOULD BE TREATED BY A DOCTOR.

APPENDIX 2

REDUCING AND MANAGING THE MOSQUITO PROBLEM BY BIOCONTROL

AIMS	PROS	CONS
To develop nationwide accelerated breeding programme for natural predators of the mosquito.	Predators such as: *Gambusia affinis,* Guppie and Goldfish – which eat mosquito larvae. Dragonflies and Jumping Spiders – which eat adult mosquitoes.	Cost. Will take years to establish. Introduction of *gambusia* upsets ecological balance of water: they take over and the native fish disappear.
To develop nationwide accelerated breeding programme for *toxorhyncites*.	*Toxorhyncites* larvae eat other mosquito larvae.	Cost. Institute's own programme supplies 1,000s of larvae to river and water authorities throughout Italy, but this is nowhere near enough. Need at least 150 nationwide breeding centres producing 500,000 or more larvae per week.

To mass-produce *bacillus thuringiensis Israelensis* (Bti) for commercial use in waterways and wetlands.	In combination with lecithins, Bti forms monolayer on water, which prevents mosquito larvae from filter-feeding.	Kills other organisms, if applied in too strong a dose. Reduces midges, which are a food source for fish and birds. Impractical and costly to produce in sufficient quantities to make any noticeable impact. Some mosquitoes have developed immunity to Bti.
To mass-produce a blue-green *algae*, into which genes from a strain of Bti have been trans-planted.	It kills mosquito larvae.	It will take several years before researchers persuade the transgenic *algae* to produce higher amounts of toxin and to figure out how to grow it commercially.
To deploy the protozoan parasite or *microsporidia*.	It produces spores in the adult female *Aedes aegypti* which infect her eggs. As a result, first- and second-instar larvae die before they mature and, on disintegrating, release spores into the water. Any third- or fourth-instar larvae in the vicinity are infected	Cost. It will take years to develop.

	and, on turning into adults, become carriers and continue the cycle of infection by dispensing the parasite to new habitats. Since it must feed its internal parasite, the *Aedes aegypti* female is not as vigorous or long-lived as normal, with the result that she does not have enough vitality to suck out that second blood meal and so doesn't infect anybody with the Dengue or Zika viruses.	
Extract oil from the seeds of the *Kochia scoparia* (a.k.a. the summer cypress or burning bush).	The oil contains a fatty acid which, when converted into a pheromone and laced with pesticide, can be used to lure adult female mosquitoes to their deaths.	